Heir to a Prophecy

Heir to a Prophecy

Mercedes Rochelle

TOP HAT BOOKS

Winchester, UK
Washington, USA

First published by Top Hat Books, 2014
Top Hat Books is an imprint of John Hunt Publishing Ltd., Laurel House, Station Approach, Alresford, Hants, SO24 9JH, UK
office1@jhpbooks.net
www.johnhuntpublishing.com

For distributor details and how to order please visit the 'Ordering' section on our website.

ISBN: 978 1 78279 754 8

A CIP catalogue record for this book is available from the British Library.

Design: Stuart Davies

Printed and bound by CPI Group (UK) Ltd, Croydon, CR0 4YY

Preface

It is of legends that I write in this story, rather than facts; for after almost a thousand years of history, what can we call truth out of the tiny scraps that survived? When men claimed descent from a bear, and people believed that dragons roamed the earth, who is to say what is fact and what is fancy? Hence, with this thought in mind, I give you the origin of the royal Stewarts, as it was handed down to Shakespeare.

It all began with the witches' prophecy.

Macbeth's friend Banquo was with him when the three witches appeared on the heath: strange, weird creatures with seductive words.

"All hail, Macbeth!" the first had said, "Hail to thee, Thane of Glamis!"—calling him by his true title.

"All hail, Macbeth!" quoth the second, "Hail to thee, Thane of Cawdor!"—giving him a title belonging to another.

"All hail, Macbeth," cried the third, "that shalt be King hereafter!"—giving voice to his secret desire.

Macbeth did not know it yet, but the second witch had spoken the truth; already King Duncan had declared the Thane of Cawdor traitor, and awarded the title to Macbeth for his courage in battle.

Then the witches spoke their prophecy to Banquo. They said:

"Lesser than Macbeth, and greater."

"Not so happy, yet much happier."

"Thou shalt 'get kings, though thou be none."

The witches vanished, leaving the pair with gladsome prospects.

All might have gone well, but Macbeth's ambitions were too strong to wait for chance to bring them about. King Duncan's life stood in his way; before long, King Duncan was murdered. The true heirs, Malcolm and Donald Bain, fled the country, thus leaving the throne empty for Macbeth to mount.

Only Banquo had reason to suspect that Macbeth was the murderer.

As of yet, however, good Banquo showed no signs of betraying his friend's secret. But as time went on, the King brooded—hating him—begrudging Banquo's every breath.

It really wasn't treachery Macbeth suspected; rather, his anger had sprung from the futility of his own position. Although he was king, he had thrown away his peace of mind, jeopardized his very soul, so that Banquo's heirs would sit on the throne he had bought so dearly.

Having gone so far, there was only one thing to do. Banquo had to be dealt with...and his son, Fleance. To that end, Macbeth ordered a great feast to be prepared, and commanded their presence as guests of honor...

1
Ambush

Fleance barely slowed his step as Banquo stopped again, removing a rock from his shoe. He and his father were already late to the King's banquet, and a half mile still stretched between them and the castle gate. It had seemed like a fine idea a couple of hours ago, taking a walk to get away from that hostile environment. There had been too many uncomfortable pauses in conversation, too many unfinished phrases, too many sideways glances. But now, dusk was quickly deepening into night, and it was getting difficult to see into the forest. There was probably a spy in every tree, for all he could tell.

The young man's curly hair blew about his face as he looked up at the treetops. High cheekbones accentuated dark brown eyes as he raised his brows to see better through the shadow. His fine square chin gave him a profile he was proud of, and he went beardless, disregarding the current fashion. But his mouth, usually so prone to laughter, was pursed tonight in frustration.

"Blast this uphill climb," he grumbled as Banquo adjusted his cloak clasp. He glanced at his father wryly; this reticence was most unusual for him. His father grunted a response, but finally shifted his belt, shaking off his lethargy. Picking up their pace, father and son strode deep into the forest.

It was a quiet night, punctuated by the crunch of stones underfoot. Not a cricket was heard, nor birds, only the sigh of leaves rustling far overhead.

"It shall be rain tonight," Banquo said.

From behind came the cry: "Let it come down!"

In an instant, three dark forms were among them. Banquo was their main target, and two of them fell upon him, slashing the startled man in the face. The worthy lord was blinded by his own blood even as he shouted, "Villains, murderers! Fly,

Fleance, fly!"

Though past his physical prime, the old warrior still was more than a match for both opponents. With a practiced motion, Banquo swept his sword from the scabbard, aiming an overhead cut at his nearest attacker's head. If the blow had hit, he would have cleaved the man's skull. But the blood was flowing so fast into his eyes that his aim was flawed. The blade only glanced off the other's shoulder, eliciting a howl of pain.

Enraged, the murderer dived at Banquo, catching him in the throat with a dagger. Letting go the knife, the man stepped back, clutching his arm; he was astounded that Banquo was still on his feet. For a moment, it seemed that their victim would respond with a last lunge. Then he staggered, gurgling, and collapsed into the arms of his murderers.

Fleance was already in motion before his father had shouted. Shoving his torch into the third assassin's face, he set the man's mask aflame. Screaming, clawing his face, the murderer went down, his feet kicked out from under him.

Fleance allowed himself a brief sneer. Then, wasting no more time, he moved toward the others when he saw the killers slashing Banquo's face. The boy hesitated, reluctant to abandon his father. But the assassins were too good at their work. Even from this distance he could tell that Banquo was already finished; his body gave no more sign of life.

It was also clear that their companion's screaming made no impression on them; the assassins must have assumed that the victim was himself. Cursing, Fleance took advantage of the confusion. He stamped out his torch, kicked his assailant once more as the man was struggling up, and ran for his life.

Murder gave the forest a sinister cast. The trees seemed to bend their limbs before him, seeking to block his way. Fleance's breath came in short gasps, heightening the pain in his side as he ran frantically the way he had come.

His first thought was to go to Macbeth and raise a search party to ride down these outlaws. Then, a deeper, more telling conviction assailed him, though he knew not whence it came: perhaps the murderers were not there by chance. Perhaps they were paid assassins, in which case he could trust no one.

He considered, leaning against a tree and catching his breath. He wasn't going anywhere without a horse, and both horses were still stabled at the castle. Going any closer to that accursed place was the last thing he wanted to do; however, he reminded himself that no one besides the assassins would know that there had been any trouble.

It was a risk. Perhaps they would lie in wait for him near the stables and finish the job. But he had a feeling that they would be too busy tending their wounds. Despite himself, Fleance smiled grimly.

He looked slowly around the tree and up the path. Everything was quiet. He took one step then another, resisting the urge to break into a run. This was no time to panic. He needed to keep his senses about him. He looked one more time in all directions, then began striding quickly toward the castle, hand on his dagger.

No one stopped him at the castle gate and Fleance went directly to the stabler's door. He knocked quickly then stepped back, looking around. There was no indication he was being followed yet.

The stabler took his time answering, his face breaking into a scowl when he recognized Fleance; he hadn't expected anyone to leave for some hours yet. But when the youth held out a coin, his mouth curled into a greedy sneer and he quickly came out, making the coin disappear as he passed.

Fleance watched him go into the stable, resisting the urge to shout at the other to hurry up. The man seemed to take an inordinately long time, then he came out… alone.

"What about t'other?"

"I only need one now. Is he ready?"

The man shrugged. "Whatever you want." He opened the stable door and Fleance sighed with relief to see that his horse was saddled. Without another word he mounted, offering no explanation for his hasty conduct and rode off, leaving the man scratching his head.

Fleance took the road away from the castle grounds. He followed unused paths through the forest, traveling all night. At first, he rode just to get away. Then, feeling safer the farther away he rode, he knew he needed a plan. If they were truly set on by assassins, home would not be safe. Nowhere was safe. What would Banquo do?

Banquo. Left dead in the forest like a wild animal.

Fleance brushed away a tear with the back of his hand. Now was not the time to cry. Nor could he bring himself to go back. To what end? His father had used his last breath to tell him to fly. His father had sacrificed himself to save the son.

But why did it happen?

By afternoon, Fleance was relieved to find himself at his destination: a small, thatched roof cottage well back from the road along the shore of Loch Lochy. A thin line of smoke rose invitingly from the chimney. Fleance unsaddled and brushed his horse, hoping to draw the inhabitant from the house, alone.

The noise did that very thing. The door burst open and a tall, balding man came out, wiping the back of his neck with a brown rag. He strode across the yard, breaking into a run as he recognized his visitor. They clasped hands; Fleance clung to the man's hand as relief flowed through him. They hadn't seen each other in years, but boyhood friendships lasted a lifetime.

"Ronald," Fleance gasped as his friend squeezed him too hard, like he had always done when they were boys.

Ronald pulled away, grinning. But his smile of welcome changed to a frown. Fleance's tunic was torn, his hair was twisted with twigs and leaves, and his eyes looked haunted.

"For God's sake, man, what has happened? Come inside," he said, pulling Fleance's arm. The other stopped him, shaking his head; he looked worriedly at the house.

Ronald's eyes followed his. "We are alone. She's fixing dinner. Don't worry. There is enough for three."

Fleance wanted nothing more than a warm meal. But he couldn't share his misfortune with anyone else but Ronald...not just yet. Ronald put an arm around his shoulders, leading him to the lake.

In a torrent, Fleance poured out the story he barely believed himself, but for the terror of the thing. Ronald listened carefully.

"Stay with us a few days," he said when the other had finished. "I'll ride out and find what's behind all this. I swear, the villains will pay."

Comforted in his friend's good hands, Fleance permitted himself to be fed, undressed, and put to bed. He slept until the next afternoon. When he awoke, Fleance sat in his bed, rubbing his eyes. For a moment, he didn't realize where he was; then the horrible memories of the day before rushed back. He almost wished he had stayed asleep forever.

Getting heavily to his feet, Fleance pushed aside the curtain divider, running his fingers through his hair and smiling self-consciously at Ronald's wife. She smiled back, pouring some milk.

"Did he make it back yet?"

She shook her head, offering him a cup.

Sighing, Fleance accepted it. "Perhaps his news will not be all bad."

He busied himself chopping wood, feeding the animals. Near dark, the brisk sound of hooves announced the long-awaited arrival.

Fleance came outside, uneasily watching the other dismount, and accompanied him in silence to the barn. Ronald took a long time brushing the horse, avoiding his eyes. It was easy to tell there was something wrong, but Fleance held his tongue, waiting for Ronald to come up with the right words.

Finally, the other straightened, putting a hand on the horse's back.

"I know you are innocent," he blurted.

"Innocent!" Fleance gasped. "Innocent of what?"

Ronald hesitated. "The word has spread that you killed your own father. The accusation is absurd; I know that."

Fleance turned away, stunned.

"It comes from the stabler," Ronald continued after a moment. "He mentioned something about your taking only one horse away, shortly after you and your father left both of your mounts with him. You didn't say anything, yet you were in a terrible hurry."

Fleance began pacing, his face filled with alarm.

His friend went on, apologetically. "I know, Fleance. What were you supposed to do, tell him you were running from your father's murderers? He could have been one of them." He coughed, embarrassed. "There is something else you should know. Macbeth, at the feast that very night, acted strangely. He kept talking to an empty chair, of murder and rising from the dead. One of the things he said was 'Never shake thy gory locks at me.' Men thought he was mad. Later, they said he was suffering from guilt." He looked sidelong at Fleance. "So you see...perhaps with time... ""

Fleance sighed, a heavy rattling sound.

"I think," Ronald said hurriedly, "most honest men suspect the King's hand in this. Fleance, I think that Macbeth had your father murdered, and intended to murder you, too. Though God knows why."

He stepped away from the horse, putting a hand on Fleance's arm.

"And yet, you must flee the country. You are no longer safe

here."

Fleance shook his head vehemently, though no words could come forth. Anxiously, Ronald's grasp tightened, communicating his tension better than words could have done.

"Listen to me," he said through clenched teeth. "If you stay, you are a dead man. How long can you hide?"

Fleance knew Ronald was really saying that he was afraid to give him shelter. If Ronald was discovered hiding a fugitive, his own life would be forfeit.

Tears falling from his eyes, Fleance nodded. "I will go."

"I will accompany you to the port, and pay your fare." Ronald sounded ashamed, but relieved.

But that meant nothing to Fleance. He was alone...more alone than ever in his life. And he was leaving his father unavenged.

2

Rhuddlan

Fleance tapped impatiently on the railing of the boat as he watched the north shore of Wales move slowly closer. He would not have chosen this backwards country as the place to ask for sanctuary. The reigning Prince, who resided in the very town they were approaching, was known to be ruthless. But this was the first ship to leave Scotland, and Ronald had insisted he take it, before it was too late.

So here he was, approaching a rustic, timber-walled town named Rhuddlan, where his future was going to be decided; he did not have the money to go farther. And he had no idea how to approach this Prince, whose name, Gruffydd ap Llewelyn, he could barely pronounce.

The wooden palace spanned the river Clwyd, giving access to the ships by a tall archway, below which their boat docked. Fleance flung his sack over his shoulder, not bothering to take his leave of the ship's captain. He didn't like the way that man looked at him.

Fleance made his way toward a large building that he guessed was the great hall. He slipped through a wide, open doorway, looking curiously around as he threaded his way between small tangles of men, who were waiting for the servants to set up the trestle tables.

The hall was larger than it looked from the outside. Two tall columns of trees supported the roof, their branches intertwining at the top. A long roof-pole was placed at the peak, and the spaces were filled in with thatch. The walls were made of stakes and wattle, allowing room for a nave on the outside of the columns, so that people had space to sleep. A long fire pit ran the length of the hall, and two rows of trestle tables were placed parallel to it. At the end, a slightly raised table faced the room.

It was common practice for nobles to daily feed a large household; newcomers were welcome as a matter of course. Knowing this, Fleance sat at the lower end of the tables as soon as they were ready; it would be his first meal that day.

Once the food showed up, Fleance was surprised at how easy it was to forget his misery. He even enjoyed this peasant fare, which he usually rejected at his father's table. After having somewhat appeased his appetite, Fleance looked up at the head table; all the places had been filled, and the servants were scrambling about with pitchers of wine and water. In the center, Gruffydd ap Llewelyn sat chin in hand, oblivious to the activity at his table. He was dressed more simply than many of his courtiers; a short-sleeved, untrimmed brown linen tunic set off muscular arms that seemed to glow red in the firelight. He wore no jewelry besides a thick gold arm ring and he drank from a simple clay mug. But there was no mistaking his regal bearing.

At first, Fleance thought the Prince was bored, but the man's restless head gave him away, moving slightly back and forth as he watched the movement in the hall. An index finger scratched through his bristly red whiskers, causing the attentive mead bearer to lean toward him inquiringly; though a shake of the fiery head sent the servant scurrying back.

To Gruffydd's right side sat his wife, a Saxon-looking lady, aloof and proud; her companions seemed to treat her too formally, as though conscious of her foreignness. On the Prince's other side sat a girl Fleance assumed must be his daughter, smiling absently while she stitched a piece of embroidery. The Princess was at that age when girlishness suddenly turns into womanhood. Her wrists and hands were tiny; glistening brown hair was cut short around the eyes and ears, like most of her country folk. Fleance found himself drawn to her.

Sighing, Fleance tore off a piece of bread and sopped up some gravy from his stew. Now that he was here, he didn't know quite what to do next. He supposed he could find some kind of work, but considering his noble upbringing, he had never been trained for labor, aside from the tasks every squire had to perform. This wasn't going to be easy. Perhaps the direct approach would work best.

Seeing a page come round his end of the table, Fleance beckoned to him. He put one of his last coppers into the boy's hand. "How difficult would it be to get an audience with the Prince?" he asked in halting Gaelic.

The page looked at him strangely, pursing his lips. "I don't know. I never tried it before." He looked at the head table apprehensively, then back at the coin. "I'll see what I can do, but it will take a little while."

The boy moved away, continuing to clear the table. Fleance watched him nervously, but forced himself to calm down, trusting to the boy's sense of his master's mood. Finally, after what seemed like hours, the page made his way to the head table.

Fleance watched as his messenger bent toward the Prince's ear, and pointed to the end of the room. The hair on the back of Fleance's neck stood on end as Gruffydd's piercing eyes looked directly at him. From this distance he couldn't tell whether Gruffydd was annoyed or curious, but he sighed with relief when the Prince nodded.

The boy returned. He would come back for Fleance when the Prince was ready.

An old man made his way toward center of the room, and the crowd began to quiet instantly, holding him in great respect. He waited until the Prince nodded at him, then broke into a sing-songy tale in Welsh, his voice rolling softly then loudly, quickly then slowly. Fleance did not understand what he was saying but was moved by the timber of the old man's voice. The tale was a long one, and there were many in the room who wiped their eyes toward the end. They had bards in Scotland, but none so melodic as this, and Fleance began to understand why the Welsh had such a reputation for their poetry.

When the story had finished, to the boisterous clamor of the guests, Gruffydd left the table and approached the bard, embracing him and complimenting him while the man bowed modestly. Then the Prince left the room just as quickly, while the more sober guests clamored for another. Someone handed the old man a harp, and he tuned it, while Fleance strained to see where the Prince had gone. He had to be satisfied with waiting a while longer.

The sweet notes from the harp fell gently on the ear, and Fleance pushed his bowl aside, laying his head on his arm at the table. He was not the only one to do so; the man next to him had already joined the music with a soft droning snore. Fleance closed his eyes, allowing his mind to wander back to Scotland...and safety.

He knew not how long he sat thus, but the music was still playing when the page was shaking his shoulder. Fleance sat up, embarrassed, and shook his head clear. The boy was tugging his sleeve. "Come," he said. "You don't want to keep the Prince waiting."

He snapped immediately to attention. Without a word, he followed the page through the same side door the Prince had used. They walked outside under a sheltered walkway that joined a smaller building. The page knocked then opened a door, gesturing for Fleance to go in, and closed the door behind him.

It took a minute for Fleance's eyes to adjust to the dark, because the wide, low-roofed room was only lit by a small brazier. The space was furnished sparsely but comfortably, evidently intended for the Prince and his family. The sleeping quarters were behind a half-wall at the other end.

Gruffydd sat alone in a high-backed chair facing the coals. He turned his chair to the side, beckoning the young man to approach.

From so close, Fleance was impressed by the strength of the proud Welshman. Heavy veins stood forth along his arms and down his thick neck. The Prince shifted his broad shoulders, as if stiff from tension.

"So. You are new here?" the Prince asked. Fleance was relieved that he spoke Gaelic.

"Yes. My name is Fleance, son of Banquo. From Scotland. I am of a noble house..." He hesitated, but decided to risk all on this first meeting. "Your Grace," he added, lowering his voice and sinking to one knee. "I have come to ask your protection. My father was cruelly murdered not a mile from King Macbeth's castle," he said, clenching his fists involuntarily, "and I barely escaped the same fate. I know not why he was killed, but I suspect treachery..." His throat tightened, and he couldn't speak for a moment.

Gruffydd scratched his beard. The Scots and the Welsh had very little to do with each other, except when their mutual hatred of the English brought them together for some profitable border raid. Still, even from this distance, the peculiar behavior of the Scots King had generated rumors.

This was the first direct contact Gruffydd had with any Scot of significance for many months. Perhaps he could benefit from some additional knowledge. He gestured for Fleance to seat himself on a bench, watching the youth recover gracefully from his fit of emotion. He found the newcomer intent but restrained, bold but cautious. Fleance looked him directly in the eye, not wavering even a second.

"I heard that the King murders his nobles," Gruffydd said.

Fleance nodded.

"I hear he rages like one who has lost his soul. What sort of sons are those who do not avenge the death of their father?"

Fleance glanced away. He thought of Banquo, bloody and struggling, expiring in the arms of his murderers...of his own flight and the guilt that plagued him night and day. With pain in his face, he turned back to the Prince, who was studying him closely. "They are the kind who wait...until sure of revenge."

Gruffydd sighed, looking into the fire. Though the boy did not know it, his own father, the valiant Llewelyn ap Seisylt, was also treacherously slain. And yet the murderer was still free, raiding the country and then slipping from his grasp. He nodded, bringing his eyes back to Fleance; in that instant a surge of sympathy and fellowship flowed between them.

"Yes. Stay with us here. Retribution will come in its own time."

Gruffydd stood, clasping Fleance's hand, and their understanding was complete.

Fleance spent his nights alongside the servants in the nave of the great hall. By day, he was permitted to ride in the Prince's train, while Gruffydd made little forays into the countryside. The Prince made sure of the grain supply and settled local disputes, and checked the condition of defense fortresses stationed along the coast. The Welsh Prince found that he liked Fleance's company, and often turned to him for comment, comparing customs of Wales and Scotland.

Before long, Fleance was allowed access to the royal apartments, and he occasionally crossed paths with the beautiful, but shy Princess. Anxious to gain her confidence, he would stop her with some casual greeting; she smiled, seemed friendly, but her answers gave him no opening to pursue. He often thought she was on the verge of saying something more, though she would always seem to think better of it. Clutching her ever-present piece of embroidery, studying the stitches with extravagant care, the girl would murmur an apology. Then, before he could stop her, she'd slip away, leaving him scratching his head.

Fleance was frustrated all the more when he would catch a glimpse of her unawares, talking to one of her maids or exchanging pleasantries with her mother over dinner. She did not appear at all ill at ease until she caught him looking at her; then she would look hastily away with a frown.

Some weeks after Fleance's arrival, the town of Rhuddlan prepared for its annual sheep-shearing festival. The Prince enjoyed this event, because he always made it a point to challenge all comers to a wrestling match. Few men were of a size to give him much trouble, but their enthusiasm made up for lack of strength.

Although Fleance had never shorn a sheep in his life, he was willing to learn. For two days before the festival he practiced, until finally he could handle the clippers without embarrassing himself.

On the morning of the festival Fleance tried his hand at the shearing, though he was quickly eliminated from the contest. He was glad that Nesta was nowhere around to see him lose, but he still felt good for the effort. After the sheep were finished, there was an archery contest, then a race, and finally the wrestling matches. Gruffydd came out, stripped down to a thin kyrtle and bare feet. The spectators formed a circle. Fleance stayed to the rear, standing on a box he had brought for the purpose.

"The prize," said the Prince, turning around, "is a full-grown ram, out of my own herd."

There was murmur of appreciation.

"Now, the rules. A man is considered beaten if his back touches the ground, or one shoulder and the opposite heel. If a man just barely escapes a fall, it is considered a foil; two foils are considered a fall. Is that clear?"

The crowd shouted yes; the rules were known to all, and Gruffydd was going over a formality.

That being done, the first man came forward; he was a large peasant who outweighed the Prince by about forty pounds. They faced each other a couple of feet apart, circling slowly, arms held out, eyes intent on the other's body. Suddenly they leaped together, hands locked on upper arms, and pushed with all their strength. Neither man gave an inch; both seemed rooted to the ground.

Then, just as suddenly, they broke apart, circling, feinting with a hand here, an elbow there. Gruffydd jerked his shoulder and followed through, wrapping his arms around the peasant's body, catching him off balance; with a swift leg around the other's calf, Gruffydd dropped his opponent heavily to the ground.

Standing up, taking a deep breath, the Prince laughed heartily, then reached down to help the man up. Cheerfully, the other accepted his hand, stood a little painfully, and walked off amid laughter, shaking his head and daring his friends to try.

There followed a much smaller man, who fell rather quickly, then a handful of others, all with the same result. Throwing up his hands, Gruffydd took a break, allowing other contenders to take the ring. He would fight the winner later.

Puffing happily, Gruffydd came over to Fleance, dropping to the ground. He took a flask of water, drinking so quickly that most of the contents spilled all over his chest. With a satisfied burp, Gruffydd wiped a hand over his mouth.

"Well, my young friend. What do you think about all this?"

Fleance smirked. "I say that most of these men need training. Their moves are awkward, and they leave a lot of easy openings."

"Oh, ho!" cried the Welshman, sitting up. "A bit of an expert, are you? Would you like to pit your skill against mine? We shall see how much you really know."

Enjoying the game, Fleance looked down his nose. "They taught me some small skill in Scotland. We are not totally ignorant. But Sire, you have me at a slight disadvantage." He looked down at his own body, nicely proportioned but of no great size.

"No more than some of those others who dared face me. And you are fresh. Come, there is no turning back now."

Expecting such a response, Fleance stood up, pulling off his tunic. He put his belt back on over the kyrtle and announced himself ready.

The circle widened as Gruffydd returned; the wrestlers broke off and backed away. The Prince stepped in, shook Fleance's hand, and crouched before him, big hands spread.

Suddenly Gruffydd was a different person.

The Scot was glad he was facing this man in friendship. Looking at those determined eyes, he saw nothing but battle frenzy, a frightful sight. There was no fun in this; Gruffydd was fighting to win, with a single-minded determination that had nothing to do with sport.

Shaken, Fleance struggled to remember all those tricks he had learned, and cursed his ego for getting him into trouble again.

But he had no time for that. The Prince didn't even waste a moment circling; he jumped onto Fleance, intending to grip him in a breath-crushing hug. He roared when his prey slipped from his embrace. Turning, Gruffydd charged again; expecting this, Fleance ducked, running away a few steps. He was breathing heavily; he needed time to think.

Surprised that the youth was still on his feet, the onlookers shouted and hooted, driving Gruffydd into a frenzy. Crouching again, the Prince dove low, taking Fleance off his feet with a great heave to the knees.

There was no getting out of that one, and Fleance barely managed to twist to one side, hitting the ground hard with his shoulder. Ignoring the pain, he jumped up, managing to leap on the Prince's back. But that was a mistake; with a shout of triumph, Gruffydd fell straight back, pinning the unfortunate Scot under his own body.

The Welsh cheered, but Fleance didn't notice. All the air had fled from his lungs, and he lay still, staring at the sky. There was a deadening pain in his left shoulder, wrenched into searing fire as Gruffydd lifted him from the ground by the same arm.

His mouth open, Fleance's head fell to one side. And for a fleeting moment, he thought he saw a look of vicious glee on Gruffydd's face before everything went black.

3

Forbidden Fruit

Fleance's eyes fluttered open, to be greeted with a most pleasant sight. Nesta was bent over him, putting a wet cloth on his forehead. When she saw that he was looking at her, she pulled back, but he grabbed her wrist gently with his good hand.

"Am I in heaven?" he asked innocently, letting her go after a moment.

Unable to help it, the girl laughed, a sound so delightful that it all seemed worth the pain. "No," she said. "You are in a little room next to my father's. You see, he was so worried about you, that he ordered a new bed for you...so you would be more comfortable." The last words came out more slowly, as his eyes caught hers and held them.

Fleance smiled. That was a long sentence for her. If this was the way to the Princess's heart, he would have to stay sick for a while. He tried to sit up, but was brought back down by a shooting pain across his shoulders and down his left arm.

Maybe he would not have to pretend after all.

Seeing his grimace, Nesta dropped a bowl onto the table and bent over him, adjusting the pillow. He grinned, embarrassed.

"Have I been unconscious long?" he asked, admiring the girl's eyelashes.

"Just since yesterday. The surgeon gave you something to make you sleep." She straightened, satisfied with her work.

"Surgeon?" Fleance nearly sat again.

"Now, do not move again, unless I tell you to."

A deep voice behind her said, "There you are, daughter. Taking care of him, I see."

Nesta whirled around.

"He seems much better," she said hurriedly, and turned once again to Fleance, "Do as I say now. I will return later."

Gruffydd didn't watch her go; he grabbed a stool and brought it over to the bed.

"It seems we pulled your arm from its socket, my son. Took a bad fall, you did. We have a lot of work ahead of us, before your shoulder feels right again."

Fleance nodded, wondering at the change in this man. Did he imagine all that savagery in his agitated state? Gruffydd seemed so considerate...so concerned. Yet he would have liked an apology. Perhaps he would approach the question from a different angle.

"You are a formidable opponent," he said.

A brief smile flickered across Gruffydd's face. "How do you think I got to where I am?"

How, indeed. Fleance had not thought of that.

"Then again," the Prince added, his grin broadening, "you showed me a few moves I never saw before. I must say, it surprised me to find you on my back."

Fleance didn't feel like smiling. His ribs were still sore from that surprise. "It did not take you long to react."

"No." For a moment, Gruffydd studied his companion. "In my position, sometimes it seems that everyone wants a chance to best me. If a man can beat me in battle, he may very well become the next prince, especially if he finds support from my fickle subjects."

He spat into the rushes. "I tell you, lad, this is not a great feeling. It is not by chance I treat every match like it may be my last. I disciplined myself until that response became natural. That is why I host the wrestling match every year: to remind people that I am a man to be reckoned with. Just in case they forget. It can't hurt to break a couple of bones in the process… there may come a time when I will need every ounce of strength and ferocity just to stay alive."

Fleance couldn't help it; what Gruffydd was saying reminded him of Banquo, blood flowing from his face. Where was his father's extra strength? Looking away, Fleance wiped his eyes.

"Aye," continued the other, "I think I know what is bothering you. Your poor father did not have a chance. I doubt whether anyone has, when it comes to ambush. I am glad, though, that you escaped. In some ways, you have come to be the son I never had."

Suddenly tired, the Prince got up to leave. He gave Fleance a look so full of affection, that the younger man forgot his anger.

Fleance stayed abed the rest of the week, tended carefully by Nesta. With each passing day, the girl's shyness receded. She read to him, an accomplishment Fleance viewed with awe. This flattered her, giving her confidence.

They both regretted the day Fleance announced himself well. He had to favor his arm, of course, but he ran out of excuses to stay in bed. In a way, Fleance was grateful for the accident. The barrier between Nesta and himself was forever broken.

There was something different about the girl. She was so full of innocence, a precious treasure whose qualities surprised him more every day. Her touch, soft and sweet, sent a new kind of thrill through his veins. This was no peasant girl, earthy and strong, enjoying physical love so naturally a part of living. Nesta was a spiritual, an intellectual being. Her mind soared above his own.

And yet, Fleance had the feeling he was crossing forbidden territory. What started as a harmless flirtation had blossomed into something he couldn't control. Nesta was a princess, thus removed from normal society. Her very existence was sheltered; she was carefully tutored and raised quietly at the palace, away from children her own age. Daughters of kings were destined to be peace makers, giving their hand in marriage to cement a political bond. Love was a luxury that wasn't considered important.

Yet he was awakening unaccustomed sensations in the girl;

watching her flourish was a delight in itself. Her responsiveness was whole-hearted, and he found himself overwhelmed with happiness... and something else. He knew he should suppress these forbidden yearnings.

There were not a lot of opportunities to pursue the girl anyway, since she was mostly sequestered inside the castle. However, the dinner hour became their favorite time, since Gruffydd allowed Fleance to sit beside her at head table, and the two youths often spent hours talking together, stretching out their time together as long as decency allowed. Ealdgyth usually came back into the feasting hall looking for Nesta before she retired to her bedchamber. Exasperated, smiling a little, she and Nesta fell into a routine where the daughter pretended not to realize how late it was, and the mother put out a hand to draw her away. Never did Nesta leave the hall without a backward glance.

One night a few months after Fleance's arrival, he slipped outside the sleeping hall for a short walk. It was long after the moon had set, but he couldn't sleep. He was anxious, his mind troubled.

Time weighed heavy on him. It had been long since Ronald had written. Why was he shamefully idle here, when he should be seeking ways to return to Scotland? Or could he more honestly be called coward? He had no money, no resources. What could a lone man do…and one who had barely reached twenty, at that? Or was he just making excuses? Did the girl have such a hold on him that he couldn't stir from her side?

Perhaps he should start out on his own—find his friend, Prince Malcolm, who was said to be in England. The Prince had need of his services; had he not lost a kingdom as well as a father? Perhaps his own aim could best be served by helping Malcolm regain the crown. Sighing, Fleance took another turn around the courtyard.

But suddenly he stopped, forgetting about his troubles. Nesta stood in front of him, lightly clad in a chemise. Judging by the way she was rubbing her eyes, she must have just awakened. Embarrassed, she smiled when she saw him.

They walked side by side, her hand resting so lightly on his arm that he barely felt it, except for the tingling underneath her touch. She turned her head to him and smiled. They talked about the stars, they talked about the land, they talked about love. Fleance loved Nesta; he told her so.

They stopped. Nesta took his hands and kissed his forehead. Then her lips moved down, found his eyes, his nose, his lips. He slipped his hands from hers, placing his palms on the softness of her thighs. With a little sigh, Nesta allowed herself to lean into his welcoming arms.

The darkness covered them, encouraged them. Fleance raised her chin, placed his lips softly against hers, then harder, seeking to purge his pent-up emotions. His tongue parted her lips, gently pushing between them. With a rush that surprised him, she met his passion, responding with her body as well as her mouth.

Fleance lifted her from the ground, feeling the heat rise to his face as she put her arms around his neck and buried her face in his shoulder. He slid through the shadows along the wall then slipped quietly through the gate, toward the river.

Finding a slight depression under a willow tree, he put her down and spread his cloak on the ground. They knelt together, and he drew her toward him.

He kissed her, pulling her with him to the ground, rolling her slender body atop his own. Without thinking, eager hands cupped around her soft bottom, breath quickened at her eagerness to settle comfortably on his growing hardness.

She moved slightly back and forth over his trembling body. No stranger to women, Fleance found himself anxious as a school boy. For so many months he had admired her, desired her, and here she was, more responsive than he had ever dared hope.

Fleance moved his hands up her back, touching her soft

breasts that lay snugly against his chest. She moved slightly, freeing them, eager for his touch. He pressed his lips against their roundness, feeling her nipples grow hard through the linen. With quivering hands, Fleance reached for the cord holding her chemise at the neck and pulled it free.

Slowly, daunted by her milky white skin, he pulled the dress down over her shoulders, revealing perfectly formed breasts. Moaning slightly, he buried his face between them.

He couldn't restrain himself any longer. Moving her to the ground, he pulled the chemise all the way down her body, off past her feet. His own tunic soon followed.

For a long moment he knelt there, admiring her. She lay still, glowing slightly against the dark cloak, hair lying loose around her face, long legs crossed.

Then he was upon her, pushing against her body so hard he must have hurt her. But she didn't let out a sound, only dug her fingers into his back.

Catching himself, relaxing, Fleance lowered his body slowly back onto hers. She was already wet, straining, a soft moan coming from her lips as she pushed upward toward him. With a groan, releasing his tension, he thrust deep inside, her own sharp cry drowned by the rush in his ears, the passion taking control, holding him. He thrust again and again; after her first convulsive shudder, she wrapped her legs around his body, giving herself to the rocking motion of his demanding passion. It was compelling, fervent, climaxing with a cry that she sought to suppress with a hand over his mouth.

No need; after that moment, he was all shudders, deep breaths, grasping fingers. Sighing, Nesta lowered her head to the ground.

She had felt the rush of his juices flowing into her. Her body ached with the pain of her first encounter, her loins sticky with blood. The ground was hard beneath her back, and sharp stones poked at her shoulder blades. But she felt good, heated, the flames of desire not yet dampened. Fleance lay across her, breathing hard.

After long moments, their breathing slowed. Nesta stroked her lover, cuddling him; he raised his head, reluctant to look at her, obviously embarrassed. Anticipating an apology about his abruptness, she laid a finger against his lips, shaking her head.

"There will be other times," she whispered. There was a hardly noticeable quiver to her voice.

The next day, Nesta stayed in her bed, protesting that she was unwell. Fleance went about his duties, worried, anxious. He was unnerved, expecting at any moment to be cornered, accused, condemned. Were they found out? Or had she regretted their lovemaking?

Nightfall seemed to take forever. When it came, Fleance waited for his beloved, wandering anxiously through the courtyard, trying to catch sight of the Princess. He wanted to soothe her, offer any protestations of sincerity she deemed necessary.

He clenched and unclenched his hands, alternately drawing his dagger and replacing it into the scabbard, until he finally threw it at the same tree that had shaded their first kiss. The blade sunk deep into the trunk. He sat upon a rock and stared at it, chin in hand.

Dawn found Fleance in the same position, as did Nesta, who stole upon him, laying a hand on his shoulder. He did not move, though she was sure he knew it was her.

"I've watched you for hours," she said, "from my window. Oh, how I fear for us… How I fear for our love."

Fleance turned, taking her hand and kissing her fingers.

"As for our love," he murmured, "we were destined to meet. We must not fault the powers that drew us together. All else will follow."

Fleance never suspected the truth of that statement. All he

cared for was the softness of her hair, the warmth of the lips that parted to accept his caressing tongue. Neither of them noticed the shade that quivered behind them: the ghost of Banquo, nodding in grave acquiescence to the witches' prophecy.

Then she was gone, afraid of prying eyes. She left behind a slight whiff of fragrance, and something else: in Fleance's palm lay a trembling pink rose: a reminder of those last few moments of bliss.

The ensuing weeks passed quickly and quietly. By night, they met in secret, always changing the scene and time. For these two, time was meaningless as long as they were together. Had circumstances been different, theirs would have been considered a great love.

Fleance forgot about returning to Scotland.

But time and again, Nesta was haunted by the vision of her father and her lost duty as princess: the pledge of her hand, made when she was still in the crib. She was betrothed to another; never mind that she had never met him. She knew that Fleance should know, but the right occasion to tell him never seemed to present itself. It was too soon to ruin the feelings so dearly come by.

The summer passed thus, in peace and contentment. There were no invasions to fight, no illness to suffer, no hardships to endure. It was a time of rare tranquility, and Wales flourished under the gentle sun.

4

A Chastisement

The sky was threatening rain that chill autumn day, and Nesta looked up at the clouds through a film of tears. She had been searching all morning for Fleance, and finally discovered him on his return from archery practice.

Before the Princess reached him Fleance knew something was wrong; she was shaking her head, gripping her cloak so tightly that her little fist quivered. When she stopped before him, trembling all over, he wanted to put his arms around her; but he dared not, fearing the unseen eyes he always felt on his back.

They walked, careful not to touch, until they found a secluded spot. Making sure no one was watching, Fleance drew her into the shadow of a small shed.

"What is wrong?" he whispered.

She burst into tears. "There is no longer any doubt," she gasped, lowering her head. "May God help us, I am with child..."

Fleance stared, unable for a moment to react. The birds called to one another over his head, and somewhere near, a child was screaming. Nesta was wiping her eyes with her sleeve. She took a deep breath, waiting for him to do something.

Reluctant to face her, he looked at the slanted roof of the shed, at the palisades beyond, at his own fingers resting on the coarse wooden wall; he noticed that the thumbnail was cracked. His fingers curled into a fist and his fist hit the wall. He had to gather his wits! What was he, a dullard? The girl needed him now most of all, and all he could think of was Gruffydd and those smoldering eyes.

"My Lord," she said, barely a whisper. "What say you, my Lord?" The entreaty pulled him back, and he noticed she was shivering. Fleance took her hand and kissed it, trying to gain time.

"We must think," he mumbled. "Who else knows?"

"Only my nurse." She withdrew her hand and pulled herself up proudly, aware in her misery that he was not going to be any help. Her eyes bore into his face and he looked away uncertainly.

Nesta wanted to wail, to throw herself at his feet and beg her lover to take her away, far away where they wouldn't have to hide any more, where they could be together and not be ashamed.

But no, she was a princess, and he a landless exile. Above all, she had to retain her dignity. So she sighed and turned away, leaving Fleance staring helplessly.

Later that day, Fleance stood dumbly near the lady's chamber, waiting patiently, seeing nothing while staring at her door. Finally, she came out, pausing at the sight of the man she still loved most desperately. Without looking around, he came up to her.

"I say we act immediately," he said hurriedly. "Let us not waste time and lose courage. I shall tell your father..." She moved to speak but he shook his head. "...and I shall ask him for your hand in marriage. He cannot say nay," he added, confidently.

Wanting to cry out in relief, Nesta was checked instead by fear. "You do not know him like I do. He listens to no one, heeds no counsel but his own. Though I love you, Fleance, I know you are not meant to be my husband. I have been promised to someone else."

Even as she said the words, Nesta knew he wasn't listening. Fleance looked at her one last time with assurance, and she stilled her tongue, knowing that in his own way, Fleance was much like her father. Her eyes pleaded with him to stay but he was retreating slowly. She wanted to beg him to come back...but she didn't try. Nesta had another to consider now; her passions could never again hold sway over reason.

Yet she knew she was ruined, for her heart was unalterably pledged to a dead man.

Fleance was not so ready to admit that he couldn't get the best of the powerful Prince. After all, wasn't Gruffydd ap Llewelyn second only to himself in strength of wit and in cunning? Surely he couldn't object to his daughter giving her hand when she had already given her heart, and to one whose noble ancestry spanned many generations.

Fleance searched impatiently for the Prince, finding him once again in the room where they first talked. Gruffydd was already half turned to the open door. The hearth was silent and gloomy, reflecting a pall that seemed to settle on the older man's face. Yes, he did seem old, Fleance thought.

"Come in," Gruffydd said wearily, motioning with a slack hand.

Swallowing his agitation, Fleance moved before him. "My father," he began, using the endearment he had long since taken up. But this time it did not cheer his benefactor. "My father, you have long considered me your son, have you not?"

After a hesitation, Gruffydd nodded.

"Then, please, Sire, I propose you make it a fact in the eyes of the kingdom as well as the eyes of our family."

The Prince straightened in his chair, his eyes flashing; Fleance stepped back a pace.

"What I mean," he added nervously, "is that I am asking your blessing to marry Nesta, whom I cherish above myself."

Gruffydd grasped the arms of his chair, pushing his body heavily to his feet. "Marry?" he asked in disbelief. "Wed you with my daughter?" He nearly roared.

Fleance stood firm. "I mean to make her my wife. I am a suitable match, by any standards."

"Suitable!" He spit the word. "I take you in, a hungry, begging castaway, and you have the bile to take my daughter from me? Of what use would that be?"

Fleance didn't answer.

"She is the key to the kingdom; with her lies the succession.

You think you carry the blood to sire kings? I cannot believe what I am hearing. Did you come merely to seek the throne?"

It was Fleance's turn to become angry. His hand unconsciously went to his sword, which it was his privilege to wear in the royal presence. Gruffydd watched him, eyes moving from the boy's face to his hand.

"To what end, the kingship of Wales?" the Scot said scornfully. "Eternally a vassal of England. I need none of that. But your daughter should be happy, not a pawn in your game of chess."

Gruffydd angrily shrugged off this statement. "It matters not. What does matter is what I say. And I forbid you ever to mention it again, ever to be alone with her again."

"Yes," he added in response to Fleance's frown, "you spend too much time together in idle pursuits. I should have stopped you long ago, but instead like a fool I turned a blind eye to your purposeless romance. I believe I will go ahead with my plan to send her away for a while, to learn some courtly manners. Especially as regards suitors to her crown!"

He stopped uneasily, as Fleance did not rise to the bait. The youth most certainly wanted to say something, but hesitated.

"Out with it!" the Prince snapped.

"My Lord..." The words came too slow. "Your daughter–it is no longer so easy."

Gruffydd's face turned red, but he waited.

"Nesta...she will have my child."

All breathing stopped, as their eyes said more than words could ever express.

Fleance braced himself, still clasping the sword hilt. He watched Gruffydd close the door, return a few paces, then stop. The Prince's anger was appalling, seething like a volcano.

"You repay my hospitality in this manner?" spoke Gruffydd through clenched teeth. "You so easily betray the sacred trust of your host, then come strutting in like nothing is amiss? You have the stupidity to face me?"

His rage burst through; in an instant he sprang upon Fleance, and the latter, unwilling to raise his hand against a prince, even at the point of mortal danger, carefully tried to fend off the grip of the huge hands. It would have been fruitless in any case; Gruffydd, savage like the country that bred him, broke the neck of the Scot and threw him pitilessly onto the flagstones. The body shivered and collapsed.

The door flew open with a slam against the wall, and Nesta looked up from her sewing, braced for the livid face of her father. Carefully she put her work aside and rose, expecting to be struck back down by a blow she hoped would end her unhappy life.

But he did not touch her.

"Is it true?" he asked, clenching his fists.

"Yes," she nodded. "You killed him, didn't you?"

Gruffydd did not answer. His usual look of tenderness was gone forever; all she could see was smoldering rage. Nesta subdued her urge to quail before him.

"Then kill me too, father, for I do not deserve to live."

"Nay," he rasped, "that is too good for you. But you are no longer my daughter. You are no longer my daughter." He choked for a second, then left her, his beautiful child, weeping pitifully as she sank to the floor.

Nesta didn't know how long she lay there. The sun was nearly gone when her mother, somber and silent, packed a few of her clothes. Ealdgyth took her daughter by the arm, leading her from the room, outside of the keep, and into the poorer section of the compound, where the Princess was to be lodged with the servants and cooks.

Ealdgyth instructed the servants to clear a space in the corner of the kitchen. Silently, they brought in a pile of hay, and the Queen took a blanket from one of her maids and spread it over the hay. Another blanket was folded and placed on top. Nesta stood by, watching her mother as if she didn't understand, and

Ealdgyth shook her head as she put a box with her daughter's clothes at the foot of the makeshift bed. Nesta sat on the box and watched her mother turn and motion for the maid to follow her. Ealdgyth did not look back.

The Princess was left alone, forsaken, and the servants stood uncomfortably around her, not knowing what to make of their new companion. She thought to herself how strange it was that she had never bothered to notice these faces before. Then she fainted.

For a long time the servants avoided her, afraid of repercussions. One day she was in disgrace; the next day, who knows? But Nesta was a quiet and sweet presence, and they all remembered her kindness in her better days. She fell into their routine, clumsily at first, but learning simple tasks without complaint, even as her smooth hands began to roughen and bruises appeared on her white arms. She had a smile for everyone, even when she seemed most miserable.

After a couple of weeks, as no notice was paid to her from the other side of the castle, an older couple, Owain and Godgifu, took Nesta into their home. They only had a corner by the fireplace for her, but it was a great improvement over the noisy kitchen. The change was lucky for her; the pregnancy was very difficult.

In time, Ealdgyth managed an occasional visit, bringing a package now and then. Once, she brought Fleance's sword, which brought tears to her daughter's eyes. But she never had a word of encouragement; Gruffydd refused to speak his daughter's name.

Finally one day, as Ealdgyth was visiting, six guards rushed in, careful not to hurt anyone but insistent that she return at once. Nesta kissed her mother one last time, then wept quietly as the footsteps diminished, grasping her stomach and leaning heavily against Owain. He picked her up and carried her to bed, calling for his wife. The others scrambled for help. A midwife was called from the village.

It was a long labor, lasting throughout the night. At dawn, Nesta was delivered of a healthy son, who she named Walter. The new mother, exhausted but smiling for once, went easily to sleep.

The servants quietly celebrated among themselves. They drank to the fortune of the new heir...the heir they knew would never reign.

5

The Weird Sisters

In the midst of a starless night, three ragged forms appeared out of the blackness. They stooped over the sleeping newborn's cradle, craggy faces dark with ageless knowledge. Old women they were, never seen apart, and even in the not-so-distant memory of the child's ancestors, they were met with, once before. The weird sisters had many names in many cultures; the Greeks called them the Fates, the Scandinavians, the Norns.

Slowly swaying back and forth, they murmured so indistinctly that no one else in the room was disturbed, if indeed they could have wakened at all. Like curls of smoke, fog crept through the shutters, under the door, and through the chimney. Wisps slowly settled into the hollows of the slumbering forms, nestling into crooks of arms, the indentations of sleeping eyes. Mist seeped into the shreds of the strangers' cloaks.

The weird sisters intoned their decree in a language known only to themselves. Then they broke into a more distinct chant, speaking directly to the sleeping boy-child:

Our eyes will be on you, our tempest-tost child,
The next fifteen years shall be awkward and wild.
To come to this point we have boiled and troubled;
'Till Banquo had fallen; Macbeth we befuddled.
We have no concern with the tragedies falling,
But must have our answers when Hecate comes calling.
"Thou shalt 'get kings" we told your grandfather;
Though thou shall not be one, you'll bring us another.
In the time that we want in the kingdom we choose
You will give us a son, and his fate we will use.
It will take many more until finally we'll see
The king who'll 'get kings that has long been decreed.

Eye of a lion, grey horsehair and bladder,
You'll act 'fore you reason until you learn better.
Wings of a bat, claws of an eagle,
Our charms will uphold you; your arguments feeble
'Gainst our interference with your life and death.
Our powers exceed those supposed by Macbeth.

No sooner were those words spoken then the witches were gone. Nesta, stirring uncomfortably, got up and adjusted the bed-clothing of her son. Kissing him, she went back to sleep.

On Walter's second birthday, the ragged crowd of friends and family, as he knew it, gathered to watch the ceremony given for every child born to a warrior. Owain held the boy on his lap, beaming and laughing as he tried to wriggle free.

Nesta carefully placed a small chunk of meat on the tip of Fleance's sword, and slowly lowered the weapon, putting the food into her startled son's mouth.

"With this first piece of solid food," she said, "may God take this child into his care, born of a father long dead but never forgotten. May he die no other death than by the sword."

Walter sat perfectly still, as if he truly understood the import of these words. And perhaps he did, thought Nesta, for often people told her they had never seen such a fey child. Strange child, she nodded in mute agreement as he chewed the morsel and craned his head at the faces surrounding him. Sometimes she wondered how he could have come from her, since she had known nothing strange or unusual in her life.

Having much to do, the small crowd was already moving away, patting the boy on the head as they passed. Nesta took her son into her arms and he patted her head in imitation of the others. Odd or not, this child was all she had to live for. Still, as always, she waited hopefully for her proud father to relent. But as the second year rolled into the third, she was forced to resign herself to the servitude he had sentenced her to. All for one indiscretion...as if losing her beloved Fleance wasn't enough.

Walter put his chubby arms around her neck.

She smoothed back his curls, thick, brown, and long, and let a finger linger in a stubborn tangle. "Let me tell you about your grandfather," she said, as the boy gazed at her with steady brown eyes. "You know who he is?" The child nodded.

"Never, at least for now, must you talk to him...never attract his attention. He is a strong warrior, a good prince." A tear worked its way down Nesta's cheek. "He was a good father, once. But he is fierce in anger.

"Remember one thing, Walter. Whatever a king does, one must never question. Ever. Even if one doesn't understand; especially even if one does, and thinks he is wrong. For a king has too many things to think about; he is, after all, responsible for the well-being of a whole country. He will be answerable to the Lord above, just like the rest of us, but more so."

Walter nodded his head, dropping from his mother's lap. He wandered to the door, pausing with his hand on the frame, and glanced back at her with that strange knowing look of his. As the boy disappeared from his mother's sight, she bit at her fingernails in consternation.

Nesta was relieved that he could not yet grasp all that she was saying, yet the time would come when she would have to tell her son about Fleance, before he heard it elsewhere. And yet, how was she going to tell him, without betraying the bitterness that gnawed at her insides? How could she keep him from hating...hating until there was nothing left in his soul?

6

Salwyn

A six year old boy sat brooding on his favorite rock overlooking a deep gully in the woods. The child was so tall and husky that he could easily pass for twice his age; but his size never seemed to protect him from the sharp jeers of his companions.

Walter shook his head, biting his lip. How many times would he have to endure those insults from the other boys? He knew that there was something different about him and his mother, something the others knew, at least in part. But try as he would, he could pry nothing from Nesta. His mother was silent about too many matters that seemed too important, and the other elders kept a wary distance from him. Just what was the mystery?

He was torn from his sulking by a trampling in the woods, and a girl's scream. Jumping to his feet, Walter looked around for a stout stick. He grabbed a long branch, but it broke when he banged it against a tree. The scream rose to a shriek as he frantically picked up first one then another stick, until he spied a suitable club sticking out from a pile of leaves. Satisfied by the object's weight, he dashed toward the commotion.

Breaking into a clearing, he surprised a wild pig in the act of rushing toward a little girl. She was frantically trying to climb a tree, and her screaming drowned the sound of Walter's approach. Intent on its prey, the pig didn't notice the boy behind it, club upraised. The beast was snarling viciously until the stick made contact squarely on its head. With a yelp, the startled animal swung on its attacker.

Walter was ready for it.

Gnashing its teeth and shaking blood from its head, the pig hardly paused before charging blindly. Taking aim, the boy swung hard, delivering a crushing blow at the jaw. He followed with a kick that annoyed the creature rather than hurt it.

The pig eyed Walter, taking a step closer, then seemed to think better of it; turning its tail, it ran into the woods. This was just as well, for Walter had broken the stick on the animal's teeth.

The girl was still clutching the tree, afraid to move. But she had quit screaming, and looked at Walter with eyes like blue saucers.

"I came upon it by accident while it was grubbing for roots," she said, starting to cry. "It attacked me. You saved me." The tears came full force now, and Walter didn't know what to do. He watched her dumbly until she stopped.

Walter knew her name; it was Myrna. Her father was a proud, retired warrior who had lost half a foot in battle; now he was a farmer. Myrna's mother had died some years ago, and Salwyn kept to himself, raising the child alone. Walter had seen her occasionally in the village, watching the goings-on from the shelter of this tree or that corner, never venturing to talk to strangers. He guessed that she was a year or so younger than himself.

The girl insisted that he walk her home, tugging at his sleeve and looking up at him trustingly. Reluctantly, he agreed. She pulled him along, across a footbridge over the river, between scattered houses to a little farm. Behind a thatched-roof house, an older man straightened from his garden patch, a broad smile breaking over his face. But his smile disappeared when the girl, feeling safe at home, broke into tears. She threw herself trembling into his arms.

Listening to her broken story, Salwyn surveyed the self-conscious boy over her head. His clear, steel-grey eyes were sharp and expressive, crinkling at the corners in a way that made him look very kind. He scratched his short grizzled hair.

"Come here, boy," he said when his daughter had finished. He pointed to a polished broadsword, leaning against the wall of the house. "Since you're so good with a stick, how would you like to learn to use such as this?"

Walter's eyes shone. He gingerly picked up the weapon, the only other one like his father's he had ever seen; and his father's sword was out of reach—until, his mother said, he was old enough to handle it.

He looked up at the old man gratefully. This was the first kindness a stranger had ever shown him. "When do we begin?"

Salwyn smiled. "Come back tomorrow, and I'll give you your first lesson."

He watched as the boy went down the hill toward his home. He knew the tales about Walter and his questionable birth; his heart had always gone out to the lad when he heard how fearlessly the boy defended himself against the other bullies. Walter needed a father, and Salwyn had always wanted a son. For years he had chafed to teach his sharply honed skills to another, since he no longer could use them. Perhaps this young boy needed a father as much as he needed a pupil.

At dawn, Walter was back. He stood at the gate, watching Salwyn take his time washing his face from a bowl of fresh water. The man put down his cloth and turned to Walter, looking the boy up and down. Then he beckoned him over, handing him a wooden practice sword; Myrna came out the door, taking her father's hand.

Walter took the sword and made a cut like he saw the soldiers do on the practice field. The weight took his arms a little farther than he expected and threw him off balance. He frowned and did it again. And again.

"Here lad," Salwyn said, while picking up his daughter and sitting her on a tiny chair. "Let me show you how to hold it with two hands." He picked up another practice sword and demonstrated, showing Walter how to coordinate both hands while controlling the hilt of the sword.

"Now, parry," he barked, throwing a light swing toward the

boy's head. Not showing the least surprise, Walter brought his own stick up and blocked the blow cleanly, as if by instinct. Salwyn smiled. This was going to be fun.

Through the rest of the morning, Salwyn taught his pupil how to cut and thrust with his practice sword. He took Walter through a series of movements designed to improve his balance and strength.

"Now, you can practice this on your own," Salwyn said, "even with a stick. Now run along home for lunch."

"I'm not hungry," Walter protested.

"But I have work to do, son. We can start again tomorrow."

Walter opened his mouth to complain, but thought better of it as Myrna ran up to him, presenting him a bunch of flowers she picked by the riverside. Walter smiled crookedly, taking the flowers. "Thanks, Myrna. I'll take these home to my mother."

Salwyn leaned on his sword as he waved good-bye to Walter. He was tired, but felt better than he had in years. He tousled his daughter's hair. "Well, child. Let's find a nice stout post for Walter to practice against. I think I'll put it in the ground over there, under that oak tree."

The next day, Walter was back for more, and every day after that. Salwyn started him off every day with stretching exercises, a workout on the post, or pell, as he called it, then some simple sparring, showing Walter the footwork he had to master before he could move on to the next lesson.

Before long, Walter spent almost all his time with Salwyn. When they weren't practicing, Walter was helping Salwyn in his garden. Myrna would tag along when they gardened, and she loved to make necklaces for Walter out of clover flowers. The older man was often and again surprised at how boisterous she became in his company; his daughter had never before come out of her shell. Walter demonstrated a patient tolerance for her, though Salwyn could see that she was more of a nuisance to him than a pleasure.

Within months, Walter had achieved a skill beyond his years. Many of his companions could barely lift a heavy broadsword. But though he started with a wooden replica, Walter was already practicing with his master's own weapon. Salwyn taught him to ride bareback on his old work horse, since a warrior had to ride to the battlefield. Soon Walter was learning the battle axe and the javelin. Lastly, would learn the longbow: the weapon of choice with any Welsh soldier.

"Yes," Salwyn would say in his more communicative moments, "you will never lack for work. Your skill at arms will be prized over all the others." And his eyes would glisten proudly.

But there was something else. There were moments that he recognized a dangerous temper in the boy. Salwyn always knew when Walter had had a particularly difficult encounter with one of the other boys. He would storm into the practice yard, grab a wooden sword and pound his post with such vengeance that his aim would get sloppy, and he would throw down his practice sword in disgust. At first, Salwyn called after him to come back, but the boy never seemed to hear him as he stomped away. The one time the older man actually blocked his path, Walter clenched his fists and glared at him like he didn't recognize his old friend. It was a look Salwyn had seen before in the heat of battle, and he didn't like it one little bit. This from a boy who was quickly learning how to be a dangerous man.

During lessons, Salwyn would try to instill every sense of judgment and restraint that he could. On a good day, Walter would listen. On a bad day, no amount of badgering would straighten the boy out, until he had physically worked off his temper. Salwyn didn't quite know what to do about it.

Nesta might have been able to explain the boy's anger, had Salwyn ever been willing to ask her. But the old soldier was intimidated by the boy's mother and he kept his worries to himself. Though she never confronted her son about his fits of temper, the poor woman knew what the problem was: Walter knew she was keeping something from him. And the strain of this knowledge was tearing him apart.

7
The Churchyard

It was All Hallow's Eve, and Walter took a quick glance at the cloudy sky as he hurriedly carted his last pailful of water up the hill. Near the top he turned his head toward a group of boys below him. "Walter, can't you hurry?" he heard, and he waved a hand in response.

He didn't exactly like all of them; though he was not quite fifteen, most were younger and certainly more foolish than he. But his good friend Gwilym was among them. He could see Gwilym's red hair bobbing up and down as he did cartwheels on the edge of the hill, and he was willing to cooperate in their plan. Walter dropped off the pail and disappeared before his mother could give him another job.

The six of them clambered through a broken wall and into the dense woods nearby, making sure no one was watching. It was most important to evade their younger brothers. They ran until they reached a little clearing, collapsing in a pile and laughing while they gasped for breath.

"Free as last," gasped Gwilym, smiling mischievously at the rest. "Now let me tell you what I finally learned about the old churchyard."

The rest were quiet at this, for they all had heard strange rumors about the mysteries of that night, of spirits and demons and unexplained happenings. But no one could seem to get the whole truth, between the older boys' ridicule and assurances from parents that they were too young.

They were impatient for adventure, exhilarated by the danger offered by unknown specters that were said to walk the earth that very night. The boys crowded close as Gwilym's voice sank to a whisper.

"I was told what we need to do tonight. Sow some hemp–seed

in the churchyard..." He looked around, savoring the attention. "At the stroke of midnight, a spirit will appear, and tell you what is going to happen in the next year. Or..." he added in a lower tone, as the others began to whisper, "you will be shown, in an apparition, the person you are going to marry."

Gwilym widened his eyes. "Also, if you put your ear to the church door, you will hear the names of the people who are going to die during the year." The storyteller sat back proudly, as they all talked excitedly, then he raised a hand.

"There's more," he crooned. "Do you remember the old caretaker, the one who was found dead on the church step three years ago? Think about it." The boy next to him shifted nervously. "It is said that he heard his name first, and died of terror on the spot!"

There was silence. The magic was working. The boys looked around, craning their necks; the sun was just setting, filling the woods with eerie shadows.

"Remember Merewyn, my cousin's second cousin?" Gwilym went on, pursuing his advantage. "She was found one morning lost in hysterics, babbling something about her husband, who had died the year before. She had to be restrained for weeks before she was sane again." Five pairs of eyes stared at the speaker; he leaned forward. "They found her on November the first, of course."

Gwilym decided that he had said enough; even he was getting scared. Someone asked if they were sure they wanted to go on with this. For a minute no one answered.

But one of the others cleared his throat. He was a smaller boy, only a year younger than Walter but undergrown and thin. He ran his hand through a shock of greasy blond hair, a gesture the others had long ago recognized as showing no good intent. Rhys squinted his good eye slyly at Walter and said, "Hem, well, maybe Walter would do it. Yes, I'm sure he should."

Everyone turned to look at the victim, inwardly sighing with relief. Walter bit his lip. He had never liked that nasty trouble-maker, especially since the day he had caught the boy pissing on his house and he had given him a sound thrashing. He always felt that Rhys was looking for revenge, but was too cowardly to stand up to him. Perhaps this night he was planning some especially interesting deceit. Well, why disappoint him?

"All right, I'll do it." He stood up. Gwilym looked at him worriedly; he knew about Rhys. But there was never a chance of stopping Walter once he decided to do something.

The rest of the bunch took to their heels as soon as they stepped from the forest, but Gwilym lagged behind with Walter.

"Don't worry," Walter reassured him. "I don't believe in all this anyway. I'm just not so sure how far that one will go." He pulled away. "I'll face the churchyard alone," he declared, hearing the other sigh in relief. His friend didn't argue but nodded his assent, already running after the others.

It wasn't the first time Walter was left alone. "Nor will it be the last," he spoke to nobody in particular.

It was an hour before midnight. Walter carefully sowed the required hemp seeds, then took up a vigil atop an old and crumbling gravestone. Tired, regretting this late-night foolishness, he buried his face in his hands, weighed down by the gloom. Little did he realize how well his bent form blended with his surroundings; some would have said he belonged there, as if he had come from the other world.

Trying to ignore the pressing darkness, his mind plunged into its habitual discontent. Although his obsession plagued him like a bad tooth, he always felt like he was closer to a resolution, the more he dwelled on his purpose.

It was time he confronted his mother with her evasions. As of yet, she wouldn't admit to him what happened to his father. None of his companions seemed to know exactly what had happened so many years ago; yet they suspected enough to treat him like a freak. Long ago he had taught them to keep their mouths under control—all except that rascal Rhys—but somehow it wasn't enough. He saw the way they looked at him. He saw them talking about him behind his back. Why was he treated like an outcast? Why all the secrets?

Owain and Godgifu were no help either, though they had raised him like their own grandson. He knew they loved him, but whenever he asked them a direct question, they would suddenly find some task that needed attention. He always knew, when they avoided his eyes, that he had come too close to the ugly truth, whatever that was.

Suddenly, although he didn't hear anything, Walter looked up and shivered; the air was permeated with a sudden chill, and the odor of decay. Through the gathering mist he saw the shapes of three old women, not close enough to distinguish, but he didn't want to see them any closer, anyway.

"Halt," he called. "What is it you want to say to me?"

The weird sisters conversed among themselves, then began to recite to him, each alternating a line. They swayed to their raspy, sing-songy verse like drunken, ragged specters.

"Walter, the boy 'got of love and deception,
Your mother the victim of Gruffydd's oppression.
Nobly born though a servant become
Your birthright a secret, her honor undone
For the love of a man whose intentions were true
Yet Fleance your father, unjustly for you
Was killed by the Prince in an outburst of rage,
His hapless revenge left for you to engage.
The blood of your grandfather shamefully slain
Murdered by one who continues to reign
Macbeth lives on yet, thus Banquo won't rest
'Till the tyrant is taken at Malcolm's behest."

The sisters began to fade, but Walter moved closer, his arm outstretched as if to ward them off; yet he wanted to know more. "These words sound strange to my ears, but somehow they ring true. What is it you would have of me?" The women only shook their heads and disappeared as if they walked into oblivion.

"Some tirade this was, and not even midnight," he muttered, kicking at the hemp seeds. There was no need to wait any longer; his most disquieting questions were answered. Walter paused at the entrance to the cemetery, swinging the gate back and forth as he listened for more sounds. But the musty odor had gone and so had the chill. The only sounds he heard were the leaves rustling over the path behind him.

The following morning, Nesta noticed a change in her son. It was nothing she could identify, only a strange reticence, a distracted air. Finally that night she sat down beside him, snuggling closer to his body for warmth.

"Son," she said, watching him stare into the fire, "will you tell me just what is on your mind?" He turned to her, putting an arm around her slight shoulders; and she suddenly noticed just how old he looked. His chin no longer sprouted that sparse fringe of stubble, but now was covered by a fine black beard, with a mouth set in a straight line: steady, bitter, and unrelenting. His eyes plunged into her own; it seemed to Nesta that they were a thousand years old.

"My mother," he said quietly, and she shivered at the tone in his voice. "Is it not time you revealed the clouded circumstances surrounding my birth?"

Nesta let out a gasp, slumping in his arms. She covered her eyes, wishing herself a hundred miles away. And yet her son waited for an answer.

"It is not an easy question to ask," he pursued. She stirred, raised her head.

"All right, I will tell you, though you may never again look at me kindly. I have never in sixteen years alluded to these happenings, but..."

She started to cry, and Walter recognized the pain he was inflicting. He embraced her gently, yet determined not to let her go until he had heard it all. Finally she dried her eyes.

"You look a lot more like your grandfather the Prince than your father," she started, then hiccoughed. "Fleance…there. I finally said his name." She hiccoughed again and started to get up.

"No," Walter insisted, pushing her back down. "I'll get you a cup of water."

Nesta watched as her son poured some water into a cup. When he turned to her she looked like a hunted animal. He gave her the water and sat beside her again. "Dear mother, you must know how I have been tortured all these years…"

"Do you think I have not?" she shot back, suddenly reanimated. "Do you know what you have done to me?"

He sat back, stricken, and she began to cry again. "No, son. I didn't mean it. Truly I didn't. I am so sorry for everything. I knew what I was doing, but your father was so loving… so exciting. And I was so lonely…" She paused. "We were lovers for one long summer, and then you came along. Walter, he paid for you with his life." Nesta wiped her eyes. "Dear Fleance. My father would never have let him marry me, but Fleance wouldn't listen. He went to ask my father's permission…"

She stopped, lost in remembrances. Walter felt a tear run down his own face. "What happened?" he whispered.

"My father killed him. It was his right."

Such a simple statement. And it hid so much pain.

"And you?"

"Punished." That was all. Nesta was not in the habit of talking very much. Walter had never seen the happy girl his father fell in love with.

"They punished you by making you live here, with Owain?"

"I was disowned. I was dishonored. I was ashamed." She was crying again.

"Mother, who is Macbeth?"

Nesta raised her tear-streaked face, shocked. She had never mentioned that name to her son. "King of Scotland," she answered slowly. "Why do you ask?"

Walter didn't want to answer. "What happened to my grandfather?" he pursued.

"Fleance's father? Murdered. Your father witnessed the murder, but he never knew why it happened. Or what happened after. How did you know?"

Still he wouldn't answer. "Tell me about my father."

Nesta sighed. "Walter, I barely remember him. He was tall, cheerful, graceful, beautiful... Our time together was so short..." She started crying again, and Walter left her alone by the fire. She barely noticed that he was gone.

The next day Walter was busy rethatching the roof of their little hut, when up walked a couple of the boys he had met with on All Hallow's Eve. He had carefully avoided them since that night, and frowned to himself as they stopped below, making a racket.

But his attention was drawn by the detested voice of Rhys.

"Come down a minute," Rhys was saying, running a hand through his hair. "You must at least tell us what happened."

Walter wiped his hands on his shirt and descended the ladder, grabbing his short sword and applying it to the whetstone. He wanted them to feel as unwelcome as possible.

Rhys edged up, poking him inquiringly on the shoulder. "See any ghosts?" he whispered, putting his lips close to Walter's ear. Then he stepped back, cocking his head to one side in mock attentiveness. Raising his eyebrows when Walter gave no response, Rhys turned to the others, shrugging.

"Or were you afraid? Did you run away before the hour had struck?"

Though Walter neither knew nor cared, Rhys had sneaked up to the churchyard at midnight to play a nasty trick on him. He was bitterly disappointed to find his prey gone, and had spread tales of Walter's cowardice to whoever would listen.

Rhys braced himself for some response, but none followed. Walter continued to sharpen his blade.

"Did they speak your name?" Rhys asked with a waver to his voice. "Did they spit in your face?"

Walter looked at him, then returned to his work. Rhys, tired of baiting an unresponsive victim, turned to walk away. "Well," he said, "what do you expect from a bastard?"

Walter's reaction was as violent as it was unexpected. Like a tiger he leaped from his stool, grabbing his enemy by the shoulder and wheeling him around. Rhys's expression of scorn turned into one of horror as Walter plunged the blade into his side. He fell to his knees coughing up blood, and choking the words that were coming to his lips.

It was just as well for Walter that he couldn't understand; for the garbled words had accused him of being the devil himself.

The bastard looked with surprise at his handiwork while the others ran howling into the village. His thrust had gone cleanly through the lung and into the heart; he had brought the blade savagely from below, just like Salwyn had shown him. His first thought was satisfaction with how well the technique had worked.

Then the fighter gave way to the human, and he bent over the dead boy in sorrow, realizing what he had done. He was sorry for all the trouble his action would cause his mother.

In less than a half hour, Walter found himself walking briskly through the forest, avoiding all paths, listening for any unusual sounds. The expression on his face did not match the pace at which his legs took him; though obviously agitated, he walked as if finally set free from a long captivity. Oh yes, he knew how free he really was, burdened already with the guilt of deserting his mother. Funny, though… somehow Nesta didn't seem surprised at the turn of events. She had kissed him and sent him away as if a long awaited and long dreaded day had finally arrived. Dry eyed and stone-faced, Nesta had leaned against the door as Walter gathered his few things.

"Search for Malcolm," she said evenly, or perhaps more accurately, with no emotion in her voice. "Malcolm is destined to recapture his kingdom; Fleance spoke of him many times. Go to London and find Malcolm."

Walter straightened, looking her up and down. It seemed her one consolation—for him to agree—so he promised to do so. Perhaps Malcolm would help him realize Fleance's revenge, after all. Or at least explain what it was all about.

It was old Salwyn who showed more emotion than usual, and hid it by presenting him with a beautiful new sword of his own making. "I was saving this for a special occasion," he had mumbled while buckling the strap around Walter's waist.

Well, Walter thought, gripping the hilt which rode comfortably at his side. No occasion could be more special than leaving home for the first time.

Myrna wouldn't see him. As soon as Salwyn told her Walter was leaving, she locked herself in her room. Walter's hurried parting words with his old master were disturbed by the sobs coming from the back of the house.

Truly, he was glad to be away from that miserable life. He was surprised that he felt no remorse for his action; but then, if he felt bad about the death of every enemy, what kind of warrior would that make him?

Finally, the long expected sound of pursuit gained momentum from the path to his left and behind him. Walter wasn't too concerned; he knew every inch of this forest. Swerving to his right, he made his way to a hidden overhang of a fallen tree long dead. He had used this hiding place many times growing up, when he wanted to run from the world.

There it was, covered with hanging vines. He hadn't needed this spot for years, and as he crawled gingerly under the vines, he was surprised to see that he didn't fit well into the space any more. But it would serve.

The men were closer, now. Walter could hear them stumbling over roots, pushing bushes aside. He shook his head. You could hear them a mile away. One of the pursuers was close enough to hear his puffing breath.

"He's long gone," the man muttered unenthusiastically. Walter recognized the voice; it was Rhys's uncle. "Let's get this over with. There's always the *Galanas* to be paid."

Walter slapped a hand over his mouth. Curse him, he had forgotten about the *Galanas*, or Were-Geld as the Danes called it. This held the kinsmen of a murderer responsible for payment of money to the family of a slain man, to the seventh degree of descent. This put the whole burden on Nesta's shoulders. His poor mother. Surely she knew what she was facing, and hadn't even mentioned it as she hurried him away.

Didn't that mean that Prince Gruffydd was also responsible? He could afford it. As though anyone was going to confront him for the actions of a bastard grandson he had already disowned...

The men were moving on, and Walter closed his eyes, fighting back tears. Salwyn had warned him about his temper, and he never really listened. Look what he had done to himself. He hated that boy for years; Rhys had always goaded the others into taunting him, the little tyrant. But he never meant to kill him. At that moment, when his temper flared, Walter had thought of nothing but his hatred: his anger at his mother, his father, his grandfather. It all concentrated itself on the point of the blade that so obligingly pierced Rhys's heart.

And now the consequences. How was he going to get money back to Nesta? She had just given him all she had, to get him started on his journey. He'd have to find a way, no matter what it took. And he'd have to find a way to control his temper.

Though he wondered at the lightness in his heart after he had spent his anger on Rhys. Maybe it was all gone?

He waited another hour until he was sure all pursuit was gone, then crawled out of his hole. For a moment he was tempted to return to his mother… but to what end? They would kill him then still extract the *Galanas* from Nesta. He would just have to find another way to make it up to her.

Walter had no idea where to go but east. Along the way he hired himself out to do odd jobs, cutting wood and such, to earn a meal or a night's shelter. Sometimes he would stay for days with a particularly obliging host. He was ever and again grateful for his mother's lessons in the Saxon language, though as a child he had always resisted.

He finally learned of an old Roman road called Watling Street, which led all the way to London. In the eastern part of England, it defined the border between the old Danelaw and the Saxon lands. Watling was a trading road from east to west, and Walter made his way to Chester, picking it up there. He was confident that he would end his trip in London. What would happen after was in the hands of the fates.

8

Earl Godwine's Return

London that day was in a particular uproar. Approaching the city gate, Walter shouldered his way through the throng, pretending that he wasn't overwhelmed by the most amazing sights he had ever beheld in his life. This was the end of a long journey on foot across all of England, but never along the way had he seen a city large enough to prepare him for this one.

Although not maintained by the Saxons, the Roman wall around London was still imposing. It was at least thirty feet tall, and a deep ditch had been dug outside the wall to repel invaders. The city had already expanded beyond the sheltering walls, and the road was lined with two-storied timber houses topped by thatched roofs. The vendors along the roadside were in a frenzy, as if they would never have such an opportunity again. Wagonfuls of vegetables and wool and breads jostled people from the middle of the road. People with makeshift tables were holding up their wares, shouting to be heard above the din.

Realizing that fighting the crowd was getting him nowhere, Walter allowed himself to be carried along. He was fascinated by the multitude of smells and sounds, and gave up trying to be indifferent. He stopped to listen to a woman hanging from her window, chattering to a neighbor. She was saying that Earl Godwine was coming up the river, then she ducked her head inside, and he heard no more than a muffled scrape. Realizing what was happening, Walter hurriedly stepped aside, and narrowly avoided a shower of sewage.

It was clear that nearly everyone was headed toward the Thames. Walter smiled as two boys pushed past him, tapping at grownup people's heels to move them aside. He followed in their wake. They pushed through Newgate and headed toward the river.

It was clear that London must be a major trading port. Walter had never seen such a large complex of wooden piers and jetties before, jutting into the river to aid the unloading of large ships. He could see boats ferried across the river at that point, going both ways, and a crowd of people on the opposite bank as well. He drifted away from the boys and slipped along some of the narrower lanes, with buildings so close together the second stories nearly touched... indeed, they seemed to be leaning toward each other. It looked like the sun barely made its way all the way to the street.

Finally, the buildings cleared near the docks, but Walter couldn't really move forward, because there was a wall of people blocking the way. He craned his neck, trying to see over their heads, grateful for his extra height, but he still couldn't tell what everyone was looking at, or waiting for. He turned toward the sound of an educated voice, which was expressing what seemed to be a popular opinion, judging by the noises of assent: "Yes, I know that Godwine is still in the King's disfavor, but consider, friend, that there are others in court to whom Edward must listen, or he may lose his throne. How long can he turn to those cursed Normans, who put their own interests before the country? The King knows that Godwine is the foundation of his throne, and God knows he makes an invaluable ally and a devastating enemy."

The companion shook his head. "You know full well that Edward holds Godwine responsible for the murder of Alfred. They put his brother's eyes out, for Christ's sake. That's hard to reconcile. And you know the King feels that the house of Godwine covets his throne. In the end, his decision stands."

The first debater was about to reply, when he was nudged aside by two Saxon warriors, who looked official enough for a path to open before them. Walter heard someone whisper that they were some of the Earl's housecarls. It was curious that the populace did not take their apparent rudeness amiss.

The warriors were tall and strong, wearing wide gold bands on muscular upper arms. Blond braids hung down their backs from beneath cone-shaped helmets, and blue eyes glistened behind a long nose-piece. Walter edged as near to them as he dared, then followed everyone's gaze down the river.

A cluster of mastheads showed round the curve, pennants flying and oars dipping in unison. A grand cheer rose from the crowd at the sight, and the cry of "Godwine" burst from nearly every throat. The vessels dropped anchor near Westminster palace, near the fleet of the King's best ships.

From his vantage point, Walter was certain he saw only one man disembark. But the cluster of spears, all he could see of the Royal troops, parted in disorder. Shortly after the single man disappeared, the spears were jumping up and down in excitement, and the name of Harold rang clearly, all the way up the shore.

Walter turned to his neighbor and asked who Harold was. The man stared in disbelief, then, looking at Walter's clothes, put a hand on his arm. "You are from the country, I see. That man," he said with reverence, "is the son of Godwine, and the finest warrior that ever lived. He will do great things for our land." He pointed at the ships. "The fate of Godwine's house lies with the King this very minute."

As if these simple words were all a stranger needed to know, the man turned his attention toward the ships. As they watched, Harold moved back onto the ship and stood at the bow, tall and strong, his hair blowing in the wind. The crowd cheered and he seemed to bask in their approval.

The two Saxon housecarls were moving away, and Walter decided to follow them. They didn't seem to notice him, or didn't care, but were deep in discussion. They were still threading their way through one of the wider streets, when the commotion began. Walter was quite unprepared, but his companions expected something of the sort, for they turned and braced themselves in the middle of the causeway, drawing their swords.

From the direction they had just come Walter heard a great yelling and screaming, and the sound of jerky hoof beats, impeded by the crowd. People were throwing themselves at the wall as two well-dressed Normans burst through, flailing with their swords at everything in their path—their horses foaming, eyes rolling, ears back in terror.

One of the fugitives aimed a well-directed blow at Walter, whose instincts were only a hair faster than his reactions; his broadsword was in his hands before he knew it, and he ducked the swing, bringing his own blade underneath the other's and sinking its edge into the man's side.

He was not swift enough to save himself from the dangerous hooves of the rearing horse, trained to attack any foe on two legs or four. An agonizing kick to his shoulder knocked him against a wall and twirled him around, just in time to see one of the Saxons finish off the enemy he had just unhorsed. The other rider got away, pursued by an angry, screaming mob. But all went black and he gratefully saw no more.

The first thing Walter thought was that he was blind. Panicked, he flailed his hands until someone struck a flint, lighting a candle. A hand slipped under his shoulders; a mug of ale was brought to his lips. He swallowed greedily and smiled, recognizing the unarmored face of one of the Saxons he was following. Now he could see that the barracks were dimly lit.

"Fine work," the fellow commented cheerfully. "I really don't know whether I would have been able to catch the rogue if it had not been for you."

Walter winced under the grip on his wounded shoulder, and the man loosened his hold. "My name is Thomas, and this is Edmund. What be your name, and whence come you?"

"I am Walter, come away from Wales, in search of a new life. I don't quite understand the issues at stake today, but if you will have me, I am your man."

Thomas glanced at Edmund, a grin of surprise on his face. Edmund pulled an arm bandage tight with his teeth, and nodded. "I see you're a lad of quick decision," he said, getting up. "Harold likes strong decisive men, willing to follow we don't know where. If you continue as we saw you today, you will do all right, I think?" He looked at Thomas and grinned, taking a long draught of ale and spreading a pallet for the night.

Neither man seemed willing to talk any further, looking much more interested in sleep. Walter was full of questions, but he knew better than disturb tired soldiers. He sighed, wondering just what quirk of fate brought him so soon to this pass, and whether he was in the winning camp. Then, his head still aching, he fell back to sleep.

For the next couple of days, Walter stayed mostly abed, but finally Thomas came looking for him, a fine new tunic draped over an arm. "Put it on," he said.

Walter slipped the garment over his head, enjoying the feel of the smooth cloth against his skin; fine linen was a whole new experience. He fastened the corded belt around his waist, and turned for Thomas's inspection.

The Saxon stepped back, fists on hips, and eyed his new protégé thoughtfully. Walter was easily six feet tall, with broad shoulders and hands that bespoke years of labor. Deep brown eyes reflected wisdom as well as sincerity—eyes that looked much too old for his years. His nose was slightly crooked as though it might have been broken in a fight. His hair was cut short in the Welsh style. His wide mouth was naturally curved a bit down, as if it was too used to frowning. However, though the overall impression was somber, the boy also seemed to be sure of himself.

"Harold will not be displeased," he said, putting an arm around Walter's shoulders. "When his other tasks are finished, he has asked to see you."

Walter blinked in surprise. His companion laughed.

"You do not understand why? It's not every day that a man takes down a Norman. You've gained some renown. Out of all the Norman bastards," he emphasized by spitting, "with all the havoc they wreaked while fleeing from London, only two were stopped. You were responsible for one of them."

Walter whistled. "Well," he asked hesitantly, "if I'm to meet the great Harold Godwineson, can I come a bit better prepared? I'd like to ask you a couple of questions."

"Of course," Thomas replied. "As long as they're quick."

Walter let out a laugh, knowing that he needed more than a little time to figure it all out. "All right, I will make it easy. Just what were those Normans in such a hurry about?"

It was Thomas's turn to laugh. "It's true, you really are a stranger. Well, to put it as best as I can, King Edward spent most of his youth an exile in Normandy. When he became King of England, he brought his Norman friends with him, and heeded their advice, instead of trusting to the sound judgment of his Saxon ministers. Edward was forgetting the laws of this country, if he ever knew them at all. The Normans poisoned the King's mind against Harold's father, Earl Godwine, until he was forced to flee the country. The King sent the Queen, Godwine's daughter, to a nunnery. Shameful! But when Godwine returned, as you saw, the Normans showed their true colors and ran like rabbits before the hawk."

"Didn't his Norman advisors try to keep Edward from allowing Godwine back?"

"Yes, but the King could not stand up against all the people in this, and England had had enough. Unlike most countries, the men of England have a voice in the government. "

"And Harold's role in all this?"

"He is the Earl of East Anglia. As you saw, the people take him to their hearts. Now hurry. We are about to see something that the world will talk about for years."

Though still a little groggy, Walter joined his new friends, and it seemed, the rest of London, to formally confirm the reinstatement of Godwine and his family into Edward's good graces. There was no place in the city large enough to accommodate the crowd, so outside the walls of London on September fifteenth, 1052, the people of England met with the King to give judgment.

The assembly was not kept waiting. At the third hour of the day, Earl Godwine and his sons preceded King Edward in a slow parade to the platform built for the occasion. A single tall throne, surmounted by a crown and shaded with a silk canopy, indicated the place of honor. The rest of the earls mounted the platform, taking their places beside the King.

Godwine began the occasion by laying his axe at the foot of Edward's throne, begging the King's indulgence in hearing his defense. The great monarch, his face soured by the loss of all his trusted Normans, had no choice but to agree.

Turning to the assembled, Earl Godwine spoke out loudly and clearly, and his voice carried a great distance. "My Lords, my countrymen...I come to you, humbled, respectful, asking leave to resume my rightful place beside your King. Of the many accusations raised against my house, I can ask you truly: from whence came those slanderous reports? From those very men who fled at the sight of my ship masts, shamed by their own deceit.

"For four reigns I have served England. Since Canute the Dane of glorious memory I have worked hard to rid our country of its enemies, and rule my earldom as justice demands. In this have I failed?"

He paused, hoping for the right response. In this he was not disappointed. The crowd, already in favor of Godwine, cheered their support.

"And so I request, Sire," he said, turning to the King, "that you grant me and mine the positions of authority we occupied before the damaging reports. And more important, you find it in your heart to be reconciled with those who put your welfare and affection… nay, the very welfare of England, before our own needs and desires."

The acclamation of the people cleared Godwine of all charges. Seeing that he had no choice, Edward assumed an air of forgiveness. Picking up the axe, he gave it back to Godwine, thus demonstrating that the powerful earl was restored to his favor.

The next point of business was to declare the wicked Normans to be outlaws, even though none were present to receive their sentences. Then it was proclaimed that England would return to the "good old laws", just as in the days when Godwine was Edward's chief advisor.

The people went home happy. They neither understood nor did they trust the Normans; they were bad for business, and they disrupted a traditional way of life. Poor Walter felt like he was the only one present who didn't fully grasp what was happening. He sighed, trying to be patient. All would be explained in good time.

As it turned out, Walter's patience was tried to its utmost. The following day was a busy one, and Walter felt shuffled aside like a sack of grain. His new friends admonished him not to move out of the compound; then they disappeared, leaving him with nothing to do. Although Walter was on his feet, he was not yet strong enough to give much help unloading the ships. He had to be satisfied with watching the river traffic along the great Thames.

The compound was located within view of the King's new Abbey, Westminster, which was under construction; they said it was a masterpiece in architecture. It was whispered that Edward should have been a monk, and left ruling to a more deserving candidate...except that he was the last of Aethelred's children. Some also said that Edward never consummated his marriage with the Queen, because she was Godwine's daughter. It looked very certain that there would be no royal heir, even though the

Queen was released from the nunnery and returned to the palace.

But Walter cared little about this talk. He was restless and bored. Two more long days passed before he saw either of his friends. But on the afternoon of his fourth day in London, Thomas rushed in, looking both ways before he saw Walter in the corner of the room. He gestured for the other to follow, and Walter wasted no time pulling on his fine tunic again.

"When Harold calls, we answer," Thomas said breathlessly as he led the way, pointing to the left down a narrow alleyway. "You get used to the pace. There never seems to be enough time to do all his tasks." The alley opened into a square before the palace gates. The pair were admitted without question. Thomas pushed through a small side door to the palace, which opened into an anteroom. Four other people were waiting to gain admittance; they glanced worriedly at the newcomers.

Thomas and Walter did not have to wait; they were shown in to the next room without a second glance at the other suitors. Harold was discussing something with three other men, bending over a table. They were pointing at a large paper drawn with boundary lines, inside of which were pictures of towns.

It took Walter only a moment to appreciate Harold's charisma. His face looked serene, his forehead relaxed, a mouth set in an unconscious half-smile, softened even more by a curly reddish beard. When he looked directly at Walter, engulfing him with deep blue eyes, it seemed like the sun had come out from the clouds. Yet at the same time, there was about Harold an unaccountable distance, a certain aloofness that made one...almost eager to curry favor. Walter shook his head. He chided himself for analyzing too much.

"I understand, Walter, that you did us quite a service the other day," Harold said. Embarrassed, Walter shrugged, yet he was pleased that this great man had bothered to learn his name.

"Come, over here. Have you ever seen a map before?"

"No." Walter looked at the paper curiously.

"Where are you from?" Harold asked.

"Rhuddlan, in North Wales."

With a strange look at the youth, the Earl bent over the table, bringing his finger along the coast until he stopped at the river Clwyd, and the little inlet that marked the town of Rhuddlan. Harold's eyes glinted.

"Is this not the home of Prince Gruffydd ap Llewelyn?" he said, as if he already knew the answer.

Walter hesitated. He didn't know how much to say.

"Yes," he began, "that is true. I only recently arrived in London."

"Hmm. What is the country like around Rhuddlan?"

Walter blinked. There was purpose behind that question. However, if Harold was going to be his new patron, he owed him his honesty. "Full of trees and streams and rivers. Very green, very hilly, very rocky. The Snowdonia mountain range divides the north from the south, and it seems to be a natural barrier."

Harold turned toward the others. "As I thought. It would be difficult to get an army through there." He looked at Walter again. "You may or may not know that Prince Gruffydd is antagonistic toward England. He constantly harries our borders. There may come a time when we need to teach him a lesson. If you serve England, you may find yourself on the other side."

Harold had a right to question Walter's loyalties. But how ironic. "Although I was born in Wales, I am a Scot on my father's side. I am the natural grandson of Prince Gruffydd, though he has treated me and my mother with disgrace. I feel no loyalty toward him."

Harold looked shocked; this was an unexpected twist. Then he looked thoughtful. Extending his hand toward Walter, he said, "Join us. Perhaps you will someday show him what you are made of."

Walter clasped his hand, neither knowing nor caring about the consequences of this newfound association. Only one thing was for certain: for the first time in his life, he truly belonged.

Walter was assigned as a page to Thomas, who undertook to train him in the duties necessary to become a housecarl of the great Earl. Walter knew this was an honor, and he was glad of the privilege. It would delay his search for Malcolm, but it was preferable to being penniless and friendless.

As it happened, chance brought Malcolm to him. One day a few months later, a lively bustle was raised at the arrival of a great northern Earl to court. When Walter discovered that Earl Seward of Northumbria was bringing Prince Malcolm in his train, he questioned Thomas so anxiously that his friend's suspicions were aroused.

"Come now, what's the interest?" the Saxon asked, elbowing Walter genially.

Ignoring the question, Walter followed with another. His friend laughed. "All right, keep your secret if you must. Malcolm of Scotland is Earl Seward's nephew. They say the old Dane means to put the boy back on his throne."

Macbeth's throne. Walter trembled, amazed at his good fortune. Once again, destiny had put him on the path the weird old women had told him about. One way or the other, he needed to find this Malcolm.

Three days after Seward's arrival, orders had been given for the housecarls to prepare for a long march. The King had agreed to send his own and a contingent of Harold's housecarls to aid Seward on his mission. The request initially had met with resistance, until it was disclosed that many of the Normans who had so violently fled from London had made their way to Macbeth. The King of Scotia had welcomed them with open arms, giving them land with which to bind them to his cause. That fact was enough to carry Seward's vote.

The barracks were a whirlwind of activity, although Walter was not yet sure he was going; Thomas said there was a doubt as to his experience. To make matters worse, Walter saw very little of his new friends; Harold Godwineson was not going on the march, and Thomas and Edmund were in charge of small contingents of their own. He was in a panic; if Walter didn't move quickly, his opportunity to find Malcolm would slip away.

In desperation, Walter made his way to the servants' quarters. It wasn't easy getting access to Malcolm, but he had an idea. He spoke closely with a maid of his acquaintance, and was soon walking down the hall toward Malcolm's door, fresh linen in hand.

The door was slightly ajar, opening into a dark, sparsely furnished room. Walter hesitated before knocking, surprised at his own nervousness. He put his eye next to the crack.

A lanky, dark-haired man stood looking from the window. Wearing a knee-length kyrtle over a loose shirt, he looked out of place in Saxon England, though he didn't seem uncomfortable. Encouraged by the rustic bearing of the Scot, Walter knocked, and the door swung open.

Seward's nephew turned to the newcomer with a genial look of inquiry on his broad, ruddy face. His hair was brushed carelessly back from his brow; a straight beard framed his square jaw, though his cheeks were shaved clean. His eyes were dark and thoughtful, and Walter found him altogether pleasing.

For a moment, Walter didn't move. Malcolm waited, sensing some purpose in the youth.

Walter shifted uncomfortably, feeling foolishly elated. On a sudden impulse, he knelt before Malcolm, taking his hand and kissing it. "My King," he said simply.

Duncan's heir, so long in exile, was not used to this respect. But he had an open, friendly heart; such an unexpected gesture warmed him toward this stranger. He raised the youth by the shoulders, embracing him in a tight hug. When he pulled away, his eyes were filled with tears. He looked closely at Walter; the other held his gaze.

"It's so very strange," he spoke softly, "you look so familiar...like someone I knew long ago."

Walter expelled a breath, releasing years of tension. "I suppose you are thinking of...of my father, Fleance. Do I look much like him?"

Malcolm gasped. For a moment the name of Fleance brought back the worst of his memories, recalling his early terrifying months of exile. Was it so long ago when he was the frightened boy who ran from his father's murderers?

He gripped Walter's arm, though the other didn't notice the pain. "I know that Banquo is dead," said Malcolm. "But what of Fleance?"

Walter's lip trembled, and Malcolm felt sorry for him. He studied the newcomer, so tall yet at least a dozen years younger than himself. The Prince felt strangely drawn to him, a bond created from mutual adversities.

"I never even got to meet him," the youth said. "He was killed before I was born."

Frowning sadly, Malcolm remembered the years they had grown up together—he and Fleance—eating and drinking, learning to fight. There had always been goodwill between their families. Many a time they had disappeared to find a pair of willing wenches, or spend the night carousing in an alehouse. He had always secretly hoped to find his friend again, but somehow had known it would be impossible.

"He was my dear friend," he said. "How did he die?"

Walter hung his head. "I am his natural son. My mother was a princess in Wales, but she loved my father and gave birth to me. The Prince killed him for what he did…"

"Prince… Gruffydd ap Llewelyn?" Malcolm said, searching his memory.

"Yes. He disowned my mother and me. We were dishonored."

Malcolm thought for a moment, then raised Walter's chin. "You were not dishonored. Llewelyn was. It takes more than an unfortunate birth to dishonor a man."

Like murder? Walter thought, looked searchingly at him. No, this wasn't the time to think about Rhys. "I came to England to find you," he said. "It was what my father meant to do. Though his life ended before achieving his goal, I mean to take it up for him." It was a shot in the dark but Walter trusted his instincts: "I've come to help avenge Banquo's death."

Malcolm smiled sadly. "Then you shall not leave my side until it is done."

Malcolm was as good as his word. Before they had left the room, word came back that Walter had been assigned to Malcolm as his aide-de-camp.

It took a bit longer to explain what happened to Thomas and Edmund. Word had traveled fast; they didn't quite know how to behave toward Walter when he came back to the barracks.

"I'm glad you are going, lad, but we didn't quite expect this."

Walter noticed that neither of his friends would meet his eye. He covered his embarrassment by tying his pack. "Prince Malcolm was my father's friend," he explained, without looking up. "My father has been dead since before I was born, but he left some unfinished business...which I hope to finish for him."

Thomas crouched at his side. "You never told us your father was dead."

Walter frowned. "What did it matter? I never knew him."

"And this unfinished business...it has something to do with Malcolm?"

The knot tied, Walter's hands stopped moving. "It has something to do with this campaign. Macbeth, you see, is the cause of my father's exile, as well as Malcolm's."

Thomas straightened, exchanging glances with Edmund. "And to think he was nearly left behind," he mumbled.

Early the following day, the proud troops of Harold and King Edward took their place next to Seward's raven banner. Malcolm rode next to the stout Earl, and at his side, chafing in his new leather armor, paced Walter on a gentle white horse, lent to him of course by the Prince.

In broad rows of six, the succession of warriors threaded their way down the twisted streets of London, waved on by cheering citizens. Scarves fluttered from windows, gay banners from upper balconies; people hung from roofs, trees, anything that could support them. Londoners poured from the west gate of the city, preceding the army and making a wide path in the middle of the road. Although the King and Earl Harold could not accompany the army, they were on hand to see the cavalcade off.

As the leaders exited first from the city, an archbishop was on hand to bless the expedition. Immediately all became silent, and everyone, from King down to the poorest beggar, dropped to one knee in expectation of their own share of divine grace. It was soon done, and mounting on their steeds, the Nobles beckoned their soldiers to follow.

Walter thought it was altogether a splendid occasion. This was the happiest day of his life.

9

Malcolm's Return

Five thousand strong, the great army marched its way north into Seward's Northumbria. Once there, it was swollen to eight thousand, the Earl's troops having gathered in his absence. The Northumbrian contingent was composed mostly of Danes.

Walter looked proudly behind him as the army stretched back as far as he could see. It was the first such sight he had ever experienced, and he was happy to be part of it.

He rode behind the proud Earl, nick-named "the Strong" for obvious reasons. Seward towered fully a head over the tallest man in his army; his shoulders were as broad as the horse he rode. This was no small feat, for he was obliged to use one of the great Norman destriers to carry his weight. Walter could see that Malcolm regarded him with respect that bordered on worship; Seward took the place of his unfortunate father.

As if sensing he was being watched, the older man turned to look at Walter. His eyes were stern, but not unkind; his great beard, parted and braided, reached halfway to his waist. Walter held his gaze uncomfortably. With a little half-smile, the Dane turned back again, speaking to his nephew Niels.

Niels was a bright, enthusiastic lad, and a close friend of Seward's son Osbeorn, who was an imperfect version of his father. Walter suspected they were as unused to battle as he was. The two of them constantly joked and chatted amongst themselves, while keeping apart from Malcolm, though the latter affected not to notice. Walter wondered if they were jealous of the Scot's easy manner, or of Seward's affection for him.

Malcolm later told Walter that his status as exile—a dependent—left him open to petty abuse. Osbeorn set an example that others followed.

"Always behind my uncle's back," Malcolm said. "He would

have forbidden their malice, if he knew. So I have kept to myself all these years; I had no friends to support me."

Walter looked at the army behind him. "You seem to have support now."

"Ha. Only because of my uncle Seward. Do you think those men fight for me? Nay. They fight for him. I begrudge him not," he added, glancing kindly at the Earl. "I love him as much as they."

"Perhaps they enjoy fighting for its own sake," ventured Walter.

The Prince smiled. "Aye, so they do."

From Monkchester, on the Tyne, the army split into two parts. The main force was to march overland into Scotland, around the Firths of Forth and Tay and north into Forfar, or Angus as it is now called. The rest would go by ship from Tynemouth to the Firth of Tay, under the command of Osbeorn. They hoped to encounter the ships of Orkney along the way, led by the great Thorfinn Sigurdson. The Orkneymen were known to be allies of Macbeth, and formidable for their courage and hardihood. Better to stop them before they merged forces with the Scottish usurper.

Near Perth, it was known that Macbeth had built a fortified castle on a high ridge overlooking the Tay. He called it Kinfauns; it was a few miles south of Dunsinane Hill, where the royal palace stood. Perched on the cliff's edge, the castle had a broad view of the surrounding countryside. Macbeth could see miles down the twisting Tay, so that no invading fleet could take him by surprise.

Here, Seward's scouts told him, Macbeth had fled to await the invading army.

It was here the land and sea forces were to meet.

The great host crossed the Cheviot Hills of Northumbria, trailing their supply wagons a mile behind them. Not in itself enough to feed such a great host, the goods in the wagons supplemented the foodstuffs acquired in the areas through which they passed.

Tending to follow the old Roman roads, the initial leg of the journey took the army west along Hadrian's Wall to the Solway Firth, where they turned northward. They marched along the River Annan. The old road stopped and started but provided them with a fairly manageable course. The road gave out at the river Clyde, so they followed the Clyde north, then veered off toward Stirling. Here, they would find a natural crossing at the end of the Firth of Forth.

At dusk, great pavilions were set up for the lords, banners fluttering and awnings staked open with tall spears. The noise of banging stakes and neighing horses added to the general hubbub. The common soldiers made do with whatever they carried, usually lying on a blanket on the ground and sleeping under the stars with their pack as a pillow.

The tents cut a beautiful silhouette against the rolling hills. The evening sky was a deep pink, and smoke from little campfires made an aromatic haze that Walter liked to sniff. If only this didn't end in fighting, Walter thought, this could be a pleasant enough existence.

Malcolm had his own red and yellow pavilion, set up near the edge of the camp. Chewing on a leg of chicken one night, spread out comfortably on a large rug before his door flaps, Malcolm was more expansive than usual. He finally told Walter about Banquo's death, and that of his own father, Duncan. He told of the relentless murders of the nobility, so that Macbeth could attach their lands one by one to the crown.

"Oh, Macbeth was a good ruler for some time," Malcolm admitted. "He created many fine laws, some of which I will keep. But sure it was that the murder of my father told on his conscience. For everywhere he looked, he saw the face of a betrayer. He tried to wash his guilt with the blood of his countrymen, starting with your grandfather." He threw a bone over his shoulder and reached for another piece. "He tried to convince the lords that he was only protecting himself against traitors, but I don't think they believe him. I feel that because of this, the Scots will flock to my banner. In fact, there are those I am depending on."

Malcolm scratched his head in thought. "By God, I hope MacDuff is still faithful to my cause. I am still waiting for his response."

Shaking his head, it was clear that Malcolm needed to change the subject. "Tell me, my friend, about the Welsh court. And Prince Gruffydd, who seems to be a thorn in the English side."

Walter sighed. "I would that I could tell you more. But my lot was as a peasant. I knew nothing about the court, never having been allowed inside the castle wall."

"Come now," Malcolm chided. "Surely you can do better than that."

The other grinned crookedly. "Oh, perhaps I found a few vantage points. Prince Gruffydd, you see, is a bear of a man, and all of us admired him from a distance. He commanded the north, but his brother in the south was always causing some trouble or other, and my grandfather was often riding out to put down some disturbance or other. They are a quarrelsome people."

"And your mother?"

Walter looked sideways at the other, but could only see sympathy. "My mother is a brave woman," he said. "But stubborn. She would tell me nothing. Until the end. Then she only told me what I needed to know… that my father was killed trying to claim her hand after he got her with…me."

"Fleance was always one to follow his impulses," Malcolm said, "right or wrong. Usually he got away with it. This Gruffydd must be a fierce man."

"I'm sure of that," Walter admitted.

"We must rescue her," Malcolm reasoned, "and bring her to Scotland."

Walter nodded, lost for a minute in thought. "And yet," he

said slowly, "I don't think she will come. She loves her father, and ever expects him to take her back into his favor. Perhaps now that I am gone, he will."

"That is not the way of Kings," the other man said.

The northward march proved as successful as Malcolm predicted. Ecstatic at the return of the long-awaited Prince, men joined him every day, swelling the army by thousands. Malcolm's happiest moment was the appearance of MacDuff, who brought a large following. The Thane quickly dismounted and threw himself to one knee, swearing fealty to his Prince and death to Macbeth.

"He sent his men to my castle," the Thane said, wiping away a tear, "to teach me a lesson. Malcolm, he slaughtered my wife and my little ones, just for spite."

Walter was horrified, and ached for this brave man, wondering how many of his grey hairs had sprung from this piece of ill fortune. MacDuff raised his head, his piercing black eyes resting on Walter for a moment before passing on to Seward.

"My old friend," he said to the Earl, shaking his broad hand. "Finally you have brought him back. And none too soon." His voice became threatening. "Macbeth has gone too far, I say, waging war on women and children. Before I am through, I shall have my hands around his neck."

"And so I believe you will," answered Seward, a hand on MacDuff's back.

Malcolm gestured to Walter, who nodded his head in respect. "This is Fleance's son, Walter."

MacDuff raised his eyebrows. "Oh," he said simply, "I wondered what happened to Fleance." Then he turned back to Malcolm. "Come, let us be off. There is not a moment to lose."

Taking his rightful place next to Malcolm, MacDuff motioned his men to follow with the rest of the army. Walter, content to ride in the next rank, wondered if he had just been pushed aside by this powerful chieftain.

But he had nothing to worry about. At just that moment, Malcolm turned and winked at him. He was just giving MacDuff his due.

It took another two days to reach the Forth at Stirling, before turning north-east toward Perth. Stirling Castle was built at the point in the Forth where the wide firth narrowed to an ordinary river. It was a motte-and-bailey castle, and protected a stone bridge. Its strategic value was great, for many recognized this crossing as the entrance into Fife.

The castle always held a strong garrison, and in this time of war it was more heavily manned than usual. But the numbers were far from adequate when faced with an enemy as extensive as Seward's host.

In the lead of the army, the great Earls surveyed the castle. They could see the heads of the soldiers craning over the top of the wooden wall that surrounded the bailey. Malcolm was all in favor of forcing a crossing, but his uncle shook his head thoughtfully.

"If I judge aright," he mused, "these men don't have the heart to fight for Macbeth. They would just as soon go home. I say we invite them to leave."

"I'd rather kill the bastards," MacDuff muttered, "but we shouldn't waste our men. We may need them all when we reach Dunsinane."

Malcolm nodded his agreement, acknowledging his inexperience. Seward sent a herald to the castle with his offer. If the garrison would surrender and leave their weapons behind, they would be allowed to go in peace.

The herald barely returned from his short errand when the gates opened and the men began their orderly retreat. It was a bloodless victory.

It took half the day for the army to cross the river. In the meantime, a local guide had shown the leaders another ancient road, which he said would take them to a shallow ford over the river Earn and directly to Perth.

Malcolm's eyes glistened at this, and he shot Walter a knowing look, though Walter did not know what to make of it.

The army now had less than thirty miles to their destination. Heartened, the horsemen quickened their pace, and settled for the night next to a little lake called Dupplin, within ten miles of Perth. It took some time for the wagons and foot soldiers to catch up with the mounted force. So for the space of a few hours, while the lords were eating and readying themselves for sleep, there was a constant influx of new arrivals.

At dusk, Malcolm took advantage of the confusion to pull Walter aside. "Bring two ponies," he told Walter, pointing at a bend in the river. "Meet me below that point. I want to avoid attracting attention if at all possible."

In a short time, they met at the appointed place, and Malcolm silently mounted, gesturing for Walter to follow. The Prince picked his way confidently along rarely used paths, fording the river and heading south. He pushed his pony faster, eager to reach his destination. Walter urged his mount forward as well, asking his friend where they were going, but Malcolm would only assure him they were almost there.

Then he pulled to a sudden stop, facing a charming little mill on a furious stream. He turned to Walter, all smiles.

"This is the May; it flows into the Earn. And this land is called Miller's Acre," he said simply. As he was talking, a door opened in the mill and an older woman came out. She was wiping her hands, preparing to offer help to the travelers. Her brown hair was pulled back and bundled into a scarf, and her face had splotches of flour on it. As she came closer, Malcolm turned to her and she slowed down considerably, as if she didn't believe what she saw.

Malcolm leaped from his horse. "Nell," he cried happily.

She let go her apron, crying "Malcolm" and threw herself into his arms. He picked her up from the ground, twirled her around until she begged him to put her down. He did, laughing, and she started crying, and Walter felt foolish all the time.

Nell wiped her eyes, while Malcolm put his arm around her and led her over to Walter, who was dismounting. He held out his hand and she took it, smiling.

"Walter, my friend, this is my mother," Malcolm said.

Nell nodded, but Walter froze, blinking. His lips were suddenly dry. He stood there with his mouth open, until Malcolm slapped him on the shoulder.

"Say something to my mum."

At least Walter managed to shut his mouth and smile. He nodded, his mind a whirlwind.

"You'll have to forgive my friend," Malcolm was saying to his mother as she led them inside. "I didn't warn him about this. Not something I could talk about in public."

His mother clucked her tongue, pouring them some ale.

"You'll forgive me if I embarrassed you, I hope," Malcolm said, passing a cup to Walter as they sat down at her table. "You see, I was touched by your story the other night, and I know how hard it must have been for you to tell me about your birth." He paused, taking his mother's hand.

"As you can see, I too am a bastard. My father took a liking to poor Nell here, and out I came. He took me in right away, though, raised me as his heir. He took care of my mother, as you can see." He gestured at the mill, which apparently gave Nell a decent living. "That was before he was king, so my birth pretty much escaped notice. His wife my step-mother may she rest in peace," Malcolm crossed himself, "apparently saw no choice but to treat me as one of her own. She was a kind woman, and never mentioned the fact that I was not hers."

Walter wondered at how matter-of-fact Malcolm seemed about the whole thing. But in a moment he was undeceived.

Malcolm leaned forward, his face intent.

"I'm telling you this because I trust you, Walter. Our friendship binds us together, in more ways than one. But you must never, never utter a word about what you see here, no matter what the cost. Others may use my illegitimacy against me, in favor of my half-brother Donald Bain, may he rot in hell!"

Malcolm looked so fierce that Walter sat back, almost sorry for the burdensome confidence. But in a moment the Prince was his old self. "But come now, let us drink to my good fortune! And to my dear mother, whom I haven't seen in years. And to my father Duncan, rest his soul, for having given her this land for her own."

They had a short but happy visit, for Malcolm's mother was a happy, selfless woman. When Malcolm told her he had come to claim the kingdom with an army, she clapped her hands together. "And a fine thing, too," she said. "But I worry about you, son, in battle."

"That's what I am best at," he returned cheerfully. "Besides, I have my standard bearer to protect me." He smiled wryly.

Walter turned his head in amazement. "Standard bearer? Surely I'm not worthy of the honor..."

"Nonsense. I must have someone I trust at my back."

Walter sighed, overcome. "I do not know how to thank you."

"That's easy. Keep me alive."

"Who is going to protect me?" said Walter.

In a few hours they were off; Malcolm didn't want to be missed. His farewell to his mother was more cheerful than Walter would have expected.

"I'm not used to having him around," Nell said at the last, blinking back her tears, but smiling. Malcolm kissed her, pretending not to notice. But when Walter bent over her hand, she put her mouth next to his ear. "Take care of him for me," she said. He squeezed her hand.

Almost before they were out of sight of the mill, Walter asked what the name of the town was. The Prince stopped his horse, turning back. Lights twinkled from some of the town windows; otherwise the only other movement was the rushing waters of the May.

"Forteviot," he said. "By God, how I love this place." Moving his pony forward, he said over his shoulder, "When I become king, I am going to build a palace here."

They made their way back in silence, for Malcolm seemed lost in thought. They parted before they reached camp, and Walter carefully tied the garrons with the rest of the mounts. When he reached the pavilion, Malcolm was safely settled; no one seemed to have missed them.

10

Battle of Dunsinane

On July the twenty-sixth, the land and sea forces met below Perth. The ships had made their way slowly up the firth of Tay, expecting any minute to be set upon by the mighty Thorfinn of Orkney; but so far, the only enemy they had to deal with was the wind. They dropped anchor at Kinfauns, well in view of the immense fortress perched high on the cliff. The army had already surrounded the base of Kinfauns Hill.

The invaders did not know how many of their enemy they had to contend with. They were sure that a large part of the army was safely ensconced between the stone walls of Macbeth's fortress; Seward had heard reports of scattered armed bands still on the move. But the besieging army was ten thousand strong by now. It was unlikely that Macbeth had been able to summon nearly as many.

The army surrounded the base of the hill, in order to cut off any help that may have been forthcoming. No challenge had been sent to the castle, nor was any received.

They hoped for battle the following day, on the feast of the Seven Sleepers. It had only happened by chance, but Walter pointed out the significance of the day: for a hundred years, the seven saints had miraculously slept in a cave, when they fled the persecution of the king. "You, too, went into hiding," he told Malcolm. "On your reappearance, the tyrant will have vanished."

"Vanished is not exactly the proper word," Malcolm answered, shielding his eyes as he looked up the cliff. "He is still there behind those stones, with his army. It could be he is laughing at us."

Seward let out a guffaw. "I do not think so. Yet I have heard that many Normans have joined him, with their cavalry. We will get a good fight out of them."

Malcolm and his other chiefs had gathered around Seward's tent, but they were moving away from Walter and the other retainers. The wind was blowing up the river from the sea, and Walter grumbled to himself as he pulled his hair back from his face. The tent sides flapped so loud that he couldn't hear every word Malcolm was saying, but the Prince was apparently disagreeing with his uncle. Finally, Seward pointed at the castle.

"Look, Malcolm. If my men were to scale that cliff, they'd be in no condition to fight once they got to the top. The road is not wide enough for an army. No, I would rather wait right here at the bottom," he said. "Those Normans will be impatient to charge into the action; they are no good hiding inside a wall, no matter how impenetrable. Nor do the Scots have much skill at archery. What could they do to us? It would be easier to starve them out than attack them uphill."

Malcolm made a face. He didn't relish the idea of a siege. "Surely his whole army cannot fit inside that fortress."

"So you are right, lad. My scouts tell me there is a sizable force in those woods." The Dane pointed at the forest stretched as far as they could see. "And we cannot forget the threat from the sea," he added, turning as his son Osbeorn approached. They grabbed each other by the upper arm in greeting.

"Well come, my son. Any word of the Northmen?"

"None," said Osbeorn, "Perhaps they will not come."

"Oh, he will come. Thorfinn and Macbeth are kin. They are both old Malcolm's grandsons, after all. It would not be Thorfinn's way to abandon his cousin."

The wind grabbed a corner of Seward's tent, pulling a nail from the ground. Osbeorn snatched the loose rope and knelt on the ground, reaching for a rock to pound it back in. "Perhaps he is out campaigning, and can't be found," he pursued, looking over his shoulder. "This is the season to go raiding, at least."

"No," Seward argued. "He's had enough warning. I say we

need to expect him any moment."

They argued the point back and forth, but finally agreed to line the ships up side by side across the narrow part of the firth, at Dundee. Though the naval force was mostly composed of fishing boats, there were sufficient numbers to make two rows, spaced one hundred yards apart. The vessels would be lashed together, blocking the firth from one shore to the other. The Orkney men, known as the best sailors in the northern waters, were formidable opponents; but their famous tactics of ramming the oars of a ship wouldn't work against these stationary targets.

"Leave only a token force aboard the boats," Seward added. "Post most of your men on the shore. Perhaps we can lure the Norsemen to fight a battle on foot, where your chances will be more even. No matter what we do, Thorfinn must be kept from Kinfauns at all costs."

Osbeorn knew when to stop talking. Disappointed to be ordered away from the main fighting, he returned to the ships with three thousand men. Seward watched him leave, shaking his head.

Malcolm stepped next to him. "He thinks you are trying to keep him safely out of danger. I hope to God he is right."

Seward grunted, his mouth set.

"But I think otherwise," the Prince added slowly. "It has all been too easy so far."

"No doubt you are right. This Macbeth is no fool. He can see down the Tay easier than we can. The moment Thorfinn appears, he will attack us with all his strength." Seward scratched his neck. "Then we will be hard put to send help to Osbeorn, if he needs it. I must remember to keep a reserve ready."

The army camped out where they were posted, using bits of pine branches for bedding. The wind blew all night, making it impossible to light a fire. Since most of the men were from the north, they were used to uncomfortable weather; but Walter heard, as he and Malcolm picked their way through the lines, snatches of grumbling because they couldn't cook any food. The Prince ordered rations of ale distributed to the men.

However, as the sun finally rose, the wind had begun to settle down and the fighters were already lined up for battle. It was an impressive sight. In the front line, each warrior was armed with a great axe or a broadsword, and he carried a tall, kite-shaped shield fitted with a long strap so it could be hung from his neck, leaving both hands free to wield his weapon. When held by the center boss, the shields overlapped, forming a solid wall to an opposing army.

Behind them stood the spearmen. The points on their shafts extended well past the shield barrier, forming a dangerous front no horse would willingly run against. The rest of the army, the infantry, waited behind the spearmen: grim warriors with their pole-axes and swords, capable of taking their place at the shield wall, or attacking an enemy that might break through.

The common soldiers, recruited from village and farmstead, swelled the ranks with their clubs and maces, slings and scythes. Though untrained in battle, they were still dangerous, for they considered the fight to be their own.

Seward did not forget his rear. Expecting an attack from the forest to the east, he created another shield wall on that side as well, in effect surrounding his infantry with a wooden barrier. Niels would manage that far post; Seward hoped to give him experience in a formation that worked well by itself, with nominal command.

The Earl purposely left a weak spot on the left flank, giving the enemy an opportunity to charge the formation to the west. The mightiest warriors were posted at this breach, hoping to trap whoever took advantage of the opening. Seward told Malcolm that there was a difference between an unexpected breach and a prepared invitation.

"Then I shall stand there, if you wish," the Prince said.

"And so I do. There will be heavy fighting at this spot, I think.

I've posted my own men in the forest to the west, and I hope to use them to drive the fighting your way. And after, turn your flank and wrap it around the enemy. Then we shall have them. When the shield wall feels your move, they shall flow with you."

Seward placed a reserve of a thousand in the Braes of Gowrie, the so-called hills rising from the river valley. They had a strong vantage point between the castle and the line of ships in the Tay, and were commanded by the valiant MacDuff. Though he wouldn't see much action, the Thane was content that Seward placed him there because he was experienced enough to act without orders. In a battle possibly so widespread, the reserve might have to act before a message could get through to them.

The sails of Thorfinn's fleet were spotted at the second hour of the morning. The scouts came with a message that Osbeorn's soldiers were at their posts, both on ship and at shore.

Seward and his captains quickly climbed halfway up Kinfauns Hill to see for themselves, making sure to stay well away from the fortress.

The Orkney fleet was led by five great longships, between 100 and 140 feet in length; the lead ship bore a large sail, with a black raven painted on it. Thirty-two pairs of oars lined its sleek sides, dipping in smooth, simultaneous motions. The prows and sterns were carved with dragon heads, brilliantly painted on long curved necks. About fifty smaller vessels followed.

Seward turned to Malcolm. "He dares to copy my banner. Mine is the true flag of Alfred, and see how the raven flaps its wings. It is said that when Alfred's banner flies proudly in the breeze, the army carrying it will win the day."

Malcolm clasped hands with his uncle, and parted toward his wing, taking Walter with him. "It is also said," he remarked to his standard bearer, "that the man carrying his flag is always killed in battle. A hard victory for the Raven-banner."

Thorfinn's fleet saw the blockade in the firth; as Seward had guessed, many ships pulled to shore, the lusty Orkneymen barely waiting for the vessels to stop before they jumped, swords upraised. Osbeorn's Danes were waiting for them, shoulder to shoulder, feet braced on the ground, shields locked, their axes gripped and ready.

The Norsemen set foot on shore and threw themselves at the enemy, slaying and thrusting, regardless of their own wounds. They met with solid resistance, as Osbeorn's men hacked at them over the shields, and thrust from underneath the rims. At first, the Northmen fell back, surprised at the ferocity of the Northumbrians, raised like themselves to fight and slaughter. But reinforced by more men from the ships, they regrouped and surged inwards, some berserking in their rage, cutting a swath through the enemy that none could withstand.

Soon, the well-defined lines between enemies disappeared into a tangle of clanging, screaming, flashing chaos. The ebbing waves of the firth were stained with blood; men were falling face-first into the foam, still gripping their swords. Others were stumbling back to their feet, dashing back into the fighting. Men were slashing first at one enemy, then swirling around to cut at another, barely pausing to see whether their blade had hit home.

No one could tell by watching who had gained the upper hand.

Thorfinn and his largest ships concentrated on the row of Northumbrian vessels. Tall and threatening, the Earl of Orkney stood in the bow of his fighting ship, recognizable by his great stature and the winged helmet he wore. He bellowed for his archers to come forward.

Placing themselves behind the row of shields along the sides, the archers waited for the shipmasters to bring the vessels astern the waiting blockade. When it was done, they took aim and let fly a stream of arrows, doing but little damage to the nearer ships.

Osbeorn stood confidently, feet spread wide, fists on hips, on the largest ship in his little fleet. He turned his head slightly, giving a message to the young pages waiting at his side.

From one ship to the next the boys stood ready, giving their leader's orders in a rapid relay. This first order was only a precaution; already the men had raised their shields over their heads, forming a wooden roof that caught most of the shafts with a dull thud. The arrows did not have sufficient force to reach the second row of ships.

Nodding at the ineffective attack, Thorfinn gave another order. His archers busied themselves for a moment, doing something the Danes could not make out. Osbeorn ordered his slingers into action. He smiled grimly, thinking that the swish of air from flying rocks sounded much more gratifying than the whistle of arrows. The stones sped over his head and over the shields. The Northumbrians cheered when they heard the cries of pain. But their elation was short-lived.

The response was far different from what Osbeorn anticipated. His attention snapped back with the flash of a fiery arrow across his vision, and its thud against the deck. He could hear cries all the down the line, as the first was followed by another and another. Soon the whole row of ships was aflame in small brilliant spots that were quickly spreading.

Thorfinn delayed a moment, his eyes meeting Osbeorn's across the water. Even from this distance the Dane could sense his enemy's glee. He shook his fist helplessly. Laughing, the tall man turned away.

The Danes burst into a flurry of activity, desperately trying to put the scattered fires out, while the Norse began in earnest to spray death-dealing arrows over the frantic host. The Northumbrians no longer had the time to cover themselves with shields; every hand was busy trying to put out fires, or cutting the ropes binding the ships together. Osbeorn sent messengers by boat to the other row of ships, commanding them to break their lashings, so he and his wounded boats might escape up river.

Chopping the lashings, running back and forth with tears

flowing from the smoke, the men worked in a frenzy, easy targets to the archers. They began to toss the dead overboard; the bodies splashed sluggishly into the river, embracing former companions in an awkward tangle. Some of the fires were put out, but others gained in their fury, beginning to spread from one ship to another. The ropes were finally cut, but it was no easy matter to extricate any one vessel from the others. The second line had the same trouble, especially as it had to work to stay upstream from the spreading ruin.

The Orkney ships were still approaching the burning boats, giving the archers an even better target. They were now near enough so that Osbeorn's javelin throwers—all he could spare—could retaliate. This made Osbeorn feel better, but he saw that it was too little too late. His small fleet wouldn't be able to sustain the punishment much longer.

Osbeorn began to panic. Shaking the sweat from his eyes, he looked helplessly at his men; all he could see was blood across his deck, the arrows passing him, men falling with hands clutched around protruding shafts.

With a jolt he staggered. Another man fell against him, pierced in the neck. Blood gushed from the wound, spraying in his face.

Strangling a cry, Osbeorn did the unexpected. He gave the command to abandon the ships.

Nothing loth, the Northumbrians began to leap for safety, putting the vessels between themselves and the enemy. The ones that could, swam toward the shore. For the rest, there were a few boats that had broken loose and managed to come downstream to rescue them. The blazing ships were empty in no time, and the Norsemen on shore, seeing the helpless Danes swimming to land, began to edge toward them.

But it was not quite so easy for them. Seeing that their fellows were in trouble, the Northumbrians redoubled their attack.

The longships had their own troubles. The burning boats,

abandoned to the current of the powerful Tay, began floating downstream. Slowly they began to separate, coming closer and closer to Thorfinn's vessels. The longships had turned to move off, but found themselves in the same situation their enemy had been in. Too crowded to organize and move quickly, they were threatened by the very ships they had set afire.

Thorfinn paced back and forth along the deck, bellowing and cursing for his oarsmen and to his neighboring ships to move on. The rowers were hard put to set a rhythm with all the others in the way.

Too late, they began to move. Some of the burning boats plunged into the longships, setting them on fire. Others dropped burning masts onto the projecting oars of smaller ships, breaking them and throwing the rowers into chaos. Experienced seamen put many of the fires out, but the burning ships kept coming on, renewing the fires until the Orkneymen pulled away, limping out to sea or to the far shore of the Tay.

After a time, the flaming boats began to sink, or just drift off, leaving a trail of smoke. For a time, the longships were out of the fight. It seemed that in his panic, Osbeorn did more damage than he ever would have done with all his training.

The second row of Osbeorn's ships, having broken free, were closing in on the battle at the shore.

At the first sign of smoke from the firth, the gates of the fortress were thrown open, and a horde of mounted Normans came thundering forth. They were clad in chain maille and brightly colored surcoats, and many carried banners that blew straight back by their rapid pace.

Seward was in the second rank of the shield wall. On seeing the Normans, he let out a yell of triumph. "Ha! I recognize the leader. There rides Pentecote, and another, that bastard Hugue. Are you ready, lads? Here is a worthy challenge. Brace yourselves, and remember: kill the horse, and the master will follow."

His men nodded grimly, the light of battle in their eyes, lips pulled tightly against their teeth. There was no more talk; the pounding charge drowned out any other noise.

The Norman knights plunged downhill in a solid wedge toward the waiting shield wall. It was a long descent; the attackers could do nothing but gain momentum, crashing through the shields in spite of the deadly spears thrust through the chests of the foremost horses. The din could be heard all the way to MacDuff's waiting forces, stamping in their impatience.

The charge carried the Normans deeply into the midst of Seward's infantry. But not all of them; recovering quickly from the shock, the foremost shield men pushed together again, blocking the way to fully half the mounted force. Dead horses and men from the initial assault had slowed the advance of those who followed. Already there was a pile of quivering bodies, smothering the cries of the living buried beneath their companions.

Locked in the midst of their enemy, the Normans fought like trapped animals, wheeling their horses and urging the beasts to bite and kick through the mass. Each stroke of the heavy Norman swords dealt death, given the extra impetus from above.

Seward was jammed in the crush of horses. Hollering for aid, he used his shield as a club, smashing it into the face of a Norman destrier. As the horse screamed in pain, he brought the butt end of his sword down on its skull, driving it to the ground.

The rider, aware of his danger, aimed a blow to the big man's head when he was jarred by the horse's fall. The mace swept harmlessly past the Dane, who was still in the midst of his attack; as his pommel brought the horse's head down, he followed with a quick sweep of the blade, driving it into the leg of the rider. He could feel the edge sink to the bone, and he wrenched it back out, sidestepping to avoid the inevitable tumble of man and horse.

But Seward stumbled into a man fighting a dismounted

Norman, knocking the poor fellow into his attacker. He heard the scream as his own man fell onto his opponent's sword. In a flash of rage and shame, Seward charged the Norman who was desperately trying to disengage his weapon. Abandoning the sword, the knight threw up his shield to catch Seward's cut when he was rescued by a horseman who attempted to run down the Dane.

Seward saw the danger and retreated, finding himself among friends, who had come to his aid. Together, four of them attacked the horseman, who reared up his mount, using the sharpened horseshoes to ward them off. He didn't see the fifth man leap up from behind and throw crushing arms around his waist. The Norman was pulled from his horse, slashing wildly with his sword. His random stroke met with flesh, but he didn't know how successful he was; a blow to his face finished him off before he hit the ground.

Seward looked for the man he had marked out, and cursed to see him already askew on the ground. Someone else had taken up his fight.

The Norman losses were heavy. Their horses' underbodies proved too good a target for those who were trained to use their dirks. Driving in low and slashing an unarmored belly, a Scot swiftly brought down a horse, spilling guts and blood all over himself. The dismounted mailed knight knew he was not as agile as the more lightly armored infantry. He covered his fall with his shield, regaining his feet under the heavy blows. His broadsword flashed out in a wide figure eight, pushing his foes back under his relentless swing. Taking advantage of their momentary confusion, he spotted a riderless horse and moved toward it, breathing heavily. He grasped the pommel and pulled himself astride the mount, kicking a Dane in the face with his spur. Invigorated, he swung his deadly sword, when this horse, too, fell beneath him. The Norman tumbled headfirst, and one of his pursuers, seeing his opening, removed the man's head with one clean strike.

Outside the shield wall, the frustrated Normans valiantly tried to reach those who had crossed the barrier. Often and again they urged their horses partly uphill, to turn and charge their foes as a tight group. But they never regained the advantage they had from the summit of the hill, and the shields stood firm.

When the fighting lulled momentarily after the Norman cavalry charge, the doors of the fortress flew open once again, ejecting a huge crowd of warriors. The second surge was badly needed by the foundering Normans; every man who had broken through the shield wall lay dead on the ground. These newcomers came on foot, and like the Normans before them, they used the momentum of the hill to plunge them into the enemy. Onward they swept past the surviving Normans, who stilled their mounts so that their allies could move unimpeded.

A smaller target than horses, most were able to avoid the threatening spears. Holding their own bucklers firmly, they crashed through the shields with tremendous power, forcing the Saxons back and breaking their strength. The weary shield men could not withstand a second such surge. Close behind, the mounted Normans pushed their way in.

In the second and third ranks, the Saxons readied their weapons, relieved to make the change from defensive to vigorous fighting.

Then ensued an even bloodier battle.

The cavalry fared the worst; fighting men kept knocking against the horses, maddening them. Every time a rider would try to move, he found himself hemmed in. The Normans never had a chance to retreat from the mob, trapped by the very impulse that drove them forth. They fought valiantly, but found themselves an especial target; the Saxons and Danes sought to enhance their prestige by taking down a Norman. Eventually, Macbeth's most formidable allies were destroyed to a man.

While Seward was struggling, the long expected attack from

the forest broke forth. Screaming like savages, Macbeth's Scots streamed across the open space before the waiting army. Wearing furs and leather for protection, the host resembled a bristling monster. Though tempted to move forward, the shield wall stood firm, braced for the impact. Niels, facing them, called for his men to be ready.

These Scots, unlike the tight Norman troops, were composed of various tribes, united under their own chiefs. The fighters felt loyalty to their own clan; but no commander, with the possible exception of the King, could order them to act as one. Here, Macbeth could have marshaled a dangerous threat, but as his presence was not evident, it could only be guessed that he had a more vital plan yet unstrung.

Yelling their own personal cries, the wild clans came on, in a vast wave of human energy. The chiefs were in the lead, surrounded by their own best men; some pulled in front of the others. Their unrestrained vigor projected a threat that overcame the lack of discipline. This was the kind of enemy the Saxons enjoyed battling with, where fighting broke down into individual blood duels, and each man felt that his own fate depended on skill and valor.

Raising axes over their heads, the leading men charged the shield wall, swiping low at the offending spears. The experienced Saxons brought up their shafts to meet the leaping fighters, impaling some, wounding others. But this action encumbered them for a moment, leaving them helpless against the two or three others that surged behind the first, ignoring the condition of the wounded men.

The infantry stepped in to help the spearmen, covering them while they pulled the shafts from their marks. The infantrymen swiftly twisted the axe in their hands, changing direction of the edge with an easy practiced motion which worked so well in close quarters. Shortly after the axes and swords began their bloody work, the spears were brought back into play, pushing the attackers back into the arms of their companions.

Unable to retreat because of the crush behind them, the leading Scots began to fall to the blades of the Saxons. This only infuriated their friends, who straddled their bodies, screaming for more room. Their own axes met the Saxon spears with a crunch, driven with muscles steeled by constant warfare among themselves.

One particularly huge Scot, striding over the mangled bodies, brought his double-bladed axe down on the shield wall. It crashed through the wood, sending splinters flying. With another heave, he shattered the shield next to the first; the momentum of his axe sank it into the chest of the shield man, spewing links from his maille.

The giant happened to choose the spot where Niels was placed, busy directing men who knew better than he what needed to be done. The boy suddenly saw himself faced by an enemy who could crush him to pieces without thinking about it. Bravely, Niels set his jaw, determined to go down without shame.

With a yell of triumph, the Scots chief strode through the breach in the shield wall, never hesitating in his fluid motions, the sharp axe blade shearing flesh and bone with ease. Following his advance were a dozen of his grinning companions, destroying another three shields. One brought his axe down on a Danish helm, cleaving the man's skull to his neck. The body fell against Niels, knocking him to the ground.

The huge leader found no opposition that could withstand his onslaught. If more men had followed, they might have turned the tide of the battle. But the man's retinue was small; other Scots scorned to accompany him.

Those he left behind attacked the Saxons who were rapidly filling the gap in the shield wall, but with less determination. The shield men, recovering from their surprise, trusted to friends at their backs and concentrated on standing firm; they faced the seething Scots, their defense powered by desire to redeem themselves.

Shouting to their neighbors, the Saxon infantry surged around the intruders, facing the Scots with three times their own number. Niels came to his feet unaided, and pushed into the throng.

The colossus found himself temporarily separated from his friends, encircled by determined men who were wary about coming any closer. Crouching, he snarled with a bloody mouth and a torn lip, exposing the lower teeth.

Taking in the situation, Niels decided to make a name for himself with one desperate action. He charged the man, taking him momentarily unawares.

Whirling with astonishing quickness, the giant brought the side of his axe against his assailant's head with a resounding crack. But he wasn't fast enough to stop the cut to his arm, already in motion when Niels was checked so suddenly. The blade sunk deep into his forearm. He twisted around again as another attacked from behind.

It took ten men to destroy the menacing hero. When he finally fell, a well-aimed knife in his throat, his bleeding body crashed upon a heap of his own victims. His followers, seeing no retreat, stood back to back, chanting their battle song, and fell one at a time, though not without taking at least their own number to the grave with them.

Niels lay unnoticed among the dead.

Seward made his way through the host, pushing toward the back of the formation. With the experienced eye of a commander, he quickly assessed the battle, smiling grimly to see his men holding. He sent his messengers off to the waiting force hidden in the western forest; it was time for them to move.

By the time Seward had rejoined his men at the forward shield wall, he heard the tenor of the fighting change. Jubilant howls of glee broke from the fresh troops that flowed from the woods. The whole line of Normans and Scots swerved for a moment, like a wave in the ocean. They saw the new threat to the west, and many of the warriors turned to face the enemy. At the same time, Seward shouted an order for the eastern flank of his shield wall to tighten up and start wrapping forward around the wide-flung Scottish army, pushing them toward Malcolm. The Saxons, with the understanding of tight discipline, held their spears aloft above their shoulders.

Holding up their shields, coming on like an irresistible force, they began to push their enemy before them. Confusion broke out in the ranks of the Scots; many, too far down the line to see what was happening, were furious at being pushed aside. The whole army was herded west toward the weak spot in Seward's wall, where Malcolm and his men impatiently waited for more action.

On the riverside, Osbeorn's men were crawling to shore, wet but happy to have their feet on solid ground. At the same time, Thorfinn's undamaged ships slipped upstream from the main fighting. Up and down the bank, boats scraped hurriedly along the rocks, disgorging a stream of fresh warriors ready for a scrap. As more and more ships pulled to shore, Osbeorn's bedraggled crew turned to face them. Fighting spread along the riverside for a quarter of a mile. Every time a boat stopped, groups of men would pull themselves from a previous fight, howling their battle cries and trying to keep the shipmen from disembarking. Undeterred, the newcomers would leap lustily into the water, hoping to take an enemy down with his jump.

But the Danes and Saxons were beginning to feel the numbers tell against them. Falling back, step by step, the Northumbrians cursed their leader and his lack of direction. Knowing they were bested, they began to fight with the desperation of lost men: deadly in earnest, but without hope.

In the midst of this confusion, no one had seen MacDuff and his reserve appear slowly among the hills. From his vantage point, the Earl took a moment to appraise the battle. He didn't like what he saw.

Shaking his head, MacDuff swore softly under his breath. Before him spread a shameful straggle of badly used men, pockets of fighting trying to merge into a cohesive unit. Where was Osbeorn?

Looking far downstream, MacDuff finally espied the commander, surrounded by a group of friends no older than himself. They were desperately fighting a score of Northmen, their backs to the water. No wonder there was no leadership; the fool was fighting for his life.

Most of MacDuff's men were on foot, but the Thane and a dozen of his best men were mounted. Quickly he gave orders for the foot soldiers to converge on the fighting directly below them. The horse would come to Osbeorn's aid, before it was too late.

From the shore, both sides were startled by shouts of "MacDuff!" that came from the throats of a thousand men, pouring out of the hills. They all recognized MacDuff astride his horse, eyes blazing and his arm ready to wield retribution.

He had judged his moment rightly. His men fanned out to join in battle the whole length of the front, and for a moment, the Norsemen fell back in surprise. It was long enough to give added vigor to the English; they pushed their enemies hard against the water.

Many of Thorfinn's archers had stayed on board ship, dealing death over the heads of their own men and into the enemy army. But they themselves had to beware; some of the Saxons climbed onto their decks while they were distracted. A couple of ships had taken fire from enemies that used their own tactics against them. Separate battles broke out on ship and shore; men were thrown into the water, only to make their way back onto the ships again.

MacDuff raged along the coast, urging his horse through the roughest conflicts, slashing those who dared to jump before him.

One man grabbed his mount's reigns, making the horse rear. Still the man didn't let go. Seeing the danger, MacDuff leaped to the ground, turning on his foe with a growl. He was too late for his horse; the Northman was sinking his axe into the animal's neck when he jumped. A moment more, and MacDuff would have fallen under the beast.

However, his enemy couldn't recover fast enough to repel the Scot's attack. Without a cry, the man fell backwards on top of the horse, his chest slashed open.

Turning, MacDuff shoved his way through the fighting, despairing of finding Osbeorn in time; when beside him spoke a voice he recognized. "Here, uncle, take my horse. I know what you need to do."

Shaking the sweat from his eyes, he took the proffered reins. "Bless you, Jamie," he said, then mounted quickly, not wasting another moment. He was not far away now...

Ahead, he saw Osbeorn, fighting desperately with Thorfinn; he parried blow after blow, retreating step by step. He could not return a single cut, and his blocks were weakening. MacDuff spurred toward him, swearing an oath, when before his eyes, Thorfinn plunged his sword through Osbeorn's heart. The boy crumpled to the ground, and his foe turned away, searching for some other foe worthy of his skill.

MacDuff fought his way toward Thorfinn, but the fighting was the thickest at his side, and his enemy disappeared from sight.

Malcolm stood before his men, axe held firmly in both hands, his eyes glinting. He was wearing a coat of ring maille, and bore a conical helmet given him by his uncle. Walter stood behind him, having tied the banner to the butt end of a short spear, upside-down with the sharp point below his hands. Proud to be the standard bearer of his Prince, he felt unafraid and unbeatable. The banner would fly, as did Seward's down the line.

He knew that his job was to stay by Malcolm, and keep him from harm. He would only use the spear defensively. Offensively, he thought as he smiled to himself; he had already managed to learn how to wield his sword with his left hand if necessary. He patted the blade at his side, making sure it would draw easily from the scabbard.

The enemy were charging them now, drawn by Malcolm's banner and the gap in the shield wall. They clashed with the din of steel against steel, and cries of anguish and victory. Malcolm was carefully surrounded by Seward's best men, but he was not about to let them do his fighting for him. His arm was strong, and he never seemed to tire, covering much ground with his strides, and cutting a wide path with his axe. Walter was hard put to keep up with him, thrusting with the standard-pole, warding off blows with its shaft.

Turning his head, Walter saw that Malcolm was heading toward one of the Scot's chiefs, easy to find beneath a simple yellow and black banner. The man was old but strong, and he crouched, beckoning to Malcolm with a grin that exposed two missing front teeth. Confident but wary, Malcolm strode forward, and the men parted, giving their leaders room to fight.

The Prince and the chief circled one another, then with a yell, the old man rushed at the younger, his sword upraised. Malcolm held his ground, then stepped aside at the last moment, swinging his axe; the blade glanced off the other man's helm. Stunned, the chief staggered, but turned around.

Backing up, the old man gasped for breath, then charged again. Blow for blow they exchanged attacks, then, expecting another rush, Malcolm retreated a step. His rival took the bait, mistaking the move for weakness, and Malcolm was ready for him. He took the blade on the haft of his axe, forcing it down, and stepped around his opponent, catching the chief off balance. Malcolm brought his axe up and then down on his exposed neck.

The head came off cleanly; then the men, howling in anger,

attacked Malcolm all at once.

Walter was ready. He pulled his sword and in one quick arc sunk it into the side of the nearest man. By now, other Saxons had caught up to the Prince, and they slashed their way to the struggling center of the disturbance, knocking their enemies down in their haste. They found Malcolm and Walter back to back, vigorously defending themselves, the banner stuck into the ground and Walter wielding his sword with two hands. Both men bled from many wounds, but seemed to ignore them.

At this new influx of enemies, the Scots quailed and broke away, giving Malcolm a chance to catch his breath.

"If you leave us so willfully," one of the Saxons said, "we will have nothing to win this battle for."

"You are right, Arthur," Malcolm gasped, putting a hand on the man's shoulder. "I must remember who I am."

He turned to Walter. "Well done," he said, watching his friend pull the banner spear from the ground.

Walter knocked the mud off the point with his boot, trying to hide his pleasure. "Is it time to move forward, my Lord?" he said.

Malcolm narrowed his eyes, looking to where the last of the Norman cavalry was falling. "You are right. It is time." He gripped his axe and gestured his men forward.

The west wing of the shield wall facing the hill had seen the least of the action, and cheered when they saw Malcolm's banner approach. The Prince came up to the captain of the van, giving the order to wrap slowly around the center.

This maneuver forced the end of the wing up onto the hill and toward the fiercest fighting, where the shield wall had broken down. Malcolm and his followers took their place at the very end of the line, guiding the way so it would hold its proper shape. For a long time, they closed on the fighting unnoticed, until suddenly their enemy cried out a warning to each other.

All along, Seward had done the same with the opposing shield wall. So that now, all of Macbeth's forces found themselves on the inside instead of the outside. And the shields continued to compress them.

Suddenly, behind Malcolm, there was a commotion; out came Macbeth himself through the fortress gates, flanked by a score of his best men. They were all on horseback, and they flew down the hill, obviously intending to cut their way through the eastern wing of the army, toward the ships. Seeing his chance, Malcolm called for his men to follow him.

But he wasn't the only one to see who had entered the scene. The men who had to face the fresh onslaught drew themselves together and met the shock with a resistance that belied their exhaustion. Thrusting their spears at the riders, they managed to unhorse two of them on the first charge, though they lost four of their own rank in the clash.

Men from both sides raced to join this new fight. Macbeth was frustrated at his failure to break through, and could be heard berating his followers. They fought fiercely in his defense.

In a short time, Malcolm had joined the battle. Keeping his eye on Macbeth, he seemed to have little interest in pausing for any lesser encounter, as the great need for revenge welled up inside him. Flooded with vigor, he knocked all opposition to the ground; Walter followed easily in his path.

Macbeth saw who was coming for him. Crying to God to sustain him, he spurred toward Malcolm equally desirous of a duel.

But he never reached his end. His companions successfully created a breach; one of them caught his mount's bridle and dragged him through, while he cursed and twisted in his saddle. But once he saw freedom ahead of him, Macbeth forgot his enemy and bent low over his horse's neck, desirous of putting as much distance between himself and death as possible.

Malcolm ran forward a dozen steps, swearing revenge at the retreating backs. Fists clenched, he bid Walter to follow him.

Macbeth's desertion had a profound effect on his allies.

Leaderless, demoralized, the Scots cried out for an end, and threw their weapons to the ground. Walter could hear the horns of surrender as he sought to keep up with Malcolm's frantic pace.

Not willing to admit that he had lost Macbeth so easily, Malcolm broke into a run. Walter was amazed at his stamina, and followed as best as he could. They ran all the way to the river, but Malcolm was forced to stop, nearly doubled over from exhaustion. Not a thousand yards before them, four of the longships pulled to shore. They knew, though it was too far to make out the details, that the fugitive was embarking on the ships to safety. And just to taunt them, the lead vessel unfurled its sail; and the black raven seemed to flutter away as the ship took their enemy to sea.

Walter put a supporting arm around Malcolm's shoulder, nearly spent himself. They leaned against each other, panting. Walter was touched by the tears flowing down Malcolm's face.

"I failed," the Prince moaned, drooping his head. "I failed my father, I failed your father, I failed the both of us. The ghosts of our ancestors go unavenged."

"No, no. Do not be so hard on yourself," Walter said, his voice scratchy. "This is not a failure. It is a beginning."

Malcolm raised his eyes. It seemed that the two of them were alone in the world. "How can you have hope, when life has been so cruel to you?"

"Because you have given it to me."

Nodding wearily, Malcolm drew his friend toward the beach. They both knew there was much yet to do.

They walked among the wounded and dead, already tended by those unhurt, and searched for MacDuff. Although some Norse ships had been crippled beyond repair, two-thirds of the Northumbrian fleet was totally destroyed. A few of the ships were still burning, run aground and abandoned; the masts of others, not entirely submerged, thrust a warning finger from the water.

They finally found MacDuff, directing the men who were laying Osbeorn's body on a litter, to carry him back to his father. The Thane faced Malcolm, his face haggard. "The Orkneymen and their Thorfinn were too much for us in the end, my Lord," he said sadly, looking around. "We failed you, God forgive us."

Malcolm smiled sadly at the man, his eyes full of tears but so affectionate that the other knelt at his feet. MacDuff did not know that he had used those same words just minutes ago. Malcolm lifted him up.

"But it is not true that you failed us. You kept Thorfinn from joining his force with Macbeth's, a truly honorable feat. I swear before you all," Malcolm said, raising his voice so he could be heard by the others, "though the traitor escaped on his cousin's longships, he left nothing behind but a few beaten clans. He shall nevermore return to these shores."

Weakly, the surviving men cheered him, though the sound was empty and hollow. It had not been a great victory. But for the moment, it was enough.

11

Hereford

Slowly, carefully, the litter bearing Osbeorn was carried to Kinfauns Hill. For the rest of the dead, two funeral biers were built, one for the Norsemen, the other for the English. The battle had been too close to the castle to leave the enemy to rot. Once set afire, and the black smoke could be seen for miles.

On arriving at the other battle site, Malcolm was relieved to find Seward busy directing the captive Scots, who were bearing the brunt of the work. The Dane put an arm around his nephew's shoulder, pleased that he was not hurt.

"I was worried about you, lad." He turned, looking over the field. "I found Niels, tangled up with a pile of dead. That's where I feared I would find you. He'll live, but he took a mighty blow to the head. They were done in by a Scot, I swear, larger than myself..."

Sensing that something was wrong, he hesitated, gripping Malcolm's arm. "My son?"

For once, the Prince was at a loss for words. He looked at the shrouded body they were carrying, and Seward's eyes followed his own. Expressionless, the Earl glanced at MacDuff, who was about to pull back the cloth.

"Nay, tell me, my friend. Was the wound in the front or the back?"

Swallowing, MacDuff said, "It was in the front, and he died by the sword of the great Thorfinn himself. I saw it, though I was too far away to help."

"Then all is well," Seward answered. "It is how I or my son should die: in battle, and with no shame."

No one spoke. Hastily, the Dane looked around him. "Hey," he shouted at someone, "That's not what I told you!" And he turned away from them, wiping his eyes with the back of his hand.

"There goes a great man," Malcolm said reverently, "and he shall be remembered for hundreds of years. Go," he added, turning to MacDuff. "Bring Osbeorn inside the fortress so he can be given his rites by the Catholic priests. And send them down here afterwards," he called after the retreating party. "They should be on hand to bless these unfortunate men, and those at the riverside."

In a few moments, a lone priest came hurrying down the hill, rearranging the cape he had thrown over his shoulders. He came to Malcolm and bowed awkwardly.

"Where are the others, my father?" Malcolm asked impatiently.

"Why, there are none, my Prince," the priest answered nervously.

"Oh, go to then."

The man scurried away.

"Come, Walter. Let us see what kind of place Macbeth has given us. We have fought so hard, and for so little."

He was still discouraged, and Walter did not know what to say. They had won by the fact that they were in possession of the field. But it was not the sort of triumph they had looked for. It was better forgotten.

But as things turned out, the victory was more complete than it originally seemed. Although the best troops of both armies bore the brunt of the fighting—and as a result the most fatalities—it was estimated that fifteen hundred of Seward's men were killed, and three thousand on Macbeth's side. They couldn't even count the wounded.

Macbeth's fortress was filled with plunder. The Prince allowed himself a grim smile. "Well, it could be worse, Walter. At least this place is undamaged. It seems that our enemy left us a peace offering, after all. I think I'll move in at once."

He lost no time inspecting the stronghold. Coming across a

large window that overlooked the cliff, he threw aside the heavy hangings and immediately jumped back, drawing his sword. But instead of attacking him, the men hiding behind the draperies fell to their knees, begging for mercy.

Taking a deep breath, Malcolm slapped his sword in its scabbard and released a shaky laugh. "Servants," he gasped. "I should have known." For a long moment he studied the pitiful supplicants.

"Come, we can't have this. I may be your new master, but I am not a butcher. You know where the food is. I have several hungry chiefs on my hands, and they will be less generous than I if they are not fed."

Stunned the men looked at him in disbelief. "Go on," he urged. "We don't have much time."

Grateful, the servants backed from the room, mumbling their thanks. Malcolm turned to Walter, grinning. "You know, I could get used to this. I suspect they will feed us well."

All the officers and chiefs were summoned to the banquet; those who could not fit in the great hall were properly fed at their pavilions, erected within the compound and on the hill. Within the great hall there was no high table, but the trestle tables were set in a U-shape, and Malcolm sat in the center; at his sides sat Seward and MacDuff. Walter served proudly as his cupbearer.

When everyone had arrived, Malcolm stood, cup in hand. The room fell silent. "Foremost," he said, his eyes misting, "I want to thank my valiant warriors for the victory you have given me. Your discipline was perfect; your command of the shield wall gave us an advantage I would never have thought possible. And you men at the firth," he added, looking at MacDuff, "gave us the opportunity to pursue this battle without Thorfinn at our throats...although I am sad you were given so unsavory a task. And yet, you held him at bay!"

The men cheered and he drank, throwing his cup away and

grabbing another. "Let us drink to my uncle Seward. And to those who died fighting so that the rightful king shall reign once again in Scotland."

The din was intense. Those outside, guessing the sentiment behind the cheering, joined in, echoing through every tent all the way to the edge of the field.

Seward stood. "And I drink to our new king. Hail Malcolm III, King of the Scots!" All stood up at this, cheering and clashing their mugs together.

Malcolm watched them all, smiling, speechless, worried. He turned to Walter, who leaned forward.

"So much responsibility... have I taken on too much?"

Walter smiled. "This is your destiny. You will know how to meet it."

Malcolm III was declared King of Lothian and Cumbria, all the land south of the Firth of Forth. In a sense, it could be said that this land was a gift from King Edward, for Lothian was considered part of England. He was destined not to be formally crowned at Scone, as King of the Scots, until Macbeth was taken and destroyed. This wouldn't be for another four years.

The first official step he took in his new reign was to grant a pardon to all the prisoners taken at Dunsinane. They were surprised and grateful; Malcolm sent a great many loyal men to their homes that day. Malcolm generously distributed the spoils taken after the battle. The amount of riches brought home excited wonder in the chroniclers of the day.

The second law he created was to grant MacDuff, and all his heirs into perpetuity, the singular honor of placing the crown on the king's brow at coronation. Like the great stone at Scone Abbey, MacDuff was to become a vital part of the ceremony. Malcolm named MacDuff, Thane of Fife, as his first Earl, thereby introducing this noble title into Scotland. The title of Earl was imported from England, and the new King intended to use it, as well as other titles, henceforth in Scotland to bind his nobles to the crown. Many deserving noblemen were given ranks such as Earl, Baron, Duke and Knight, according to their merit; the old titles were kept by some, but were not renewed by the crown.

The Northumbrians marched home the week following his coronation. Seward took his leave with words of affection and a promise to return as soon as possible to finish the war with Macbeth. But for now, Malcolm had enough on his hands to consolidate his position in the south. Macbeth would be no trouble to him for quite some time.

However, the great Earl was destined not to keep his word. Broken by the loss of his eldest son, Earl Seward died in his bed a few months later. He railed bitterly at his ill fortune: a warrior should find his end in battle, not on his back in sickness, "like a cow". So his companions dressed him in his armor, and the Earl of Northumbria died; garbed at least as a warrior, he clutched his great axe in his hand.

Many of Edward and Harold's troops were left behind to aid their ally in consolidating his position. Walter was permitted to stay with Malcolm for a time; there was a great need for his skills. Malcolm's methods, although workable, needed a little polishing.

The son of Duncan was a fighting king: resourceful, vigorous, popular with his new subjects. He was not afraid to make changes; he was willing to stand firm against all opposition. However, Malcolm could not read.

But with Walter's help, royal charters and decrees began to issue forth from his temporary center of government at Kinfauns. Men who had lands confiscated by Macbeth either had them returned, or were compensated for them. Disputes were smoothed out, pardons were issued. Wrongs had to be righted.

Walter was still discouraged to see Malcolm leave imprints of his teeth in wax as a royal seal. But he had to admit that it would be difficult to duplicate such a thing…

But Walter's happy sojourn did not last very long. He was still in Harold Godwineson's service, and by October he received a summons to return to London, with a thousand of the house-carls.

It was a sad parting between the King so shakily seated on his throne and the poor retainer loyally attached to his cause. Both of them knew it would be long before they would meet again. Malcolm's swarthy face took on a sad but regal look as he gazed thoughtfully at Walter.

"Go. Earn your fortune, my friend, while I earn my kingdom. It will be much harder without you, but you shall show the world what a true Scot is made of; for that is what you are in your heart. Come back to me when you can, and I will give you a worthy homecoming."

Walter departed with many a backward look. He knew that he would return, but he felt deep inside that he would be a much changed man.

Away from Malcolm's influence, Walter was once again just another of Harold's men. He was content to ride with the messenger, who was full of gossip. For a while, Walter barely listened to the man's prattling, until finally he came to the reason for the troop's recall.

"When Seward died, I guess you know, he left behind him a younger son, Waltheof, still a child. So King Edward called together a Witenagemot, where it was decided that the Earldom of Northumbria would go to Harold's brother."

"Tostig?" Walter asked.

"That's right. The third brother. Tostig is a great favorite of King Edward's; they hunt together, you know. Personally, I wouldn't give you a broken half-penny for the fellow; they say he is cruel and greedy. But he was the King's choice."

"What about the child...Waltheof, did you say?"

"Right. Who knows? Someone will take care of him. His father was well loved, they say. Anyway, Tostig's appointment met with some resistance, especially by Aelfgar, who was made Earl of East Anglia when old Godwine died. You can be sure that he was loth to see more power go to the house of Godwine. Aelfgar was so violent in his objections that he was exiled from England."

"You mean Aelfgar, son of Leofric..."

"The Earl of Mercia. That is right," finished the messenger, proud of his knowledge. Men like himself were the forerunners of the court Herald; they would come to know the genealogy of any family of importance, and could recognize at a glance the coat of arms borne by a knight.

Walter fell to musing over his own relationship to the man they were talking about. Aelfgar was the father of Ealdgyth, which made the Earl his own great-grandfather. In these days, when children were born to parents who were almost children themselves, a great-grandfather need be of no great age. Aelfgar, now an exile like himself, probably didn't even know he existed.

"This outlaw," continued the well-informed messenger, "prompted an even more unfortunate reaction. Aelfgar was furious at the way he was treated, so he sailed to Ireland and gathered a force of mercenaries, mostly Danes. With eighteen ships he found a haven in Wales and formed a mutually profitable alliance with Gruffydd ap Llewelyn."

He looked down his nose at Walter. "You do know who that is, I suppose?"

"Yes. Go on."

"The Welsh Prince is ready enough to break his treaty, even without the support of an English ally. Aelfgar is his son-in-law, you know. As I was saying, forming this alliance, the two of them proceeded to ravage the borderlands of England, killing innocent women and children, despoiling farmland, burning whole towns."

Walter nodded. He almost felt guilty, related as he was to these troublesome people. Or was he? They would never claim him as one of their own.

But what a surprise to this fellow if he were to discover Walter's accidental connection with the guilty parties.

When Walter entered Harold's chambers, he was glad of the foreknowledge. He was expecting to see the Earl in a state of activity, but the agitation of everyone in the room had taken on an even more frenzied aspect. Harold was pacing the floor, extremely irritated; the other men in the room stood uncomfortably silent, afraid to interrupt him.

Harold espied Walter as soon as the door was open.

"There you are," he said, breaking the tension. "Much has happened since I have summoned you. How goes it with Prince Malcolm?"

Walter gave his report, though he noticed Harold was barely listening. After he had finished, the Earl looked at him from the corner of his eye. "Very well," he said. "That border is secure, at least for now. We must turn to the problem of your grandfather."

Walter frowned, uncomfortable at Harold's biting reference to his relationship with Gruffydd. This was quite a different man from the one he met that first day.

The Earl had turned away, resuming his pacing. "As I'm sure you have heard, Gruffydd has been causing serious trouble on the borders. But he has finally gone too far. He has ravaged a city very important to the King, a strategic point in the defense of England."

The Earl turned. "The city of Hereford is near the Welsh border. It is under the protection of King Edward's Norman cousin, Earl Ralph." Here Harold stopped and spat, as if the very name was distasteful to him.

"There was a battle. Ralph, it seems, scorned our honest Saxon tactics. He wanted to use horses, as cavalry. Never bothered to train them to face an army, I guess, even an army as straggling as the Welsh."

Harold managed a bitter smile. "One look at the Welsh, and the whole cavalry turned tail and fled, taking Ralph and his Normans right along with them.

"Gruffydd and the traitor Aelfgar entered Hereford unopposed. They burned the city and destroyed the church, murdering the seven priests trying to block the door."

Everyone in the room murmured in horror, crossing themselves. Walter was disgusted.

"And of course, they didn't hesitate to plunder the church, taking all the holy relics. Worse yet, five hundred Englishmen were killed, yet not a single enemy was lost."

Harold walked to Walter, placing a hand on his shoulder. "So you see what we need to do," he said. "The King has appointed me as general in charge of an army to rid us of that damned Welsh Prince. You speak their language. You know how they fight. Walter, I'm going to need your help."

Harold's first excursion against the Welsh was begun cautiously; never before had the Earl faced such a foe. The Welsh were a hardy race, and difficult to contain. He gathered his forces at Gloucester, and ventured past the Welsh border, marching into the hills. Harold sought a strategic place to do battle.

But there was no enemy to be found. Tribal people, the Welsh were not trained to stand and do battle. They fought often amongst themselves, but in small contingents, preferring to strike and disappear. Knowing that it would be disaster to face the invaders, the mobile forces melted away at the first sight of the English. And burdened as they were with their heavy armor and horses, the Saxons could not pursue the fugitives over unfamiliar ground.

Harold was not one to waste his men on a fruitless venture. They retired to what was left of Hereford. The town's easy defeat was made possible because its previous Earl preferred to trust the safety of a stout castle rather than a defensive wall around the town. The castle could only protect its owner. When the town fell, however, the fortification went with it.

This time Harold put his men to work digging a trench and constructing an earthen rampart around the settlement and began rebuilding. Meanwhile the town was repopulated with some of Harold's men. In time, masonry would replace the earthen wall.

The Earl had learned a valuable lesson on his short campaign. It was time to refit his men, and teach them how to maneuver in the mountains. They were going to have to give up their heavy battleaxes, and trade them for javelins and spears. Instead of planting themselves behind a shield wall, they would learn how to keep moving. The Saxons were going to discover that the fiercest fighting began when the enemy was in retreat. The Welsh must be brought down from afar.

Walter was given the task of teaching the methods he had learned from the ablest of Welsh soldiers, his old friend Salwyn. His progress slowed when it came to train the housecarls for archery. Nobles used archery in the hunt, and not for warfare. It was a skill for the lower classes, not to be taken seriously by a highly-specialized warrior. He did was he could, but the Saxons were unenthusiastic students with the bow.

Even though the cold weather made fingers less responsive, Walter was at the archery butts with a handful of others one December afternoon. Hearing Harold call him, he reluctantly hung his bow on a tree limb. Whenever the Earl came to town, it surely meant trouble; he never bothered to make a social visit.

Harold stood alone, watching his men's progress. "They need much practice," he said conversationally.

Walter looked at them doubtfully. "Their hearts are not in it, I'm afraid. They still view the bow as a serf's weapon, or at best, to be used only for hunting. They still don't realize how important this skill is against the Welsh. But we will keep at it."

"Ahem. Good. Meanwhile, Walter," he said, putting an arm around his companion's shoulders, "there is something I would ask you to do. You are under no obligation, of course. But I think we can get Aelfgar to parley with us. I know where he is, right now; he is separated from Gruffydd. Have you ever met him?"

Walter shook his head, secretly enjoying the disappointment on Harold's face.

"No matter. It would have been easier if you were acquainted. Anyway, if you can get Aelfgar alone...perhaps we can persuade him to abandon his worthless cause."

"It may not be worthless to him."

"Ravaging English land? Can you really justify that?" Harold pulled away from Walter, to the other's relief.

"It is not for me to justify anything. You seek to deal with Aelfgar, remember. What do you want me to do?"

"Talk to him, argue with him. You can see what I am getting at, surely!"

Walter understood well enough, but he wasn't going to make things so easy for Harold. "Oh, I see. When you said 'we', I thought you were coming along."

"Of course not. It would be too dangerous to place myself in his power."

"But less dangerous to me..."

"As kin, Walter! He will not harm you."

Considering this, the other reluctantly agreed.

"I think you will find yourself a welcome guest. King Edward has authorized me to offer Aelfgar back his earldom...and total forgiveness. Losing his position is what angered him in the first place. I doubt that he'll refuse."

Not a moment was wasted. Harold had obviously planned on Walter's acceptance, because a horse was standing ready by the new gates of Hereford. A spare blanket and pack were securely attached to the saddle, and a man stood nearby, shifting from foot to foot in an attempt to stay warm.

"This is your guide, Walter. He is native to these hills."

Walter looked warily at the Welshman. His natural animosity rose against any of his own countrymen to the south; although Gruffydd had politically unified the whole country, it was much harder to get the two halves to peacefully coexist. The man was swarthy, dark haired, thin and wiry, but there was no indication of treachery in his steady gaze.

The stranger swung himself into the saddle of a sturdy Welsh Cob, and led the way without a word. Walter followed, with a last look at Hereford as the gates swung quickly shut behind them.

They traveled up and down hills without count; Walter soon lost track of the way and was forced to rely completely on his guide. He hoped that Harold had paid the man well.

By dusk, the glow of firelight betrayed a camp. Walter sighed with relief when he and his silent companion were stopped by six men who suddenly appeared from the trees, surrounding them. The leader stepped forward, taking the reins of Walter's horse. Someone else did the same with the guide.

"You must tell us what you are seeking." It was an order, not a request, put to Walter in Welsh, though he had to concentrate to cut through the southerner's dialect.

He looked down at his captor. "I seek Earl Aelfgar, with a message from Harold Godwineson."

The others growled at the name. "We have no business with that man, unless it be in battle."

They were undoubtedly hostile. Walter glanced at his guide, who sat impassively on his horse, staring ahead. Clearly he was not going to be any help.

Sighing, he addressed the leader again. "Nonetheless, it might be wise for him to meet with me. I have news of import that he might find agreeable."

The other laughed shortly. "And maybe you come to assassinate him?"

"It is hardly likely. He is my great-grandfather."

This surprising announcement met with a lively discussion between Walter's captors. The man holding Walter's horse turned back to him, a semblance of respect on his face. "You are Welsh."

"And what of it? His daughter married Gruffydd ap Llewelyn. All Wales knows that."

The men conversed among themselves again. Finally, they decided to lead the strangers to the camp, making signs to other scouts that all was well.

A large, conical tent covered with furs was their destination. As Walter dismounted, the door parted, and out walked a blond man in his late fifties. He was cloaked in a thick, wool garment which was thrown carelessly back over one shoulder, exposing a rich fur lining. A fairly new beard covered his chin, grown evidently to protect him from the cold.

He observed the new arrivals curiously, more out of boredom than anything else, then raised an eyebrow at Walter's guard. By the respect with which he was treated, it was clear that this was the troublesome Earl.

"A messenger from Harold," the man said. "He claims he is your great-grandson."

"Oh?" The curiosity became more genuine. "He is not known to me."

The Welshman grabbed Walter's arm. "Then I will dispose of him."

"Not so quickly." The Earl gestured with a languid arm. "Perhaps he is descended from one of my bastards."

Walter reddened. "Not unless you call Ealdgyth one of those."

Aelfgar became rigid and strode up to Walter, his face close to the younger man's. He studied Walter's features with narrowing eyes. After a moment, his mouth softened into something like a smile.

"You speak boldly, for one who is in such danger."

"Harold thought I would be safe with my own kin."

The Earl took a sharp breath. Then he turned on his heel, motioning for Walter to follow him. The others started to come also, but he waved them back. "I will speak alone to this man. Stand guard nearby, in case I call you."

Walter wrenched his arm from his captor's grasp, returning the man's glare with such fire that he stepped back. Aelfgar held the tent open for Walter.

The flap closed heavily behind them, shutting out much of the cold. A single candle burned on a tree trunk, lighting the interior with a weak, sputtering flame. Aelfgar gestured for Walter to seat himself on a pile of furs.

"Abominable conditions, for a man of my rank," he said, sitting on a bench. "But I must make do with what I can, as long as I remain outside the law."

He paused, staring at Walter.

"What is this about Ealdgyth?" His eyes glittered in the candlelight, and there was a spasmodic twitch to the edge of his mouth.

"She is my grandmother. You must know that Nesta had a son."

"Ahhh. So that is it. You are the bastard that brought the poor girl such shame."

Walter clenched his fists. The last time someone spoke so derisively, he had killed him. But he brought his anger under control, reminding himself that it was Aelfgar's own granddaughter who came to ruin.

"Harold is right," the Earl continued carelessly, "I will not harm my kin, no matter what side of the blanket they come from. But I'm sure he sent you for more than a pleasant introduction." His twitch turned into a sneer.

Frowning, Walter wished himself far away from this unpleasant man. "Earl Harold sent me with an offer."

"Oh?" The sneer gone, the other side of his mouth began to jerk.

"He says that he received King Edward's permission to offer you back your Earldom, if you cease these hostilities."

The man jumped to his feet, knocking over the bench. "At last! They have finally seen reason." He stopped suddenly. "Harold is offering this Earldom? In what capacity?" The jealousy in his voice was unmistakable.

Walter cursed his ineptitude; negotiation was not his strength. "Perhaps I spoke in error. Harold made the offer, but the King alone has the power to raise the sentence of exile."

Aelfgar strode across the tent, turning at the door. "Perhaps I should not make too much of the details, when I stand to gain so much. I can leave this God-forsaken place, and go back to the comforts of England." The last words were to himself. For a moment, the Earl studied his hands.

"Very well. Go to your Harold, and tell him I accept his terms. I will present myself to the King at Gloucester...with an escort suitable for my rank." He pushed his way out of the tent.

Walter sighed, relieved. He was ready to return that very minute, but his guide thought otherwise. The man was among friends, insisting that they spend the night. So Walter checked on his horse, recovered his blanket, and found a place to sleep.

At dawn they were off. Aelfgar had already spread the word of his change of fortune, instructing his mercenaries to take their share of booty and return to where they came from. The camp was bustling, and Walter took his leave of the Earl without ceremony. As he was riding off, Aelfgar shouted after him.

"Tell Harold that I have won this time." His sarcastic laugh ran through the woods.

Back in Hereford, Harold listened to Walter's story with amusement. "Well, that is the end of this campaign, at least," he said, chuckling to himself. "He really told you that he had won?"

Walter nodded. "He seemed to be a man of action, not of thought."

"You are right about that. The fool gets no more from Edward than he had to start with. But he has proved one thing: he is less troublesome as an Earl who will be constantly under watch, than a wild rebel."

Nodding, Walter excused himself; his greatest desire was a hot dinner and bed. But Harold stopped him with a hand on his arm.

"I want to thank you, Walter. No one but you could have accomplished that mission. You have saved many lives."

Walter stared. Never before had Harold spoken so kindly to him. The Earl tightened his grip for a moment, then went off with his companions, leaving Walter mystified. No wonder he commanded such loyalty. When he wanted to, Harold could be most charismatic.

Satisfied for the moment, Harold went back to the business of governing his earldom, leaving a garrison of housecarls in Hereford. Walter stayed, too, instructed to carry on with his training.

A new bishop was appointed to the episcopal see at Hereford; he was a favorite of Harold's named Leofgar. He was a bit of a non-conformist, having insisted on retaining his moustache throughout the whole of his priesthood. Leofgar belonged to that new breed of warlike prelates who preferred the sword to preachings of peace.

Prince Gruffydd had disappeared just long enough to recruit more fighters, then his border raids began again. By June, the Welsh had ranged close enough to Hereford that Leofgar declared it was fine time to challenge them to battle. Walter was pessimistic, and obtained an interview with the Bishop.

The worthy prelate was issuing directions for a supply train. He beckoned Walter to a bench at his side, although the constant stream of servants didn't slacken.

"Out with it, lad," he said, his manner businesslike. "I am very busy, as you can see."

Put on the defensive, Walter was at a sudden loss as how to begin. He was in no position to argue with one so clothed in authority.

Seeing his predicament, the Bishop gave him his full attention for a moment. "Oh, you are the Welshman who has been instructing our soldiers in the new methods of fighting. They have improved admirably, I have been told."

That was better. Walter mumbled his thanks. "It is because of their training I have come to see you. Are you sure you would venture with so small a host into enemy territory?"

"Oh come now. The Welsh are a bunch of untrained savages, who fight amongst each other when they are not fighting the English..." He coughed, remembering that he was speaking to one of those savages. "Sorry, lad. I didn't mean all of them. But we have a highly trained army, thanks to you, of course, and we will not be cowed by a sudden foray and loud blasts from their horns. It takes more than that to threaten a housecarl."

Walter sighed, seeing what he had to deal with; the man was partly informed, and had come to his own conclusions. But he had to try again.

"With your Grace's permission, I disagree. They might seem untrained to you, but these Welsh are raised to fight. Even as boys, they are trained to withstand great hardships; they climb mountains to gain endurance, existing on poor rations. They…"

"That is all well and good, son, but need hardly concern me. I mean to avenge the rape and plundering of this city, and will do so this very month...with or without your help!"

There was nothing more to say. Walter got up to go, and bent to kiss the Bishop's ring.

"But stay...Walter, is it? There is some value in what you say. It may be that we could use more men. Listen to me. Harold is in Chester with the King. Go to him, and ask for reinforcements. I'm sure he will oblige. I intend to go straight west, but I shall send scouts to tell you where you may join me. Now leave me son, and

Godspeed."

Walter was glad to be away, for he had little faith in this new enterprise.

Harold was indeed in Chester, and seemed surprised to see Walter. But when he heard the purpose of the unexpected visit, he cursed bitterly.

"I should have known that Leofgar would try such a thing. He was ever ready to fly off on some adventure or other. And knowing you, you tried to persuade him against it." He gave Walter a wry smile.

Reddening, the other couldn't help but smile back. "Well, yes. But he wouldn't heed me. Although he at least considered my objection that his force was too small."

"And sent you to me for reinforcements. To get rid of you, rather! But no matter. You are here, and I shall send more men, if only to bring him back to answer for his foolishness. Unless, of course, he fares well."

"Somehow, I doubt it."

"So do I. It will take me two days to summon a new force. I think I can get the King's help in this. Five hundred will do nicely, I think."

Walter was impressed. That would double the number of men who were to go campaigning with Leofgar.

Walter was assigned as a guide—to his amusement, for he was unfamiliar with south Wales—and interpreter to the new captain. Harold was too occupied to take charge himself, but he assured his captain that he would follow as soon as possible.

Leofgar was as good as his word about the scouts. Walter met with the first messengers as the small force was leaving Chester, and a steady flow of information kept them on the right track.

However, the messages stopped by the third day. The reinforcements had a good idea where to search, and progressed cautiously, expecting trouble.

They were stunned by what they found. In the valley of

Machfwy, many miles west of the border, they came across the remains of a terrible battle. Bodies were strewn all over the rocks, and blood still flowed into the valley's stream, turning it red. They hadn't missed the fighting by more than a couple of hours.

There, in the center of the thickest pile of corpses, lay the banner of Hereford, toppled over and trampled.

Walter shook his head, aghast. "They met the Welsh in full battle. This is unbelievable. The Welsh rarely ever confront an army."

The captain of the army looked around, pointing to the crags along both slopes.

"It looks more to me like an ambush. Look above; there is plenty of room for a few concentrated men to throw down a steady flow of rocks. The damage from those heavy stones is terrible all by itself. Add to this an attack from both ends of the valley, and you have a panic-stricken host, trapped and crushed together, at the mercy of falling rocks and organized assault. The advantage was all on the side of the Welsh."

Walter followed this man's unemotional conjectures, while considering how much he still had to learn about strategy. Yes, it was very possible. They picked their way to the valley floor, discovering a number of men who had been injured by the rocks but had survived the battle. They were duly taken care of, and horse litters were lashed together to take them back to Hereford, using cloaks stretched between two branches for support.

Searching through the pile of bodies near the banner, Walter was the one to discover the hapless Bishop. Dead with a deep gash in his head, Leofgar lay on his face, still clutching his mace. Men crossed themselves, while calling him a fool.

A detachment was sent back with the wounded and the body of the Bishop to Hereford, while the main force, still four hundred strong, continued in search of the Welsh. They could not be talked out of their revenge, so Walter reluctantly continued with them in his new role as guide.

But they found the Welsh no easier to engage than the last time. Rather than stand firm to press a futile attack, Gruffydd's men constantly led the Saxons forward. Showing themselves in a screaming, trumpeting mob, they would pour down a hill, launching darts and javelins at their enemies, then immediately run away, shooting their bows behind them as they fled. The Saxons were not yet fully re-outfitted, and no matter how intent they were on chasing the Welsh, they were so encumbered that they soon fell behind.

The lightly armed mountainous people were ever attacking the rear of the English line, first one side then the other. Come night they would strike at the camp, wearing down the Saxons with ceaseless vigilance, constantly moving from place to place so that both the soldiers and their animals succumbed to sickness and weariness.

Harold showed up just in time, accompanied by Earl Leofric and Bishop Ealdred, Leofgar's replacement. The Saxons were relieved, on the verge of giving up. The skilled negotiators promptly sent messages to Gruffydd, offering to parley.

It seemed that the Prince felt he had little more to gain from this expedition, and he agreed. Perhaps he was buying time. No matter what the reasons, he civilly gave his oath of fealty, swearing to be a faithful under-king to Edward. He was also compelled to forfeit some lands previously granted by the King.

All parties knew that they were going through the motions of peace; Gruffydd would break oath again whenever it suited him.

The ensuing six years were a time of rare peace in England. Harold went on pilgrimage to Rome. King Edward finally declared an heir, realizing that his marriage was all too barren. He recalled his nephew Edward the Exile from Hungary along with his wife Agatha and three children: Eadgar, Margaret, and Christina. But the exile died almost as soon as he set foot in England, leaving the country in a worse predicament than ever:

the only surviving male heir of the house of Alfred was the child Eadgar.

Earl Leofric of Mercia, peacemaker and father to Aelfgar, died the same year as Edward the Exile. The earldom went to his errant son, despite all his antics. But three years later, Aelfgar died as well, and the earldom was inherited by his young, inexperienced son Edwin. Gruffydd was deprived of his nearest ally.

Harold considered that frontier much safer now, too.

For the moment, Walter was content with training the Saxons as they continued to master their new practice of warfare. They became adequately refitted with lighter armor. Their heavy ring maille and chain maille was replaced by lighter materials: usually leather scales. They wrapped their legs from the knees down with leather straps and wore soft boots on their feet. The Saxons were becoming more mobile and better suited to mountainous terrain.

12

Harold's Christmas Campaign

Walter looked up from Malcolm's message, torn between joy and envy. His eyes took in the new mortar wall, and beyond that, the fields outside of Hereford, golden and ready for reaping. While he had been marking time in Harold's service, rebuilding his border town stone by stone, Malcolm was busy winning a kingdom.

After four years, Malcolm had finally reached his goal. Macbeth had been tracked down to Lumfanan, in Aberdeenshire, with only a handful of followers in his service. And after a brief and pitiful struggle, MacDuff killed Macbeth single handed, finally avenging the death of his wife and family, as he had long ago promised.

The deed having been done, it was long past time for the coronation. Malcolm bid Walter to come north at all speed, to witness this most special day. Walter would find him at his new palace at Dunfermline on the Firth of Forth.

What a quandary! Walter couldn't just leave. He summoned his fastest messenger, and promised a reward if he could deliver a letter to Earl Harold.

For once, all went well. Harold was in London when the messenger reached him; he already knew about the coronation. Since he wasn't aware of the close friendship between Walter and Prince Malcolm, it never occurred to him to send his young captain north. But this provided an opportunity to be represented without having to go himself.

Sending the messenger back with a proper retinue, Harold gladly granted Walter's leave of absence.

Malcolm welcomed Walter with open arms then rushed him off, with the rest of his party, to an inn at Scone, where a few rooms had been reserved for them. There was a running to and fro like Walter had never seen, and Malcolm was so busy he hadn't more than a moment to talk.

"Wait for me at your room, tonight," he managed to say, before he was interrupted by a half-dozen men; without even a backward look the Scot was gone.

Scone was a charming village in the midst of rolling hills, located between Perth and Dunsinane palace. Its abbey had been the site of coronations since the time of Kenneth II, when that great King had the Stone of Destiny transferred there from Dunstaffnage in 846.

Walter spent a rowdy evening with his companions in the inn while waiting for Malcolm to show up. The place was packed with Scots of all ranks, who left social distinctions outside at a time like this; when there was a lack of lodging, a man couldn't afford to be too choosy. Spirits were high; a man might see a coronation perhaps once or twice in a lifetime.

Finally, deciding that Malcolm had probably forgotten about him, Walter staggered off to bed. He was the first one to retire, and was suspicious to see a shadowy form leaning against the wall beside the window.

Walter felt for his dagger, forgetting that he had left it in his bedroll. A deep chuckle responded to his movement.

"Is that how you greet an old friend?" The man leaned forward, lighting a lantern.

"Malcolm!" Walter burst into laughter. "I didn't expect you here."

"Oh? Did I not say that you should wait for me in your room? Do you think I could have found you downstairs without being recognized?"

Walter hiccoughed. "I'm so sorry. That was stupid of me. But even so, I'm not sure even I would have recognized you in that garment."

They both laughed. Malcolm was wrapped in a dirty cloak,

with a floppy cap on his head.

"It's no matter. I needed a few minutes alone. Come outside; I think you need some fresh air."

Malcolm supported his none-too-steady friend down the steps and outside without drawing much attention. The chill night air had its desired effect on Walter.

"This is not very distinguished of you, Sire."

"None of that Sire talk in private, Walter. I'm still the same man I was, you know. This isn't the first time we've stolen away together. But stand, let me look at you. You seem to have grown in stature."

Walter stepped back while Malcolm opened the lantern, nodding approvingly.

"You've filled out some, without a doubt. Married yet?"

"In that wasteland? The only women who settle in Hereford are already married, and I don't have the time to search the hills for nice Welsh peasant girls. There always seems to be fighting to do somewhere in the marcher country."

They began walking. Still talking, Malcolm led Walter through the Abbey gates, alight with many torches. In the churchyard, workmen were placing a stone into the seat of a tall-backed wooden chair. Behind the throne stood an old stone Celtic cross.

Malcolm moved slowly forward, sobered by the scene. He removed his hat and cloak, revealing his more regal clothes. The men recognized him and backed away, bowing with respect.

The Prince beckoned Walter forward. He ran his hand reverently across the battered red surface of the sandstone seat.

"Lia-Fail..." he whispered, "the Stone of Destiny. Look closely, Walter. Wherever this stone resides, there the Scots are destined to rule. It is my heritage."

He pulled an iron ring from its recessed groove, placed there many centuries ago for carrying.

"They don't bring the Lia-Fail from the abbey until the last minute. Someone will stand guard over it all night. It weighs 300 pounds, Walter, and yet it was brought all the way from Egypt, a gift from Pharaoh's daughter thousands of years ago. It is said that upon this very stone, the angel stood with flaming sword and expelled Adam and Eve from the garden of Paradise."

Walter touched it gingerly. A large crack ran across its surface, threatening to split it apart.

"On this stone I shall sit tomorrow," went on Malcolm, "and take oaths of fealty from all my chiefs in Scotland. It will be a great day."

His eyes sparkled in the torchlight. "And I shall have a crown placed on my brow...a custom never used before by a King in Scotland."

Coronation day, April the twenty-fifth, 1057, dawned cloudy and misty, as did most days in Scotland. As Walter arrived with his delegation to take their places on the ceremonial path, he marveled at the size of the crowd that had gathered. Beyond the church yard rose a great hill, called the Mount of Belief; there stood the majority of people who could gain a foothold. Bright splashes of color vied with each other for attention, constantly in motion. And near that rose Moot Hill, accommodating the rest of the congregation.

How simple the churchyard looked, and yet there was no mistaking the royal seat; the back was draped with purple silk embroidered with gold.

The voices hushed as the procession started from the church, led by the Bishop of St. Andrews and the abbots of Scone. Malcolm followed them, led on both sides by MacDuff and another of his Earls, and surrounded by his highest thanes.

The Prince was draped in a heavy cloak of purple velvet lined with ermine; he wore a simple white silk tunic edged with pearls that reached the ground and dragged behind him.

Malcolm was led to the Stone and seated upon it. The Bishop, turning to the crowd and giving his blessing, proceeded to pray for the King and anoint him.

Walter's attention began to wander, but snapped back as the Earls carried forward a pair of spurs and a regal sword which they presented to the King. They removed his cloak and replaced it with one made of cloth-of-gold, and gave him his orb.

The King stood, facing outward. "I swear as your King to be faithful to the people of this land, to uphold your rights and protect you from your enemies, so help me God."

He knelt, gesturing to the Bishop. MacDuff stepped forth, carrying a cushion, on which sat a brilliant golden crown. The assembled murmured in surprise. In a simple movement, the Earl picked up the crown and held it over Malcolm's head.

"Bless, O Lord, the substance of our Prince," the Bishop intoned, while MacDuff held the crown over Malcolm's head, "and let the blessing of the Lord be full upon his children; and let him dip his feet in oil, let his horns be like the horns of unicorns, with them he shall push the people together to the end of the earth, for let Him who rideth upon the heaven be his help forever. Amen."

Amid the hush, MacDuff lowered the crown on the King's brow. Then he stood forward, shouting to the heavens, "All hail, Malcolm Canmore!" The assembled Scots shouted their approbation. The Highland Sennachy, Scotland's most revered professional genealogist and historian, sang to the King, in his guttural Gaelic. His chosen lay, the Albanic Duan, was an epic poem about Scotland's past. It was a most solemn honor, which served to unite both ancient and modern Scotland under one head.

And it seemed to Walter, shouting amidst the great crowd, that Malcolm's eyes rested on him alone, and sparkled.

The first week of December, 1062, Hereford swelled with preparations for the visit of Harold Godwineson. They hadn't seen him since his pilgrimage, yet no one was fooled about the purpose of this trip.

Gruffydd had started a fresh rash of excursions over the border, and all knew that Harold was determined to make an end of him, once and for all.

Walter was nervous about the imminent meeting; there was something unsettling about this particular offensive. It was unseasonable for an aggressive campaign into such an inhospitable country; there were no available crops to forage in passing, no wealth of livestock to tap. He busied himself in readying the kitchen for a heavier load of meals, and in checking the inventory for plentiful supplies. But he couldn't shake a heavy foreboding, which weighed down on him with each passing hour.

Finally the day came. Harold rode up with suitable pomp, accompanied by fifty of his picked housecarls, his banner flying proudly in the breeze. Walter was cheered by the sight of Edmund and Thomas, riding side by side in the second rank. He flew to greet them as they entered the gate.

As they dismounted, Walter's friends looked approvingly around themselves. The bailey was built on a tall motte, a manmade mound surrounded by ditches and palisades. It commanded the countryside, being built on the tallest hill, and the valley of Wye twisted away from it in both directions. In the center of the bailey, the keep rose large and comfortable, with plenty of room to accommodate all the troops. The servants and followers resided in smaller side-buildings, still within the confines of the outer wall.

Walter's old friends filled him with news as he took them to their lodgings. King Edward had passed much of the burden of government onto Harold's willing shoulders, thus keeping them all busy. The Earl often signed royal documents alongside the King's name. And foreigners were starting to call him Duke of the English.

Walter listened hungrily, but sensed they were keeping

something back. "Let Harold tell you himself," Edmund said. "In fact, I'm sure he is waiting to see you."

Walter reluctantly agreed, leaving the two of them to unpack. He walked slowly to the Earl's chamber, wishing he could find an excuse to stay away. By now, he was sure he was in for bad news. After hesitating at the door, he took a deep breath, then knocked.

"Come in," a familiar voice said. Walter opened the door, startled by the alteration in Harold's visage when the great lord looked up. The fine gold hair had grey streaks in it; there were wrinkles in the once flawless complexion. The pressures of so much responsibility were taking their toll.

Harold held out a hand in welcome.

"Pleased to see you, my Lord," Walter lied, taking a seat across from his chief.

Harold looked at Walter closely. "You have done a great bit of work for me," he said after a moment. "The troops are at their best. I'm sure this time we cannot fail."

Walter nodded, waited silently.

Harold continued, "I feel that now is the moment of greatest opportunity. Christmas is coming, and with speed, we can catch the fox in his den. I mean to attack Gruffydd in his palace, during his holiday festivities. He is sure to have his defenses down. It is no time for campaigning, and I mean to do no such thing. A quick journey to Rhuddlan, the easiest capture one can imagine, and a fast retreat back to Hereford.

"It can take a fortnight at the most. We will spend a week here resting from our journey, then resume our traveling, fitted out with enough supplies to last the duration."

He hesitated, trying to sense Walter's reaction.

The latter sat motionless, betraying nothing on his face. It was a feat he was used to, for Harold was an expert at reading men's emotions.

Harold added more slowly, "I will take a hundred men from

your garrison, along with the fifty I brought. Of course, I don't expect you to come. You can stay here in readiness for our return."

Walter heard the last words, but only through a fog. Rhuddlan, his home! His mother! He thought of her often, but suddenly realized just how long it had been since he last saw her. He imagined her dead, burned by Harold's rampage. His sad eyes looked at Harold, and the Earl saw the suffering in them.

"I care nothing for Gruffydd," Walter said bitterly. "But you are right. My place is here."

Harold sighed in relief. "Thank you, my friend. We shall talk more later. Right now I must rest."

Walter closed the door, glad to be alone. He locked himself in his chamber. "Friend," he said aloud to himself. "He is no man's friend, least of all mine." Those were the last words he said the rest of the day.

But his mind wouldn't rest. He sat at his window, watching the sun set. He pictured the long afternoons of his childhood, while his mother taught him to read and write, taught him languages he didn't necessarily want to learn. He remembered her smile as she tucked him into bed.

He recalled her haggard face just before he left her. Her eyes had begged him to stay while her lips told him to leave before it was too late. He thought of her anguish when she told him the story of his father's death.

When his head was throbbing and the light was gone, he fell senseless onto his bed. He didn't remember dreaming, but the next morning Walter awoke with a new resolve.

For the rest of the week, Walter was rarely left alone. No one bothered him, but he was quick to notice the furtive eyes watching from every corner. Even in the middle of the night, on opening his chamber door, he saw the shadow of a sentry pacing at the end of the hall.

Harold saw no need to explain the situation to him, and

Walter didn't have to ask. The dilemma was clear to the Earl, and he didn't want to insult Walter by pretending he wasn't taking precautions.

Walter busied himself with readying supplies, purchasing food stores from the area. In a week the small force was ready to venture forth. Harold took his leave of Walter, but no unnecessary words were spoken.

For a long time, Walter stood before the gates and watched Harold's little troop ride away. Little by little the others went inside, and he was left alone with his thoughts.

Finally, he turned back.

Great was his surprise when, on closing the gates, Walter saw Thomas waiting for him. The Saxon put an arm around his friend's shoulder and suggested they have a cup of wine together. Walter nodded.

When they were alone, the two friends gazed at each other. Thomas was the first to break the silence. "Well, I guess Harold thought it would be a lot less difficult if a friend would perform the insulting task he put me to. You know how vital this campaign is."

"Of course," Walter retorted. "It will go a long way toward furthering his career."

Thomas didn't respond at once. He took a drink, steadying himself.

"When all this is over, perhaps you can end your service with Harold and go back to Scotland, where you really want to be. Your time is nearly up anyway."

Walter's cup shook. "To hell with that. What about my poor mother?"

"Your mother? Ah, lad, I was afraid of that."

Walter looked at him hopefully. "Perhaps when Gruffydd is captured, he will spare the rest."

The other shrugged doubtfully. "I don't know that capture is his aim," he said, then stopped at the look on Walter's face. "Is that what he told you?"

The other nodded, less convinced than ever.

Thomas looked troubled. "Then perhaps it is so, after all."

He thanked Walter for his kindness and left the room, appointing a guard, nonetheless. Walter barely noticed.

The second night after Harold left with the army, Walter woke Thomas in bed. He had avoided his friend since their hesitant talk together, but the time had come for him to make a move. He had waited for his moment, then lowered himself from his window, scaling the wall to Thomas's own. Projecting logs made the task fairly easy.

Thomas woke immediately and sat up, not the least disconcerted.

"I was expecting you," he said, making room for Walter to sit on the bed. "Come, we must talk. I have been thinking a bit myself."

Walter hesitated; he didn't know where to begin. "Thomas, we have known each other these seven years..." he started. His friend leaned back, motioning for him to go on. "I know Harold trusts you. But how can he expect me to sit here and wait for him to massacre my kin?"

Thomas interrupted him. "I thought you didn't care about Gruffydd?"

"Oh, not that one," Walter said. "But there are more than just my mother who are important to me. I can remove those innocents without raising the alarm."

Thomas frowned. "You talk as though you are already on the way there."

Walter grabbed his hand. "My old friend," he pleaded, "I know what a dilemma this is for you. I cannot stay. I must go, even if it means you have to try to kill me."

Closing his eyes, Thomas debated with himself. When he opened them, he saw the face he loved all those years, and knew he couldn't let Walter down.

"I guess Harold misjudged me," he sighed. "May God forgive me."

Walter let out a sigh. "I must go tonight."

"I know. Perhaps you won't even make it there, and I won't feel quite as guilty."

Walter gave Thomas a hard look, but the other looked away.

"Perhaps." He stood, looking around. "Must I give you a blow on the head to make it good?"

"No. Harold will never believe it. I shall tell him you escaped in the middle of the night, that's all."

Walter moved to the window, then hesitated. "Come with me. We will make our way to Scotland."

The Saxon shook his head. "I cannot lose so much honor. Though he will punish me, I must stay with Harold, for he is my Lord."

Walter threw a leg over the windowsill. "I don't know whether I will ever see you again, but remember this: you have helped a guilty son save his mother from destruction." He paused, then added, "And I am ever in your debt. If I can, I will repay you."

Thomas turned from him, lying on his pallet. "Go. I hope I never see you again."

It was hard to leave with those words still in his ears. But there was nothing else to say. Making sure there was no one in sight, Walter crawled from the window.

He knew every stone, every alleyway in this city. Harold should have known he couldn't hold him. Walter crept to the stables, finding the bundle he had secreted earlier. Then he harnessed a horse, taking the animal through a rear postern. The door opened with a key he had secretly made for himself, long ago.

Mounting, he took one last look at the place he had called home for six years. Then he disappeared into the night.

Walter was glad to turn his back on Harold's service. This portion of his life was over. But then, he had been ready to leave for a long time.

Harold had a good start on Walter, and the fugitive knew it. Walter guessed that the Earl planned to march north on the English side of the border, taking the easier, though longer route. This left no choice but to go directly north through the heart of Wales, taking the more treacherous paths that would inhibit an army's progress.

Walter wasn't nervous at the prospect of the grueling trip ahead of him. The thought of going home, seeing his beloved mother's surprised face gave him extra incentive to brave the cold wind blasting him in the face.

His horse wasn't as eager. There were times when Walter had to dismount, taking the reins and walking his steed over treacherous ground. Sometimes pulling, sometimes pleading, he managed to goad the beast into action. On a good stretch of ground they flew forward, the movement giving the horse warmth and its rider a surge of excitement. On a bad stretch, there were innumerable hills to climb, crisscrossed by rapid streams and intertwined roots. Sometimes it seemed like they were making absolutely no progress.

The nights were worse. Anxious though he was, Walter knew he needed sleep to endure. But these lands were rarely populated, and the traveler had to content himself with a pitiful fire and the warmth of his horse to keep from freezing to death. In the matter of three or four hours he was moving north once again.

Walter continued thus for four days. Finally the ground became more level, the tall hills receded. Rhuddlan was finally in sight. There was no destruction. Harold had not yet come.

13

A Timely Warning

Christmas festivities were well advanced as the door to the feast hall swung open, bringing in a blast of cold air. But no one seemed to notice; there was already a constant flow of people in and out of the room. And what was one stranger more or less?

Grateful for the obscurity, Walter inched along the wall, eyes darting worriedly here and there. He looked at the head table without hope. The Prince and his noble lady were lavishly dressed for the festivities. Ealdgyth, still beautiful despite her forty-five years, sat tall and elegant in her throne. She looked at him from the corner of her eye.

Walter was searching for Nesta, Princess of the realm, dishonored daughter of the great Gruffydd ap Llewelyn. The longer he looked, the more frantic he became. It had been eight long years since a frightened, lonely boy had fled from his homeland and all that he knew, leaving his mother to face the consequences of his violent actions. Although he had written some letters along the way, he never knew whether they had reached their destination. Where was she?

Before he entered Rhuddlan, he had purchased another horse for his mother's use. Secreting the animals in the woods, he had entered the village with a pounding heart. First, he went to the hut where he had grown up, knocking softly. There was a long pause, then unfamiliar steps inside approaching the door. The door cracked open.

Walter's mouth was open in a half-smile, ready for a startled greeting. But an old woman filled the doorway, scowled at him then slammed the door shut. His mouth wouldn't close. He felt stupid, then horrified, then angry. He wrenched the knob, but it held against him. No one responded to his banging.

Then, hoping his grandfather had taken pity on his helpless

mother, he ran toward the great hall, encountering no one he recognized along the way. Had Harold already taken such a toll on the Welsh people that Gruffydd's few favorites were already destroyed? No, Walter told himself, he would find them celebrating the holiday.

And his surroundings did look cheerful enough, even though the distraught man didn't share the sentiment. The walls were hung with gay wreaths, wrapped in fine ribbons. Extra torches stood grouped at every corner, fluttering slightly in the breeze. As he trod silently across the courtyard, snow fell around him, blanketing the white ground with a fresh layer.

But the feasting hall didn't give any more clues to his search; rather, it fed the growing unease churning his insides. Not wanting to be recognized, Walter left quickly.

Keeping to the walls and heading for the river, he tried one last refuge, afraid that he might find his old friend Salwyn already in the grave.

As Walter neared the house, a grim smile came to his face. Unmistakable signs of Salwyn's presence were still intact. But the shutters were shut and locked. Walter went around to the back of the house, rapping quietly at the door.

At first there was no movement inside, and Walter feared a repetition of the scene he had experienced at his own house. But finally someone stirred, and the door flew open, revealing a warm, well lit interior.

The woman holding the door gasped, putting a hand to her mouth. She was the most beautiful creature Walter thought he had ever seen, though he immediately recognized his frail little playmate. Despite himself, he smiled. With a little cry, she threw her arms around his neck, dragging him inside.

Walter was intensely relieved to find his old teacher in seemingly good shape, snugly wrapped in a blanket near the fire. Salwyn slowly rose from his chair, coming forward to grasp his hand. Walter gathered him into a hug. There the three of them stood, wrapped in one big huddle, all talking excitedly and crying at once.

Such was Walter's homecoming.

In a few minutes, he was comfortably settled with a cup of steaming milk in his hand, caressing Myrna's golden hair and admiring Salwyn's new leather quiver. The urgency of his need lay heavily on his heart, but he was unwilling to ruin the magic of the moment.

But the old man knew that Walter's was not a social visit. After hesitating, Salwyn cleared his throat; he looked at Walter searchingly.

"You don't know, do you?"

Walter's heart sank. He shook his head. Salwyn looked pained.

"You knew she wasn't going to have an easy time of it, after you left," he added, almost in anger. "Well, there wasn't much you yourself could do. But her father could have helped her."

Walter looked confused, almost scared. His old friend sighed.

"This isn't easy to tell you," he said. "You mother had to pay the *Galanas*... you know, compensation. Rhys's life was valued at three sheep, four hens. A silly price for a human life, right? But it was a fortune to your mother. In paying back Rhys's kin, she labored night and day. Wouldn't give herself any rest.

"The *Galanas* was paid, all right. But her health was gone. The next winter, she took ill and died of a fever...I'm sorry, Walter."

Walter didn't hear the end of Salwyn's long speech. Now she was gone and it was all his fault...all his fault. He had to shake his head to clear the guilt; now was not the time to wallow in self-pity.

He sat for a long time, staring at the fire, until Myrna fidgeted uncomfortably. He looked at her, his eyes filled with tears. She was also crying, and he gathered her to him, putting his face in her hair.

Salwyn painfully got up from his chair, and went in to

another room, returning with a sword. Walter recognized it as his father's.

"She asked me to give it to you," the old man said. "It was all she had left, but she said you'd come back for it some day."

Walter took the gift, and the grasp of the weapon reminded of him of the purpose of his visit. He shook off his despair, preparing to deal with it at a less dangerous moment. He leaned forward.

"Listen to me," he whispered. "Harold Godwineson is coming to this court, to surprise Gruffydd and destroy him. No one will escape his anger. Come out of this place with me. I will take you somewhere safer."

Myrna jumped up, looked around the room in agitation, ready to act but not sure where to start. Her father didn't move, as if he didn't hear the message. Walter knelt at his side.

"Did you hear me, Salwyn? The man will not spare an aging old soldier. That is why I came. I have abandoned my master, turned traitor to save my mother. Don't let me destroy myself for nothing."

Salwyn heaved a great sigh, looking at Walter with eyes that spoke of sorrow for things past, and a willingness to end a miserable life. Walter had never seen that look before, but he respected it. The old man shook his head.

"I cannot go. Even if I wanted to, it would hinder you so that you might never escape. But take my daughter to safety. Take my Myrna. I long to join my wife."

Walter looked at Myrna, and she threw herself onto her father, begging him to come. In some confusion, Walter decided to step outside for a moment, and leave those two alone.

Unobserved, he threw a mantle over his shoulders, and left the house, closing the door softly. Looking around, he started when a shrouded figure moved away from the gate; but in a surge of protectiveness, he strode forward to confront the stranger. The unknown quickly threw back the disguising hood, revealing the chiseled features of Ealdgyth.

"What does this mean?" he asked suspiciously. "Does the husband send his wife to arrest the intruder?"

"Don't be a fool," she said scornfully. Then, in a milder tone, she added, "He did not see you." She hesitated a moment; it was the first time they had ever spoken together.

"I recognized you, you know," she said softly. "You have your mother's eyes. She would have been proud to see you so handsomely grown."

He jerked his shoulders angrily. "And what have you to say, you who allowed her to die?"

"Silence!" she cried imperiously. "You know nothing of what you speak. Think you she would have paid the wergild without my help?" In her anger she lapsed into her native dialect.

Walter pursed his lips.

"Her father never knew," she finished. "It was enough that my daughter died in peace. Where were you when she needed help?"

Shamed, Walter lowered his head. He knew she was right. His grandmother put a hand to his chin, lifting it so she could see his face. "But I came not to chastise you. You are here for some unknown reason, and I may be able to help."

He looked into her clear eyes. She was so strong. "I met your father," he said.

Ealdgyth jumped; the suddenness of his statement took her off guard. Her father, her loving father who wept when he sent her off to be married. The thought that this boy knew Aelfgar brought him closer to her.

"I negotiated with him for Earl Harold...brought him back from his outlawry."

Her sigh came out as a sob. "I did not see him before he died. I loved him so much."

Never had Ealdgyth seemed so vulnerable. She had always been to him that stern, distant queen; but now she was only a bereaved daughter. Without warning, a new resolve formed in his mind.

"I was going to let Gruffydd rot where he sits..." he began, when the fiery woman interrupted him:

"Speak not so of your Prince! With all his faults, he is a great man."

"Then let him go to hell!" Walter cried, pulling away. He made three steps then stopped, turning. Ealdgyth had not moved.

"I am telling you this so you may save yourself from destruction. Get thee gone!"

He said all his conscience would allow. But the woman restrained him from leaving.

"Your mother and I have a distant relation in Brittany," she whispered. "His name is Alain le Roux. He is Earl of that great land. He remembers Nesta fondly." Her voice broke. She fumbled at her neck and pulled a necklace over her head. "Here. Go to him. Return this to him. He gave this present to your mother when she was a child. She always wore it. I removed it when she died and kept it..." She crumpled up the fine silk cord and put it into his hand. "This will give you an introduction. Perhaps you can find a place at his court."

Walter pulled away without looking at her, shoving the necklace into his pouch. He remembered playing with it as a child, but was shamed that he never asked his mother where it came from. When he had reached the door, he turned to thank Ealdgyth but she was gone.

Reentering the cottage, Walter saw with relief that father and daughter had come to some sort of understanding. Although they didn't seem to be talking, Salwyn was packing a few things, and Myrna was putting away his dinner dishes. In these ways do we deal with our torments, Walter thought.

"We must go now," he said, and the others stopped, looking at each other.

"Are you sure you will not come?" Walter ventured, but the

old man's look silenced him. Myrna took her pack and pulled Walter with her, pausing at the door to look back. Salwyn wouldn't raise his head, but Walter fancied he saw a tear stain his sleeve. The two left in silence.

Already the castle bailey resounded with activity. Walter did not want to be found near the Welsh he had so timely warned. He wrapped Myrna into a warmer mantle and, provided with the extra horse, they rode quietly away toward the south.

Ealdgyth took Walter's vague warning seriously. Sensing that they had little time, she hurried back to the feast hall. She slipped into the room unnoticed, and hurried to her husband.

Gruffydd was emptying a large goblet when his wife bent over his shoulder.

"Oh, there you are," he said, grabbing her around the waist. "And why did you desert me, without a by-your-leave?" Smiling, he pulled her onto his lap.

Ealdgyth allowed the frivolity, because it would bring her closer to his ear. "My husband," she whispered, "we are in grave danger."

"Eh?" He pulled back, looking at her face. "What is it you say?"

"Tonight I received a warning to leave this place. I think we should heed a message given by such a source."

Gruffydd shook the muddle from his head. "Stop, woman, with your riddles. Speak plainly. Who has given you this warning?"

"Nesta's son."

"Pah. The bastard seeks a reward."

"Will you stop it? Can't you see, he came to save his mother? He didn't know she was dead."

"So why would he warn us?"

"I followed him." Ealdgyth looked around, half-expecting the doors to burst open. "For once in your life, give the boy credit.

He is already gone; he wouldn't take a reward from your hands."

"Wife, I think this is foolish, but I can't afford to take any chances. Let me up."

Sobered by Ealdgyth's words, Gruffydd stood; the room immediately quieted.

"The festivities are over," the Prince announced. Hearing groans of disappointment, he became angry. "You will do as I say! We have been given a warning: there is a threat to our safety this night. We can either stand and fight, or flee. But since we are ill prepared to fight, I suggest you leave this place. We don't know the extent of the danger. Gather your families and go. Now."

Motioning for some of his favorites to follow, the Prince gave orders to ready the boats.

It took very little time to load the boats, always ready docked below the archway of the palace. Gruffydd didn't take the strange warning too seriously; though nervous enough to suspect treachery at every turn, he little expected to be attacked during the most sacred holy festival. But he trusted his wife's good sense and intuition, which had helped him in the past. And she was so certain that something was amiss.

They launched the little vessels, making their way to the mouth of the Clwyd and into the sea. The cold wind blasted into their faces, and Gruffydd silently agreed with the grumbling of those who regretted leaving the warmth of the feast hall.

"This is colder than a witch's teat," one man mumbled, pulling a blanket around his shoulders. The boat pitched, nearly throwing him overboard. "Damn it, man!" he shouted at the rowers. "Can't you control this thing any better?"

"They're doing the best they can," the man's wife retorted. "The poor men are no more sober than you are, never expecting to be dragged away from their drinks in the middle of the night."

"Aye, and for what?" someone else shouted over the wind. "Are we to be startled into flight at the least rumor of trouble?"

That was enough to get a reaction from Gruffydd. He turned angrily. "If I say as much, you will jump into the river on my command!" He was about to add more but he hesitated, confused. No one was looking at him; rather, they were staring over his shoulder. He turned back, following their gaze.

At first, Gruffydd could only distinguish a reddish glare on the shore: the kind of glow that meant only one thing. He watched, frozen like the rest of them, while the glare turned into distinct flames. He listened as the silence of his friends gave way to cries of horror.

Perhaps, amongst them all, Gruffydd's mute grief was the most bitter. He watched his splendid palace burn, and saw the last beacons of violence light the sky from the remainder of his precious fleet. They were still close enough to hear the screams of his peasants, murdered in their homes.

Gruffydd sat motionless in the stern of his boat, his mind's eye seeing Harold pacing disappointedly back and forth before his pillaging troops. He, Gruffydd ap Llewelyn ap Seisylt, had been outsmarted by this cursed Saxon. He had barely escaped, thanks to the timely warning from his bastard grandson.

But the Earl was having his revenge. The Prince of Wales would never see his beloved Rhuddlan again.

Ealdgyth sat beside her husband, enveloped in her own silence. She was not sorry to leave a place of such bitter memories. The bones of her daughter were safe. But her mind kept straying back to her grandson, with his brooding black eyes.

She knew with a surety born of kinship that some other time in the midst of disaster she would see him once again.

It was still many hours from dawn. Myrna lay wrapped tightly in her cloak, snuggling close to Walter for heat. Their little fire had burned down, and he was afraid to light it again.

Thousands of thoughts raced through his mind, making it impossible to sleep. He envied the repose of his companion, though he pitied her tearstained face. It was a brave thing to leave her father, but he knew she would suffer the rest of her life because of it. She would always wonder what she should have said to convince him to go.

He looked over at her round, silken face, admiring her beauty; Myrna was only a year or so younger than himself, yet one could hardly tell. Walter put a hand to his forehead, tracing a barely hidden scar over one brow. Surely he must seem twice her age.

He turned away, trying not to notice the inviting warmth of her body. What was he going to do with her now? Take her to Scotland with him? And then what? He knew that she was still attached to him, now more so than ever. He was all she had. Having torn her so abruptly from everything she knew, she would turn to him for solace, for her very support. What had he gotten himself into?

He supposed there was always marriage. She was beautiful, and gave him an odd sort of comfort, reminding him of home. But Myrna had always been the silly little girl, forever haunting his steps, never leaving him alone. Even now he felt she was a burden.

There really was no choice. He would take her to Scotland; it was only a few days travel overland. More importantly, all these years he had thought longingly about Malcolm, desiring to take his rightful place—or so he considered it—at his sovereign's elbow. He had been gone long enough. But this decision brought on an even worse thought. What would Malcolm think of his actions? Would he scorn Walter's traitorous behavior toward Harold, or would the King understand what he had done?

Malcolm had lost a parent to violence. On the other hand, Harold had helped him regain his kingdom. If Malcolm came to despise him, Walter wondered how he would manage to go on. There would be nothing left for him, either.

Rolling himself into his cloak, Walter closed his eyes to the cold. It seemed that he had just fallen asleep, when he felt a nagging tug at his shoulder. Dazed, he cocked his ear sideways, trying to distinguish the whispering sounds of the forest from the murmurings in his head. In the corner of his eye he fancied he saw those three forms, always so clearly etched in his mind. Myrna lay like one dead.

One of the sisters waved her hand over his head, forcing him to close his eyes. "Sleep," said the sister next to her, and the other said "Dream".

Walter dreamt. The weird sisters led him through a land of rolling green hills, where the sun seemed to always shine and a breeze caressed his skin. They kept beckoning to him, although at times they faded altogether.

Before long he was within sight of a tall, stately stone castle, perched on a hilltop. Banners fluttered from its turrets, sentries paced its walls; a drawbridge was down over a wide moat.

The women suddenly surrounded Walter, breathing into his face, encircling him with their arms. He struggled to break free, but they held him fast.

"Walter," they all whispered in his ears,

Where are you going, our tempest-tost child?
Our thoughts have been with you, our actions were mild.
You may not go on so without any thought.
You must use your judgment like you have been taught.
Alain has a daughter in Brittany land
We send you to seek her and ask for her hand.
And place on her finger a gold wedding band.
Our will shall not vary though you be afraid.
Your destiny's path has already been laid.

The sisters disappeared, giving Walter one last look at the castle, so he could memorize its features. Then he awoke, sitting up and looking around. Everything was as before, including Myrna's attitude in sleep. His hand went to his pouch and he pulled out his mother's necklace. Although his couldn't see the amber stone, he ran his finger along its smooth surface then hung the necklace around his neck. It gave him a little comfort.

He sighed and lay back. Was that really a dream? Somehow he doubted it.

After taking a lean breakfast, they quietly made ready to move on. Walter was worried about Myrna; she soon gave him good reason. Mounting her horse, she turned its head in the direction they had come. She looked challengingly down at Walter.

"You know I cannot leave without seeing if my father is alive or not," she said quietly.

Walter had dreaded this moment, though he wasn't surprised.

"You know," he said, "that you will be walking right back into the danger we were running from last night."

She nodded.

"And," he added, "there is a good chance that if Harold is not there, he will have posted some men."

She nodded.

"And if he catches me, I am a dead man."

Myrna burst into tears. She sobbed uncontrollably for a few minutes, and Walter busily adjusted his saddle, unwilling to give in. He peeked at her from under his horse's neck. She looked like a child.

Glancing up suddenly, she caught him watching her. Straightening, Myrna wiped a hand across her face and pushed her horse forward.

Walter mounted quickly, catching up to her. He said nothing.

"Don't come with me," she said finally. "I will follow."

"Impossible. You will be lost in a minute." He sighed. "Believe me, I understand. If only I had known that my mother was dead..."

"Then you wouldn't have come, and I would be slain."

Or worse. There was no answer to give.

They dismounted while still in the woods, and surveyed the town from the refuge of the trees. Myrna gasped; unlike Walter, she was unused to seeing man's capacity for destruction. There was absolutely no sign of the Saxons; they had left as quickly as they came. But they had certainly left their mark.

What was once a grand monument to Gruffydd's accomplishments was now a pile of charred embers. A few sturdy pillars stood to mark the site of his great hall, with smoke rising around them in curls. Some of the peasants were picking through the ruins.

Walter could hear the wailing of wives for dead husbands, and he saw the slow train of carts moving toward the burial ground. He felt responsible, but there was no time for guilt.

Myrna was already running for her father's house; the fire had not spread over the river. Walter cursed to himself, then ran after her, but it was too late. She came to a dead halt before her door, and Walter barely reached her in time to stop her fall.

Salwyn lay face down, half in and half out of the doorway, still holding his bloody sword. His death had cost the enemy dear; three Saxons lay on the ground around him.

Walter lowered Myrna to the ground, holding her until she regained consciousness. She came to with a gasp and a sob, then pushed away from Walter, staggering to her father. Walter helped her turn him over. Though the old warrior had a violent end, his face looked strangely peaceful.

They buried him next to his wife, then Myrna packed a few more of her things and carefully closed and locked the door to the house. She offered no resistance when Walter led her away. In fact, she showed little life at all for some time.

14

Exile of Gruffydd ap Llewelyn

Gruffydd and his following had no choice after their close escape but to take shelter in the mountains of Snowdonia. They found refuge with Gruffydd's two brothers Bleddyn and Rhiwallon. Perched atop a tall crag at Harlech, their castle overlooked the ocean on one side, and the mountains on the other. From there, messages were sent, summoning the loyal Welsh to the defense of their Prince.

Gruffydd had to admit that he felt jealous of the comfort of Bleddyn's home. Watching for ships, the Prince cursed bitterly to himself for the hundredth time that day, kicked a clump of dirt and contemplated its fall to the ground far below him. He derived a malicious satisfaction watching the startled sea gulls flap noisily away.

His beloved Rhuddlan was gone, and he hadn't the means to avenge its destruction. With the first sign of trouble the southern Welsh were sure to ally themselves with the English; they would use any means to destroy him if they could.

It was always this way. The Welsh were their own worst enemies. Constant turmoil, with chief against chief and north against south, kept them from uniting against the real enemy: the English. None of them trusted each other; they were always watching for an opportunity to take advantage of a rival's weakness.

And the English were so numerous...there was no keeping them out. Harold had the King's army to use, if he needed it. This time, the Prince knew, Harold meant to finish his task; Gruffydd would, if he were in the Saxon's place.

Hearing a noise behind him, he turned to see his wife. She was picking her way slowly toward him, gripping a heavy cloak against the wind. She smiled wryly.

"You always seem to find the coldest spots."

Gruffydd moved to Ealdgyth, engulfing her with his own mantle. He brushed a few strands of hair from her eyes, thinking with surprise that he seldom stopped to notice how beautiful they were.

Ealdgyth had taken their troubles so impassively, so uncomplaining, that he was constantly amazed. But then, she had always been full of surprises, since the first day he saw her, a wide-eyed twelve year old bride, yet totally unafraid of her whole new environment.

"I know I don't say this very much, Ealdgyth, but I think you are the best thing that ever happened to me."

To Gruffydd's delight, she blushed a deep red. He drew his wife closer, nestled her head under his chin. She sighed, leaning into the comfort of his arms. It was rare these days that Gruffydd relaxed enough to hold her like this. And yet his need for comfort was great.

As they stood thus, the Prince was looking at the sea. Ealdgyth felt him stiffen, and broke reluctantly away, noting his sudden intense stare. Her eyes followed his.

Away on the horizon, they saw a sail. For a long time they watched, but it continued north without veering from its path.

"You fear invasion, then?" she asked, knowing the answer already.

"We are safe enough for now, my dove," he said after a moment. "Harold will not campaign as long as it is winter. But he will be back. And I don't know if I can stop him."

Ealdgyth shivered. Never had her husband spoken this way before.

As the winter passed, recruits gathered at Harlech. Throughout north Wales, the people were busily repairing weapons and armor, and restocking crucial hidden strongholds in the mountains, in case the royal party found themselves under siege.

By the end of May, Harold was ready. He and his brother Tostig planned a joint invasion by land and sea. From Northumbria, Tostig crossed overland with a large army, and along the north coast of Wales, toward the island of Anglesey. He left a path of fire and devastation behind him.

Harold put together his force of housecarls at Oxford, marching to Bristol. From there they launched a fleet, traveling around Cornwall then north along the coast, in case the Prince were to try escaping by ship. He joined Tostig at Anglesey.

As Gruffydd expected, the southerners capitulated to Harold. No sanctuary would be found there.

When the two Earls met, they began a systematic sweep of the country southward, in what was considered the most revolutionary campaign of all time by the English. Nothing was left undone, no crops unburned, no enemies left alive. Following the Welsh practice, Harold ordered that prisoners' heads be severed from their bodies.

The Welsh despaired against what seemed a remorseless attack.

And yet they held out valiantly for the duration of the summer. Gruffydd moved from camp to camp, rarely staying long enough to use all the food supplies. And when Harold thought he had trapped his game, he was furious to discover only abandoned fires and half-eaten meals.

Continuing their guerrilla attacks, the Welsh would sweep down from the hills, creating havoc and killing the English with the desperation of a trapped creature. Then they would seem to melt away into the trees.

But no defense could withstand the systematic destruction of all their sustenance. Every time Harold would win a battle, he would erect a stone cairn with the inscription "Here Harold Conquered". The Welsh became demoralized, and Gruffydd found his little band of warriors shrinking every day.

Finally, there were only a handful left. Late one night, after the camp retired, Bleddyn and Rhiwallon pulled aside a crusty warrior named Madog Min. Moving outside of everyone's hearing, they made him a proposal that would bring the purposeless game of cat and mouse to an end.

"Listen carefully," the older brother said. "It is time to negotiate with Harold. Go to him with this offer: Gruffydd's head, in exchange for our joint rulership of Wales. As underlords to the English King, of course."

Madog's eyes glistened greedily as he listened.

"Oh, and make whatever deal for yourself as you can," the brother added. "After all, it will be you who will show Harold the prey."

Min rubbed his hands together, nodding in agreement. He soon left under cover of night, but everyone just took him for another deserter.

The following morning, Gruffydd and Ealdgyth were having breakfast. Furtively, she eyed him worriedly; the once burly and confident Prince seemed to have shrunk along the way. There were hollows in his cheeks, and his green eyes, that once shot fire when angry, now appeared clouded and dead.

They had camped on the shore of the river Afon Llugwy, next to a cheerful waterfall called Rhaeadr Ewynnd, or foamy white falls. The falls were short but swift, and the river was wide in this valley so secluded by the protective mountains. Though the sound of water drowned out the noise of possible danger, yet the natural obstruction was more secure than most. And visibility from halfway up the hill was good. Gruffydd, too, was confident in the men posted to watch, though there were all too few of them.

Or maybe he just doesn't care anymore, thought Ealdgyth. The Prince seemed too depressed to take an interest in his own safety.

She sighed, getting up to wash her underdress in the river. Ealdgyth was unused to these chores, but her servants had long past taken their leave, apologizing with eyes averted. She couldn't really blame them; their situation was getting desperate.

And they hadn't moved camp for a week. They were comfortable here…too comfortable. She was sure that trouble was close, but today Gruffydd didn't listen to her.

"My husband," she said nervously, "haven't you even noticed that your brothers are missing today?" The Prince looked up dully, his eyes bloodshot. He glanced around, then went back to eating his breakfast. "You are going to do nothing?"

He shrugged his shoulders.

Ealdgyth hung her dress on a tree branch. "Ah, my husband," she sighed, "what has happened to your old spirit?"

She never heard an answer. At that moment, a hand went over her mouth, and another grabbed her arm, wrenching it behind her. Her cruel captor turned her around, showing her what was happening to her husband.

Gruffydd didn't feel a thing. In his near stupor, he never heard the stealthy footsteps behind him, nor the swish of a broadsword through the air, before the lethal blade cut right through his neck, severing his head cleanly from his body.

Ealdgyth screamed through the hand that clamped her mouth; she fainted as the blood spurted from Gruffydd's neck, showering her and her aggressor. But she was conscious long enough to have recognized the leering face of Madog Min, gloating over the bloody deed he had just done.

The last of the Prince's stout defenders had faded into the forest when they saw Harold's men making their decisive move upon the hidden camp, led by that traitor, Madog Min. The Welsh were a practical people. They knew that the chase was finished, and didn't relish dying with the man who, at the last, had caused them so much misery. Gruffydd met his end alone and betrayed, his only companion his ever faithful wife.

Harold sent Gruffydd's head to King Edward, along with the beak of the Prince's master ship and a few other incidentals. He took Ealdgyth along with him, intending to marry her in the hope of keeping peace with her brothers, Eadwine and Morkere, those English Earls whose support he needed.

To Madog Min he had promised the value of three hundred head of cattle for the deed. But when it was over, he scorned the supplicant as a traitor and sent him on a ship to Dublin, empty handed but glad to keep his worthless life.

But another fate was in store for the murderer. On the way to Dublin the ship sank in a storm; the chroniclers said that there was no loss of life except for one Madog Min.

15

A Short Reprieve

It was not seasonable for a crossing of the English Channel. No vessel was yet designed to do such a thing; in the winter, even the Norse pulled their dragon-ships onto the shore and passed their time warmly inside their lodgings.

With the words of the weird sisters still in his mind, Walter determined to spend the winter with Malcolm. At least he could explain himself in person, before his friend heard rumors of his betrayal from the wrong sources.

Malcolm had built a royal palace at Dunfermline, a few miles north of the Firth of Forth. He lived in what was called the Royal Tower, a stone building three stories tall with a full attic. The palace boasted more than twenty-five chambers, plenty large enough for the royal household. It perched atop a tall, steep hill, only reachable by a long road resembling a ramp; at the base of the hill ran a crooked stream. The entrance was on the second story, accessible by a staircase and over a drawbridge. It was a secure place, without the necessity of building massive outer walls.

The trip to Malcolm's royal residence took the pair across Scotland to the firth. They traveled slowly east, staying at night in small inns. No one bothered them, assuming they were brother and sister. They had to ferry across the wide expanse of river, then picked up their pace, feeling the rush of a traveler near the end of the road.

Walter and Myrna stood at the foot of the steps, looking thoughtfully at the structure. It was very unlike anything they had seen in Wales, and for Myrna who had never been outside of Rhuddlan, it was a complete novelty.

Walter was relieved that she had finally begun to show some life; her youthful curiosity was gradually overcoming her mournful mood. Although she missed her father terribly, nature had begun its long healing process. She even dared a smile now and then, though she usually caught herself.

Although Walter felt terribly sorry for her, in a way he envied her feelings. As is usually the case, he didn't realize until too late that he must have given his mother up for lost long ago. The shock of hearing about her death didn't affect him as deeply as it should have. It was already as if he had done his mourning; as if now he could finally put an end to worrying about her. But he was saddened that he found no tears. He felt remorse, a sense of guilt at not having done something for her sooner. But no grief. He wondered what was wrong with him.

He took Myrna's hand, leading her forward. Suddenly, two soldiers stepped from inside the building, spears raised, and demanded the names of the visitors. But one of them recognized Walter. With a yell, he leaped down the steps, grasping Walter's hand. They both talked at once, laughing and joking, the soldier making eyes at Myrna and asking her name. She blushed furiously.

The other disappeared inside, and a moment later Malcolm dashed out the door, forgetting his regal manner. He flew down the steps and gathered Walter in his arms, in a hug that nearly smothered his friend.

And then Walter's tears came. He was too happy to be embarrassed about showing his feelings; this was a moment he had waited for, a long time. Standing arm's length apart, Walter grasped Malcolm's shoulder, unwilling to let him go. It seemed to him that in all this world, the King was the only person he loved. They had fought together, worked together, ate and drank together, struggled for the same cause.

Malcolm swore his surprise, smiling wide enough to burst his face. He was in splendid condition, ruddy skin, black hair full and wild, shoulders filling his tunic with the unmistakable temper of finely tuned muscle. His black eyes twinkled.

"I'm delighted, Walter," he exclaimed. "God's blood, it's been too long."

"Five long years," Walter finally responded. He smiled sadly "I've wanted to be here all along."

Malcolm put an arm around his shoulders. "And I've needed you all along," he said. They began walking toward the tower as the King gestured to one of the guards to take care of their mounts. They almost left poor Myrna behind, when Walter stopped, embarrassed. He turned Malcolm around.

"I've brought someone with me," he said.

Malcolm misunderstood. "Aha, a little wife you have. And how pretty."

Myrna blushed, and Walter laughed. "No, my Lord. This is Myrna. I've known her since we were children." Malcolm looked at his friend, a half-smile on his face. He was confused, not knowing what to say to the girl.

Walter took her hand. "It's a long, sad story," he said, "and one I'm not very proud of. I must tell you about it. But right now she is shivering."

Malcolm laughed, forgetting that it was still winter, and not everyone was able to ignore the cold. He led the way into his home.

Soon, the travelers were comfortably settled. Malcolm wanted his guests to join him in the feast hall, but Walter insisted that he couldn't, at least that night.

His heart misgave him; he wanted most of all to tell his story. Only then could Malcolm decide whether his guests were still welcome. This was the only place in Britain that Walter could, or would consider his home, and he wanted to preserve it.

Though Malcolm was often insensible to subtleties, he seemed to understand the gist of Walter's plight. He perceived that something was wrong, and was willing to give Walter his undivided attention. So the King ordered a private dinner to be served to the two of them, in his own chamber.

Malcolm was perfectly happy to start off by telling Walter his own experiences.

"Well," he began, "you know about the end of Macbeth. Of course, killing the leader doesn't mean there were no more enemies. Faithful to the fallen king, his retainers thought I would find them and kill them. Stupid fellows. So they got hold of his son, or his stepson, I don't exactly know which..." he bit a haunch of lamb.

"The pretender's name was Lulach. Lulach the simple, people called him. He was a perfect tool for the traitors. They took him to Scone and put a crown on his head. Don't quite know how many crowns there are in Scotland. I thought I had the thing." Malcolm wiped his mouth, grinning.

"Anyway, they declared the fool king. It took me seven months to find him, but we finally overtook the boy in Strathbogie and put an end to that travesty."

Malcolm stopped, taking a draught of wine. "Drink, Walter. Anyway, by then Earl Thorfinn had died. Actually, he died before I caught up with Macbeth. To tell you the truth," he added, lowering his voice, "I think I would have had a much worse time of it if Thorfinn had been there, especially since I didn't have my uncle Seward at my side. Don't tell anyone I said that. Those Orkney men fight like devils, you remember. But once their chief was gone, they preferred to fight for me, their natural king.

"I took Thorfinn's widow, Ingibjorg, in marriage, to retain their support." Walter sat up, surprised. "Oh, no, Walter. She died a few months ago, dear lady. But she gave me a fine boy, who I named Duncan, after my father."

Walter congratulated him on having an heir, embarrassed that he knew nothing of it.

"It's no matter. With your help, we will make him valiant and strong.

"But to continue, even the death of Lulach did not deter some of the others. They persuaded one of my most noble retainers—

and I will not tell you who," he added with a look of warning. "That is also no matter, as I will explain shortly."

He stuffed some bread in his mouth. "As I was saying, they persuaded this ungrateful fellow to join in their secret plot to murder me. But fortunately, praise God, I was warned in time.

"I planned a hunt to resolve this thing, and invited the man to come. When I had a convenient moment, I pulled him away from the rest, and took him to a hidden valley."

Malcolm stopped, looked at Walter. He leaned forward, suddenly very serious. "Walter, I have never told this to anyone. You must not let this story leave the room. Swear it!"

Walter promised to be silent, frowning. He remembered the last time, with the miller's daughter.

"All right. I pulled this man in to the valley, as I said. He seemed to suspect nothing, but suddenly I turned to him and confronted him with what I knew, upbraiding him with his lack of gratitude for all I had done for him. Then I leaped from my horse, pulling my sword.

"'Now,' I said to him, 'we are equally armed. If your design is to kill me, do it fairly instead of sneaking around like a coward!' I was ready to fight, to give him a chance. But for all that, he was so astounded that he threw himself at my feet, begging my forgiveness."

For a moment Malcolm looked satisfied with himself at a task so well done. Then he became serious again.

"He promised to be a faithful vassal, and he has been, ever since. But I learned a cruel lesson regarding the instability of man's loyalty."

Walter put his face in his hands, shaken by the turn the conversation had taken.

Not noticing, Malcolm had gone on. "But that was the end of the rebellion, as far as I can see. Scotland has been at peace ever since, and the people have been content...Walter, what is it?"

Walter raised his face, and the King was struck by the change his emotions made on it. "Speak up man," he said.

Swallowing, Walter said, "I am guilty myself of a breach of loyalty. It's what I've been wanting to tell you."

Malcolm was at a loss for words.

Walter took a long drink of wine. He told Malcolm about Harold's plan to invade Rhuddlan, and how he destroyed the Earl's chances by his warning. "And you know the worst of it," he added. "I'm upset by what you might think of it, not because of Harold. For him I still feel no remorse."

Malcolm shook his head. "It was a grievous thing for him to invade your birthplace. It was only understandable for you to want to save your mother. But you have done great wrong to betray your Lord." Malcolm paused. "Just why did you give them warning? You could have accomplished what you did without that."

Walter shrugged his shoulders. "I felt something that I never would have expected. When Ealdgyth was standing there, so pitiful yet so strong, I felt I was sending her to her death. And I remembered that she and even Gruffydd were my kin. They are my grandparents, Malcolm!"

He stopped; ever since they met, he refrained from using Malcolm's first name.

But the King still looked puzzled. The explanation didn't satisfy him.

"There was something else," Walter added, standing and walking to the wall. He ran his finger along the stitching on the tapestry. "When I was a child, I don't remember how old, my mother told me to remember one thing. Whatever a king did, she said, one had to accept, whether it was right or wrong. One could never make judgments, no matter how much it hurt. She said that ruling a country sometimes meant that the king would have to do things that normal men wouldn't have to face.

"I guess she always believed that, until the day she died. I think if I had let Harold kill Gruffydd, I would never have forgiven myself, because my mother wouldn't have forgiven me." He put his forehead against the wall.

Malcolm came up behind him, put a hand on his shoulder.

"If you are looking for absolution from me," he said, "I cannot give it to you. But what your mother said was right. I am beginning to find that out for myself."

He turned Walter around. "As far as I am concerned, you have done me no offense. My feelings toward you are as they have always been. You are my loyal subject, and more than that, a good friend, which is something a king rarely gets to say. Whatever is between you and Harold, you'll have to straighten out yourself, if you ever get the opportunity."

Walter grasped his hand, flooded with relief. "That is good enough for me."

Pouring more wine, Malcolm sat again. "Now tell me what else has happened to you."

Walter relaxed, feeling like a burden was lifted. He nearly smiled. "Are you superstitious, Sire?"

Malcolm shrugged his shoulders. "Most likely."

"There is more to this than I can explain, but maybe you can help me. This also I have never told anyone else." He raised an eyebrow meaningfully and Malcolm drank to him.

"But actually, this goes back to when I was sixteen. In fact, this was the cause of my original troubles." Walter put a hand to his neck, touching his mother's necklace; he hadn't really thought about that peculiar night for many years. "It was All-Hallow's Eve, and I was a boy. I was involved in one of those pranks boys do, you know, on nights like that. But it didn't go as planned.

"I saw an apparition. Three old women appeared to me, almost as solid as you are. They told me…" he nearly choked. "They told me I was a bastard and that Fleance was my father. They told me to avenge Banquo's death." He put his hands over his face.

Malcolm sat on the edge of his seat. "Is this how you found

out?"

Walter nodded. "I confronted my mother and she admitted everything. I was enraged. And when one of the others called me a bastard… well, I killed him. I couldn't help myself. And in fleeing to the safety of London, I abandoned my mother."

The King coughed uncomfortably. "That's an unearthly story, Walter. But why are you telling me now?"

"Because I saw them again, just the other night. After… Rhuddlan. When I warned Ealdgyth about Harold, she told me to go to Brittany. That night the three weird sisters appeared to me in a dream, and told me the same thing. Honestly, I don't know what to believe. But I do know that the first time, they told me the truth of something I never knew. Now, they want me to do their bidding. I'm afraid to go against their will, because I don't want to arouse their anger."

Malcolm crossed himself. "They may curse you or something worse," he said. "God forefend. By all means, do what they say. Perhaps they mean well for you. But," he added thoughtfully, "that means you will have to leave me again. I don't mind telling you that I would hate for you to go."

"I feel much the same," Walter answered. "But something tells me that I am not fated to settle here yet. Though you can be sure that I will return in sooner than six years this time!" He laughed. "But that brings us to another problem."

"I can guess what it is. That pretty little thing you brought with you."

Walter nodded. "I took her away from Rhuddlan, and now she has nothing. Still, I can't bring her to Brittany."

Malcolm shook his head. "But don't worry. Perhaps we can persuade her to stay as hostage. Anyway, I need someone to take care of my little Duncan. I'm not much of a tutor."

Walter laughed, knowing that Malcolm couldn't read or write. "Perhaps I can persuade you to talk to her about that. Besides, we have the rest of the winter to worry about it."

It was a few days later that Malcolm did what he promised. Myrna was beginning to blossom again, considering all the attention the guards were giving her; she was taken with little Duncan, who so desperately needed a mother. The little boy followed her around, tugging at her skirts to be picked up as often as she would allow it.

King Malcolm sought for Myrna one day, finding her putting the child to sleep. He took her for a little walk outside of the tower. She was subdued and awestruck at the attention given her by such an important person. They stood on the edge of the hill, looking at the bright pink sunset. He pointed out the Forth, and its opposite shore, where she could just make out a few buildings atop a cliff.

"That is called Dun Edin, now Edinburgh," he said. "Dun means hill, just like Dunfermline. Let's see. Ferm means crooked, referring to the little stream below, and Line means cascade...see down there, the little waterfall? Our ancestors, the Celts, were ever a practical people.

"Someday I intend to build a castle there, at Edinburgh, to have a better grasp of Lothian. You wouldn't believe how much trouble crossing the Firth of Forth with an army can be." Malcolm paused, then turned to Myrna decisively, his eyes troubled.

"Actually," he said, "I have a very important question to ask you."

She shivered, pulling her cloak closer. "Anything, my liege."

"Well, it concerns Duncan...and Walter."

She looked at him questioningly.

He squinted into the sun. "He'll be leaving me again."

Myrna gasped.

"Not exactly tomorrow, but soon enough," he added quickly, looking down at her. "Something about a prophecy, a dream. Oh, you'll have to ask him about it yourself." He paused, embarrassed.

She put a hand to her mouth, turning away. "I don't think he would tell me," she said, so softly that he had to bend to hear.

Malcolm felt sorry for her. His temperament was best suited for facing an enemy on the battlefield, not the tears of a woman, especially one so young. Wishing he were elsewhere, the King started to put out a hand in consolation, but pulled it back. He coughed.

"I think you ought to stay here," he said. "Myrna, will you help me take care of my son?"

Turning away from him, she said, "Yes, perhaps I should, at that." Malcolm awkwardly put an arm around her and led her back into the tower. He knew she was crying, and left her as soon as they were inside.

As it turned out, when spring came Walter couldn't bring himself to leave. There always seemed much to be done and Malcolm kept encouraging him to stay. The King absented himself often to tend to business in other parts of the kingdom. Walter always accompanied him in his travels. There were minor disputes to be settled, and the King took pleasure in presiding over this or that court, making decisions and setting up laws. More difficult was the settling of land disputes. The proud rebellious nobles were never willing to relinquish a claim to land, even if it had belonged to someone else for generations. These discussions often came to blows; there were times when a hand as sure as Malcolm's wasn't always enough and he saw trouble on the horizon.

And too, Walter reasoned to himself, he had to make sure that Myrna was settled. Indeed, she seemed to be adapting well to the role of nursemaid. It may not have been an exciting prospect to her, but she knew that she was suited for little else. Duncan was, after all, a Prince; she had been given an important task.

Before Walter knew it a year had passed, and it was too late to make the channel crossing. He was secretly relieved, though for some reason he couldn't shake the guilt that hovered about his heart like some evil omen. His mother's necklace was a constant reminder of a task undone. And there was more: ever since the season changed, his dreams started coming. One recurring dream, in fact. It was the same one he experienced after Rhuddlan; always the weird sisters were showing him the castle in Brittany. He had memorized every inch of its face by now. Night after night he paced the same steps, never varying. Every morning he woke up shaking, exhausted.

Spring came late to Scotland, but by March Walter had decided to go. If he ever wanted to sleep in peace again, he must do the bidding of the old crones.

He told Malcolm of his dreams.

The King crossed himself. "By all means, Walter," he said, a little too hastily. "By all means. Do what you see fit."

Walter nodded, for he knew how the King felt. Malcolm didn't want to discourage his friend and bring the same curse on himself.

The day before Walter left, Malcolm took him aside.

"Tell me true, Walter. Have you discussed your leaving with Myrna?"

Walter shuffled his feet a little. "Well, actually, no."

Malcolm frowned at him, a rare sight in a usually cheerful face. "Now listen. I'm the one who is stuck with the lass. You've seen how she drags her feet, and won't talk to anyone. I insist that you tell the poor girl something, anything!"

Seeing that Walter looked ready to make an excuse, the King put a hand on his shoulder. A heavy hand.

"It's the least you can do."

Making a face, Walter agreed to find the girl.

He didn't have to search far. Myrna was sitting at her favorite spot near the fireplace. She had a piece of needlework in her hands, but didn't seem to be looking at it. When Walter sat beside her, the linen fell to the floor.

"Oh dear." She bent to pick it up. When she straightened,

there were tears in her eyes.

"Myrna," Walter started, but found he had nothing to say. What was he going to tell the girl...that he was going off to find a bride? He didn't half believe it himself.

She saved him the trouble of starting the conversation. "Walter, I just don't understand. I thought you were happy here."

He sighed. "This is my home, Myrna. But there is something I have got to do."

"But what?" Her voice was shrill, whining. Walter winced.

"The night we left Rhuddlan...you know, the night I took you away. You remember I left you and your father alone for a while. When I was outside your house, I found my grandmother waiting for me."

Myrna was interested despite herself. "The Princess?" she asked in awe.

Walter nodded. "She told me of a relative I have in Brittany. She said...that he was fond of my mother. She gave me something to return to him." He pulled out the necklace as a confirmation. "Perhaps I'm still trying to make up for what I did to her...by seeking out her last remaining kin."

Myrna shook her head; it was evident that she wasn't convinced. It certainly didn't seem likely enough to Walter, either.

He leaned forward intently. "Myrna, do you remember the time my mother told us about destiny: how some people believe that our life is already determined, even before we are born? Well, I believe that my destiny lies in Brittany, somehow. I can't rest until I find it."

He sat back, impressed by his own words. Though they may have been spoken with the intent to soothe a young girl, now that they were said, the words seemed somehow right. In a strange way, he found comfort in their expression.

The next day, Malcolm and Myrna accompanied Walter to the

ship in silence, trying to smile but not succeeding very well. Myrna absently held Duncan's hand, who kept pulling at her to move closer to the water. Walter's heart was about to burst, but he put on a brave face in saying goodbye.

"You know I'll be back, my Lord," he said to Malcolm. The King nodded.

"I warn you, come back in one piece."

He gave Myrna a quick kiss. "Take care of him," he said.

They all knew he was talking about Malcolm.

16

Alain Le Roux

Still young enough to enjoy traveling, Walter soon turned his eye forward rather than back to his beloved Scotland. Sad he was to leave Malcolm, but that emotion eventually gave way to a sense of euphoric freedom. The channel winds gusted, cold but fresh, across the deck. He turned his face into the blast, willing the elements to try and overwhelm him. Or was he hoping that in struggling with the forces of nature he could purge the turmoil within himself?

The winds favored them; they crossed the channel in a day and a half. The pilot was as seasoned as he was good-humored; he knew well enough where Count Alain le Roux lived. The mighty castle was a bit inland just south of the Baie de St. Brieue, where he could easily put in. Brittany was full of good ports, the captain said, not like that treacherous Scotland they had just left. Walter leaned eagerly on the railing, watching the coast move closer.

It took very little time to settle with the captain and take his bearings. Smiling at the gaily dressed children as they scurried across the road in front of him, Walter shifted his bag to one shoulder and set a quick pace along the southerly path.

Walter was glad of the French training he had managed to glean from Malcolm, who learned Norman French at William the Confessor's court. Ironically, he was soon to learn that he could have managed without learning French. The Welsh and Bretons shared a common ancestry; Wales was anciently settled by people from Gaul in which Brittany was a part. Its language, though evolving independently, still retained enough of its roots to make itself understood in its mother country.

The captain was right: the castle was only three miles from the port. He came upon it as he was topping a hill, and the shock of recognition made him step back a pace. He knew by now that he should have expected to see what was in his dream, but it was so intense, so vivid. It was as though he had actually traveled here before, not seen it in his mind.

But there it was before him: the tall stone castle, the moat, wide and clean because it was a stream and the castle stood on an island. Bright red banners fluttered from the towers, and the drawbridge was down, as if in welcome.

"Ahhh..." Walter said aloud. He was overwhelmed for a moment. Castle building had not become an art yet in England; men—even kings—lived in timber structures usually all on one level. But here was a masterpiece in stone...and the largest fortification he had ever seen.

Walter stopped before the drawbridge. At the far end stood two sentries; they eyed the newcomer suspiciously, but did not move forward. He decided that he was at least safe in crossing over to them.

As he neared them, the sentries moved together, barring his way with their spears. Walter asked if this was the castle of Count Alain. They nodded yes; he told them who he was, and his relation to the Count. The guards seemed unimpressed, but sent someone inside with a message.

No one returned right away, and Walter craned his neck to see inside the compound. There was an outer bailey, more of an open space between the tall crenellated walls and the castle itself which was scattered with barracks and workshops. The space bustled with activity, and no one stopped to pay attention to the stranger.

Finally a page came with an answer, bidding Walter to enter and follow him. The guards soberly parted, nodding Walter in but not bothering to notice him further. Looking backwards at them, he moved a bit too slow for the page, who tugged at his cloak. Smiling, he obliged.

They passed through another archway, and Walter found

himself in a large open area, called the inner bailey. Living quarters and the great hall opened into this space; it was thronged with servants passing back and forth, each intent on his own chore. The place was very busy, efficient, and noisy. The page hurried him through a little side door, up a spiral flight of stone steps, then down a narrow hallway flanked on the bailey side with tall, arched windows.

Counting three doors from the end, the boy showed Walter a small, austere room. It had little furniture in it besides a small bed with a straw mattress. There was a table and bench and nothing else. But Walter was used to a lack of comfort. He turned to the young boy.

"What is your name, lad?"

"Antoine," the boy said, picking up an empty pitcher from the table.

"How old are you?" Walter pursued, trying to set a conversational pace in his awkward French.

"Oh, ten, sir. I have been here for two years, so I can learn courtly manners."

Walter looked surprised. "It is a common thing here," Antoine added. "You will find many others like me, and some older. Our family sends us here. My Lord Count receives the earnings from our wardships in return for the great service of training us to become squires. In time, if we are brave and good, we might even achieve knighthood."

He looked curiously at Walter. "Don't they do the same where you come from?"

The other shook his head thoughtfully. "That is quite an exchange," he said. "And at the same time, the Count insures peace from his vassals."

"I suppose that is true," the boy said. "Though I never thought of it that way."

"It is no matter," Walter added hastily. "But I thank you for your help. Do you sleep in the castle?"

"Oh, yes. I share a large room with the other pages. But I must go now. I shall return when my master is ready to meet you."

Without another word, the boy left the room. Walter paced the floor. Having traveled so far, the last thing he wanted was to be shut into a little space. There was a small window near the ceiling. Pulling over the bench, Walter stood on it and found that he could just barely see over the sill. He looked out curiously.

The blank outer wall cut off any other view. Below him, there was a pen of stout hogs, which were probably tonight's dinner. He wrinkled his nose, then got down thoughtfully. These weren't the most dignified quarters he had ever been given. But then, he had arrived unannounced...and a total stranger, at that. He supposed he could have gotten worse treatment.

It wasn't long before Antoine came back, carrying a candle holder and sticks made from tallow. This at least was encouraging; candles were a luxury in England.

"My Lord will see you now. Come." Walter followed the boy, amused at his sense of dignity.

They walked quickly through many corridors, and across a small room. The cool breeze of the nearby sea blew gently through the tiny windows as they climbed another staircase. Reaching a wide landing, the page rapped on a heavy wooden door.

It opened, and Walter was surprised to see a girl coming out, looking backwards. She nearly collided with the Antoine.

Laughing, making excuses, she happened to glance at Walter. The smile froze on her lips, and she stared at him, more in curiosity than rudeness.

She was a pretty girl, hardly sixteen. Though by no means beautiful, vivacity gave animation to her face; indeed, she showed character for someone yet so young. Strong chin, high cheekbones, wide forehead were nicely set off by deep blue eyes. Pulled back from her face and braided with ribbons, her long hair looked soft and luxurious. Her lips, a dark shade of pink against her pale skin, contracted into a puckered circle of wonder.

Walter sighed. Her surprise looked suspiciously like recognition. Was this the girl he had come to marry? Had she, too, been given some kind of forewarning?

He didn't have much time to think. The girl picked up her skirt in embarrassment, and ran down the stairs, taking a quick look behind her. And Walter heard a voice from inside the room, telling him to enter.

Nodding, the page motioned him inside, closing the door. Walter looked curiously around. The room was small and comfortable, and there were shelves on the wall, holding at least a dozen books; this was surely a king's treasure. The arched window behind Alain's back gave a breathtaking view of the sea, with its bobbing ships snugly anchored in the bay. The Count sat at a wide, oak table strewn with parchment, the only sign Walter had seen of disorder. Alain hadn't as yet looked up from his work; he was busy writing.

The man was stocky, though not as tall as Walter. He had shocking red hair that glowed in the sunlight, and a full red beard. His hands were large, but he managed the fine quill with ease. Carefully dipping the tip into an inkwell, he penned a beautiful script, which Walter bent to admire.

"Do you write then?" Alain asked, and Walter guessed that his host had been watching him out of the corner of his eye. The Count sat up, his face serious, but his green eyes twinkling. Big pink cheeks, full lips, broad forehead all gave him a pleasant appearance that put Walter at ease. He guessed that the Count was about forty years old.

The younger man smiled. "Yes, I do, sir. My mother taught me."

Alain sat still a moment, thinking. He leaned his head slightly to one side.

Then he spoke in Welsh. "My guards told me you claim a kinship with me. Is this so?"

Walter answered in the same tongue, "Yes, my Lord. On your Welsh side, as you guessed. I am the son of Nesta, daughter of Gruffydd ap Llewelyn ap Seisylt. My grandmother Ealdgyth told me to come here. She said that you were fond of my mother, and would be glad to meet me."

Alain seemed to consider this. "What you say is true. I am very much fond of her...you speak in the past tense...Do you mean she is with us no more?"

Walter nodded, saddened. He pulled the necklace off and handed it to the Count. For just a moment he felt the urge to snatch it back. But the look on Alain's face shamed him. The Count clearly recognized the trinket, and his hand shook a little as he accepted the gift.

"I did not know. This is very sorry news indeed."

He paused, wiping an eye. "She was a sweet girl. It has been many years since I saw her...at least twenty. I visited her in Rhuddlan, after her dreadful mishap. Imagine her father treating her that way."

Of a sudden he leaned across the table. "But wait. That would make you the little whelp I saw...her bastard."

Walter was embarrassed. It was rare he let someone speak thus to him, but it was clear Alain meant no harm. Among the nobility, at least, illegitimacy was not such a rare thing.

"But no matter. You shall tell me about it anon. Have you eaten? No? Excellent. Antoine!" He seemed glad to change the subject.

The door opened, and Walter's little page stood there, evidently not having moved from his post. "Some food for me and my guest, quickly." Antoine scurried away.

Alain turned to Walter, smiling. "I keep them prompt, my boys, from the earliest age I can train them. We are at war more than at peace here, and I want them to be able to respond to my orders at once. It may make the difference between life and death, their training. Ah, here he is."

They sat in silence, while Antoine laid out a tray with a large flask and two goblets. He bowed, then left quietly while Alain studied his young kinsman, hardly noticing the interruption. "I have been out of touch. Tell me what happened to her."

Walter relieved his awkwardness by pouring some wine. He looked at the Count as he handed over a cup, somewhat heartened by the man's kind face. "It is a long story," he said, "and not a happy one. I fear I am the cause of all her troubles…" He paused. How much should he admit to?

He looked at the Count, a kindly man. It was good to talk to kin; he had so few of them, and so far none had been friendly.

"It was long before she...told me of my birth. I took it ill, for I was just sixteen, and treated by everyone as if I had the plague." He bristled defensively, despite himself. "I was very confused then, and it so happened that I quarreled with a boy...an enemy...and killed him. I left the country then. Left my poor mother to pay my *Galanas,* though I didn't understand just what that would do to her." His voice cracked. "She died, working herself until her health was gone, so she could raise the money to pay my accusers. And I never knew until years after she was dead and buried." He turned his head away; retelling the story brought back the pain with a new surge of guilt.

Alain felt sorry for him. The murder was none of his concern; killings of this sort were all too common, especially when the victim was a serf. But if he had felt any doubts about Walter's identity, the man's agitation dispelled them. He'd seen this kind of remorse destroy a person.

"Look here, Walter," he said at last. "Don't you think your mother knew about the *Galanas* all the time...and sent you away without telling you of it?"

By the look on Walter's face, Alain suspected he never thought of it from that point of view.

"If he were half a man, Gruffydd would have taken care of it for her. I always thought him a *nithing*." The Count spat into the rushes.

Walter's fists clenched involuntarily, then relaxed; he looked with wonder at the Count.

"I knew your mother, remember," Alain pursued. "She would have put your needs before her own, knowing full well the cost. Do not lessen her honor by taking the blame on yourself."

Alain was glad to be interrupted by a knock on the door. Antoine entered with a steaming tray of food, and the Count helped put things in order while Walter regained composure.

When they were alone again, Walter sighed heavily, leaning back against a wall. "Thank you, my Lord. It has been long since my mind was so easy."

The Breton was pleased with himself. "It is the least I can do, for a kinsman and guest. I think we are fourth cousins, you know...you bear a great resemblance to your mother."

Walter's hand shook slightly, thinking about Ealdgyth. "No one ever told me that before," he said softly, "except for my grandmother."

"Uh, well you do. Now let me guess...your visit here. You said your grandmother prompted you to it?"

Walter swallowed. "Yes. When I discovered about my mother's death."

"And you came to tell me of her death...as a sort of pilgrimage?"

There was an aspect of truth in this. Walter nodded.

"And where do you come from?"

At this, Walter smiled. "I have been at the court of the King of the Scots, Malcolm III. I tell you, my Lord, that he is among the most enlightened of monarchs."

"Oh," said Alain, unconvinced. "Of course, conditions are different there."

"Much more crude than this." Walter looked admiringly around the room. "There are few stone buildings in all of England. And yet, King Malcolm spent much of his younger years in King Edward's court."

"So he is influenced by the Normans, as a result?"

"I doubt that he could help it."

They both laughed.

"Are you passing through, or do you intend to stay for a while?"

Walter smiled. "It is a pleasure to talk to such an educated man. If it pleases you, I would like to serve with you for a time."

Alain nodded. "We shall see. I can always use another good man."

They ate a couple of minutes in silence. "So what of Gruffydd?" Alain asked, interested in spite of himself.

Walter managed a wry smile. "I think his days are numbered. Harold Godwineson campaigns against him, with King Edward's blessing."

"The Earl of Wessex? I hear he is a great fighter. Would like to meet him someday." He stopped, considering. "The Welsh have always been a thorn in the side of the English. But they are a strong people. They will retain their independence, no matter how much the English think they are conquered. For that I respect them.

"Walter, you are welcome in my home. I apologize for your poor lodgings, but I was unprepared for you. And I needed to be sure of who you were. Tell me: what are you best equipped to do?"

"I am most comfortable when training others to fight. Like these boys you call wards."

Alain laughed. "I forgot. This is not a custom in England. But it will be, in time." He put down his goblet. "Very well, I can use another trainer. Walter, I think we will get along very nicely together. But forgive me, I still have much work to do. Tomorrow at dawn, will you ride with me? I must go visit my half-brother Alain le Noir. Good. Antoine!"

Early next morning, Walter found himself astride a large black gelding, greater in height and girth than any he ever saw in England. He rode next to Alain, followed by a small entourage. Much to Walter's surprise, the pretty girl he saw the day before rode on Alain's other hand. Her laughter was lively, and she spoke quickly—too quickly for Walter's taste. The words tumbled one after another. She looked teasingly at Walter from her father's other side.

"Is it not time, father, to introduce me to this fine stranger?"

Alain looked from his daughter to his young kinsman. "I'd quite forgotten. Isabel, this is your cousin Walter...a distant cousin, I'll grant, but kin nonetheless."

Isabel inclined her head sweetly. "Will he be staying with us long?"

"I don't know, silly girl. Ask him."

"Let me change sides with you, father, and I'll do just that."

With an indulgent chuckle, Alain made way for his daughter.

Walter could see that this one was not shy. Restraining a grin, he looked politely at her.

"Oh now, I've forgotten what I meant to ask you. No matter. It'll come to me."

Alain laughed out loud. "Subtle you are not, Isabel. Go on...keep your young man occupied, whilst I talk with my captain."

Reining his horse back, Alain rode beside the man who bore his banner. Walter watched him for a moment, then turned to Isabel.

Once alone with him, she lost some of her bravado. "Will you be staying long?" she asked, but not in jest.

Walter could not help but smile at the irony in the question; was it not for her that he came? "I suppose I will be here for a while. You father is...charming."

She smiled. "That he is. And he spoils me so."

"You are an only child then?"

Asked in all innocence, Walter was mortified at the expression on her face.

"Yes." It was almost a whisper. "My mother died, bearing me. I thought my father would have told you. He has been so good to me about it, not blaming me like he might have. It was my fault, after all."

Walter shook his head. "Do not talk so; it is not the truth."

She looked at him for a moment, unable to hide the pain in her eyes. She bent over her horse's neck, patting him. When she straightened, the look was gone.

A kindred spirit. If only he could disguise his feelings that well. How different she was, from all the others. How soon they had broken the barrier between strangers. He found that he liked this interesting girl.

Too soon, Alain was back with them again. He told Walter why they were traveling to his brother's castle. There was a campaign in the making, directed against Count Conan of Brittany, who was besieging the city of Dol. The city was held by the Lord Rhiwallon against Conan, his immediate chief, in favor of Duke William of Normandy. William was coming to their aid, especially since Conan had chivalrously sent a message, challenging him to war.

"The fool," Alain said blandly. "Now William will come to meet him instead of the other way around. The Norman bastard makes short work of men like Conan."

Isabel was bored; looking at Walter, she was disappointed to see him so interested in talk of war.

"Dol has ever been friendly with me," continued Alain, "and I have always been at odds with this Conan. This is our great chance, my brother and mine, to meet William and fight alongside him. I tell you Walter, this Norman Duke is hell fire. I would be his friend. He has good ideas and knows how to get what he wants."

Le Noir lived in a respectable stone castle, not quite half the size of the Count's. And compared to the other's castle, this one seemed a sorry imitation. Animals roamed about the grounds; the smell of waste was ever present. The walls were in need of repair, and Walter saw that it was the result of neglect rather than warfare.

Le Noir came out to greet them; he was a quiet, solitary man about Alain's size. But the resemblance stopped there. Where the Count was all smiles, his brother seemed not to smile at all. His eyes and brows were heavy, and when he looked to one side, his whole head moved, like a cow. In fact, all of his actions were slow and methodical. He had a bushy black head of hair and a black beard equally unkempt.

But their welcome was warm enough. Le Noir nodded in interest to his brother's story, and ushered them into a large room, laid out with food and drink for his tired visitors.

"So Conan has pushed Duke William too far, you say? I say that the time is right to bring some order to our country. This Conan looks greedily on our own lands. He would be duke, I think. So when do we move?"

"Saturday next, I am hosting a hunt. Our allies will gather there. The following Monday, we leave for Dol."

"Let me see," Le Noir said, counting his fingers. "That is ten days from now. I shall be ready, with two hundred men. You are staying the night?"

Alain nodded. They plunged into more discussion about the campaign, but Walter's attention began to wander.

His eyes met with Isabel's; she had been staring at him, and blushed to be caught so easily. She looked so lonely there, that he wished he could find a way to pull her from the room. But at that moment, two girls burst into the hall, running up to their cousin. They were followed by their mother, a stout, cheerful woman who greeted Alain with a boisterous hug and a smacking kiss.

The girls threw their arms around Isabel, all talking at once.

Walter was amazed to see Le Noir smile at them. So he did

have a heart, after all.

The ride back to Alain's castle was pleasant. The clouds parted early and the sun shone benignly across a land looking green and plump. Count Alain watched Isabel and Walter as they rode together, knees almost touching. He didn't really mind Walter's attentions to his daughter; the girl had been so lonely all her life. But he felt a pang of grief for his beloved lost wife.

No, he admitted to himself, reclusive was more the word he should use regarding his daughter. Underneath the girl's cheerful exterior lurked a heart that ached for a mother, as he ached for a wife. There was nothing he could do would fill the void. He couldn't bring himself to marry again, and one daughter was all he had.

It was time for her to be married—past time—but one thing Alain couldn't do was strap her to a husband that would make her miserable. She was unhappy enough without being used as a political tool. So he had decided to let her make her own choice. Even if she chose a man in straightened circumstances, he had money for a generous dowry.

The Count smiled, thinking about the fights he had had with his brother concerning this very issue. That was one thing about Le Noir: his concern about the family make up for Alain's own lack. Le Noir had found at least a half-dozen prospective matches for Isabel. He, too, sincerely cared for the girl, and was annoyed to be politely refused time and again. This was one subject that never failed to prompt a reaction from the man.

It never seemed fair that people of his class, who could buy just about anything they wanted, were refused the most basic happiness of life. The opportunity to choose one's mate was a privilege even the poor were allowed.

"It's true," he thought to himself, "my feelings about this are ridiculous. But then, I've never been a predictable sort. I suppose it would have been different if Isabel was a man."

He looked at his daughter chattering happily with Walter, who seemed unable to squeeze a word in. What about this stranger? He was respectful enough, for sure. And the way he looked at Isabel resembled more an awe-struck boy than a wolf. She could pick much worse.

But what about the man's past? And his unfortunate birth? Alain shrugged. It would be up to Walter to prove himself.

Unaware of the Count's thoughtful stare, Walter was engrossed with thoughts not totally compatible with Isabel's conversation. He felt like an intruder here, come to steal away a man's only child. And she was a child...too young for thoughts of marriage.

Or was she?

He looked shyly at the girl, watching her small, round breasts bouncing ever so slightly with the motion of her horse. The look she returned, through lowered eyelashes, certainly didn't exist in any childish vocabulary.

"But I've been talking about myself enough, Walter," she said. "What about yourself?"

"I don't know that there is much to say. I've lived much of my life in England, as a soldier. On the borders between England and Wales."

"Oh, Wales," she broke in wistfully, "My father talks about that country often. I do so wish I could go there."

He looked at her thoughtfully. "Perhaps you will, some day. It is a wild, untamed country, totally unlike Brittany."

"Tell me more."

"The people are proud, but quarrelsome. They fight among themselves, giving the English a weapon to use against them."

"And what do the English want with the Welsh?"

Walter blinked, surprised. The question was deeper than he expected from her. "The English seek conquest. They mean to make the Welsh vassals, to direct their revenue to the English crown."

"You speak bitterly."

He was surprised again. He didn't expect her to sense what he sought to hide even from himself. "I do not altogether agree with their methods. England covets her neighbors and will not let them live in peace. If you want to know the truth, my love is for Scotland, which suffers as much as Wales does. I have lately been in the service of King Malcolm, who is my closest friend."

"Then what are you doing here, so far away?"

He sighed. "Sometimes I don't know myself. It's as if there are things I have to do first, before I can settle there for good."

She digested that, then dismissed the thought, changing the subject. Walter was relieved. This girl was more complex than he thought. He would have to choose his words more carefully.

He smiled, inwardly pleased.

It was dark when they returned. Antoine was immediately summoned, and Alain told him to show Walter to his chamber. Walter was confused when the boy led him down a different set of corridors, then surprised that Alain had changed his room. The Count had been generous; the new chamber was luxuriant.

"Will there be anything else?" Antoine smiled, for once.

"No. My thanks, lad."

The boy, ever in a hurry, disappeared.

The room was at least double the other one in size. A wide bed with a feather mattress took up most of the space; at its foot stood an oaken chest. Though there was only a slight chill to the air, a crackling blaze in the fireplace threw shadows on the rich tapestries, giving them animation. The windows were cut larger than one would expect for a castle, but were placed high in the tall chamber.

"I hope you like it here."

He whisked around; Isabel was standing in the doorway.

"I'm down the hallway from you. Look, I embroidered this cloth myself." Isabel walked to the bed, running her hand over the soft linen cover.

Walter tried to control the heat rising to his face. Her close proximity had its effect on him; he ran his eyes over her slim body, draped clingingly in a white dress. She turned to him, the skirt moving gracefully around her legs. The firelight cast a glow in Isabel's face, making her seem older, seductive.

"I just wanted to make sure you were comfortable. Until tomorrow, then."

Holding his breath, Walter watched her approach him. But she merely held out her hand for him to kiss, then slipped silently through the open door. He followed, seeing her disappear into a room halfway down the hall.

Walter found a pitcher of water on a table, and gratefully poured its contents into a clay bowl. He splashed his face, cooling off.

He was unused to women; he had schooled himself against such cumbersome thoughts. And here was a chit of a girl, a total stranger, creating such unwelcome sensations in his loins. Was he under a spell? Was he always to do what those old hags told him, whoever they were? Did he have no control over his own life?

"Not I, God's blood," he said out loud, bringing his fist down on the table. "I will not be anyone's puppet."

17

Isabel

The next morning he woke with a new resolve. No longer would he let this girl bother him; no longer would he feel like a deceitful guest. He went in search of Alain, finding him in the kitchen giving instructions for the upcoming hunt.

"Ah Walter. Come, I'll show you my dogs. Have you hunted much?"

"Not at all. I have had no time for it."

They went outside.

"You would enjoy it, I'm sure. Look: these dogs are my pride and joy. Well trained, they are, and rigorously exercised. I have men here whose sole job is to tend to the hounds."

He pointed to the front door of the kennel. "That door is only used for the hunt. So the dogs know what is expected of them. See, there are the spaniels. They are for bird hunting, not for big game, like we will be going after. Saturday we shall use the bloodhounds for tracking the game, and the greyhounds for running it down. You will see.

"Ah, there is Isabel."

Coming round the corner of the kennel, Isabel was leading a pony, covered with sweat.

"Good morning father...Walter. I had a nice ride. A beautiful day, is it not?" She was looking at Walter.

"Indeed," Alain answered. "I have been showing Walter my dogs. Where is your favorite?"

Giving Walter the reins, Isabel disappeared into the kennel, re-emerging with a squirming puppy in her arms. "It's a cross breed, a mistake." She giggled as the dog licked her on the chin. "Papa was going to get rid of her, but I insisted on keeping her for my own. She doesn't belong here, but she's still nursing."

She held the pup up to Walter, letting it lick him. He tried to look stern, and was hard put to suppress a smile.

"Poor Rusty. Walter doesn't like you, it seems."

Isabel went to put the dog away. "Damned nuisance," said Alain. "At least I gave away all the rest of the pups to my serfs. Come, Isabel, take your horse. I must show Walter the rest of the place."

Isabel took back the reins, touching Walter's hand. "You will ride with me tomorrow, won't you?"

"We shall see."

Alain took Walter into the outer bailey, where there was a fenced off area reserved for sword practice. It was roofed against the rain. Already there were some squires practicing, using a thick wooden stake as a pell. Others were engaged in a bout with wooden sticks.

"I feel like a bit of exercise. How about you, Walter?"

The other agreed readily. Alain had quilted tunics on hand for protection, and several light helms. They chose blunted iron swords and small round shields.

Alain took a defensive stance, his legs shoulder distance apart, shield held out, sword back. Walter followed his lead, and they circled each other, taking measure. Although a taller man, Walter crouched so low that he seemed shorter than Alain.

Walter took the first shot. Aiming for the other's head, he struck lightly, experimentally. Alain responded easily, raising his shield. Then he followed with a triple combination of his own: a cut to the side, then to the thigh, arching around to the opposite side of Walter's head. Walter blocked all three then stepped back, impressed. He was facing a skilled swordsman.

He stepped in, trying to grab Alain's shield with his own, to open him up for a thrust. The Count was surprised, but followed him rather than pull against his move. He did not hesitate to respond with a wrap-around shot to Walter's head, which almost connected, except for the other's timely dodge.

Walter disengaged, crouching lower. The two circled again,

unaware of the crowd that was gathering to watch. Alain closed this time, using combination after combination, which were answered by well-aimed cuts and thrusts. Crashes and bangs of sword against shield echoed from the castle walls, competing with shouts of encouragement.

But Walter's youth held him in good stead; the older man's breath was coming in ragged gasps, his sword striking with less force. It was becoming a contest of endurance.

This was no good. As they paused for breath, Walter backed up, threw his shield to the ground. He tore off his helmet, laughing.

"We don't have to get all our practice in one bout!"

The Count removed his own helm, face red but smiling. "I meant to test your mettle, Walter, and by God that's what I did! I haven't fought like that in some time."

The onlookers gathered around the two, laughing and thumping them on the back. They accepted Walter respectfully; not all of them had held out so well against the Count.

Walter was grateful. Alain had made it easy for him.

He spent the rest of the afternoon in the practice yard, teaching some and competing with others. When he had finally had enough, he moved away toward the water barrel.

As he was taking off his helm, Walter saw Isabel standing before him, a dripping ladle in her hand. Cursing under his breath, he took it from her, pouring water on his head.

She laughed. "I thought you were supposed to drink it."

He gave the dipper back for a refill. She gladly cooperated, but the smile fell from her lips at his expression.

"Walter," she faltered. "Is there anything wrong?"

"No." He drank, feeling her eyes on him.

"Yesterday we were so friendly, and today...we are like strangers."

"Isabel..." She looked so pitiful, like a puppy that was scolded without knowing why. All this wasn't her fault. He was the fool...foolishly besotted with her. And after only two days. "I'm just tired, that's all."

"Oh." She wasn't convinced. "Will you at least sit beside me...at dinner tonight?"

"Of course."

Her look of relief was enough to make him regret his boorish behavior. She squeezed his arm then ran off before he could change his mind.

Later, washed and changed, Walter joined Isabel like he promised. The Count kept a large household, necessary for a man of his status. Dinner every night was a banquet. Much food and wine was served, for there was little else to do at night but drink and eat.

He found a place saved for him at head table. Since word had already spread that he was Alain's cousin, for lack of a more distinguished guest his place at the Count's table was not unduly resented. As he sat down he noticed that Isabel's demeanor was...different. He couldn't quite figure this girl out. Polite, smiling, she was the perfect companion, her conversation general.

There was no doubt about it. Isabel was on her guard. Although Walter felt guilty about imposing such restraint on her, he was relieved.

He and Alain stayed up late together, drinking, long after Isabel left for bed. She stood up, kissed her father, and turned to Walter. For a moment her resolution faltered, her eyes taking on the same look as that afternoon.

"Walter...will you ride with me in the morning?"

He knew that he shouldn't agree, that this was a decisive moment to assert himself. He looked at Alain, but the worthy man smiled, nodding.

"Take Antoine with you. He needs to practice his riding. The boy spends too much time inside."

It was settled. He would go with Isabel, and the boy's presence would hinder any...unwelcome discussion.

"This is too much," thought Walter as she walked slowly away. "I'm not in control here, and I feel ridiculous."

Alain refilled his cup, sat back. "A sweet girl. And pretty." He looked sideways at Walter. "Well. My first knights should be showing up in a few days. We must find room for the troops. There is only space for a couple of hundred in the outer bailey."

Happy to change the subject, Walter asked, "And in the town? St. Brieue?"

"Yes, that should take care of most of them. But I must quarter the chiefs in my castle. Would you forgive me, my boy, if I were to take your room away again? Just until we are off. These Lords take it amiss if they are crowded."

"Of course. The chamber is more than I warrant, anyway."

"Nonsense. You are my kin. But if you will, I would quarter you with my boys. The squires, you know. I'll delay it as long as possible."

"Think no more of it. I am satisfied."

They drank in silence for a moment. "Walter," the Count said, "have you ever had a command?"

Surprised, Walter reddened. "Well, I commanded the garrison of a border town in the Welsh marches. What made you ask?"

"The way you carried yourself this afternoon with the boys. The way you gave directions, they followed you naturally. Why didn't you tell me of this command?"

Walter shrugged. "I am not proud of it. I was in Harold Godwineson's service, you see."

Alain put his cup down. "This is news. I thought you were in Scotland."

"Afterwards." He didn't want to continue, but Alain was not so drunk as to lose track of the conversation.

"So how did this happen?"

Walter sighed. "When I ran away from home... when I killed that boy I went to London. I signed up with Harold, and that's where I met King Malcolm, who hadn't regained the throne yet. I had yet to complete my service with Harold, and he sent me to Hereford, on the border.

"You see, Harold campaigned against the Welsh for years. As long as the fighting stayed on the borders, I had no real problem with it. I have no love for my grandfather." This last was almost a growl.

"But Alain, he made a sudden descent on Rhuddlan...I couldn't just stand by and let him destroy everything."

He drank deeply, searching for comfort in the bottom of his cup. He looked at Alain, whose face was more serious than he had yet seen it.

"Walter, your mother?"

"I thought she was still alive. Abandoning my post, I raced Harold to Rhuddlan, hoping to take my mother away before they killed her. Harold shows no mercy to the Welsh."

Alain put a hand on Walter's arm. But he couldn't stop now.

"She was dead. Long dead. Ealdgyth saw me...followed me. Alain, I couldn't leave without warning her. It would have haunted me the rest of my life."

He laughed, a hoarse bitter noise that did not sound like mirth.

"Of course, it's haunting me anyway. I warned them, and they got away. I abandoned my men, my service, turned traitor to Harold, and for what?" He laid his arms on the table, putting his head down. "For nothing. No matter what I did, it would have been wrong."

Alain filled Walter's cup, shoved it into his hand. "Drink, son. No man should have to face such a decision."

Walter complied, grateful that the alcohol was taking effect.

"And Rhuddlan? What of it?"

"Burned to the ground. People murdered everywhere. Harold was thorough, if nothing else."

"Rhuddlan gone. Poor Ealdgyth. I know how she loved it."

Walter looked at Alain. Expecting scorn, he saw only compassion. Grabbing his arm, Walter said, "Now you know why I didn't tell you. It's not something I am proud of. I hope you'll forgive me."

"God's teeth, man, there's nothing to forgive. Your life has not been easy, Walter. But I'm no man to judge another. In your place, I might well have done the same thing."

The younger man stared. "Do you mean that?"

"Of course I mean it. I never lie. If anything, I respect you the more for telling me. Even if it took you a while. Every man has things in his past he would rather bury...we live in a violent age. But you must take care of your kin first, or there would be nothing to depend on."

Walter's heart went out to this man. It was twice, now, that Alain had given him comfort.

But the Count was stumbling to his feet. "Enough for now, Walter. It's time we were abed."

Walter awoke, his head pounding. It was not often he allowed himself to get so drunk. He shook his head, but the movement brought him pain. Look what he let slip! He never meant to tell Alain of his treachery.

But it was too late now. The worst was over, and he was glad.

A knock at his door brought forth a groan. Antoine came in without waiting for an answer.

"Isabel told me we were to go riding with her."

Remembering his promise, Walter groaned again.

"Are you all right?"

Walter waved him off. "Yes, yes. Give me a moment."

He poured more water in his bowl, ducking his whole face. He lifted his dripping head, and managed a small smile. "Better now."

Isabel pretended not to notice Walter's scowl as he paused at her door. "I'm ready." She smiled sweetly. "Father said you may use the same horse you rode the other day."

Once in the fresh air, Walter's headache gradually went away. He even began to enjoy himself, rocking with the smooth gait of his horse.

Antoine dropped back a few paces, leaving them alone.

"Are you looking forward to the hunt?" Isabel ventured.

"Uh, yes I am. Are you going?"

"Usually only men are allowed. But this time, father said he is going to make an exception and allow the women, too. I'm very excited."

Walter smiled at that. "It seems you are always excited about something."

She blushed, looking away.

"Oh, I didn't mean to insult you. What I should have said is that you are filled with such love of life...an enviable quality, for sure."

"What do you mean?"

She was so young, so naive. "Not everyone is as fortunate as you. Some people have a hard life, from the day they are born. Their very existence is a struggle."

Isabel looked thoughtful. "You must be right. I am lucky. Though I've always been so lonely, I thought I was very unfortunate indeed."

"I suppose it is true that we never seem to get what we want."

"Oh, don't say that!" She put a hand to her mouth, embarrassed. That came out too quickly.

Walter looked behind them, at Antoine. The boy was out of hearing.

"Isabel...look at me."

She obeyed despite herself.

"Do you know where we seem to be heading?"

"I...don't know what you are saying."

"Please, don't pretend. Isabel...we seem drawn toward each other. I feel attracted to you...like, like I've never felt before.

Isabel, I'm ten years older than you."

"I don't care." There. It was said.

"I have nothing to offer you. No land, no titles...I am beneath your status."

"I care nothing for that. Don't you see, Walter? I'm just a poor, lonely child, like you. I can't describe it, but when you are near me, I feel like everything is as it should be. Oh, you'll never understand."

He understood all too well. "But this is all too soon. You know nothing about me."

She looked at him, her eyes full.

"Like the fact that I'm a bastard," he said.

There was silence between the two of them. Walter could hear cows lowing in the field.

"I know."

Walter was amazed. Again, he seemed to underestimate this girl.

"My father told me. But Walter, that doesn't change anything."

"It should. I can offer you nothing."

"Oh, come. Let's canter."

Isabel sank her heels into the pony's flank, leaping forward. Walter was not far behind.

She rode like she was born to it, urging her mount ever faster, hair flying behind her. He marveled at the girl's perseverance. Why was she interested in him? And why couldn't he resist her?

Suddenly, he heard a cry from behind him, and a thud. Wheeling his horse around, Walter's first instinct was to stop the boy's riderless mount. He urged his horse forward, managed to grasp the reins as the animal slowed down.

He dismounted, worried. Antoine was lying flat on his back, the wind knocked out of him.

The boy forced a wry smile. "This is embarrassing," he gasped after a moment.

He sat up, rubbing a shoulder. Isabel came up behind them.

"Are you all right?"

"I think so," said the boy, getting painfully to his feet.

"I'm so sorry. It's all my fault."

Walter helped Antoine back onto the horse. "Perhaps we should go back."

"By all means," Isabel said.

The pace back was much slower, but Isabel was content to hover over Antoine like a cat with her kittens. The boy was trying to hide his pain, and it was clear that the attention was welcome. Walter fell back a little and watched her. She was much more sure of herself when she wasn't paying attention to him. He knew he was making her as nervous as she was making him.

When they returned, the first of the guests were arriving. Isabel gave Antoine her reins and waved goodbye. There was a household to run, and she knew she had a job to do.

The rest of the week was hectic, with new arrivals coming all hours of the day and night. Provisions had to be made, lodging found. Isabel, as hostess, kept a brave face and performed her duties remarkably well. Walter meant to tell her so, but couldn't find the opportunity.

He was soon ousted from his chamber, which he didn't mind. He was sorrier to be moved well down the table, making way for men of rank. Content with the talk of the fighters and squires, Walter had to admit that he missed Isabel's attention.

The evening before the hunt was a busy one; Walter was at the kennels watching the stir, for the hunters were already at work. He couldn't do much to help, but he was curious about each of their jobs. Here, he thought, was the heart of the hunt; the hunters did all the work, while the nobles reaped the rewards.

As Alain had explained, the front door of the kennel opened and out spilled the hunters and dogs, one man to each animal. Bloodhounds and greyhounds gathered around Alain, and the

Count inspected them proudly.

"You look very good. I anticipate that we will have a fine hunt on the morrow."

He was answered with a murmur of agreement.

"Our meeting place will be the same as last time: in the clearing of the forest, by the little stream under the willow." There, Walter knew, the nobles would gather to await the reports of the hunters. Then, as Walter watched, Alain assigned to each group a specific spot to await the stag for the whole night. It was during the morning feeding that they would locate the game, in the fields surrounding the forest.

The hunters were an elite group, having received this post after a long apprenticeship. They were dressed in a green tunic, slit up the sides, and wore heavy leather leggings for protection against thorns and briars, their feet clad in soft boots. They carried a leather thong for slapping against their boots to encourage any lagging hound and a horn around their neck to summon the dogs or communicate among themselves. At the pommel of their saddle hung a sack of bread, from which to feed a tiring dog.

The hunters initially gathered at the assigned clearing, securing the hounds there and appointing a few men to keep watch, lest the dogs untimely warn the game of their approach. They found their assigned spots and settled for the night, munching on some bread for a quick dinner, and indulging in a little watered wine from their flasks. Joining a small group, Walter found this interlude a pleasant break from the cold castle.

Just before dawn, he was awakened by a quick shake on the shoulder. A hunter bent over him, finger on lip, and pointed to the field. There, munching on the tall grass, stood a magnificent five-pronged stag, unaware of the human eyes on him. They waited for the animal to finish, and noted the point where the buck entered the forest. No one made a move until the animal was out of sight.

Then, at a sign from the leader, the hunters followed him to the place where the stag had fed. Carefully, they marked the spot with a little pile of twigs, while one of the grooms collected the stag's droppings. Their work done for the moment, they returned to the gathering place.

Already the had participants met in the forest, to breakfast on cloths spread on the ground. At the head of this assemblage sat Alain, glowing with pleasure; Isabel sat beside him, trying to look like a countess. One by one, each team of hunters brought their droppings for scrutiny; as the Count studied them, they told him the size of the stag they had followed.

Out of the five groups sent to observe, three had found their prey. It was up to the Count to determine which one to hunt that day. While choosing the stag, Alain offered everyone a moment to sit and eat. The hounds were fed bits of bread sopped in milk, so their stomachs wouldn't be too full.

After breakfast, the whole company followed the hunter to his chosen spot. The dogs pulled their grooms along, excited at the prospect of the chase. When they found the marker, the bloodhounds were released to snuffle the spot.

Walter joined Isabel and rode well to the back of the group; her father, of course, was in the front. So far, the nobles could do nothing but wait for developments. After a time, the bloodhounds caught the sent and turned silently to follow it. They had been trained to get within sight of their prey before giving chase.

Now and then, the dogs lost the track. It took a bit of wandering, and showing the hounds where the scent might be picked up before they spotted the stag, head up, eyes wild at the sight of hunters. In a moment it was gone, but the chase was on; the greyhounds were slipped from their masters' grip. Almost crazed by now, the dogs flew quickly after the prey, passing the bloodhounds like they were standing still. As though not to be outdone, the bloodhounds gave tongue to encourage their fellows.

The hunters followed at a gallop, blowing their horns. Everyone else joined in, prepared for a day-long chase. For a time, the forest was filled with excited shouts, baying of bloodhounds, the crashing of charging horses. The horn was busy calling back any over-eager and lost dogs, echoing through the trees with jubilant sounds. But as the hours passed, many of the guests dropped out of the race.

By silent accord, Walter and Isabel decided to do the same, unnoticed by eager huntsmen and women who flowed past them. They turned their mounts back toward a stream they had passed earlier.

Finding the spot secluded and pretty, they tethered their horses, listening as the clamor died off. Walter spread his cloak on the ground for Isabel and sat beside her. She lay back, looking at the trees.

"You did well, my dear little chatelaine."

She sighed. "It was very hard work. Though I hate to see my father and you leave, it will be a pleasure to see the rest of those men off."

Walter was at a loss for something to say. There was so much they needed to talk about, but where should he begin? He had already bungled things once, the other morning when Antoine fell off his horse.

Isabel closed her eyes. He stared down, looking at her chest rise and fall, and the little hand placed on her throat. Was she waiting for him to make a move?

Almost independently, his hand wandered to her cheek, stroking it. He marveled at the softness of her skin, and found himself bending over. He kissed her on the lips. Isabel put an arm around his neck, waiting for another kiss.

But nothing came. Her eyes fluttered open and she sat up in surprise. Walter was gazing at her in consternation. They faced each other, breathing hard. With a trembling hand he touched her forehead, moving his fingers down her face. Isabel closed her eyes, only to feel him pause again. Curiosity overcame impatience; she gently took his hand, kissing it.

"Something still bothers you, then," she said softly. "Tell me."

With a great heave of his chest, Walter squeezed her hand. He looked over her shoulder.

"Yes, you are right. May I ask you something that will probably sound quite strange?"

She nodded uncertainly.

"The first moment you met me, you looked surprised, like you recognized me from somewhere."

It was Isabel's turn to look away, though she didn't speak.

"Please tell me," he pursued, "is there anything in what I say?"

"And what of it, if there is," she retorted, challenging.

"Please, Isabel, this is important to me. There is a reason for what I ask."

She hesitated. "Yes, in truth, it is as you say." She hurried on, not noticing his intake of breath. "If you must know, I have dreamed about you. Your face, your voice...it was not often, but a couple of times in the last two years. Every scene was different, but it was always your face.

"One time, we...married."

She put a hand to her forehead, as if to push away the thoughts.

Walter scrutinized her closely. "Is it as terrible as all that?"

"Oh no, oh no," she cried, throwing herself into his arms. "I'm just so frightened by it all. It was different when I never knew you, but now..."

He held her close, feeling the warmth of her body, her face against his shoulder.

Then she pulled back, disentangling herself from his arms. "Now it's your turn. What is it you are getting at?"

But Walter wasn't finished with his questions. "Did you see them in your dreams...the old women?"

"No," she shook her head. "No old women."

"There was no one leading you in your dreams?"

"Why, no. What are you speaking of?"

"I just don't understand. It doesn't make sense."

"You don't make sense!"

Walter ran a hand over his forehead. "I'm sorry, Isabel. But you see, I too had a dream. Several dreams. About Brittany. About a wife. But I never saw your face."

She gasped.

"But it was somewhat different from your dreams. You see, these three old women came to me and spoke of my future...on more than one occasion. The first time, they told me the truth about my past. The second time, they told me to come here. 'Thou shalt 'get kings' they told me, 'though thou be none.' I don't know what to make of it."

Isabel shook her head, baffled.

"My Isabel, my heart," he said, leaning forward to take her hands. "They sent me to find you. To marry you, Alain's daughter. I can't explain it, but I don't know how to resist them."

"Resist!" she cried, insulted. But after a moment she followed another thought. "Who do you think they are, Walter?"

"I never know whether to speak of them. But they interfere too much!" He turned around, half-expecting them to appear. "Isabel, sometimes I think I go mad.

"For a long while, I did not know what to think. But all the signs tell me that I have been visited by the Norns."

She looked at him questioningly.

"I forget," he added, "you are Christian. Well, I tell you Isabel, there are other religions in this world, even older than your own. They, too, are powerful when a people believe in them."

Isabel crossed herself, twice.

"Forgive me for speaking like this. But the old Pagan religion still heavily influences my people. The Norns seem to have an interest in my future. I believe in them."

Isabel was shocked; she had never heard such heretical talk.

Walter continued. "The Norns are very powerful; they rule the course of time, and determine a man's destiny. Like the Greek Fates, you could say. One of them is named Urd, for *fate*. Another is named Skuld, for *being*. The third is named Verthandi, for *necessity*. No man can gainsay them.

"But see you, Isabel, I do not know whether I would willingly do their bidding the rest of my life."

Confused, she looked dumbly at Walter. But in a moment, his last statement penetrated her thoughts.

"What say you, Walter? You would not have me because these hags of yours sent you here against your will?"

Pained, he saw how she was taking this.

"Do you not see, Isabel? I cannot help it. My heart is already yours. It is my head that gives me pause."

"Then why did you come here?" she exclaimed, standing up and brushing her skirts with hard, fast strokes.

"I...was afraid not to."

Flushed, this time in anger, Isabel towered over her reluctant conquest. Walter never thought he had seen her so beautiful.

"When your head comes to an agreement with your heart, then we shall talk. Until that time, I do not wish to pain you with my company."

With a little toss of her head, Isabel walked away. Walter watched in silence as she untied her horse and climbed easily into the saddle. She left without a backward look.

Walter was still walking his horse back to the castle when the grooms passed him, two by two, carrying the quarters of a buck, strung along a stout branch. He barely remembered the feasting that night, except for trying to catch the eye of Isabel, who sat glumly next to Alain, picking at her food.

He wasn't angry with Isabel. Indeed, he hardly expected her

to understand what he didn't comprehend himself. Why should he balk at the wife the weird sisters had offered him? She pleased him very well. So far the old women had done him no harm...at least, none that he knew of.

18

Campaign in Brittany

The ride to Dol was not long; it was about fifty miles to the east. Their road took them a little to the south of the besieged city; the Bretons did not judge their force of two thousand large enough to attack alone, so they continued east, hoping to join up Duke William.

As the Normans were crossing the treacherous river Coesnon, to the south of Mont St. Michel, the two armies met. Count Alain and his brother went alone to meet the Duke, leaving the troops stamping restlessly behind them.

Seeing their example, William rode forth from his army, bringing one other they did not recognize, but who wore his hair and dress different from the Normans. Walter sat in the front ranks of the Breton army, with a clear view of the proceedings. From the distance, he fancied that he recognized the stranger, and his heart pounded even though he told himself it could not possibly be so.

William the Bastard dismounted ceremoniously, acknowledging the newcomers with open arms. The Duke was a large man, who towered a head above nearly everyone else; certainly he looked down to Count Alain. After his welcome, William introduced his companion. Alain seemed interested, throwing up his arms and nodding his head. His brother did nothing.

In a few minutes, Alain returned, giving orders for his army to join William's. As the men moved forward, he turned to Walter.

"I have finally met your Harold Godwineson," he said in a low voice. "What a figure he cuts! On my soul, just a little while ago he saved a Norman soldier, single handed, from sinking into the marsh the other side of the river. Pulled him from the mire with the strength of his own arms, when the others would have left him there to die. He seems to command respect, that one."

His worst fears confirmed, Walter bit his lip. "What is he doing here?" he grumbled.

Alain shrugged his shoulders. "I do not know. William seems to be treating him like an honored guest, at least."

Within two hours they were within sight of Dol. An ancient city, it stood on a slight rise above the flat plains, with walls that looked like a great crown atop the hill.

At the foot of the hill had lain the army of Conan. But the siege had only been half-hearted; Conan ordered a retreat at the first word of William's approach. Now, the Normans were greeted with a great cheering from the liberated city and the smoldering fires of a deserted camp.

In their hurry, Conan's troops left some of their larger pavilions behind. The Normans and Bretons settled happily into the same place, preparing to savor their easy victory. In fact, they were hungry, and seemed to stay hungry for several days, eating all the local food that Dol could provide.

Reaching the point of desperation, the city's governor presented himself at William's pavilion. The Duke received him graciously.

The man bowed, first to William, then to Harold. "My name is Rhiwallon," he said respectfully. "We are grateful to you, my Duke, for your timely intervention. But I must report that Count Conan's siege has reduced our resources to nothing. My Lord..." the man's eye flashed momentarily. "I ask you this. What does it matter to us if we are plundered by our friends or our enemies? The result is the same."

Having made this bold statement, the man stood with bowed head, expecting to be struck down. But William admired his courage. He turned a wry smile to Harold. "The man is right. We are doing no honorable deed, here. All right, then. We will march in the morning."

Obviously relieved, Rhiwallon backed away.

"Wait!"

The governor froze, betraying his fear; thinking himself absolved, he had dropped his defenses.

"Never use such an attitude with me again, or I will burn this town to the ground myself."

For a moment the man looked at William with disbelief. But seeing the Duke's expression, he scurried from the tent.

Even Harold was a bit shocked, but William's face quickly relaxed, and he even smiled. "That man will never cause me trouble, I assure you," he said in answer to Harold's questioning glance. "There are times when a simple reminder is enough. Besides, he is right. We have spent enough time here. Sufficient scouts have returned to assure me that Conan is headed back toward his town of Dinan. We can take him there."

Count Conan had taken advantage of the time he was given, and planted his army securely in William's path. He chose a field that was flanked on both sides by a dense forest, and spread his army from one side to the other with a front about eight men deep. Ditches were dug facing the approaching army and sharpened stakes projected from the mounded dirt. Alain told Walter he was sure there were more of those hidden inside the ditches themselves.

William didn't seem perturbed by the ugly scene. He ordered his archers forward.

Walter watched in amazement; this was the first time he ever saw archery used in a pitched battle. The archers calmly knelt on one knee, pointing their arrows into the sky. What they took aim at was impossible to tell, but the shower of arrows coming straight down upon the enemy did tremendous damage. Howling, dashing back and forth, the men didn't seem to know how to escape the raining destruction. Not all of them had shields to hold over their heads; many of the host were merely peasants, drafted into feudal service.

William's first wave of foot soldiers started forward, assured that the arrows flying over their heads were too disruptive for the enemy to stage a successful defense. They approached with spears and long swords to try and knock aside the threatening stakes, working quickly and efficiently; evidently the Normans were used to acting against this type of defense.

Quite a few gaps were created before Conan's men crept up onto the dirt mounds, throwing javelins and slinging stones to hinder their work. Meanwhile, many of William's infantry had worked their way through the woods around both flanks of the defense. They attacked simultaneously while the cavalry jumped the ditches in front. Conan's footmen fought furiously, while the Normans beat them back step by step.

Heavily clad in their chain maille, the Normans skillfully whirled their destriers about to deal heavy blows with axes and swords. They smote quickly and deftly, wasting little energy and trampling those of the enemy less heedful of their horses' hooves.

The battle was straight forward from that point. Walter fought at Alain's side, impressed by the agility of that stocky man. The Count favored the mace, like William, using it with astounding power. Few men rose from a blow received by that weapon. Walter was kept busy enough with his own two-headed axe; men shied away from his weapon, for it was rarely seen this side of the channel.

All of a sudden, Walter found himself face to face with Harold. From behind the nose guard on the Saxon's helmet, Walter could see the Earl's eyes widening in shock. Harold's sword was half-lifted, but he stayed his arm. It seemed that the two of them were momentarily removed from the battle, engaged in their private struggle. They were frozen, unable to move.

Then the spell was broken; Harold was whisked away in the fray. Suddenly, William loomed up in his place. The Duke gazed curiously at Walter for a moment, the knowledge of what had just passed written on his face. Then he, too was gone.

After that, the battle was soon over. Conan was leading his men in a frantic flight for the safety of Dinan.

They set up camp near Conan's town. Later that night, as he was arranging his bedroll, Walter wasn't surprised when Alain put a hand on his arm, and told him Duke William wanted to see him. "You fought well, lad," he said a little jealously, "but I didn't know you looked that good."

Walter smiled grimly. He knew what the Duke wanted.

As soon as Walter entered the Norman pavilion, William dismissed his entourage. They left without question, directing suspicious glances in the newcomer's direction. Once alone, William looked at the other appraisingly. This was the first time Walter had seen him close up, and he could understand why everyone was so impressed with this man.

It was his presence that one noticed first, commanding respect. This was no unconscious thing; William cultivated his image. The man's physical strength was intimidating; even his lower arms bulged with muscles. Fierce eyes glared from slightly jutting eyebrows, darting this way and that; they were restless, consuming. His lips were parted in an unconscious way that appeared to precede a snarl.

Walter guessed that Alain already told William about himself, but he wasn't sure Harold had said anything.

As if he had read his mind, William spoke up.

"Harold doesn't know you are here. Nor did he see me behind him, you know."

He leaned forward, motioning Walter to sit down.

"As you are Alain's kin, I will suppose you are on my side. For loyalties are what we are talking about here."

Wondering what kind of assurance was expected from him, Walter opened his mouth to ask a question, but thought better of it. The Duke did not miss the expression. He sat back again, leaning against his saddle.

"If you are wondering why Harold is here, I assure you he did not come as my guest. He was shipwrecked on one of my vassal's lands, and I rescued him from a dreadful imprisonment." William laughed, a low rumbling sound that boded ill will.

"So now he remains as my guest. And you," he said, thrusting his jaw forward. Walter thought he looked like a mastiff. "What is his quarrel with you?"

Walter did not answer. He was not ready to trust the Duke; nor did he wish to be made use of, for William's private aims.

The Norman watched him, eyes narrowing. But he did not get angry. "I know it wasn't my imagination."

Walter licked his dry lips. "I am Welsh, the grandson of Gruffydd ap Llewelyn, Prince of Wales. I served for a time under Earl Harold, but my presence to him, and his to me was... unsettling."

The Duke had not taken his eyes from Walter's face, and still he was unsatisfied. But he knew when a man wouldn't talk. "Ah, Gruffydd," he said, seeming to relax. "Harold told me about the man. A great leader, evidently. Therefore trouble to the English. Harold finally caught up with him, you know." Seeing Walter's surprise, he followed it through. "Or maybe you didn't know." He smiled, enjoying his advantage.

"The Prince hid in the mountains for many months. But he was deserted in the end, betrayed by his own men. Harold sent his head to Edward."

Walter shivered, ignoring the subtle triumph on William's face. He looked up finally. "Did he say anything about Ealdgyth, the Prince's wife?"

William seemed disturbed. "He has her, I think he said. Didn't say what he did with the widow."

Walter frowned, remembering the kindness Ealdgyth showed his mother. He stood to leave, but William told him to wait.

"There is that question of loyalties we need to answer. Look here," he said as he leaned forward. "It is no secret that King Edward promised me the English throne on his death. And I mean to have it!" He hit his knee with a fist.

"I think Harold wants the throne. He would keep me from it, if he can. Do you want to see him king?"

Walter was shocked; this was something he had never considered. He thought of Rhuddlan in flames; he remembered Myrna's father, sprawled on the doorstep of his house.

He shook his head. "No."

"Then you are with me. Good."

William waved his dismissal at Walter, turning to a cold dinner.

When Walter returned to his tent, Alain was waiting for him. The look of jealous curiosity disappeared when he saw Walter's face. He held out a hand to the younger man as he sat heavily on his pallet.

"What said the Duke... are you all right?"

Walter sat heavily on his pallet. "Sometimes I think I will never be all right. Don't worry. All is well with the Duke. I just wonder how far William will go, to reach his ends. And who he will drag with him?"

But Alain wasn't really listening. He was already throwing a cloak over his shoulders. It was already getting to be a routine every night, that the Count would attend William until late.

Left alone, Walter lay back on his pallet, listening to the sounds of the camp. Voices lifted in song, sometimes in argument; he noted the crackling of fires, the occasional shuffling as someone searched his tent in the dark.

He found himself wide awake. Try how he might to avoid it, his mind kept reverting to Isabel and those last days. Over and over again, he dwelled on that precious moment when he held her in his arms... the feeling of her body against his, her face against his shoulder. It was like probing a sore tooth, making it worse.

Rolling onto his side, Walter stared into the darkness. He kept remembering the anger on her face, when she left him so abruptly. And her averted eyes, when they said farewell. Perhaps she was glad to send him away, never wanted to see him again.

There was no taking back what he had said to her, but he was beginning to regret the intent behind his words.

The more he thought about it, the more he decided that he had been wrong—grievously wrong. No matter what the design of the weird sisters, Isabel was a prize that he should never let slip away. She had become precious to him, all the more so because he might lose her.

The army moved to surround the town of Dinan. It was a poor choice for Conan's refuge. Although the town's summit held a proper motte and bailey castle, the city walls were made of timber. Duke William looked at it with satisfaction. He turned to his captains.

"We will surround the entrance, for now, and give the man his opportunity to surrender. But he had better be quick about it. I will waste no time here."

So, properly dressed and carrying William's banner, his herald calmly waited at the gate for an answer. The response was not long in coming; clods of dirt and rocks sped the messenger to the safety of the army. William's face was red.

"Conan was lucky he didn't kill my man. We shall only burn down his fortress."

Taking this for an order, which indeed it was, the Normans set about gathering wood and straw. They quickly piled the kindling at the base of the walls, setting fire to it without waiting for further parley. William had learned long ago that action alone got the response he wanted.

The smoke told the watchers where the fire was spreading, propelled by a brisk wind. Soon, tall flames shot through the black clouds. It was not long before the gates opened a crack and a spear was thrust forth, the city key dangling from its tip. William gestured for Alain to retrieve it.

Pleased by the honor, Alain rode forward. He faced the doors, ceremoniously plucking the key away, while still mounted.

Watching, Walter momentarily saw a mist before his eyes; there was a rushing sound in his ears, drowning out even the roar of the fire. Dizzy, he swayed in the saddle, clutching the horse's mane. Then it passed, and Alain was handing the keys to William.

The ceremony being done, the gate flew open and the inhabitants poured out. Conan was quickly recognized and brought before the Duke.

Alain took his place beside Walter, who grabbed his arm worriedly. "That could have been a trick," he said. "You might have been killed."

"Nonsense," the other said. "It is traditionally the sign of surrender. They wouldn't dare such an act."

Conan stood submissively before the Duke, who enjoyed making the man squirm under his deadly gaze. The prisoner looked up with a mixed expression of scorn and resignation. He clearly didn't expect to live.

Finally, William spoke. "You have learned your lesson, I think. For your act of aggression, I will be content to receive your forfeited lands, including this Dinan and the town of Dol. Make sure this never happens again!"

Amazed at this unexpected reprieve, Conan bowed and limped off, hoping not to attract further attention to himself. William turned to Alain, accepting a wineskin.

"I'm sorry you were so easy on him," Alain said. "Trouble follows that man like bees to honey; you will not have seen the end of Conan."

William looked bitterly after the retreating man. "When you have to deal with as many rebellions as I have, Alain, you learn that if you killed every one of the instigators, there would be no one left to rule. Sometimes, you will get what you want with mercy."

Dismounting, he strode to the gate, where most of his men were posted. Refugees were pouring out of the fortress, leading their livestock, pulling carts. The Duke pushed his way through the throng, as unheeding of them as they were of him.

Looking on, Harold Godwineson stood with his few friends. William called his name, and begged him to kneel. The fire still raging behind him, he drew his sword and knighted the Saxon without another word.

How dramatic, Walter thought, watching the Earl bow his head; the Norman towered over him as he tapped both shoulders with the flat of his blade. He marveled at the web Duke William was weaving around his captive.

This was more than a simple knighthood. From now on, Harold Godwineson was William's sworn man, honor bound to put his Lord's needs before his own. And that included the throne of England.

In two weeks' time, the Norman and Breton Lords assembled at the Duke's castle in Bayeux. Count Alain and his brother were asked to accompany William this far into Normandy after Dinan. Walter was obliged to attend as well, obeying the express wishes of the Duke.

On entering the great hall, the attendants were greeted with a strange scene. A tall table sat in the middle of the floor, draped with an embroidered cloth. Facing the table were the chairs of state; across from these were benches for the guests; they numbered about ten score. The Lords of Brittany and Walter were directed to the first row. Duke William was nowhere to be seen as yet.

But his appearance was not long in coming. As soon as everyone was seated, the doors flew open with a fanfare. In a gaudy procession of priests and bishops, Duke William entered, brilliantly dressed in a white velvet surcoat edged with gold trim. He wore his ducal coronet on his brow.

At William's side paced his tiny wife Matilda, taking two steps for every one of his long strides. Behind the ducal pair strode Earl Harold, conspicuous in his brown linen tunic cut short to his knees, and golden bands above his elbows; he must have known that the Normans found his style ludicrous. But his look of majesty made gaudy trappings seem unnecessary; even William in his angry splendor could not match the simple elegance of Harold's manner.

All stood in the hall until the Duke was seated. Harold waited next to his chair, but William asked him approach the table, upon which the Bishop was placing a Bible. Harold laid his hand on the holy book and looked at William for instructions; his face was expressionless.

"My friends and nobles," said William, pacing before the assembly. "Earl Harold would return to England, despite my protests. But ere he leaves, I have asked him to swear an oath, before my assembled Lords." He turned to face Harold, who had already broken into a sweat.

"I would have you swear, my Lord Harold, that you will espouse my daughter Matilda as soon as she is of marriageable age."

After a moment, Harold said, "I swear."

"Secondly, I would have you swear to give up to me, this day, your castle at Dover, so that I may garrison it with Norman soldiers." The corner of his mouth turned up into an almost unnoticeable sneer.

Harold looked up at the ceiling, sighing. "To this also I swear," he said evenly.

"And thirdly, lastly, I would have you be my man in England, and uphold my claim to the throne of my friend King Edward upon his demise. In return for this, I swear to give you all the highest honors in England, and allow you to retain your earldom." William's eyes narrowed, willing his prisoner to acquiesce.

Walter gasped aloud. He knew this was madness. Even if he would, Harold had not the power to give up the royal castle of Dover. But of his own free will, to help the Norman become king?

Harold stood silent for a long while. Perhaps he was searching his soul, to gauge the extent of his own damnation.

"Swear," shouted William, filling the room with his voice.

Shaking his head, Harold firmly put his hand on the Bible. "I swear," he said with a slight tremor to his voice.

"Speak the words, Harold."

The Earl looked at William, hate shooting from his eyes. "I swear to be your man in England, and speak up in your support. Now let me go."

Walter sighed. He alone, with the possible exception of William, knew that the Earl had just forsworn himself.

Harold started to leave the room when William called "Wait" in a voice that brooked no denial. The Saxon turned to face him, impatiently.

Walter was surprised to find William's eyes turned to himself. Then the Duke nodded intently; there was no mistaking his meaning. Gulping, cursing the Duke, he slowly rose, responding to the man's summons. Harold looked at him in shock, not having remarked his presence in the room.

"Walter, pull the linen from the table, and bid your countryman to come forward."

Harold drew to the table, not needing to be told. He already suspected the surprise William had set for him.

Hands shaking, Walter obeyed the Duke, then turned away, burying his face in the cloth. The Earl paled, as he sank to one knee. William turned triumphantly to the assembly.

Inside the table, carefully cushioned between folds of silk, lay the holy relics of the saints of Normandy. Harold knew what he had done. Though shameful, it was no great matter to swear false oath on the Bible. But devastating would be the retribution of these holy men, whose bones he had made a mockery of.

Still shaking, Walter helped Harold to his feet, leading the stunned man from the room. He handed the Earl over to his attendants, then hid himself in an alcove of a window, waiting for a feeling of sickness to pass. Although he knew nothing of the relics, he felt he had betrayed Harold once again.

19

A Betrothal

The welcome at Alain's castle was a noisy one; everyone was happy to be back, and families lined the road, running after their loved ones' horses. Isabel was waiting at the end of the drawbridge, and her father dismounted, giving her a hug.

Walter watched this reception nervously. What a difference his feelings were from when started this campaign. Back then, he was relieved to get away from her. But now...it was as if his very happiness depended on a glance from those scornful eyes.

Isabel was relating to her father some incidents that occurred during his absence: the birth of a new foal, the visit of their local abbot. She had not yet acknowledged Walter, so with a sigh he took the reins of Alain's horse, offering to bring it to the stables. He was stopped by her voice, calling his name.

Walter turned, holding his breath. Isabel had control of the situation, and she knew it. How proud she looked; and well she should be. She was chatelaine while they were gone, and had run the castle from day to day. This was quite a job for one so young.

"Wait, Walter. I'll come with you. I'd like to show you the new foal."

Smiling, Alain waved them carelessly on.

They walked in silence to the stables; Walter was afraid of starting off badly, and could not interpret her expression. Her face held a mixture of sadness and anger and hope, but which of the three was foremost it was impossible to tell.

He unsaddled the horses quickly, mindlessly, brushing them and throwing some grain in their buckets. She showed him the foal without comment, and they left the stables, heading aimlessly along the outer bailey. The sun was setting, putting the area next to the wall into an early dusk.

Neither was willing to make the first move. But Walter knew

that this problem was of his making, and it was only right that he should make amends.

"Isabel," he said, and was surprised to hear his own name at the same moment. They laughed, relieved. Walter put his cloak around her shoulders, and took her arm in his. "Isabel, my heart, I was wrong for what I said. How can I make it up to you?"

For a moment, she didn't answer. "Is that all you can say?" she finally asked.

"No, that is not all. I must tell you where I stand. There is this matter of the weird sisters. I will do their bidding, as I always have, because I want to. If the time comes that they ask of me what I will not give, then I shall face the issue once again. Perhaps that time will never come."

She made a shrug of impatience, pulling away.

But he would not have it. He stopped, turning her around to face him. She did not fight.

"Isabel, I want you. I want you to be mine. In the time we were away, I could think of naught but you. I yearned for you, Isabel. I ached, I fretted, I cursed myself for my folly.

"The weird sisters did me a favor, bringing me here, for I never would have come, otherwise. But if you will have me, I give myself to you, heart and soul."

He paused, relieved to see her mouth soften. "Isabel. I have never felt this way about a woman before."

She put her head on his shoulder, and he pulled her in to an embrasure. Engulfing her in his arms, he whispered her name over and over, kissing her eyes, her cheeks, her lips. She gave back his caresses willingly, hungrily. The passion in this girl was intoxicating, and so much more than he expected.

Walter stopped, breathing hard.

"Will you marry me, my love, of your own free will? Never mind those recurring dreams."

"Need you ask?" she said in her little breathless voice. "I was yours from the moment I saw you."

"And yet you hardly know me, Isabel."

"That is no matter. Our fates are already interlocked. I will heed the message of your Norns."

"Your father..." Walter's eyes betrayed his uneasiness. "My illegitimacy. Will he accept me as his good-son?"

Isabel seemed sure on that point. "My happiness is closest to his heart. He will not gainsay me in this."

They were moving back to the castle. "We shall ask him tonight," he said. She was already ahead of him, in her excitement.

But Walter still felt uneasy. There was so much more to say.

"One more thing," he added, pulling her back. She stopped, questioningly. "I must return to Scotland, sooner or later. King Malcolm needs me there, and I, too, would be nowhere but at his side. Can you leave this, your home, and live in that cold land to the north?"

She looked at the ground uncertainly. "But Walter, what of these sons of yours, who would be kings?"

"What made you think they would be kings of Brittany?" he said softly.

His eyes burned into hers, the conviction in them carried through mists from the other world. For a moment she saw in his eyes the faces of many men, faces unmistakably bearing the traces of Walter's features. Whether they were of the past or the future, she could not tell.

She staggered against him, shaken by the burden of all those lives. Then he was her own again, caring for her, the look in his eyes gone.

She didn't know the answer. Other possibilities had never crossed her mind.

Walter considered her carefully. "We will wait before telling your father," he said quickly. "There is no rush. You have to be sure."

"You...will not stay here with me?"

"In Brittany? No. Not forever. That much is certain. I would have you with me, Isabel. But return to Scotland I shall. My place is there, not here, no matter how much I love you and your father. And I do love you. Never doubt that."

"Then so be it, Walter. I can never let you go."

Was it the responsibilities of the last few weeks, or the pressures of their relationship? Or had Walter's perceptions changed over time? No longer did Isabel seem like a child. She had become a woman, more than ever solid, dependable, insightful. Walter was glad they had come back together.

Alain was already buried in his work. Walter found him putting things in order, and took a second to watch him handle his parchments and manuscripts with care, as if he had terribly missed them.

"Did you see the foal?"

"Oh...yes. A pretty little bay filly. She will be big, I think..." He trailed off lamely.

Alain put a book on its shelf, then took a piece of straw to the fireplace, lighting it. He carefully set the flame to a candle.

"That's better. Sit, Walter. How goes it with my daughter? Everything sorted out?"

Walter sat down, surprised. "How did you know that we quarreled?"

"Oh, come. I would have to be blind not to have noticed."

The other coughed, embarrassed. "Yes, we have made that up." He paused, summoning his courage. "My Lord, there is something I would ask of you, if you would be so kind."

Raising an eyebrow, Alain said, "Certainly my boy. Anything at all."

Walter wondered whether the worthy man might regret his statement.

"It regards your daughter. We have more than made up our quarrel."

"Oh?" the Count said conversationally. "Well, I am glad to hear it."

"Well, sir, there is more to it than that. I have come to ask her hand in marriage."

At that, Alain's face brightened up. "My son, my son! This is wonderful news."

Amazed, Walter remembered to close his mouth. Alain's reaction was totally unexpected.

The Count was pouring them a drink. "We must celebrate."

Unbelieving, Walter accepted a goblet. "Alain, you took me by surprise," he laughed shortly. "I'll admit it: I expected you to object."

Alain sat down, more serious. "Did Isabel think so?"

"No. She said you would do whatever made her happy."

"Well, there you are. If she wants you, she will have you."

Walter sipped, still doubtful.

"I never expected you to argue with me. Take your treasure and be happy with her."

"May the Gods bless you, Alain. Your generosity goes beyond my understanding. I'm not used to such good fortune."

"You wonder why I accept you, a bastard, for my only daughter?"

Walter flinched.

"Well you should ask, Walter. This sort of thing does not often happen." Alain was obviously pleased with himself. "What do I care of the disposition of my lands after my death? They can go to my brother, for all it concerns me. Except for the lands I give to you, um, in her name, of course. In her dowry. The revenue will support her in comfort. My daughter's happiness is all that I want.

"You have proved yourself a brave warrior. You can take good care of her, I dare say."

Dubious, Walter held out his chalice as a toast.

"Oh, come, man! Surely you see that I support Duke William,

a bastard if there ever was one. How can I in good conscience support one, if I deny another the hand of my daughter? I am many things, my son, but hypocrite is not one of them."

Walter sat up to bang his cup against Alain's. "Now that is reasoning I can understand."

Laughing, Alain called for Isabel.

As if she were waiting outside the door, Isabel glided into the room, her head held high. She listened as her father gave his blessing, then turned an eloquent look to her beloved.

"Do you accept, my daughter?"

Laughing, she dropped into her father's lap. "With all my heart."

Alain hugged her, then gently pushed her off. "Come, dear, Walter and I have much to discuss. Join us in an hour's time."

They watched her leave. "By God, I think you have a worthy wife, Walter," Alain said wistfully.

"And just as worthy a good-father. I will not let you down."

"I know, my son. I know."

Isabel was back at the end of the hour, bringing a platter of cold meats and bread. Walter forgot that they hadn't eaten yet.

"Thoughtful girl," Alain murmured, stuffing a piece of meat in his mouth. Walter followed his lead, offering some to Isabel.

As they were finishing, a knock on the door reminded Alain that he had other business.

"That will be my grounds-keeper. Leave me, my children. I'm sure you have much to talk about."

Walter and Isabel were perfectly willing to be alone. She kissed her father good night, and they left together.

The night was cloudless and moonless, and they went up to the top of Alain's tower, to watch the stars.

The battlement of the tower was as tall as a man, cut with openings about chest high. For a time they leaned over the edge, looking at the stars reflected in the moat.

Isabel pointed across to the far tower. Upon it paced a look-out, merely a shadow in the darkness.

"Do you think he can see us?" she giggled.

Walter pulled her toward him, his back to the protecting rock. "Not now."

He covered her mouth with his own, releasing himself to passion for the first time. He pulled her tight, holding her as if never to let go.

She came to him, pressing against him with her whole body. Opening her mouth, she coaxed his tongue forward and he responded eagerly, searchingly, lost in unknown sensations. His hands slid forward, pressing against the side of her breasts. As she moved in response to his touch, he could feel her hard nipples against his fingers. She let out a soft groan as he carefully rubbed them, enjoying her firmness.

But finally he stopped, letting her go. She was radiant, happier than he had ever seen her. Backing up, pulling her dress into a semblance of order, Isabel kissed him quickly, then pushed him back against the wall. She leaned forward onto him, enjoying the feel of his body pressed against her.

"This is no place for such activities," she said teasingly. "Perhaps we should find a more...comfortable spot."

Taking a deep breath, Walter brought his cravings under control. "My love, my sweet. Think on what you are saying."

She stepped back, her breath a sharp staccato.

Reaching for her hand, he stood straight up. "As much as I want you, and I do... do not doubt it." He brought her hand against his hardness, as if to stress what he was saying. She let him guide her, eyes opening in lust. "Isabel, Isabel, I will not dishonor you."

Gently, reluctantly, she pulled her hand away, placing it instead against his cheek.

"Remember, I am a bastard," he breathed, reluctantly forcing the issue. "No matter what I do, I cannot alter that fact. Can you imagine what I have done to my mother?" He almost choked on the words, so intense was his conflict. "Never did I understand what possessed her to do such shame until now!"

He gathered Isabel into his arms, not wanting to give up her soft yielding body. Her breathing was fast, hard, hot against his ear. "I will not do the same to you, and bring another, such as myself, into the world."

There, it was said. Still he wouldn't release his hold on her; still he pressed his manhood against her. He kissed her hard, possessively.

But this, too, passed, and he allowed her to untangle herself from his arms. She did this none too willingly. But realizing the threat to her honor if they were caught, she acknowledged what he said.

They stared at each other for long moments. Embarrassed, she looked away.

"You are a passionate woman," he said softly, "and even more do I love you. You can teach me how to take pleasure from life."

Isabel bit her lip, overcome with the glimpse he gave her of his soul, his intense unhappiness. There was so much she didn't know about him.

20

A Change of Weather

For a time, Walter enjoyed his new status as landowner and head of the household. Marriage was an unimagined pleasure, and their first year together was filled with activity.

Isabel's father was a frequent resident, often preferring their company to his own. He was always welcome, bringing news of the outside world with him as well as a rush of activity and gaiety. Walter and Isabel declared themselves happy as the winter set in.

Alain cheerfully complied with Walter's request for training as a mounted warrior. He taught his good-son all he knew. When his own knowledge was exhausted, he brought others who gladly shared their experience out of love for the Count. Walter's old training aided his new, sometimes providing him with strategy unthought-of by the others.

But as their second winter began, Walter began to feel a craving for his old life. He missed Scotland, he missed Malcolm; he even caught himself thinking fondly about Hereford. Isabel eyed his growing restlessness uneasily; she would have been happy to continue forever like this.

So it was with relief on his part and anxiousness on hers, one day late in January, when they saw Alain ride in, flushed with excitement. He dismounted from his horse, gave it hastily to a groom and dashed into the house. The Count grabbed Walter by both arms as Isabel closed the door behind him.

Walter broke into a grin at the look in his good-father's eyes; the sense of approaching warfare communicated instinctively between the two veterans. Isabel sighed in distress and left the room, her dog Rusty following.

"Walter, you will not believe the news," the Count said, as Walter offered a chair near the fire. "Old Edward of England died on the fourth day of this year, and the following day, on the Epiphany, they placed the crown on..."

"Harold's head," Walter interjected thoughtfully.

"Oh," said Alain, disappointed. "So you've already heard."

"Not at all, father. I guessed it. I'm sorry...please go on."

"Humph, well," Alain went on, slightly mollified, "yes, it was Harold. It seems they had to proceed quickly with the coronation, because the next high church feast day isn't until Easter. They didn't want to go so long without a king, I suppose. But really, Walter, they went from the funeral right to the coronation. Such haste!"

"Yes," the other said, deep in thought. "I suppose your William is throwing a fit."

"Well, yes, and more." Alain stopped, savoring his mysterious message.

"And?"

"And after scowling and cursing and calling Harold forsworn, William has vowed to take an army and conquer what has already been promised him."

"Conquer! Transfer a whole army across the English Channel? Has he gone mad?"

Alain shook his head. "Why no, Walter. He is very sane. Caesar did it, didn't he? And I, for one, have promised to accompany him. This is what I came to tell you."

"Then you have lost your mind as well," Walter retorted, stomping back and forth across the room. "I can't believe his troublesome nobles will follow such a mad scheme. And leave Normandy to the wolves."

"Actually," Alain continued, ignoring Walter's rancor, "he is prepared to promise a lucrative reward for every man that goes with him. How do you fancy an Earl for a good-father? For he has promised me no less."

"An Earl of someone else's land."

"Tut, man, that is what war is all about! After William is done, there will be plenty of lands without masters, I would think."

"And his nobles have agreed?"

"It hasn't come to that, yet. William wanted to secure the support of his neighbors before he approached his own countrymen. Of course, Conan has thrown his offer back in his face. Said he would invade the moment William leaves Normandy."

"Which is what I would expect," Walter answered. Coming to a stop at the window, he threw back the shutters, letting in a rush of cold air.

Alain said, "I suspect the Duke has his own ways of dealing with such recreants."

"Perhaps he does, at that."

"There is one point in William's favor, concerning the invasion. He has sent a representative to the Pope, asking for his support. In return, he promises to hold England as a fief to Rome."

Walter turned, a grim smile on his face. "That Duke is wilier than I expected. A sly move, that. Once the conquest of England is known as a religious war, poor Harold doesn't hold a chance."

"Poor Harold? I thought he was your enemy?"

"No more than William," said Walter under his breath.

"What was that, my son?"

Walter sighed. "Only that William might not stop at England. He may threaten Scotland, as well."

"Conjecture will get us nowhere. Listen, Walter. Will you join me? I have need of your talents."

The other pulled up a stool, facing the Count. "Think on what you do. If we go, it is possible neither of us will return. Especially myself. I will be too close to Scotland to leave it, ever again."

Alain shivered, looking at the window. "Then we shall still be neighbors, and I will come often to visit you, at Malcolm's court."

"No!" came a decidedly female voice. Both men looked up guiltily, seeing Isabel at the door. Her face betrayed how much she had heard.

Walter got up, putting his arms around his wife. "I can deny your father nothing," he said, although it would be more true to say that Malcolm was first in his mind. "Before we married, I told you I would return to Scotland. Have you forgotten already?"

"No." She broke out of his embrace, closing the shutters, to Alain's relief. "I just hoped it wouldn't be so soon."

Her words were lost on her father, who got up, clapping Walter on the shoulder. "Let us drink! I am parched."

Her husband, looking at her painfully, allowed himself to be pushed from the room.

Isabel knew he wouldn't reply to her sentiment. He had already made up his mind, and she had promised to go with him. Was it really so long ago?

Toward the middle of August, Walter and Alain rode hard toward William's encampment, half a day ahead of Alain's three thousand men. As they topped a large hill near the river Dives, the two men pulled their horses to a stop, whistling in admiration.

The rumors they had heard about frenzied ship building during the summer were not exaggerated; for a non-naval country, Normandy had amassed a considerable fleet in a remarkably short time. As far as they could see, ship masts stood like a forest of trees, rocking slowly back and forth in the tide.

Spread out in a colorful array along the coast, riversides, and into the hills, were the many knights' companies. The first-come had naturally picked the best spots to pitch their gaily bedecked pavilions.

"So we guessed rightly, Walter," the Count said in satisfaction. "It was good that we got a head start on the rest of my men. My thirty ships will do all right for themselves, but I am most concerned with keeping my army together.

"There," he said, pointing to the mouth of the river, "I see the leopard of Normandy. William gave himself a good vantage point. Come, maybe he reserved a spot for us."

Walter followed his good-father patiently, willing for the moment to forego his usual comments about the Count's servility to the Duke. It was really the only aspect of Alain's personality that he had objected to. Often and again he would argue that a man of Alain's rank should bear himself with more self-respect, but always the Count shrugged off his words with a sheepish smile. The last time it came up, Alain had finally admitted that he was in awe of the Duke, and couldn't seem to help himself. Though he didn't like it, Walter had to accept his honest answer. And it was true that a respectful deference flattered William, so that he was inclined to favor his Breton friend.

Duke William turned at Alain's approach with a genuine smile of welcome. "I'm glad you are here," he said. "So what do you think of all this?" He waved his arm to encompass the whole scene. "The best muster I have ever commanded. Six hundred and ninety-six ships I will have counted, including your thirty; you are the last come, except for a few stragglers." He smiled again.

"Of course," he added in a lower voice, bending to Alain's ear, "I hope you brought a few men. You are singularly alone, except for your fine good-son."

Alain laughed. "Three thousand are coming. I hope you have room for them."

"That space is waiting for you," he said, pointing to a generous area near his own pavilion. Alain had guessed correctly; there was a large area set aside that could easily accommodate all his men. William had obviously hoped for generous support from Brittany, and in this he was not disappointed.

"Of course, we may be here a while. Since two days gone, the wind had been blowing from the north. It shows little sign of changing as yet." He paused in thought, his keen grey eyes on the horizon.

"Right now, Alain, my primary concern is feeding the troops, while we wait for the wind to change. Remember...there will be absolutely no pillaging of my land between times. Any man caught stealing, burning, or otherwise causing trouble will be hanged. No exceptions. I will absorb the cost of feeding the troops.

"You will make sure your men understand?" His eyes glittered, and the Duke seemed to grow taller, more threatening. Then he smiled, putting an arm around the Count's shoulders, and drew him to the table, explaining his work. It was though a cloud had passed.

Finding himself dismissed, Walter went to prepare the camp as best as he could.

It took the whole next day for Brittany's contingent to settle. The air was filled with hammering and shouting, as neighboring soldiers came over to investigate. No one expected to be there long, so they viewed their stay as a holiday. By evening, campfires were set, glowing cheerfully against the faces of those who eagerly bent over pots of soup.

Once his chores were finished, Walter went to look at the fleet.

Compared to what he saw of Thorfinn's ships, these were a sorry imitation. They were constructed in the same manner, that being the only style of ship-building known in this part of the world. But unlike the sleek longships, these were wider, more cumbersome. Even the largest, which he guessed to be about seventy feet, was only half the size of Thorfinn's own ship. They were single-masted open boats, and most of them ranged about forty-five to fifty-five feet long, though some were as small as thirty feet; the average ship had nine or ten pairs of oars.

Walter guessed that the ships without oars would carry the horses, relying totally on the wind to carry them to England. No wonder William was so worried. Of course one couldn't fit both horses and oarsmen on the same narrow vessel. Many had a smaller boat tied behind them, to carry supplies.

Near William's pavilion rested a beautiful ship with the name *Mora* painted along its side; a checkered sail gracefully fluttered in the breeze. Its prow bore a boy made of gold, blowing an ivory horn. Someone told Walter the ship was a gift from William's wife Matilda.

One of the more interesting sights was the group of carpenters, hammering and shaving away on the beach. Closer observation showed that they were constructing prefabricated fortresses, to be thrown up within hours of landing.

He couldn't deny it to himself; Walter was impressed with William's efficiency.

Wandering through the encampment, Walter discovered that much of the army was composed of mercenaries. There were several younger sons, hoping to make their fortune in England. Many of the men fought under no banner; some spoke an unknown language.

In the days that followed, Walter identified some of the Normans that composed William's army. Here by the riverside was William Fitz-Osbern, the Duke's closest friend. He was the first to make the great pledge of ships; in fact, he was the man who tricked the other Normans into following his lead. His camp was in constant motion, alongside his sixty ships.

Over there was Roger of Montgomery with sixty more vessels. Another sixty were brought by Roger of Beaumont; next to him were the sixty ships of Hugh of Avranches, the future Earl of Chester. Nestled in the hills was the contingent of Hugh of Monfort, with his sixty knights; there was no mistaking his own fifty ships.

Walter Giffard, the Lord of Longueville was there, the elderly knight who presented William with his gallant Spanish stallion. His pledge was thirty ships and a hundred knights.

By far the largest showing was Count Robert of Mortain, William's younger brother, who brought one hundred and twenty ships. It was said that William greeted him with a truly magnificent feast.

But the most ostentatious display was that of Odo, the Bishop of Bayeux, William's powerful younger brother; his contribution was a hundred ships, hung with blue sails of the finest silk. This was the man destined to instill a hatred in the English hearts exceeding even that for William himself, so brutal and cruel were his methods. He was most admirably suited for the Duke's purposes, having earned the reputation of a formidable mace fighter. This was the one weapon his religious vows would allow, considering that it was outside the restrictions forbidding him to draw blood by sword or spear.

Walter considered himself lucky to have identified so many important Normans; but his knowledge was spotty, and he finally gave up trying to count them all. He wondered if Harold would command such a formidable array.

A few nights later, Alain came to bed with such a smug look on his face that Walter sat up, intrigued. Snickering to himself, the Count enjoyed his companion's curiosity, until the other lay back, showing signs of boredom. Laying down, pulling his blanket tight underneath his beard, Alain said, "Ah, yes, my boy, I did hear some news this day. It concerns my old enemy Conan...remember him? The one who threatened to raid Normandy, once William left for England? Well, it seems that his life came to a sudden end, this week past."

"Dead?" Walter said in a low voice. "How convenient."

"Well, yes. He was making an entry into the fortress of Chateau-Gontier, which had just capitulated to his siege, when he fell off his horse, a corpse."

"Poisoned!" the other said, a bit louder.

"Shhh! Not so loud. In fact, it is already rumored that an envoy smeared his gloves and bridle with poison. It was only a matter of raising his hand to his mouth."

Walter let out a breath. "I like this not."

"I liked *him* not, I assure you. It was well done, no matter who ordered it. But I saw William's eye, as the tale was told. He looks much less nervous now that Conan's threat is gone."

"I would imagine so."

"Can you blame him for appreciating the loss of an enemy? Come now."

"No. I merely scorn the method."

"Walter, it will never be proven. Grow up, boy. There is much at stake here."

"This game of conquering and duplicity does not sit well on my stomach. But you are right. I must accept things for what they are. But must you be so happy about it?"

"Why not?" Alain scratched his beard. "I benefit, without carrying the weight of a crime on my soul. I do not disapprove of this act. If Conan were smarter, he wouldn't have given himself away like that. He has only himself to blame."

"Had," Walter said. "Good night, father. I've had enough to think on for one night."

"Good night," the other murmured. "Perhaps you think too much as it is." Walter didn't answer, but Alain didn't really expect him to, anyway.

The south wind delayed so long, that even the seamen exclaimed of it. It was a bad omen, and William was hard put to keep a good face about it. One month passed thus, before there was a suggestion of change.

It was an exciting day when the flag was found flying the opposite way.

William gave the order to board, which was met by hearty cheers. Then began a scrambling, frenzied race to see who could embark first. Ships were brought right to the shore, so the horses could leap over the short sides. Two days' rations were quickly packed, and lumber was loaded into the little boats tied behind the big ones.

Men brought only the weapons they could carry: axes, swords, bows, maces, javelins, spears, slings. No siege weapons would accompany the army.

It was September the twelfth, 1066. By late afternoon the army was boarded without a bit of trouble.

The whole day had been blessed with a steady northbound breeze. The sun was bright, making the sea sparkle with thousands of glistening caps on the water. Unencumbered by horses, William's *Mora* started ahead of the rest, the golden boy pointing directly at England.

Walter leaned on the side of the ship, looking eagerly forward. He and Alain were on a medium sized vessel, carrying horses like the majority of the others. His mind wasn't filled with the glories of battle, or the plunder they were promised. He had fought alongside Harold's finest housecarls, and experienced the stubborn resistance of the shield wall. Walter knew what they were up against.

His thoughts were on none of these things, except in passing. Walter was picturing his beloved Scotland, which was coming closer every minute.

The hours passed thus, in peace, when after sundown they spotted threatening clouds to the west. The Normans were not used to the sea; they were out of their element. Land was not in sight, and few knew what monsters lurked in the vast ocean. Many among them who would welcome their end in battle felt a terrible fear of drowning; most never learned how to swim.

The grumbling became frantic as the wind rose. They tied down what they could, but the horses were another problem; the animals were picking up their nervousness, stomping the decks, shifting their weight. As the wind began to pitch the boats, the horses began to rear, pulling at their leads.

The clouds came in fast and thick, blocking out the stars. Walter suspected that the helmsman was having a difficult time, and moved to help him at the side rudder. There were no oars on this vessel and the large square sail was not designed to be used crosswise against the wind.

The first stinging drops of rain were coming down, fast. Alain ordered the men to start bailing.

Already, Walter had to shout at the helmsman to be heard. He could see the man's neck muscles straining, and his knuckles gripping the helm. The man was staring ahead, unseeing, until Walter shook him hard by the shoulders. Slowly he turned dull eyes to the sky.

"Never sailed this far from land before," he finally said loud enough for Walter to hear. "I don't know what to do. Can't see the stars."

Walter straightened up; already they were losing track of the other ships. The waves were becoming dangerously high. "Then you must steer eastward with the wind. We'll find land again, and take shelter in some harbor."

With the mention of land, the man perked up. "Right," he said, shaking water from his eyes. "We have no other choice. Take the ropes on the sail, and bring it around a bit. The wind will bite, drawing us quickly home."

Hoping that the man had a good grip on himself, Walter grabbed a rope, pulling slowly, learning as he went along. The rain had already drenched his clothing; the shrieking of the horses and the shouting men grated on his nerves. But shortly, the wind filled the sail, and he could feel the tug of the ship to the east. Filled with relief, he strained his eyes to where he hoped to see the shore.

It seemed to take forever, with the screaming wind in his ears, and the stinging rain against his head, before Walter made out a darker line in the distance. He shouted to the helmsman, who nodded his response. They continued north along the coast, searching for some kind of harbor, frustrated at their nearness. They knew the danger in coming too close, where hidden reefs could destroy all hopes of safety.

Walter was glad that Alain and the others were busy bailing. More than once, he spotted a tell-tale white sail, sticking up crookedly from the water, where some other ship was less fortunate than they. He wondered how many others were lost.

Ahead, they finally spotted a harbor and made for it, exhausted and trembling but grateful. The gusts were beginning to diminish when they slipped into the natural harbor in what proved to be the river Somme, at St. Valery. Walter could see that other ships had made it ahead of them.

They were on land belonging to William's vassal, Guy of Ponthieu, the very man from whom William rescued Harold Godwineson.

The following morning, when the storm died, the wind began to blow from the north.

Duke William was relieved to see Alain safe, and Walter even fancied tears in the Duke's eyes at this happy reunion. "I feared for your life," he said, taking the Count by the shoulders. "My heart nearly failed me when I saw so many ships go down."

"Ah, my Lord, I imagine it won't turn out as bad as it seems now," said Alain, flattered. "At least you are in one piece. Without you, all would surely be finished. You are the heart and soul of our venture."

"Indeed, Alain." William pulled Alain forward a couple of steps, still looking at the ground. "I am the expedition. They went because of me. And now that we have suffered adversity, will I lose as many from desertion as I have from accident?"

As the day stretched on, more ships that had sheltered in less satisfactory spots found his harbor. William sent messengers up and down the coast on horseback, searching for other survivors.

Activity seemed the best cure for the Duke's discouragement. He appointed men to pray under Bishop Odo's direction in St. Valery's minster day and night, imploring God to change the wind in their favor. He sent crews far and wide to purchase provisions. He gave secret instructions to bury the dead, washed ashore from the storm.

Every day William could be seen mixing with his men, spreading enthusiasm. He increased their food rations. When he wanted to, the Duke could be the most charming man around; his manners were perfect, his words inscrutable, and his compliments ready. When not among the ranks, the inexhaustible man was praying in the minster. His only betrayal of doubt was the constant turn of his eye to the weathercock atop the tower, and the momentary droop of his shoulders at its unwavering direction.

One day a jongleur came to call on William, offering to tell his fortune. Bored, William obliged. The man stood before him, bells jingling from a parti-colored hat, and started with a few ordinary juggling tricks, but the Duke shook his head impatiently.

"Come now," he said, "what's this about my fortune?"

"Ah." The man dropped a pile of twigs at his feet. "From what this configuration tells me, you shall conquer England without a blow. Harold will come and bow to you as his rightful sovereign."

"Take this man off, give him a good meal, nothing more," William said to his attendant, turning his back on the man. When his brother Robert questioned him on his abruptness, he said, "No one knows Harold more than myself. I say to you, he will fight until there is no more blood in his veins. I need no one giving me false hopes."

More to his liking was his own personal jongleur, Taillefer. This strange little man, almost too serious for one of his profession, thought of himself as more than an entertainer. He always seemed to know when and where he was most needed. Witty comments were interspersed so cleverly that they unfailingly managed to break the tension.

Taillefer worked almost constantly; when he wasn't near the Duke, he could be found mingling with the army: juggling here, singing there. He was followed by smiles wherever he went, and succeeded in raising spirits even where William failed.

Notwithstanding the ongoing prayers, fifteen days passed. It was clearly the end of summer; despite William's encouragement, men were grumbling that the invasion was at an end. Everyone knew there wouldn't be the resources to launch another.

Duke William was desperate. In a last effort to attract God's favor, he begged the Abbot and monks of St. Valery to bring out the sacred bones of their holy patron.

The next morning, William's army lined up, expectantly awaiting the holy ceremony. A long carpet was laid on the ground. To the hopeful ears of the army came the soothing, droning chant of the monks. A magnificent procession appeared, in the midst of which glowed the golden shrine of the saint; it even seemed to have an inner light about it.

The shrine was placed on the carpet amidst a hush. As if with one mind, all of William's host fell to their knees, praying fervently to St. Valery to intercede in their behalf and bring the south wind they needed to complete the holy campaign. One by one they showered the shrine with golden coins, until soon both the carpet and its treasure were buried beneath the generous offerings.

As though their prayers were heard, the wind changed in the middle of the night. The early dawn broke with the weather-cock pointing in the opposite direction.

It was the morning of September the twenty-seventh, two days after Harold won the battle of Stamford Bridge; though William knew naught of that.

21

Pevensey

Alain and Walter were just stirring when they heard the shouts. A moment later, the door of their pavilion parted; William stood tensely in the opening.

"It is time!" he said. "The wind has changed. Alain, you and Walter come on my ship today. We will not be separated like the last time."

In a moment he was gone. The Count was all smiles at his new privilege.

They stepped from the tent, watching the Duke walk arm in arm with Bishop Odo toward the minster. Alain turned to Walter. "What do you think of the good Duke now?"

Walter shrugged his shoulders. "I will admit to some grudging admiration. He carried this thing off with the strength of his will."

Alain was satisfied with this admission, and exhorted Walter to hurry.

The camp was an immediate frenzy of activity. Even more than the last time, everyone was worried about losing the wind. Men harnessed themselves to carts and wagons, in their impatience to load. They were singing and calling to each other, shouting at the horses to get them aboard. Tripping over each other in their haste, they left much behind. The only essentials seemed to be the casks of red wine, which were loaded first.

By late afternoon, the fleet was ready as William's *Mora* led the crossing of the English Channel. The Duke told the pilots to keep a light burning on their ship come evening and follow William's beacon, a lantern hung from the top of his mast, to make sure they kept together.

Everyone's eyes were forward, and morale was high. Come late evening, one by one the crew fell into a slight doze. Walter kept watch for a long time, but the pilot tapped him on the shoulder, assuring him it was all right to rest. He immediately fell asleep where he sat.

At dawn, a cry from above brought Walter quickly to his feet. He looked at the top of the mast, where a man was leaning dangerously away from his support, straining to search the sea behind their ship. Walter looked in the same direction, jolted by a frightful sense of aloneness; there was nothing to be seen but empty water.

The pilot was looking up from the foot of the mast, querying the lookout, when William's gruff voice made him jump.

"What is the meaning of this?"

The man turned, nervously. "My Lord, we have not spotted the others."

"I can see that much for myself. Where are they, in God's name?"

Trembling, the pilot did not dare an answer. Spinning on his heel, William gestured impatiently for his men to go back to work.

Odo moved worriedly toward the Duke as his servants set up a table. "What are you going to do?" he asked, breathing the question no one else dared.

"Why, eat breakfast of course. Order them to drop anchor and lower the sail. Come, join me, Alain, and you, Fitz-Osbern!" he called loudly. "I'm told we have a splendid breakfast prepared for us. Let us not waste it."

Alain, who was talking to Walter, shrugged, then smiled at the apparent joviality in the Duke's tone. A handful of men sat about William's little table, awkwardly passing food no one wanted to eat, and not daring to speak. Finally, William forced a smile. "She is a fine ship, don't you think, Odo?"

The Bishop swallowed a large mouthful. "Splendid, splendid. I have been meaning to ask you from whence it came."

Everyone knew the answer, but William was relieved to break

the tension. He leaned forward, as though to stress a point. "Even the sails were hand-sewn by my wife, Matilda. Indeed, she presented the whole ship to me as a present, complete with the finest hand-picked crew."

As the listeners murmured their appreciation, William turned aside and whispered in a low voice to a sailor, who climbed up for another view. They pretended not to notice this subtle betrayal of nervousness.

Finally, halfway through their meal, the lookout shouted that he saw four sails on the horizon.

"Good work," William called up. "Keep searching. I doubt not that we will be rewarded."

And so it was. In another half hour the man called out that there were so many masts, they looked like "a forest upon the waves."

William stood up from the table, declaring his thanks to God for their deliverance. When the sailor came down from his post, he was rewarded with a gold coin.

"I almost feared we were the ones who were lost, and the others on their right path," the Duke said, in Alain's ear.

It was only then, that the pilot was pulled aside, and reprimanded so colorfully that his face turned red.

William ordered the sailors to unfurl his great checkered sail, and proudly led the way to England. Hence, around nine o'clock in the morning of Saint Michael's Eve, the Norman fleet came into sight of the bay at Pevensey.

Knowing Harold's thoroughness, William fully expected this spot to be defended. As they neared the coast, everyone stood in breathless anticipation of a roaring Saxon army, willing to defend the land with their life's blood. What they saw instead was an empty beach. Not a single human voice was raised in challenge; only the screaming of sea gulls announced their presence.

"Where is everyone?" came the often repeated question

among the ships.

For a brief time, William wondered if the Saxons had set a trap. But he knew Harold too well for that. "It is not his way," the Duke declared finally. "He is not here. The Lord God is on our side."

Men quickly donned their hauberks, and readied the horses for the difficult leap from ship to land. Weapons were tested, ships run ashore, masts were lowered. The Normans waited for William's ceremonious disembarkation.

The first armed man to touch English soil, William confidently leaped from his ship. Perhaps he should have judged the distance more carefully, or maybe he was simply too sure of himself; but as soon as his foot touched shore, it slipped from under him and he pitched forward, landing on his hands.

A horrified gasp took the watching army. Men crossed themselves, crying out that it was a bad omen.

But William quickly recovered his footing—and his wit. Grabbing two fistfuls of sand, he held them up, crying, "By the splendor of God, I have taken seizen of my kingdom. The earth of England is in my two hands."

As everyone let out their breath, the relief was audible. Of course: the new lord would take seizen of his property. Leave it to the Duke to turn a disaster into good fortune.

As the tension broke, the archers were first to leap from the ships. Carefully, they surveyed the immediate hiding places in town, to pick off potential ambush. But it seemed that the townspeople, at least, had either fled or hid themselves away.

Next off were the knights, encouraging the destriers to leap from the boats. Once the animals were ashore, they mounted, taking formation and making a wide sweep of the area. These, too, reported no activity.

Finally the rest disembarked, pulling the ships onto the sand. William immediately ordered a crew to begin digging a ditch, for the creation of a hill on which to build his first prefabricated fortress.

It was discovered that only two ships had been lost during the crossing. One of them carried the fortune teller who so displeased Duke William. He looked wryly at his brother.

"Some soothsayer that was, who couldn't even predict the time or manner of his own death. Take that as a lesson, my friends, not to believe such agents."

The men didn't have far to go to forage their first meal; they rounded up all the livestock abandoned by the locals. While William explored the vicinity with a small attachment of twenty-six picked men, the rest prepared a happy celebration.

Before long, the scouting party returned on foot, cursing and leading their horses by the reins; sheepishly, they nodded at the good-natured laughter that greeted their appearance. It was noted that the Duke was carrying on his shoulder the chain maille hauberk of Fitz-Osbern, as well as wearing his own.

It seemed that the surrounding land was either too marshy or too rough to support a cavalry. There was only one main road leading from Pevensey, which was not enough to support an army. Nor was there enough food to last more than a couple of days. The men grumbled at the unwelcome message that they would have to move on the morrow.

William's main concern was with the activities of Harold. A few local captives told him all they knew: King Harold had waited all summer for William, then suddenly hurried with his army to the north.

William listened carefully, nodding. Then he turned to his followers. "I think it is time we showed Harold we are here."

The next morning his army began to move forth from Pevensey. The cavalry took the thirty mile track through the marsh, two abreast, eastward around the harbor. The infantry was ferried across the bay, walking ten miles to Hastings along the coast. William loaded the equipment and supplies onto a few ships, including his own *Mora,* to make the crossing by water;

these went farther out from the shore. He didn't want to make another difficult landing with his whole army, and thought that if he split his force at this stage, they would manage without danger.

He was only too right; only the Saxons suffered damage. The Normans left widespread devastation in their wake. Towns and farms were burned, livestock taken; the destruction was systematic and thorough. William reckoned that Harold could not stand by and watch his precious England succumb to the invader, piece by piece. Perhaps he could be lured south before he was ready.

The ships were the first to reach the town of Hastings. It was as deserted as the other town. Wasting no time, the workmen disembarked with their supplies, and immediately began erecting another fortress.

It was in the midst of this activity that a letter reached William, dispatched by a Norman named Robert, known as the son of Wymarc, one of Edward's close advisors.

"Listen to this, Alain," said William, his jaw jutting out in displeasure. "The coward tells me to turn back, since Harold is returning triumphantly with a hundred thousand men from his victory at Stamford Bridge. They are in Northumbria, I believe. It seems that he killed both Harald Hardraada and his brother, Tostig.

"Quite a victory," he added to himself. "This Robert tells me that we can't match the power or numbers of the English army. To meet them in battle would lead to our certain destruction.

"Some help he is, my kinsman." William tore the letter angrily. "I refuse to believe him. Harold must have lost many men at that battle. If he rushes south, he will lose many more.

"Alain," he added decisively, turning to his friend, "pen a letter for me, will you? You script is so much better than mine."

Alain bowed, moved to get parchment and quill.

"Tell this Robert that I thank him for his interest," William said, ironically emphasizing the last word, "but if I only had ten thousand men the quality of my own sixty thousand..."

Alain looked up questioningly.

"Yes," William said, "why not exaggerate a bit? If I had only ten thousand, I would still not draw back. I came to claim my crown, and by God's splendor, I shall not hesitate until I have it. Tell him also for me, Alain, that he were better off not degrading the Norman might. That sort of kindness does not sit well with such as myself. Fill in the details, Alain."

By October the fifth, Harold had made his marathon forced march the two hundred miles from York to London. Exhausted, wounded, emotionally drained, the King relished at least a few days' pause while waiting for fresh levies to come in.

William, however, wasted no time. He sent his first message to Harold, reminding him of Edward's choice for the succession—himself—and of Harold's oath. Bring the case before judges of either England or Normandy, he suggested, and they should all be satisfied with the results. Or, failing that, William challenged Harold to single combat to decide the matter.

The King of England was incensed at the suggestions. Nonetheless, he calmly wrote back that Edward's final choice from his death bed had been Harold. This superseded any promise he might have made to William in his lifetime. Moreover, the Witan, which was the highest authority in the land, had already decided in Harold's favor. He requested that William leave the country, or else friendly relations between their two people would be broken forever.

"Enough is enough!" Duke William cried, exasperated. "Odo, the time has come to inform Harold of the Pope's excommunication."

Everyone within hearing took a deep breath, crossing themselves. That dreaded word carried with it the fires of hell for the person to whom it was directed, and for anyone who had converse of any kind with the damned. Harold and his whole army were already under the interdict. It only remained for them to be told.

It was a week before Harold started his rapid descent from London. He waited futilely for the promised troops from the north, the very men he had just defended. Losing patience, he decided to move forward and let them follow as they might. He had already chosen the spot where he would make a stand, and detached a work group to start ahead of the rest of his army.

William made his scout repeat the message once more in front of Alain.

"The Saxons are building a wooden palisade along the base of Senlac Hill," the man said with bent head, "which is by the ancient hoary apple tree. As far as I can tell, this hill lies directly in your path to London. Given all the marsh in the surrounding area, he will be impossible to circumvent."

"That is not our problem," said William to Alain, as he dismissed the scout with a curt nod. "I do not want to avoid Harold, but neither did I want to fight him on land of his choosing. The wily fox intends to force me to come to him. And fight uphill. Ah, Alain, I get my just deserts for underestimating him. I never expected such speed."

"But my Lord," insisted the Count. "You couldn't have moved on London without distancing yourself too far from your ships. You might have cut yourself off from any possibility of retreat."

"There will be no retreat from this campaign! It is all or nothing, don't you understand?" William turned on Alain, fire in his eyes, but the Count for once refused to flinch.

"I'm sorry," he said finally, turning away. "I take out my frustrations on the people who understand me the most. You are right. I somehow thought I could lure him to us...but I was wrong. Well, we must make the best of it. What's done, is done. We shall move tomorrow. Perhaps we can make him quail at the sight of our horses. He knows the might of my cavalry, even though his stubborn countrymen do not. Yet."

And so it was that the army moved to barely within sight of Senlac Hill on Friday, October the thirteenth, just as Harold's army was making camp. Spies were sent out by both parties, and the story was later told of the man who informed Harold that the Norman army was composed mostly of monks. Knowing the peculiar haircuts the Normans preferred, Harold had laughed. He told the man that he would find the monks to be of a particularly formidable breed.

Late that night, Walter volunteered for watch duty. His companions were busy composing themselves for prayer and confession, an activity he was singularly uninterested in. From across the marsh, he could barely hear snatches of singing and laughing; and for that night at least, Walter wished himself among the Saxons.

His heart ached when he thought of his dear friends Thomas and Edmund, somewhere within that glow of firelight. Sending a prayer to the goddess Don, Walter begged not to be forced to face his friends on the battle field.

As the night drew on and the prayers of the Normans began to cease, Walter stiffened as he heard the sounds of footsteps coming from the Saxon army. He stepped behind a tree, sword in hand, when he recognized the voice of Harold himself.

The King of the English was accompanied by another man Walter did not recognize. Hesitating for a moment, Walter decided to follow the pair until he could form a cohesive plan in his mind. He matched their footsteps with his own.

His betrayal of Harold four years ago had always tugged at his conscience, no matter how he tried to rationalize it. And suddenly, the opportunity to make peace with his old chief rose like a specter before him. Despite himself, his whole body trembled while he frantically decided how to present himself.

Harold and his companion stopped, in full view of the army;

Walter crouched in the darkness, nerves on end, picking up all the sounds around him except for their whispering. Finally, after a long time, they turned to leave, passing the concealed spy by only a few feet.

"Perhaps you were right, Gyrth, after all," Harold was saying. "Seeing this Norman army sends shivers down my spine. I never would have expected William to bring so many horses with him. I tell you...his knights are more powerful than you could imagine."

"And what of it," the other said impatiently. "We must fight them with whatever we have."

"But I wonder," Harold said slowly, "maybe we should retreat back to London, and await Eadwine and Morcar. They should be here any day."

"Retreat back to London! I don't believe my ears." They stopped, glaring at each other. "After all my arguments for you to stay there and for me to carry on instead, since I haven't been cursed with this damned oath...And you insisted on leading the army, not listening to a word I said. Now you want to turn back? Never for the world. They will call you a coward till this island sinks into the ocean."

Gyrth turned back to the Norman army. "No, my brother, you have made your decision, and now we must abide by it."

Walter decided that this was his moment, and stepped out, allowing himself to be seen. Harold's companion noticed him first, and leaped between the intruder and the King, drawing his sword. Walter didn't move.

In a moment, Harold recognized his old captain. He placed a hand on the other's arm, saying "Wait" and moved forward.

"Walter. I never thanked you from extricating me from that dreadful room."

Embarrassed, Walter shrugged that statement off. For a moment he couldn't find his voice. Gyrth, enraged, started forward again, but was waved back imperiously.

"Harold," Walter began. "About Rhuddlan..."

"I know. It no longer matters. It was my own pride that I must blame, not you. I was punished for thinking that, out of love for me, men would turn against their own blood kin. I do not hold you at fault."

Walter sighed. "I am at fault, then, for not expecting you to understand." He paused. "Know then, Harold, that I fight here for my good-father, Count Alain le Roux, because I cannot refuse him, rather than for the cause of William. I care naught for him."

For a moment, Harold looked lost in thought. Then he spoke. "For this I forgive you. I have made my confession; I will not stain my soul by a last unworthy thought.

"One boon alone, I ask: if you survive the battle, make sure that Thomas is not left wounded on the field. I have treated him wrongly in the Welsh matter. In my smallness, I could not bring myself to absolve him of guilt."

Walter bowed. "And in turn, I swear not to mention this meeting to anyone. In this we are finally even."

Seething at Harold's side, Gyrth could not contain himself any longer. He grabbed Harold's arm.

"What nonsense is this? Kill the man, before he brings the others upon us."

"Silence!" commanded Harold, turning an angry look on his companion. "Remember, that though you are my brother, I am still your King! This man had given me his word. Had I extracted it from him on another occasion, much else might have turned out differently. Come. We are off."

Without another word, the two brothers disappeared into the night.

Mentally exhausted, Walter leaned against a tree. Harold had forgiven him. And tomorrow, he was fighting against him.

Not so sure he was on the right side, Walter cursed the forces that brought him to this pass.

There was no rest for him that night.

The following day began cloudless and cool, the perfect weather for a battle. Duke William received communion in full view of the army; then, after a good breakfast, he summoned his men for the usual speech.

"Normans, Bretons, French, and all the others who have joined this holy pilgrimage, now is our day, when God had called us to defeat our unworthy adversary. This Harold, who is forsworn, excommunicated!

"As you all know, we have been graced with uncommon good fortune. We have crossed the channel unhindered, and landed unchallenged. But now we are faced with great battle, which will finally determine our future on this soil. Know you there is no turning back! Your honor and safety are in your own hands.

"But see you: this is a sacred endeavor, blessed by the Pope himself. We will not fail. So go forth, smite our enemies, spare no man in their hostile ranks. And when we are done, our exploits will be celebrated from one end of the earth to the other, for all time!"

With that, the Norman host broke up, leaving William surrounded by his captains. "The left division, composed of men from Brittany, Maine, and Anjou, is to be commanded by Count Alain le Roux," he said. These were most untried of his army, so they were given the mildest ascent.

"The right wing will be led by Count Eustace of Boulogne, composed of the French and Flemish troops," he added. "Bishop Odo will command the center, alongside myself, leading the Norman knights.

"The first line of our army will be the archers, the second line, the infantry, and behind them, the three thousand cavalry."

He searched their ranks, looking at these men he trusted with his future. "Ralph de Conches," the Duke called, "do you claim your hereditary right to bear my gonfanon?" The talking lessened for a moment as the valiant knight shouldered his way forward and knelt before his chief.

"My Lord, please forgive me, but I respectfully decline this honor. Today I declare that I must keep my hands unencumbered, even by the standard of the holy Apostle, so that I may smite your enemies with all my power."

William looked disturbed, but could not fault such a sentiment. The honor of carrying the standard was fraught with much personal danger, as well as lacking the singular pleasure of unhindered warfare. With a thought, he called for Walter Giffard, the man who gave him his valiant steed. Again, the others stepped aside, as a proud, white-haired man appeared, carrying his helm in the crook of an arm.

"My Lord," he said slowly, "I am an old man, and cherish the thought of wielding my sword in what may be my last battle. The honor of carrying the banner deserves to be filled by someone younger and stronger than myself."

Nodding in reluctant acquiescence, William turned irritably to the others. "By my hilt, will no man carry my standard, then?"

Giffard cleared his throat. "I believe," he answered, his rich voice filling the silence, "if you would permit, that a kinsman of mine, Toustain Fitzrou le Blanc, will not cause you shame." A perk young man detached himself from the others, coming to kneel at the Duke's feet.

"By the rood, he seems gallant enough," William said, mollified. He grasped the youth by the hand and raised him up, as everyone sighed with relief. The Duke turned as his squire brought up his beautiful white horse, and stroked it affectionately on the neck.

Just then his last scout rode up, panting. "We have seen the Royal standards in the midst of the enemy," he said, breathless. "One was the Dragon of Wessex; the other was Harold's Fighting Man. They are in the very center of the ranks, where the King's housecarls are the thickest."

"Why, the fool seeks to determine the future of his country in one single battle," exclaimed William, looking at those around him. "By the grace of God," he knelt, "I do vow to erect a holy abbey on the very spot where those banners fly, if He but grant me victory this day."

Moved, William's companions knelt also, mumbling a prayer.

Crossing himself, William got up, turning to put on his hauberk. In his hurry, he accidentally donned it backwards. Seeing the error, the nearest man gasped. The sound drew the others' attention, and they burst into a worried groan, declaring it another bad omen.

But the Duke was just as quick as before with a response.

"Can't you see, my Lords," he cried. "With this action, you see your Duke changed into a King."

A general agreement eased the tension, as they broke away to their own men. Finishing his armament, William lifted a curious talisman on a leather thong. He looked it for a long moment, then kissed it and pulled the cord over his head. It was a loving gesture, for truly Duke William felt that God was on his side; from his neck hung the finger bone of a saint over which Harold had made his fateful oath.

22

The Field of Hastings

William sat astride his destrier, helmet on, iron shafted mace in hand. Above his head floated the consecrated gonfanon of the Pope, alongside his own standard. He surveyed the difficult line of attack.

Harold had indeed chosen his spot well; the army was spread across the summit of a hill perfectly suited for his somewhat reduced numbers. They were ten or twelve ranks deep, all on foot. Both of Harold's flanks were impassable. To the west was a ravine, cut by a small stream and banked with mushy ground; to the east, the incline was precipitously steep.

Their post was purely defensive. The Saxons could not move from their firmly entrenched spot. William nodded to himself. His own mobile force could attack in waves, allowing them alternate periods of rest, while the solid English line would be forced to defend themselves almost continually. It was only a matter of wearing them down.

However, Harold did have a distinct advantage on his side. With tremendous energy, the Saxons had erected a wall that effectively enclosed them in a fortress. There were only three openings in the otherwise solid wall, to allow for possible forays. Charging uphill into a wooden palisade was no easy task.

The housecarls were concentrated in the middle, directly opposite the Norman division. Both wings were composed of shire levies, less experienced men, grimly clutching their axes and bills, homemade swords and daggers, clubs, rocks tied to a stick for throwing, slings, studded maces, or farm tools; they were crude, but effective enough. Their protection was minimal, but they stood, along with the rest, behind the kite shaped shields, a second line of defense beyond the palisade.

William glanced down as he felt a tug on his stirrup. Standing beside him, brilliantly dressed in parti-color, was his favorite jongleur, Taillefer—Cleaver of Iron—who had kept him amused for so many hours in their long wait across the channel. William's smile faded at the serious look on the minstrel's face.

"I beg a boon of you, my Lord," the man said. William nodded. "The time has come for me to prove my mettle, Sir Duke. Would you permit me the first blow, so that the name of Taillefer shall always be remembered in remembering your own?"

William hesitated, moved by the man's request. "You know what that means," he said, bending low over his horse's neck. "You will never make it back to our protection."

Taillefer made a gay little leap, belying his fears. "Why Sir, what is that, next to immortality?"

Sighing, knowing that he would lose many more of his supporters before the day was over, William gave his consent. He looked at the sun as the jongleur armed himself. It was about three hours before noon.

In moments, Duke William watched his minstrel ride out into the open space between the two armies. He gave the order to be ready for the attack. The archers would go first.

Meanwhile, Taillefer rode forth on his little pony, singing songs of Roland and Charlemagne, to the astonishment of both armies. Spellbound, all watched him give the most momentous performance of his life, throwing his sword in the air and catching it with a practiced whirl.

He rode through an opening in the palisade, rearing his horse theatrically, when suddenly he brought his mount to the ground and charged forward, killing two men before their comrades came to their senses. In a flurry of axes, jongleur and horse went down.

At that moment the cry was given for the Norman archers to advance. In all three divisions, the first line moved into range, planting their feet wide, taking aim and showering the Saxon line with relentless shafts. However, the trajectory was uphill; the arrows did little damage.

Soon, the archers fell back, and the infantry was ordered to attack. Theirs was the most perilous work; in range of javelins and missiles, they had to apply all of their strength, attempting to tear down the stout palisade.

In places they succeeded. Breaking through, holding up their shields, they surged forward to pit themselves against the unmoving Saxon shield wall. Meanwhile, others continued the laborious task at the palisade.

However, the Saxons proved a formidable enemy. Unbeaten in battle, they smote with practiced confidence. Fierce as the attack was, the defense was fiercer, and the infantry was driven back by a combination of blows and well-aimed stones. They gave way to the next wave of attack.

It was the cavalry's turn to try their best. The most awesome fighting men ever seen in England, the ponderous knights gave vent to their impatience, thundering past the infantry in their difficult uphill climb.

They were still hindered by the palisade, though the weaker spots were damaged further by the charging horses. Holding their spears before them, they crashed against the unyielding shield wall, crying their slogans, cursing the enemy.

The Saxons gave not an inch. Horses reared against each other, having no space to turn back. The Saxons were prepared; a well-aimed sweep with the poleaxe could bring down both man and horse in one blow. Unarmored, some of the horses fell on the first charge, pierced by English spears. The steep ascent proved too much for the Normans in their preliminary attempt. They retired in order back to their starting point.

This was more of a probing attack than an all-out assault. William had not committed all of his army to the first thrust, nor had he himself joined in. From his vantage point he was able to gauge the places of most serious resistance, and weakness, of the Saxon line.

William had his answer. Judging from his set expression, the strength of the English was every bit as menacing as he had supposed. With a stern shout, he ordered a second assault.

Once again the archers tried their skill, followed by the infantry. The attack was fiercer this time, their shouts of "God help us" answered by cries of "Out, out!" from the Saxon ranks. Still, they made no headway. Again they fell back, unsuccessful, to make way for the cavalry.

The Breton contingent was divided into three sub-commands: that of Alain, his brother Le Noir, and Walter. They found that the untried levies on the wing resisted as stoutly as the housecarls.

Amazed, Alain determined to break through this second time. With a cry of "A Brittany" the leaders spurred forward, followed by their undeterred troops.

But this time their anxiousness betrayed them. Charging through the infantry, no one in the rush, from commander to rear horseman, noticed that in their gentler ascent they had greatly outdistanced the Norman contingent to their right.

Intent on their immediate targets, the Bretons crashed into the shield wall again, meeting with a fiercer resistance than before. Heavy missiles flew at them, meeting their marks with a deadly thud. Sturdy Englishmen met their swords with sweeping axes, cleaving through blades and limbs.

Screaming horses lashed out in pain; men plunged through the shields only to be thrust forth again or pulled from their horses. All mingled in a chaotic roar. Slipping on fresh spilled blood, tripping over writhing bodies, the well-organized line broke into scattered tangles.

Suddenly the foremost knights realized that their right flank was undefended. A few men drew back in confusion, yelling their dismay.

From one man to the next, the word spread that they were unprotected. Bewildered, wanting only to get away from the onslaught, the inexperienced riders reined off, intent on a moment's reprieve.

Walter felled a man with his sword, and looked up to see men pulling away. Jerking his horse's head around, he dashed through the pandemonium, yelling for them to turn and fight. Slapping men with the flat of his blade, he cursed, admonished, threatened, but to no avail.

Like an avalanche the retreat gained in momentum, until all the men, losing their heads, shot away from the fighting. In short order they overran the infantry. They passed the Norman line, still struggling forward, spreading terror through their ranks as well.

Some of the Bretons found themselves in worse shape than ever; stumbling into the mire on the edge of the field, their desperate scrambling rooted them even deeper. Many tumbled into the ravine, pushed by their companions who couldn't stop soon enough. Terrified horses kicked their riders senseless.

Walter found himself beside Le Noir at the rear of the retreat. They did not give up; grabbing men by the shoulders and jerking them around, they finally managed to force a small group to turn back. But it was not enough; from the midst of the confusion came the rumor that Duke William was dead. The battle was over.

Progress came to a halt as the few men milled around in confusion. Walter spotted Alain and rode toward him, leaving Le Noir to make some sense of the commotion. Between them, they shouted some sort of order into those within hearing. The best they could do was halt the retreat.

But a new clamor came to their ears. Turning, Count Alain saw that a group of Saxons were breaking ranks, itching to turn the retreat into a slaughter. Forgetting the safety of the shield wall, they came streaming down the hill.

At the same time Alain heard an even more familiar voice. The Duke spurred directly toward them, helmet off, thrusting at the recreants with a spear. "Madmen!" he shouted at the Bretons.

"Behold me. Are you insane? Your retreat means death. Victory lies ahead. See you, cowards! Your Duke is before you!"

William struck more fear into the Bretons than the Saxons did. Turning toward the English, even the most fearful saw the charging men, and they were struck by their opportunity. Yelling their battle cries, the Bretons dashed back into action.

Gathering the fleeing Normans, William led them toward the headstrong English, cutting off the sundered warriors from the safety of their army. Seeing their plight, the Saxons gathered atop a little hillock in the midst of their enemies, fighting desperately for their lives. Their gallant stand, back to back, while they fell under the avenging swords of the Bretons, went farther than any other incident toward demoralizing their companions.

Then followed a brief reprieve, during which both sides managed to repair their disordered ranks. Just as expected, William rode up to chastise the unsteady Bretons, who had nearly lost the day. But the anger was gone from his face. Looking steadily at the men who had learned such a bitter lesson, he tried to boost their spirits.

"Well, my lads," he spoke evenly, "there is no need to tell you what you have done. But remember..." he raised his voice, "there is no glory in running from a fight. Even were I killed, I would expect you to continue, if only to maintain your honor. There will be other battles after this one!"

He paused, moving his horse among them. "Perhaps not all bad has come from your panic. See how they mourn their dead on that little hill. Methinks we will try the same ruse again; mayhap you can redeem yourselves. But on my order this time! Not before."

The men cheered, encouraged. William spurred his horse back to the center and gave the order to prepare for another attack.

In ten minutes they moved again. Flowing through the breaches in the palisade, they widened the openings each attack. The Saxons never moved forward to block their way.

This time the Bretons fought valiantly, but the glory in this onslaught went to the Norman division.

In the middle, before the Royal standard, the fighting was the fiercest. William himself was the most apparent, appearing everywhere on his white horse in the midst of the worst exchanges. The pile of bodies was thickest here; making headway on a horse was laborious. William spotted Harold laying about with deadly blows from his poleaxe and surged toward him.

But his movement was checked by a most unexpected attack from Harold's own brother, Gyrth. Seeing the King's plight, the Earl of East Anglia heaved his spear, throwing it with tremendous strength. The shaft pierced the heart of William's gallant steed, and the beast sank, nearly pinning the Duke beneath it.

But a man trained in cavalry fighting must also learn how to clear his fallen mount. Leaping skillfully, the Duke fell heavily on the ground, but regained his feet before anyone had a chance to attack him.

William had not gained his formidable reputation for no reason; he was known to be as deadly on foot as he was on horseback. Shaking the stun from his head, he looked around, searching for his antagonist. With the instinct of a born warrior, he found him; momentarily, the Duke's eyes locked with those of Gyrth.

Inaction was followed by swift reaction. Determined to avenge this insult, William pressed forward. On his right a man attempted to stop him; a sure sweep of the mace crashed into the unfortunate's face, dropping him in his tracks. And still the Duke moved on, seeing that his opponent was waiting for him, sword in hand.

They met with a clash of steel on steel. The force of William's blow would have reduced a lesser man, but Gyrth withstood it, bending slightly at the knees to absorb the shock. He tried to follow his block with a swing to the head, but William easily stopped it.

In anger the Duke swung his mace in a full circle about his head before crashing it into Gyrth's shoulder; the man's grimace betrayed his pain. Staggered, the Earl responded with an ineffectual thrust, but he knew the fight was over. In another moment the war club was brought down in a skull-crushing arc, and the valiant Earl's life force had run out. It was no dishonor to die under the hands of so mighty a foe.

Shortly after, William saw Gyrth's brother, Leofwine, fall under the mace of Bishop Odo. Brothers were killed by brothers. William gained a dark satisfaction in knowing that Harold had witnessed the slaying of his own two siblings.

But action cut short his unworthy thoughts. He was not as comfortable on foot, and disentangled himself from the Saxon crush, looking for a handy horse to borrow. He spotted a likely steed, mounted by some Maine knight whose name he did not know. The Duke called to the man, requesting him to relinquish his horse. Scorning the thought, perhaps not recognizing his sovereign, the man refused.

Already fired by the fighting, William seethed at his abrupt treatment. Striding forward, he struck the man such a blow that the knight fell from the horse. He leaped on the animal's back, leaving the rebel to his own devices.

William was as active as ever, for still he had not taken a major wound. But the same luck did not hold for his mounts. Again, William's horse was killed under him; again he wreaked revenge on his aggressor. This time, Count Eustace offered his own steed, and the Count in turn was given a mount belonging to one of his followers.

Deciding that the charge uphill was in every respect useless, William determined to find a way past the shield wall. He sent a message to Alain instructing him to command a feigned retreat with his whole division. He did not expect them to take long in obeying.

The Duke was not disappointed; shortly afterward, the Bretons took to their heels in a very convincing show of chaos. Forgetting their recent lesson, the inexperienced Saxons charged howling after them, taking nearly a third of their line.

Walter led a portion of the men in a different direction from Alain, scattering the Saxons even further. Then, when he deemed that the pursuers were sufficiently cut off from main army, he shouted for his men to turn.

Reeling their horses in a sudden reversal, the fugitives became the attackers. Realizing their error, the Saxons tried desperately to band together, but many were too late. They were cut down in their momentary bewilderment.

Those in the rear saw the danger; a certain number of them got together on the hill that had already proved so fatal to their fellows. But this time was different. There were more defenders on the hill; they were better armed. Throwing stones and darts, they killed many of the Bretons that were trying, once again, to attack uphill. The Saxons managed to hold the summit.

Other Saxons charged to the hidden ravine, so dangerous to the Bretons in the last incident. They turned on the edge and took a stand, followed by horsemen who hadn't witnessed that fatal scene, so intent had they been on their own flight.

The Bretons tried to careen to a sudden stop, but their horses were not so nimble as men, nor could they halt those charging behind them. Over and over, horse and man toppled into the gully, crushing those underneath them, and being crushed in turn by those coming after. It was said that the corpses filled the ravine until level with the ground.

Walter's men had not moved far; faced with the most defiant Saxons who held their ground, the fighting continued without a break. Clean battle-lines had melted into a surging chaos; individual struggles replaced organized assault.

A burly peasant pulled Walter from his horse while he was

fighting off two other men. The frightened animal reared, chasing off the first two Saxons who otherwise would have finished him in a moment. Walter twisted from the man's grasp, swinging wildly with his sword.

The peasant saw the movement, easily evading the badly-aimed cut. With a heavy club, he struck Walter in the side of the head, sending him reeling against his horse. Grinning, the man took a step forward when his face changed to a grimace of pain and his arms went out. The club fell to the ground, and the Saxon with it, blood spurting from his back.

Walter looked up, stunned. Through a fog he saw Le Noir circling him. "Be more careful, my boy. You were lucky your good Breton helmet saved you."

The knight recovered the reins of Walter's nervous horse, and held them out. Walter took them, but leaned heavily against the charger's neck.

"Get out of the fighting," the other shouted, then was gone, not wanting to miss too much action.

Walter heaved himself onto his mount's back and followed Le Noir's advice. Not until his head cleared did he wonder how he managed to maneuver without harm.

Duke William got what he wanted. With the mad pursuit of the Saxons, the continuity of the shield wall was forever broken. They left a large gap at the top of the hill, and the Normans were quick to take advantage. Charging crosswise before the shield wall, the cavalry reached the summit of the hill for the first time all day.

Now, they merely had to attack eastward into the teeth of Harold's housecarls. The remaining Saxons quickly brought the shield wall around to face the new threat. But the Normans were no longer hindered by that difficult climb; their attacks were more powerful, given the easy footing. The summit, however, was too narrow for all of them; there was still much activity along the slope.

The lack of space on the hilltop also inhibited the movements of the Saxons. No man had the room to make a full swing without stepping out from the safety of the shield wall. It was said that the dead were held up by the living, so tightly wedged were they.

The fighting had gone on for nearly six hours without a stop. William was able to alternate his troops, following archery with infantry with cavalry. Where one tactic was weak, another was strong. The English, however, were forced to stand in one place, frustrated, watching their neighbors die beside them while they were constrained to hold themselves back in a defensive posture. The palisade was almost completely destroyed. The day was evolving in favor of the Normans.

But the outcome was still far from certain. If the Saxons could hold out until nightfall, the battle might be over.

At one point, Duke William found himself faced with an adversary as powerful as himself, who nimbly ducked his tireless attacks. Evading a particularly deadly blow, the man turned and smashed his axe down on William's head, denting his helm and nearly knocking him from the horse. But the Duke held his seat, then aimed another blow before noticing that the man merged himself among his companions.

However, a group of Normans, always willing to curry their master's favor, charged toward the fellow, transfixing him with their spears. Seeing this, William turned away, shrugging off his ill luck.

The Duke never succeeded in getting close to Harold. Another Norman almost reached the Saxon King; Robert Fitz-Erneis galloped toward the royal standard, smiting those who dared try to block his way. But the Saxons were too quick for him; they surrounded his horse, striking him until he fell off and was trampled underneath. His charge brought him to within a few feet of the banner.

More and more English abandoned their shield wall,

preferring to die in a more actively offensive manner. Anything was better than standing for another minute crammed together. This change in tactics brought the fight back into the Saxons.

William surveyed the field for a moment. Then, with a burst of inspiration, he ordered the archers forward, commanding them to shoot up in the air, so that their arrows would fall like rain on the defending troops. "Aim especially for the royal standard," he added.

Calmly, the bowmen stepped within range, pointed their bows into the sky; it was a tricky maneuver, depending mostly on luck and the wind. There was a danger of wounding their own men if the arrows were badly aimed.

At first, the Saxons didn't pay much attention to the arrows. But like magic, the new threat drew their sight upward, threw them into a panic. Men were pierced in the face, in the throat; screaming in fear and frustration, they raised their shields, leaving their lower bodies defenseless.

Suddenly a burst of activity below the Dragon of Wessex relayed the message that one arrow, at least, hit its mark. Rumors spread instantly through the ranks; Harold was pierced in the eye.

Twenty of William's knights spurred toward the spot, pursued by angry housecarls intent on having their revenge. All but four of the twenty were cut down in this last charge.

But the four reached the fallen King: Eustace of Boulogne, still intent on revenge for an earlier affront; the son of Guy of Pointhieu, Harold's earlier captor; Hugh of Montfort; and the younger Walter Giffard.

Seeing that Harold was still alive, they leaped from their horses, intent on dealing the fatal blow. One of them pierced him through with a spear. Another struck him with a sword, below the fastenings of his helmet. Harold was stabbed through the chest by a third. But, most unchivalrous of all, the last man cut his leg clean through, and flung it far from the body.

In the struggle, Harold's Fighting Man went down, trodden into the mud. The royal gonfanon was carried off.

Enraged, the housecarls doubled their vigorous attacks. But the Normans, as well, were heartened by this crucial death. The day was won; all present knew this. Harold's valiant fighters, his most personal friends, were prepared to die on the field, defending their own honor to the end. Their only intent was to take as many Normans with them as they could.

Around the spot where the standard had fallen, fighting lasted into the dark. But elsewhere, as the banner fell, men who had farms and families waiting for them lost heart. Theirs was not a soldiering life; they were not used to sentiments like dying in battle. First by ones and twos they fled, then the whole field was moving with men streaming to safety, some throwing their weapons in their haste to be off.

The fighting became a race; the Saxons became fugitives, and their enemies the pursuers. But the English unwittingly had the advantage; it was dark. They knew the land, and could traverse the marsh, while heavily laden horses slipped and floundered. Spotting their opportunity, the pursued turned again, wreaking their last revenge on the premature victors.

Many Normans lost their life in that treacherous marsh, later called Malfosse, just at the moment when they thought themselves safe. It was an omen, if only they could see it; herein were displayed the problems facing William in dealing with this, his conquered people.

23

Victory

From the edge of the field, Walter watched the Bretons chase the unhappy Saxons from the field. Hearing a curt order to hold back, he turned to see Alain behind him; it was clear the Count was too weary to enforce it. All was over; both their horses stood, legs spread and heads lowered, gasping huge gulps of air. Walter sat none too steadily in his saddle, reeling with a thunderous headache and a dizziness hard to ignore.

When they had caught their breath, Alain urged forward, anxious to see how the Duke fared. They could hear the sounds of massacre behind them, and assumed it was more Saxons meeting their fate.

Alain was drawn by the sound of William's voice, shouting orders to erect his banner on the spot where Harold's flew. He sounded as fresh as when he started the day. William espied Alain as the Count dismounted.

"Ah, my valiant Breton. Your stouthearted troops overturned their shame. Well done," he shouted, then turn back to finish his orders. "Clear the carnage from this spot. I want my pavilion erected here, so I may oversee the field of triumph."

"But my Lord," someone warned him. "Perchance all the Saxons are not dead. There could be those who lie in wait, to kill you as you sleep."

William turned. "Oh, it's you, Giffard. Lived to see yet another battle won, eh my friend? No, our good Lord has seen fit to give me the victory this day. He will not fail me now.

"See here, my squires. After my tent is up, see to it that you lay a meal fit for a champion, so that I may cheer my good friends with a worthy celebration. Alain, Le Noir, join me presently if you will."

Men dragged the dead away as though they were as many

sacks of flour, flinging them down the hill to make room for the Duke's camp. The blood had mostly soaked into the ground, but they threw down fresh marsh grass atop it. A bonfire was soon flaring near the Duke's pavilion; it was a beacon in the blackened battlefield, lighting the way for stragglers.

The echo of tent stakes hammered into the ground gave a staccato to the groans of the wounded. Bodies lay strewn haphazardly, entangled in places where the fighting had been the worst, with upturned eyes sightlessly watching the forced gaiety of the victors. Already the vultures had come: the poor, the hungry who emerged when the battle was over, compelling the dead to relinquish their valuables.

Not heeding these greedy harbingers of futility, the Normans settled as best as they could among the dead. Ignoring the pathetic poses of the vanquished, the weary soldiers tended their wounds and ate a cheerless dinner before falling, exhausted, into their bedrolls. As the night drew on, a heavy fog rolled in from the sea, shrouding the dead and the living in a comfortless blanket.

The morning sun burned away the enveloping mist, exposing the battlefield in its ugly entirety. The number of dead and wounded were countless, the stench of death almost overpowering.

Walter crawled from his blanket, head reeling. He had fallen into a deep sleep, forgetting his hunger and pain. And now, though somewhat rested, he felt stunned. But his promise to Harold, and, moreover, to Thomas himself, overcame his physical needs; he felt ashamed to have delayed his search so long. Even now, Thomas may be lying somewhere dying, exposed to that damp, chilling air.

He threw a cloak over his shoulders and hung a waterskin from his belt. Straightening, Walter blinked in the sunlight, shuddering at the scene before him. In the countless battles he had fought, never had he seen such devastation.

He groaned when he saw how the space had been cleared for William's pavilion. This was where he had intended to search; how much harder his job would be now.

But Walter set his jaw, persuading himself not to lose heart. Grabbing a bite of bread, he set about his work, systematically pulling body from body on the hill where they were thrown. As the morning drew on, he was joined by others; they separated the living from the dead, while carrying the corpses to the bottom of the hill. Laid side by side, the bodies could be more easily identified by their loved ones, who already received permission to carry them off for private burial. The only one exempt from William's magnanimous gesture was Harold.

Gytha, Harold's mother, had come up to the victorious Duke, tears flowing; it didn't matter, as the hardened man barely noticed her grief. Kneeling before him, she begged him to let her take the body of her royal son, and even offered his weight in gold. Moved by this last gesture, William nonetheless refused to give in.

"What need have I of your gold?" he said. "Listen to me, my Lady. Your son died unshriven, excommunicate. He may not be buried in consecrated ground. But I will do this for him: I will bury him on the south shore, overlooking the channel he guarded so diligently. It is not so shameful an honor..." he hesitated. "That is, if we can find his body."

Unconsoled, Gytha joined in the search.

Looking through the mass of bodies, Walter began to despair. He had been at it for hours; his movements were mechanical, numb, and his head was pounding. Straightening for a moment, wiping his face with a rag, Walter froze at the sight of a woman standing helplessly before him.

As if feeling watched, the woman looked around, starting in surprise. Her dirty face was streaked with tears, her hair straggled around her stooped shoulders. It was four years since he had last seen her, years that had taken their toll on her handsome face, deepening the wrinkles around her eyes. Eyes that looked haunted.

As if breaking a spell, Ealdgyth fell weeping into Walter's arms.

"What has happened to you?" he whispered.

She was unable to answer, and her grandson tightened his hold, waiting for the tears to slacken. Activity went on around them, as if they weren't there.

Finally, Ealdgyth composed herself. She backed up a step, taking the proffered rag and wiping her face, smearing the dirt even more. Walter took the cloth, poured water on it and wiped her cheeks.

"Do you know what happened to Gruffydd?" she asked hoarsely. "What they did to my love?" She was crying again.

"Shhh," Walter tried to comfort her. "I heard something of it. Enough, I warrant. But what did they do to you?"

She looked at him, surprised. "You do not know, then? Harold took me as his prize. He married me to appease my two brothers, Morcar and Eadwine. A lot of good that did him," she added bitterly. "Where are they now?"

Trying to absorb all this, Walter shook his head. "And yet he swore to marry William's daughter," he said to himself.

"What was that?"

"Nothing. Did he mistreat you, though?"

"Oh, he treated me well enough," she said unconvincingly. "I carry his child. It is my only solace." She patted her swelling belly.

Before Walter could interrupt her, she pointed at the field, forcing him to look. "But see there, that woman in blue. Eadgifu the Fair they call her. His mistress for years. Flaunted her in my face...me, the wife of a better Prince than he. And there she is, looking for his body by the marks that only she and I know." Her voice was bitter.

"Ealdgyth," said Walter, with enough intensity to recall her attention. "You are pregnant?"

"Yes."

"You must leave this place! Remove yourself from William's grasp. Can you not see that you aren't safe, if William discovers your presence here? You are lucky he doesn't know you, or your life would be forfeit."

"William?" she said dazedly.

"Hear me, I say. This is important. If he discovers that you carry Harold's heir, he will be forced to kill you, lest more rebellions rise in his name. Can you not see that?"

"Rebellions," she repeated. Then suddenly, what he was saying pierced through her misery. "Oh my God. Walter! Can you help me?"

Without another word, he looked around. Satisfied that he wasn't being watched, Walter grabbed Ealdgyth by the hand, leading her to the horses. Hastily, he untied and saddled a mount, and placed her securely on its back. He handed up his cloak and water, and led the horse away from the hill.

"I regret that I cannot accompany you, but I have a sworn task to finish. I might be missed, as well, then you surely would be in danger. Go, grand-mere. Go to your brothers. And may good fortune attend you."

She bent down to kiss him. "This is the second time you saved my life. I thank you, Walter."

Too moved for words, Walter slapped the horse on the rump, sending them on their way. Ealdgyth turned one last time, waving her hand.

Heaving a sigh, Walter turned back. Glancing at a pile of bodies off the road, he gasped, seeing the object of his search. Clutching a sword, Thomas lay across two other men. Blood was still seeping from a gash in his side. Walter ran to the spot, his heart pounding, and carefully turned his friend over.

The movement expelled a breath from the prone man's lung. Then he coughed, and took a deep gasp.

Letting out a cry, Walter cradled Thomas in his arms. For a few minutes they sat like that, until the Saxon's breaths moved from jerky to smooth. Finally, Thomas's eyes opened.

"Walter," he said so softly that the other had to bend to hear him. "I never thought I'd see you again. You should have let me die." At that he fainted.

Looking around desperately and seeing no one, Walter picked his friend up and carried him to Alain's pavilion, hung with the Count's banner. Aware of nothing but the stricken face of his burden, Walter ignored a voice repeatedly calling his name from somewhere behind him.

He entered the tent, laying Thomas across his blanket. The flap rustled behind him and Alain moved closer, bending to study the wounded man.

"My friend, father," Walter said. "He ruined himself for me, and I swore I would make it up to him, if I ever had the chance."

"But he's a Saxon, my boy," the Count said, looking around, just in case there was someone within hearing.

"I care nothing for that! I must save him."

"All right. But keep quiet about it. Don't bring trouble on our heads." He got up to move away, when Walter grabbed his arm.

"Bring a surgeon, please," he begged. Alain pulled uncomfortably away, but nodded.

Walter's head dropped, as he fought to stay conscious. But Alain was as good as his word. Within an hour, a doctor came in, muttering to himself. He glanced at the unconscious man.

"I have our own wounded to attend to," he growled, seeing that Thomas was Saxon. He turned to leave.

With extraordinary energy, Walter leaped past the man, blocking the door. "I don't care if he is Saxon, Chinese, Genoese, orange, yellow, or green. You will care for this man, or I swear you'll be in need of care yourself!"

The surgeon glared at him. Though he didn't have a weapon in his hand, the threat in Walter's eyes was real. The man nodded, begrudgingly, and went to work on Thomas under the careful eye of his overseer. He cleansed and stitched the wound, then forced a liquid down Thomas's throat. Recovering his nerve, the surgeon stood, straightening his cloak.

"His lung has been pierced. There will probably be a fever. I do not know whether the man will survive." Brushing past Walter, who was already kneeling at his friend's side, the doctor turned at the door.

"Duke William will hear about this!" he snarled.

Walter jumped up. "Get thee to hell!" he shouted, and the man scurried away, grateful to escape.

Left alone, Walter dropped to the ground next to his friend, and lay on his side. He kept his sword within reach, intending to watch over the wounded man. But his own injury proved too much for him; he fell asleep instantly, shielding Thomas with an arm over his chest.

Nearly dusk, Walter awoke to a shaking on his shoulder. His head shook with pain and he groaned, covering his eyes.

"Walter, are you all right?" He recognized the voice, but it sounded very far away. "Walter, my son...Walter." The voice was fading, but Walter was too tired to care. "My God, they're both feverish."

Walter felt a cloak spread over his body, then someone lifted his head, pouring a hot liquid down his throat. He tried to say something, but no sound came out. "Sleep," Alain said. Walter slept.

Many images crossed his mind. He saw Gruffydd talking angrily to a man who looked a bit like himself. The Prince crossed the room, closing the door, then turned, murder in his eye. He grabbed the man and wrapped an arm around his neck, breaking it with a great surge of strength while the other struggled, trying to ward off his grasp. Walter tried to scream.

Then he saw the same man again, walking through the woods with an older person. Amid the trees lurked three men, holding knives. Again Walter tried to shout, but his silent cries went unnoticed. Suddenly the hidden men dashed forward, catching the older man unawares, while the younger turned on his attacker. "Fly, Fleance, fly!" the other shouted, as the murderers drove their knives into his breast. Momentarily uncertain, Fleance ran for his life. The scene went dark.

Then his head was filled with eerie voices, chanting in an unknown language. But the three faces that glowed from the void were familiar to him. "Your grandfather Banquo," they said, each in turn.

"But the slayer was avenged." Walter had found his voice. "Why do you torture me with these things?"

They didn't respond to his question. "Who are you then?" he pursued. "Why do you order my life?"

The weird sisters responded, each in turn:

"You must know the past
As we know the future.
Your life is yet destined for much greater things.
We order you on
As your task is written,
Descendants of Banquo, their fortunes we bring.
Your good sense has brought you
The rewards of courage.
We send you to serve beside Malcolm your King."

Relieved that they required no other tasks from him, Walter rallied as they faded. In his dream, he sat up, reaching toward them.

"Is this the last time I'll see you? Tell me why you have chosen me."

The weird sisters faded for a moment, then came back.

"Thou shalt 'get kings,

Though thou be none..."

This they all spoke together, when their whole bodies appeared, and they motioned from beyond with their arms.

Out of the darkness appeared Banquo, this time not bloody and dying, but dressed in his best court gown, bowing to Walter as he passed. Following him walked Fleance, who bowed and called Walter his son. In his hand he carried a glass globe, and he held it up.

The sphere's insides glowed with an intense light, dimming as other bodies passed it. Walter squinted, seeing man after man follow and bow in respect. As a number of them passed, those that came after wore crowns on their heads, and carried scepters.

Little did Walter realize that this was the same vision shown to Macbeth so many years ago, and with such a different reaction.

For Walter marveled at the great plan, of which he was only a small part; like a link in a chain, he was essential to the whole.

All faded from sight, just as he woke up.

Alain was bending over him, carefully placing a wet cloth across his forehead. Still wondering at his vision, Walter smiled weakly, trying to sit.

"You spoke many strange things in your delirium," the Count said, pushing Walter gently back.

"Delirium? How long have I been unconscious?"

"Two days, my lad."

Walter sighed. "It only seemed a moment."

"It always does. But for a while there we thought we had lost you. You stopped breathing."

Remembering Thomas, Walter felt at his side. His hand touched another body, still warm. He closed his eyes, relieved.

"Yes, your friend is alive, though he still does not wake. But I think he will survive. You almost killed yourself, searching for him in your condition. I didn't realize you were so ill."

Alain smiled. "You gave the surgeon quite a scare, you know.

He wouldn't set foot in this pavilion again, no matter how I begged. Had to tend you all by myself, with the help of my brother."

Grateful, Walter reached for his hand.

"Anyway, William returned to Hastings, ordering that the rest of us move as soon as our wounded are able. When you are up, perhaps we can fashion a litter for your friend, here, though I know not what we are going to do with him."

Walter knew, but was too weary to talk.

"Rest, my son. You took quite a blow to the head."

In the days that followed, the battle site came to resemble a camp that dwindled with every sick body able to move ahead. Alain spent most of his time at Walter's side.

"Did they ever find Harold?" Walter asked.

"Finally. His mistress, Edith Swan Neck, recognized him, mangled though he was. One leg was missing."

"Mangled," Walter said scornfully. "And these are the best of William's cavalry."

"You are no harder on the scoundrels than William was. It was not difficult to find out who treated his body so shamefully. They bragged from one end of the camp to the other. William threw one of the culprits out of the army, and gave the others a tongue lashing they won't soon forget."

Alain hesitated. "Walter, can you travel?"

"I may, but not my friend."

The Count coughed. "There is something I have to tell you, Walter. The surgeon told William about your incident." He paused.

"And he forbade bringing this Saxon into his camp, is that it?"

Alain nodded, embarrassed.

"Father, I won't cause you any more trouble. My place isn't here."

The Count shook his head vehemently. "No, my son."

"It cannot be. I will not leave Thomas, and he wouldn't go to the Norman camp anyway. But that is not all." He sat up, folding his blanket. "My place is with Malcolm. I do not like William and his ways. I would leave, anyway. This just makes it a little sooner."

Alain muttered to himself, brushing a hand through his hair.

"Alain," Walter continued, "My life is with Malcolm. He is my friend, and he needs me. I will not stay away any longer."

"I suppose I lose my daughter, too."

"No! You do not mean that. There is no reason why you can't be with us."

"We shall see, Walter. Perhaps, after all, it is for the best."

"I am sure of it."

The next day, Alain departed with his brother, leaving Walter and Thomas a generous supply of provisions, as well as three horses. "I feel as if I am deserting you," Alain said, embracing Walter.

"Nay. You will know how to find me, when all is settled."

He watched them ride off, then entered the pavilion. Looking down at his friend, he was delighted to see his eyes open.

"I heard all that, Walter. Why did you stay behind?"

"I have no heart for William's cause," Walter said, sitting down. "I did my duty to my good-father. Now I must do it for you."

"Good-father?" Thomas tried to sit, but fell back, coughing.

"Stop, you fool. Yes, I married a pretty little Breton girl, before all this happened. When the call to arms came, I went with Alain, who is a count in Brittany."

Thomas looked away, ashamed for his friend. Walter was hurt.

"It was something I felt I had to do. I made my peace with Harold the eve of the battle, though I suppose you won't believe me. I need not make it with you, too!"

That made things worse. He felt guilty that he had lashed out at his friend. Thomas frowned, still looking away.

"I'm sorry, Thomas. I never felt right about it. But how could I refuse my good-father?"

"It really doesn't matter now," Thomas said finally. "I knew Harold went to the Norman camp the night before. I didn't know he saw you." The effort to speak cost too much; he closed his eyes.

"That's enough talking for now. Just listen to what I tell you. Harold said something else."

Thomas's eyes fluttered open, but Walter placed a finger over his friend's lips. "He asked me to search the battlefield for you, to make sure you weren't left wounded there. He said he treated you badly after the Welsh incident."

Thomas's head was turned again, this time in intense sorrow. Walter went on, "I can only suppose he took you down in rank."

Thomas nodded, tears running down his face.

Walter got up, poured a flask of water. He offered it to his friend. "His regret was genuine," he added lamely. "Though it can be no more than I feel myself." Thomas didn't move.

"I told you I would repay you, if ever I had a chance. Please don't deny me this little bit."

After a moment, Thomas accepted the water, though he refused to look at Walter. Not really expecting any other response, Walter left the Saxon to his grief.

For three days Thomas did not speak a word. All this time, Walter sat by his side, offering a hot bowl of gruel now and then, which his friend absently accepted. The Saxon spent most of his days staring at nothing, though it was not difficult to tell that his thoughts were directed inward; the conflict was reflected on his face. But his body, regardless of his state of heart, refused to waste away. Before Walter's satisfied eyes, his friend began to rally.

On the third night, as Walter was settling down to sleep, his companion finally spoke to him in a careworn voice.

"I find that I am not worthy to judge you, Walter. If Harold had forgiven you, what right have I to pursue the argument?"

Containing his relief, Walter stayed silent.

Thomas let out his tension in a rattled sigh. "Walter, will you take me with you to Scotland? I have no desire to live in England under foreign rule."

Afraid to betray himself, Walter merely said yes. Then he rolled over to sleep.

It was another two weeks before Thomas was fit to ride a horse. Then Walter insisted that they move to a local hostel. He got no argument from his companion.

As Walter was packing his horse pouch, he discovered a bag of gold coins secreted in the bottom. Laughing, he pulled out the bulging sack.

"That thoughtful fool," he said to Thomas, who was saddling his own horse. "He knew I wouldn't take it, so he put it where I couldn't argue with him. But yes, we are sure to need it before we are through. I do miss him already."

The Saxon stopped, leaning on the horse and staring at the spot where Harold was killed. "Perhaps you should have left me for dead. I am nothing but a burden to you in my state."

Walter followed Thomas's look thoughtfully. It was true that his friend was still not himself, so that he constantly needed to be prodded from his brooding. He was forever lapsing into a reverie of sorts.

"No," he finally stated firmly. "Once we are away from this dreadful spot, you shall shed some of your pain. Now, no more talk of leaving you for dead, I beg you, or you shall break my heart."

The other managed a grim smile. "You are right. One broken heart is enough." It was the last thing he said until they were well out of sight of Senlac Hill.

As Walter had suspected, once away from the stagnant air of death, Thomas seemed to breathe more freely. The proprietor of a nearby hostel gave them a room on the top floor. The Saxon healed much faster, and was ready to travel in a fortnight.

The countryside showed no signs of change yet, as if the Normans were only a bad dream. Walter and Thomas rode leisurely north, content to assuage their pain in the beautiful scenery and the joy of companionship. The refugees could not possibly know of William's southern campaign, though they suspected he would be waging some sort of warfare against his conquered subjects.

By little twitches Thomas seemed to reanimate until finally he was content to hum and whistle. In bits and pieces his story tumbled out: how Harold was furious at Walter's escape, and dismissed Thomas forever from the rank of housecarl. Harold refused to speak to him for years, until suddenly he allowed Thomas's presence near him after his return from Normandy.

Thomas spoke of Edmund's death during the Welsh campaign—dear Edmund, who remained one of his few faithful friends after his disgrace. "It was more of a dreadful accident than anything else," Thomas said. "You see, the mountains could be most precipitous. Edmund had taken the rearguard; it was drawing toward dusk. We hadn't caught up with the Welsh for days, though we knew we were drawing near them. Their campfires were smoldering the day before, which meant that we almost trapped them."

Thomas grimaced bitterly. "We thought ourselves so tough...so well trained. The more the fools we really were. Sneaked around behind us, they did, those Welsh on the run. We were so overconfident we never considered that possibility. Before the front of the line knew what was happening, half a dozen of our men had arrows in their backs. Edmund escaped the first onslaught, but overreached himself trying to save another from plunging down the slope. The man was probably dead already."

The Saxon wiped his glistening brow. "My poor friend balanced on the edge with his burden, but the rocks gave way from under his feet and down they both went. Walter, I was thirty feet away from him...too far to help."

He paused. "The Welsh soon disappeared, as they always did. Harold stopped while we recovered our dead and wounded. Edmund had a broken neck; he fell beneath the man he was helping, almost straight down for two hundred feet."

Walter was horrified at how far the ill effects of his flight reached. Thomas shook his head, reading his friend's thoughts.

"It was something you had to do, Walter. I could not in all conscience hold you back, any more than you could manage to restrain yourself. Do you regret your action?"

Walter shook his head.

"All right then. It was well done."

After a long silence, Thomas encouraged Walter to tell of his own exploits. Their old affinity was returning; they lost track of time, not really caring how long they took. In his future years, Walter would often look back to those carefree weeks as the most peaceful time of his life, notwithstanding the terrible battle.

But Walter was still anxious to see Malcolm.

24
Dunfermline

Walter remembered all the roads to Dunfermline well; as they neared their goal, he quickened their pace. Thomas could not bring himself to object to their speed, but one momentary look at his pale face brought Walter to a quick stop, apologizing for his forgetfulness.

"Now you look like the eager boy I once know," the Saxon said fondly. "Look at you, leaning forward in the saddle like you'll never get there."

Walter laughed, and was glad that he felt able to. "I suppose Scotland does that to me. It's the only place I ever called home."

"Well, I'm right glad of it. Will we reach the palace soon?"

"Presently... look there! Edinburgh. Malcolm started building that castle a year before I left for Brittany. Commands all of Lothian, it does. What a sight, perched upon that cliff of stone as if it was part of the rock. Why, it is hard to say where one comes to an end and the other begins." He turned to Thomas, expecting reinforcement of his admiration. Instead he caught a gleam of amusement in his friend's eyes.

"Oh, come on. We are nearly there."

Summoning the last of his strength now that the end was near, the Saxon spurred his horse to match Walter's speed.

The huge gates to Edinburgh castle opened to Walter's summons, for this time the traveler was recognized and welcomed in a style more becoming a retainer to the king. Ceremoniously, he and his friend were led into the great hall, where Malcolm sat upon his throne, chin in hand, attending a dispute between two noblemen.

As always, the King preferred informality. Although placed higher than the others, he allowed them to sit in his presence. His crown was set aside, along with his cape, and he was dressed in a plain tunic and soft boots. But majesty belonged to his person; there was no need for adornments to emphasize his rank.

Still, he was ready to impress with his surroundings. He had built his new castle of stone using a style learned from the Normans. Tall, highly placed windows let in plentiful light. Large banners adorned the hall, the royal lion of Scotland hanging above the throne. Giving their due to his Earls, he hung their family arms along the walls, putting the oldest arms nearest his own banner. Under his vast roof, men felt insignificant.

"Splendidly done," thought Walter to himself as he admired the hall.

Then Malcolm saw him. He stood up, smiling broadly, and the two men turned to look at the source of their interruption.

Excusing himself to the nobles, Malcolm strode forward, placing his hands on Walter's shoulders.

"Well come, Walter. I've been worried about you. When I heard of William's battle, I suspected you might be there. That was many weeks since!"

Walter was gratified by his concern. "I nearly lost my life at that battle, Sire, and needed some weeks to recover...as did my friend Thomas. He wishes to take refuge in your country..."

Malcolm gave the Saxon a searching look, then clasped his hand. "You'll find that some of your countrymen have made their way here already. You are all welcome to my court. I am glad you are recovered, Walter, but it looks as though Thomas still needs tending to.

"Wallace," he called to a servant. "Get this man a surgeon. A few more miles, and he might have had sore need of one."

Blinking, Walter turned to Thomas. It was true; in his excitement, he had forgotten his friend's condition. Even now the brave warrior was swaying. He put out a steadying hand.

"Go now," Malcolm said gently. "More of this later." He strode away, soothing the ruffled feelings of his abandoned petitioners.

Later that day, after they had finished a meal and Thomas was safely installed in his bed, Malcolm sent for Walter to join him in his chamber.

"By God it is good to have you back," the King said. He sighed happily, gathering up a white cat who had followed Walter in. "Where is your lady wife?"

"Still in Brittany. I will summon her if it's all right with your Grace."

"Stop the 'your graces' in private, please, if you don't want to gall me. You have been spending too much time in William's company, I suppose."

The other laughed. "You are right. He does so love to be feared. My good-father Alain fears him, even though he is a fine warrior in his own right."

"It will probably get him far, in William's service. And what of yourself?"

"You need not ask," Walter answered bitterly, straightening his tunic. "He disliked me intensely, and I him. There were times I wondered what side I should have fought on."

"It helps to be on the winning side. Ask your friend Thomas."

Walter looked askance at the King.

"Never fear," added Malcolm with a short laugh. "I have not turned mercenary. But when it comes down to it, Harold lost England to the invader. He failed in his duty. A king is not allowed excuses." He glanced quickly at Walter. "Remember that, my friend."

Walter shook his head.

"No, Walter, listen to me. As king, I will—and have—committed acts you may or may not approve of. I blunder now and then...can't help it. But losing one's country is unforgivable. No matter what the excuse, that kind of failure takes away his right to be king. I heard all the tales, Walter...I saw where he made his mistakes, excusable though they are in a lesser man..."

After a pause, he added, "Though you know, I don't like this

William." He glanced sideways at Walter. "You are staying this time, are you not?"

"I am your man. I would not leave again."

"Good. I have work for you. Since you wrote me about mounted warfare on the continent… yes, I found someone to read the letter." Malcolm smiled. "I have been thinking. It is time we came to understand this art. I have already purchased two score of good, solid horses. Tomorrow we shall cross the firth, and I will show them to you. They are in Dunfermline."

Leaning back, Walter savored the comfort of Malcolm's presence while the Scot launched into a tirade of all the wrongs he expected to receive from the Norman. Malcolm would forgive him if he didn't manage to follow every word. Tired and grateful to be alive, Walter was busy reveling in the novelty of relaxation.

Early the next morning, Malcolm was eager to be off. He jostled Walter onto a horse, then trundled the ferryman out of bed.

Splendid though Edinburgh was as a defensive fortress, Malcolm still preferred the comfort of his tower at Dunfermline. He spent as much time there as possible, considering it his real home. For the rest of his life, he was to ferry back and forth between the two.

"Come old man," he shouted at the ferryman's house. "We have work to do." In a moment, there was a fluttering of shutters, and in another, a short wrinkled man hurried out of the door, pulling on a cloak. He muttered apologies as the King handed his horse to a groom; there would be other mounts at the opposite side, always standing ready.

"I keep him around because he amuses me," Malcolm said aside to Walter. "He's rarely prompt."

The Firth of Forth was wide between Edinburgh and Dunfermline. Larger than the Firth of Tay, an army couldn't be transported across without using boats. The closest ford was more than thirty miles to the west at Stirling, where the firth narrowed into a river.

The morning was bright, the current relatively calm. Once set upon the opposite bank, the pair was galloping cheerfully to Malcolm's palace.

Walter was comforted to see Dunfermline unchanged. The King was concentrating his building efforts on Edinburgh. As they clattered up to the drawbridge, Myrna appeared at the door, holding the hand of a chubby boy who was waving frantically. The woman's own gesture of welcome froze when she recognized Walter.

Duncan pulled free from the slack hand of his guardian and raced laughing to his father. Beaming, Malcolm reached low and pulled the boy to his saddle. Seeing that his friend was reluctant to look at Myrna, he tried to fill the uncomfortable silence. "Fine boy, wouldn't you say?" he called.

Walter nodded, then pulled himself together. He dismounted and walked up to his old companion, taking her hand and kissing it. "I'm happy to see you," he said, then paused, embarrassed. She was gazing at the child.

"Come, Myrna," said Malcolm, exasperated. "Is this any way to greet your friend?"

"Forgive me," she said, taking a breath and looking at Walter. "Your coming was such a surprise."

Walter frowned. He hadn't expected her reception to be so cool. But he reminded himself that Isabel was quite likely a bad blow to the girl's hopes.

Malcolm handed the child back to Myrna. "Come, Walter. I'll show you the stables I built to house our gallant destriers." Pulling the horse's head around, he led the other around the rear of the hill. Walter was glad to turn his back on that situation.

When he saw Malcolm's purchases, he soon forgot about women. Malcolm had indeed chosen his horses well. They were all large, at least double the size of the ponies native to Scotland. Proud, deep-chested with thick necks and heavy legs, they looked like they belonged together, for twenty of them were white, and twenty were black. They snorted and shook their heads as the two men walked through the stables.

"It was a fancy of mine to choose them for their colors," Malcolm said, patting one familiarly on the neck. "But you can see that not one is inferior to the others. Forty is all I could afford to start with; as it is, it takes an army of grooms to care for them. I hope my example will persuade my stubborn noblemen to buy horses of their own… I am glad you came back, because I would rather have you training them than someone from the continent…" His eyes met Walter's. "You were long overdue, my friend."

It was a few days before Thomas was ready to leave his sickroom. Once he was well enough to move around on his own, he refused any offer of help. When Walter offered to show him the new stables, his face brightened.

The Saxon was nervous about the rocking ferry boat, for he had never crossed such a large body of water before. Slightly pale, he was the first to jump to land.

Though he had never fought on horseback and refused to learn to do so, Thomas had a natural affinity toward the animals. Today, the smile on his face transported him, giving him the rare beauty Walter had always envied in their early friendship, though Hastings had added a somewhat poignant expression never seen before.

Taking an immediate liking to a large black stallion, Thomas threw a halter on the animal's head and brought him into the sunlight. He clipped a line to the halter and led the nervous animal into a pen. Stepping back, Thomas let the rope slip through his hand while he coaxed the horse into a circle. At first the stallion resisted the man, but Thomas spoke softly to it and led the animal quietly, willing the horse to relax and cooperate. Finally, Thomas brought the horse to a halt. He turned toward

Walter, but his stare was directed behind his friend. Walter swung around, curious.

There she was, standing behind him, holding a child's hand. Myrna absently tried to restrain the hair blowing across her face.

Holding his breath, Thomas lost himself for a moment. Impatient, the stallion tossed his head, trying to pull away from his captor. The Saxon didn't respond, taken in by the girl's soft, brown eyes.

Walter looked from one of them to the other in wonder. She, too, seemed captivated, ignoring the tugging at her hand while the child strained forward. Walter was thrilled; before his eyes unfolded the cure for the unhappiness he saw wasting his friends.

He took the child from Myrna, breaking the spell. "Myrna, meet a very dear friend of mine, Thomas. He has come to stay with us. Thomas, this is my childhood friend, Myrna. The Prince Duncan is in her charge."

Remembering his manners, Thomas bent purposefully to the boy, shaking his hand. Then he straightened up, taking the girl in with a thorough examination. Her face was flushed.

"What a pleasure it is to meet such a beautiful woman in this wild country. I feared I would be forced to look at such as Walter for some time to come."

Myrna laughed. "I wouldn't be here but for him. You shouldn't seem too ungrateful." She finally smiled at Walter.

The boy was clamoring to ride the horse, but Myrna explained that Malcolm had purchased a special pony for Duncan's use. That was where she had been heading, for they went riding every day. Thomas looked eloquently at Walter.

"Yes, please, Thomas. Go with them. The air will do wonders for you." Walter said lamely. "I'll take the horse." Happy at this unforeseen turn of events, he took the lead line and stood watching as the others moved away, chattering as if they were old friends.

His immediate reaction was of amazement, for never had he seen Thomas with a woman. His next feeling was one of loneliness, and a distinct yearning for Isabel. He would go to the port that very day, in search of a ship to Brittany so he could send for his wife.

It was clear what Walter's duties were going to be, and messengers were sent out to the noble families, offering to train their eldest sons in the art of chivalry.

Sending their boys to court was an unknown practice in this isolated country. It took some persuasion to convince the hardheaded lords that this wasn't just a ploy to hold their sons hostage. Many of the older nobility ignored the offer, though most of the new earls agreed readily.

As soon as he had a handful of pupils, Walter started their training. All of the boys had experience riding, and some practice with weapons, but Walter and Thomas had their hands full teaching their students how to fight as a team. Much time was spent breaking up quarrels.

But as the weeks drew into months, the young men began to enjoy the camaraderie of working together, and identifying themselves as the "King's men."

He did his best to ignore his own loneliness, while waiting for Isabel to arrive. She had much to do to arrange the estate, and it would be some time before she was ready. Meanwhile, he fell easily back into his old working habits with Malcolm.

One morning, on their way to inspect a third new palace under construction at Forteviot, he happily told the King that Isabel was due to arrive in one week.

Malcolm was delighted. "I feared Thomas was making you jealous," he laughed. "He seems to be making such progress with Myrna."

Walter shook his head dubiously. "Madly in love though he is, he seems jealous of me."

"Oh, it is understandable that Thomas is jealous," Malcolm said. "The poor girl still dotes on you. Perhaps she thinks you'll forget your foreign wife."

Walter smiled, thinking of Isabel. "She will learn otherwise soon enough. I'm grateful to Thomas for taking her mind off me. The shock won't seem so bad."

"I hope so for his sake. It is said that when a man falls in love so late in life, he falls hopelessly so."

Walter moved his horse a little closer. "So when will it be your turn?"

"For shame, teasing your King so!" Malcolm cried, racing away.

Isabel was surprised and pleased at her reception. As the boat docked her eyes searched out her longed-for husband, resplendent in a velvet tunic. Next to him was a man she guessed had to be the King; though he wasn't wearing a crown, he aptly matched Walter's description. Close by stood a grim Saxon warrior, to whom her husband spoke with more than casual familiarity.

And near the blond Saxon stood, as if rooted to the ground, a beautiful woman, who looked at Isabel with such enmity that the Breton couldn't move her eyes away. Walter had never mentioned another woman, but with the intuition that never leaves one who loves, she knew that this girl was a rival.

Once the landing plank was clear, Walter jumped aboard and grabbed his wife in a hug that squeezed her breath away, lifting her from the deck and twirling her in a most undignified way. He put her down just in time for Malcolm to follow his lead, until the poor woman was gasping and laughing at the same time. Her dog, inseparable from his mistress, was jumping about and barking, though no one paid notice to the clamor.

The King rewarded the surprised ship captain for landing her safely, then whisked the small party off the boat. Isabel was introduced to Thomas, whose eyes were kinder than she supposed. Then Walter led her to Myrna, who looked ready to run away.

But Isabel, in her sweet manner, took the girl's hand, voicing her happiness to find another woman near her own age to make the transition easier. Myrna was not vindictive by nature. Despite herself, she smiled shyly.

As Walter happily led the way to the Tower, Thomas lagged behind with Myrna. He knew how the girl felt; for weeks his heart had suffered, as much for his own sake as for hers. While Myrna longed for Walter, she would not give him the chance to speak his love.

Thomas wondered if his recent grief made these feelings so strong... or was it truly his heart? He felt as though he would die a second time if she wouldn't have him. He chided himself for such immature emotions, and yet he couldn't help them. Wisdom came from experience, but love never seemed to learn. However, experience had taught him one thing: slavish affection like hers for Walter wouldn't last forever if not returned. Especially if one was still young.

At first Myrna walked by his side as if in a trance, her thoughts in turmoil. Just when Thomas was wondering if she was aware of his presence, she stopped him. Turning to face her, his heart leaped at the new look in her eye.

"I feel... rejected," she said, not noticing the tightening of his hand on her own. "And yet... a new sense of freedom." She looked at him questioningly.

"Think of it as a release. That woman's presence severed the old bonds between you and Walter forever." He faltered, hoping she wouldn't resent his presumption.

Considering this, Myrna didn't seem to mind. "I wasn't good enough for him. But you... knowing this, you would still accept me?"

Had he been so obvious?

"Can that possibly concern you? Myrna, you are beautiful, you are good, you are intelligent. If that wasn't what Walter wanted, it doesn't mean no one else would cherish you. I only hope you will accept me."

She shook her head wonderingly. "I have always been alone, Thomas. There are many things you will have to teach me."

Taking that as an assent, he took her in his arms, twirling her just as the others did Isabel. This had never happened to her before; Myrna's eyes were glistening when he put her down.

"I would like to feel... loved by a man. Can I truly be happy?"

Thomas laughed, and felt surprised at himself; he never thought he would laugh again. "You are so like a child sometimes... and see, you made me laugh. Perhaps I, too, can learn to be happy."

As if they suddenly understood each other, the couple chose to stray away. No one remarked at their absence.

Walter and Isabel couldn't give justice to Malcolm's dinner; in a way, they felt as if this was a wedding banquet. The others teased them about the upcoming night; their eyes laughing, they felt a little foolish. The King toasted the reunited couple.

As soon as they could, the pair slipped off. When Walter showed Isabel into his room, she shivered, despite the comfortable blaze flickering cheerfully in an oversized fireplace.

"It will take me a while to get used to the chill," she apologized.

"All the more reason to gather you into my arms," her husband murmured, wrapping her securely in a blanket and pulling her down onto the bed.

Softly, then with more intensity he kissed her, recalling his former desire in a rush of longing suddenly set free. With a maidenly blush she resisted for a moment, then gave in lustily as was her wont. After months of untimely separation, the newlyweds exhausted themselves rediscovering their long suppressed emotions. They fell happily asleep in each other's arms.

The next morning, Isabel woke to the careful caress across her cheek. Her eyes opened lazily, to see Walter gazing at her as if afraid she would disappear.

"My cherished prize," he said softly. "We shall never be separated like that again."

She sighed. "Until the next war, my love. At least we are on the same island. What of my father? Did the conflict suit him?"

Walter laughed. "He was a new man. William was proud of him. Alas, I have heard nothing from him since we parted."

"Well, in that at least I have the advantage. He wrote me a letter from London, telling me how terrible English food was, and how he missed our gentle sun. I received it just before I left. More to the point, there was a sorry demonstration by the Saxons, who elected Eadgar Aetheling as the new king. Though he hasn't been crowned."

Her husband sat up in bed. News like this brought out his warlike instincts. Word traveled slowly to Scotland, and was often contradictory. "I knew that would get your attention," she laughed.

"The Aetheling," he said thoughtfully. "Edward the Confessor's nephew, I think. He was the rightful heir all along, though not as suited to kingship as Harold. Too young, I had heard. So the Saxons still had some fight in them?"

"Not much, from what I could gather. Dover had already surrendered without a blow. The Norman spared them as much as he could, though his army lost control and burned half the city. From there, William laid waste to Kent, or at least to those parts that haven't submitted to him.

"Once he devastated the land north and west of London, William settled in at Berkhampstead, requesting London's submission and the Witan's acceptance of his claim to the crown. Evidently they deposed Eadgar and sent him along with the embassy to greet the Conqueror."

They were silent for a moment.

"We understand that the northern English purposely withheld their aid to Harold," Walter said, seeing that Isabel spoke all she knew. "It was a poor thing for them to do to their country, but they probably hoped that William would leave them alone, since he has no argument with them. If he leaves them alone, maybe he will leave us alone..."

It seemed that Walter and Isabel's conversation was often repeated by others, as everyone had an eye turned toward England. Some days later, Earl MacDuff came to visit the King, and his concern was most evident.

Walter hadn't seen the bulky warrior since Dunsinane so long ago. Prosperity had filled out the man's frame, until he looked more happy to sit before a well-filled table than astride a horse. But the look in his eye was enough to convince one that the spirit was willing, though the flesh might be slower to respond.

"Wait," Malcolm said to the Earl before they went inside the palace. "I want you to see what my squires are doing. Walter, go get our ten best lads and saddle them up." He put a familiar arm around MacDuff's shoulders, walking him back to the practice yard.

"I tell you, Sire," the Earl started, "I think that horses should be used to take a man to the battlefield, but no farther. Our ground here is marshy, and where it's not wet, it's full of stone. Your horses will be broken under such conditions."

Malcolm nodded, watching the boys saddle their mounts. "I agree that much of the terrain is unsuitable. But not all... especially at our southern borders and into Northumbria, where our enemy most surely will be mounted."

MacDuff sighed. "Northumbria. Yes, that's why I'm here. I would know what your plans are. Better that we take Northumbria than that cursed Norman bastard."

"Ah," Malcolm shook his head. "We speak only of our defense, for now. At least," he added in a lower voice, "as long as

Eadwine and Morkere are still in control. But I fear that will not be for long. William cannot be safe from revolt if they are left to themselves.

"Perhaps I should have tried harder to make him my friend," Malcolm spat. "But I did not have the stomach for it. But I do fear for Scotland, MacDuff. Having come so far, why should William be satisfied with only England?"

"We should fight him, my Lord. Those are my feelings."

"With what? A handful of thanes and a throng of clansmen? I can't keep my own people from fighting amongst themselves."

The other nodded. "What you say is true enough."

"And this is why I am training their sons," Malcolm pursued, willing him to understand. "Come, have a look at our new tactics."

MacDuff crossed his arms, taking a hard look. "All right. I remember how those Normans fought at Dunsinane. They were a formidable enemy."

Malcolm gestured for the boys to start. The large practice area was arranged with posts from which round shield were hung by straps. Each rider carried a spear, aimed for the shield. If he managed to break the straps with the force of his blow, he achieved his aim. Nine out of ten hit their mark the first pass, and two of them broke the ligaments holding the shield. They ran the course twice more before the King brought his guest away.

"They look reasonable, Sire," the Earl said thoughtfully. "But I do not have much faith in this project. We Scots have always fought differently, and it works for us. So why change our ways?"

Malcolm gestured impatiently. "You cannot count on it, I say. We must do everything we can to protect our land. I was hoping that you and my good thanes and earls would follow my lead. Once these men are trained, they could go out and teach these skills to others. Then we can confront the Norman with an army equal to his own.

"I fear it, MacDuff. I feel, truly, that some day, perhaps not in my lifetime but in my children's lifetimes, our dear Scotland will be caught at the throat by the sons of William. I wonder if it were best to take on the ways of our enemies."

MacDuff was appalled. "Is it not enough that you have borrowed their titles? I can stomach being called an Earl, but I will be damned if you'll catch me cutting my hair short like a monk."

"And a damned sight you would be, too, my friend!" Despite himself, Malcolm roared with laughter.

It was only a couple of months until Thomas and Myrna announced their betrothal. Since she had no father to ask, Thomas approached Malcolm for Myrna's hand. Pleased, the King offered a dowry for her.

"On one condition, Thomas," he said. "That I do not lose my son's teacher. Not yet, at least. I am very comfortable with her. When he's eight, in two years... then I'll let her go." He laughed, eyes twinkling. "But then, if you formally join my service, I won't lose either one of you. As captain of my personal guard?"

Thomas was momentarily stunned; an unfamiliar burst of gratitude took him by surprise. Flattered, his face broke into a wide grin. He had forgotten how good it felt to serve an appreciative master. Perhaps, after all, it was time to accept Harold's death. Perhaps he didn't have be ashamed to bury the dead and find a new reason for living. He bowed, a graceful gesture in one so lean. "With pleasure, Sire. It is time I put my rusty skills to use."

The appointment came as a surprise to Walter, though Thomas was hard put to believe it. "Come, Walter," he said, "you must have persuaded him to do it."

"Why, no, I swear by all that is dear to me. The King saw your merits, as well he should. Your talents as a warrior are no secret."

Another surprise was in store for Walter that night, while he rested comfortably in his wife's arms.

"This is indeed a blessed day, my love," she said. He agreed, murmuring into her hair.

"Come, Walter. Surely you've noticed that I have been feeling poorly these last few mornings."

He raised his head. "I thought that our dreary Scottish food was bothering you."

"Dear, sweet fool of mine. I'm carrying your child."

He sat up in bed, a look of consternation on his face. Fatherhood was something Walter had never considered seriously before.

"What is it, Walter? Does that not please you?"

Smiling worriedly, he took her carefully in his arms. "It's the second best thing that's ever happened to me. The first was marrying you. But I don't know what to do."

"What is there to do but love me as you always have? The rest comes naturally enough. And stop holding me like I'm going to break."

But Malcolm thought it only natural. "By God, Walter, Fleance would be so proud!"

Fleance. For a second, Walter was confounded. The word sounded strange to him, spoken out loud. And yet, Malcolm had known his father; he blessed the name, speaking it so lovingly. He brought to mind a gallant young man, strong in his will to live, unsullied by shame of deceit...

Walter thought he would never love Malcolm as much as he did at that moment. For with a single kind thought, the King had legitimized the child of a bastard.

25

The Saxon Exiles

Late one night, the peace of Malcolm's household was shattered by the arrival of five hungry, exhausted men; they had evidently ridden hard for many days. Consistent with his widely known hospitality, Malcolm always made his guests welcome, the more so when they felt bound to him out of gratitude... and unfailingly hostile to King William of England.

Although by now, exiles in search of sanctuary had become a common occurrence, this group was different. Their clothes may have been torn and dirty, yet their bearing bespoke noble birth. Gratefully eating a late meal, they proceeded to introduce themselves to Malcolm, Walter, and Thomas.

One of them the King already knew: Cospatric, his cousin, was an energetic man a dozen years younger than Malcolm. Descended from Earl Uchtred of Northumbria, Cospatric carried himself like a dispossessed nobleman. Dark of eye and hair, he had high, hollow cheeks and a thick drooping mustache. A missing front tooth marred an otherwise not unpleasant countenance, which, however, favored an expression of scorn. Walter did not trust him.

The King was startled by the name of the second gentleman. He was Eadgar Aetheling, the unfortunate heir who never managed to get closer to the English throne than a hasty election, even more hastily refuted. Malcolm leaned forward, a scanning look of recognition on his face.

To study the young man, one could understand why the Witan had no faith in their king-elect. Perhaps aged about eighteen, the boy had nervous, shifting eyes in a pale face, and a weak chin which he sadly attempted to cover with a scant beard. Eadgar's naturally thin blond hair was already balding. He cracked his knuckles constantly.

The Aetheling's fidgety manners were understandable, however; one could see the result of too many changes of fortune. As a child he was raised in Hungary, only to be taken, along with his mother and sisters, to England when Edward the Confessor chose his father Eadward as heir to the throne. Unfortunately, Eadward the Exile died mysteriously within a month after his arrival in England, and once again the family was dependent on a King's charity, as they had been in Hungary.

This time, the children were brought up under the careful eyes of their adopted countrymen; for Eadgar was the last true heir to the throne. But misfortune seemed to follow the boy; Edward the Confessor died while Eadgar was an adolescent. England's position was too precarious to trust to an unstable boy, so he was passed over in favor of Harold.

The rest was recent history; not ready to give up the elusive dream of sovereignty, he was able to attract a loyal following: those willing to go to any length to retain a king of royal Saxon blood, even one not native born.

Sitting back, Malcolm slapped his knee. "Of course," he stated decisively. "I remember you now. You shared an exile with me at Edward's court, though you were only a child."

Eadgar seemed happily surprised, as if he suddenly met with an old friend. "Why yes, with my two sisters and my mother Agatha. I think I remember you...You came with Waltheof's father." He pointed to a large boy sitting next to him, about his own age, who looked at Malcolm with intelligent eyes.

"My God. Waltheof, Seward's boy!" the King exclaimed, jumping up. He grabbed Waltheof by the shoulders, holding him at arm's length.

"Your father was so dear to me...and I never expected to meet you. By my soul, you are welcome, cousin. I should have recognized you."

As the two looked at each other, Walter nodded in silent agreement. It was true; Waltheof bore a strong resemblance to the great Seward. His face was round and wide; he persisted in the Danish style of a long braid and forked beard. Waltheof's clothes were of skins and furs, roughly tied with rawhide; they barely covered his bulging muscles.

The other two men, named Syward Beorn and Sheriff Merlesweyne, were not of Malcolm's acquaintance. They were of old Saxon blood; Merlesweyne had been greatly trusted by Harold, who left him as governor of York after Stamford Bridge.

"Sire, I don't know how recent your news is," began Waltheof, "but it came to pass that King William has given the earldom of Northumbria to one of his own creatures. Yet he still thought to fool us with a native born."

Malcolm sat back, stimulated by a sense of action. At long last he could make plans about the Norman, knowing where the conflict was beginning.

"He chose a man called Copsi," sneered Cospatric. "A friend of Tostig's. It didn't take long for the Northumbrians to kill him."

In the break that followed his words could be heard the sharp intake of three breaths. The others leaned forward.

"Northumbria was ready for revolt," Eadgar whispered, showing more spirit than Malcolm expected. "Unfortunately, William anticipated it. Before we knew it—" His companions jerked their heads angrily at his use of the word 'we', "—his soldiers were upon us. We barely escaped."

Malcolm let out his breath slowly. This confirmed his suspicion that William was every bit as dangerous as he thought. Deciding not to betray any insight, he asked them what their next plan was.

"There are rumors of another rising, given time," answered Cospatric. "He has already appointed Copsi's successor, a Robert de Comines, one of his companions from Flanders. However, Durham belongs to us. It seethes with discontent. Once they revolt, York and the rest of Northumbria will follow."

The King looked uncomfortable. Expecting them to ask his

help, he was trying to think of a polite refusal. Essentially, their plan was sound. Unless William was willing to devote his entire army to the North, he would find the Northumbrians a surprisingly stubborn bunch. No, Malcolm's doubt lay in the leadership; it wasn't difficult to size up the temperament of these men. This was not a good time to jeopardize his shaky standing with William over an enterprise that could well fail. They had abandoned their first attempt too easily; perhaps they learned a lesson. If their second rebellion proved more successful, they might find the Scottish King more amiable.

"We ask nothing of you at all, except food and shelter for us and those who follow," Eadgar said quickly, divining Malcolm's thoughts. "And the use of Lothian to gather support."

Relieved, the King assented. Since his thoughts had already been directed toward his southern borders; perhaps this ruse would serve to expand them. Durham, located sixty miles north of York, was close enough to Scotland that Malcolm was under the jurisdiction of its Bishop. Why not annex it altogether?

Malcolm nodded. Yes, perhaps these troublesome men could lay the groundwork for his secret plans to invade Northumbria.

Gathering aid did not take long; it seemed that Malcolm's assent had been taken for granted even before it was given. As the men poured in, they brought fresh reports about Comines's insolence. Cospatric had, after all, properly assessed the situation. The Norman Earl wasn't really interested in ruling the North. Preferring the role of a tyrant, he carried on like the Northumbrians were a conquered people and killed as he chose, stealing what he wanted. He was totally insensible to their anger as if they were of no account.

Finally, late in the spring, the long-expected word came. Comines had attempted to enter Durham with seven hundred men. Knowing the peril, intent on keeping the new Earl safely outside the walls, Durham's citizens barred the gates to the city.

But as soon as they thought they were secure, the townsfolk were betrayed by their own Bishop, who opened the doors and let the Normans in.

Without delay, the army began to plunder the city, as if its residents were enemies. Setting fire to houses, raping wives and killing children, they spent one long night enjoying the slaughter and ruin of Durham's hapless inhabitants.

Comines had added that necessary ingredient which released the brooding rage, simmering for so long. Just as the Normans were settling to rest after their exhausting frenzy, the gates burst open from the outside, spewing a flood of angry men. Their entry was bloody, intent on revenge.

The outnumbered residents of Durham, encouraged and strengthened by their countrymen, turned on their aggressors, wreaking havoc that matched their own fury.

Comines and his nearest companions saw how desperate their situation was, and took refuge in the Bishop's palace. But they did not flee unseen; howling their revenge, the attackers flowed toward the building, bearing torches. Before long, the palace was in flames.

In a last desperate stand, Comines and his men burst forth, swords flying. The crowd momentarily fell back at the energy of their onslaught, but overwhelming numbers gave them courage. Comines went down, shouting and cursing, taking a number of enemies with him.

For his men, there was no question of escape. Treated with the same scorn they showed their victims, the garrison fell to the weapons of the Northumbrians. All but one of the Normans was killed; the last man was allowed to escape so the story would spread.

With hours, it seemed, the whole country knew what had happened. York, always ready for revolt, flew into a passion of revenge. As if in imitation of their neighbors, they attacked their own Norman garrison, driving them into their fortress.

When the news came, the Aetheling was ready. Thanking Malcolm briefly and hurriedly, the leaders of the growing Anglo-Saxon power hastened south from Scotland. The King was not sorry to see them go. He politely accompanied his guests to the border, attended by the few local lairds he could summon, and they all watched wryly as Eadgar crossed into England.

"I wish I could say good riddance to them," he murmured to Walter, as the Scottish entourage turned back. "But methinks this Eadgar is like a poor cousin, who shows up at the dinner table as soon as his pockets are empty. We will not have seen the last of him."

The King fell into thought. Indeed, this Eadgar promised to cause him more trouble...of this, he was certain. King William knew what was going on; how long before he demanded that Malcolm turn the exiles over to his ruthless justice?

Meanwhile, not caring to think beyond his visions of glory, the Aetheling marched to York. As he passed through Northumbria, all the dissatisfied, all the angry thousands swelled his ranks, intent on throwing the Normans forever out of the North. The gates of York flew open before them, as he expected, and Eadgar made his entrance proudly, convinced that the cheering was meant only for him. Celebration was held for the city's deliverance, while the Normans were besieged in their fortress.

Eadgar looked to the right and to the left, while someone took the reins of his horse and led him to the Archbishop's palace. He tried not to notice how ragged the townspeople were. Occasionally, someone would touch his heel, or his leg, and he would bend down as though to bless them, hoping no one would notice that he didn't really know what was expected of him.

Archbishop Ealdred was waiting at the top of his steps while the little cavalcade approached. He smiled grimly as Eadgar dismounted, and held out his ringed hand for the requisite kiss.

"Come," he said shortly. "There is much for you to do."

Eadgar looked at his friends for support. Ealdred was a formidable man. The Aetheling knew him from before, during the panic after Harold's death while the Witan scrambled for a successor. Even then, Archbishop Ealdred barely acknowledged his rule; how was he going to act now, when Eadgar played the role of usurper?

The Archbishop had already turned his back on the deliverers of his city; Eadgar and his companions followed him into the house at a respectable distance. They were somewhat relieved when Ealdred led them into a room full of burghers and merchants; at least they wouldn't have to deal with him alone.

The assemblage paused in their conversations at the new interruption, and bowed respectfully as the Archbishop passed, nodding his greeting. He mounted the steps to his throne and sat heavily, then studied Eadgar for a long time.

"It is you who must lead this war against the Normans," he said finally. "You are the true heir to the throne of England. I speak this, mind you," he added to them all, "as a Saxon, not as an archbishop. I must take no part in this uprising." He held up his hand as the Yorkists objected. "No, my sons, I cannot help you. Whether I wanted or no, I consecrated William the Norman as king, and I cannot go against such an act. But I will not hinder you either, in your work."

Eadgar opened his mouth and then closed it. He suddenly felt as though the ground had dropped out from under him; all eyes had turned to his face, and he could see that every man in the room expected him to answer. But what was he to say? He had always depended on someone else for guidance, yet even Cospatric, usually so outspoken, was cowed in the Archbishop's presence. It was all up to him, now.

"Where are the Normans?" he began, and flinched at the quiver in his own voice. He coughed, and started again. "Have they attempted a parley?"

This was enough to break the silence, and Eadgar sighed with relief when everyone talked at once.

"Burn them out, before they send for help, I say!" shouted a man with a long stick.

"It may be too late, by now," answered another. "I say, send a messenger to them, demanding surrender."

"No!"

"Not yet."

"Make them suffer!"

The men tried to outshout each other, while Eadgar looked from one to the other. "Give them what they gave us!" shouted the man closest to him. Eadgar nodded, eliciting a cheer. He began nodding even more vigorously, happy with their reaction.

It seemed like the decision had been made. But then a large man stepped forward, dominating the assembly; he was fully armored, and judging by their response, the others knew him well. He looked hard at the man next to Eadgar. "And what of the fortresses?"

"Burn them!" the man shouted fervently.

The giant grabbed his arm. "And what use are they to us, burned to the ground?"

"Yes," someone urged, "he is right. Drive them from the castles, then take them ourselves."

"No!"

"Too dangerous!"

"We cannot hold York without fortresses!" The man's voice carried across the room, even though he wasn't shouting. Eadgar frowned, but didn't dare object.

The others grumbled uncertainly. Someone turned to the Archbishop. "What is your opinion, your Grace?"

But Ealdred shook his head wearily. He sat back in his throne, glaring at Eadgar, as though urging him to take control. But the Aetheling did not dare look him in the face.

The big man noticed Ealdred's look, and he, too, turned to Eadgar. "What do you say, then, Prince Eadgar? Should we starve them into submission?"

Many of the men felt too strongly about this question to hold their tongues. "Burn them out! Starving will take too long!"

And the shouting started over again. People kept tugging at Eadgar, talking into his ear, arguing with one another. The big man faced the Aetheling squarely, but Eadgar did his best to ignore him, too.

But his adversary would not bear this affront. "Enough!" he shouted, and the room fell silent. "We are not getting anywhere. Perhaps Eadgar Aetheling needs time to think." He spat then stomped out of the room. After a moment's hesitation, the others followed him, scowling at Eadgar as they passed.

The Aetheling watched the room empty out, until there was no one left but he and his small following, and the Archbishop Ealdred. He finally dared a glance at the prelate, but was not reassured by the man's expression.

"You just succeeded in alienating Thane Archill, the most powerful man in Northumbria," Ealdred said. "Eadgar, you will have to do better than that."

The Archbishop's scorn provoked the only reaction Eadgar knew how to handle. His face grew sultry, and he shrugged in disdain. "A lot of help you were," he retorted. "What kind of man are you, to let me endure such behavior, before I even knew what I was up against."

The Archbishop sighed, suddenly weary. "It is something you are going to have to get used to, if you want to be king. Right or wrong, Eadgar, you must learn to take a stand!"

Before the Aetheling could respond, the Archbishop was on his feet, gesturing a dismissal. Then he walked from the room by a side door. Eadgar blinked at Cospatric for a moment, then some servants entered and bowed. Relieved, Eadgar pushed past his friends and followed the servants from the room. No one spoke to him as he passed.

The next three days dragged on in much the same manner, until it looked like the Yorkists were going to lay siege to the garrison, mostly because they couldn't decide on another course of action. By now, Eadgar had lost half of his council including Thane Archill, but he was too sullen to care. No one could get a word of advice from his lips, so the men started making decisions for themselves.

Cospatric decided to become the Aetheling's spokesman, and he made a pretense of consulting Eadgar before sounding his own declarations. It was all the same to Eadgar. He nodded his agreement when someone suggested they position men outside the city walls. He frowned when someone else counseled a parley, but no one paid attention. There was a constant flow of people in and out of Archbishop Ealdred's council chamber, and Eadgar watched the movement detachedly. In fact, he was happy to be relieved of the burden; he didn't have the vaguest idea what to do.

Bored to tears, Eadgar barely noticed the young man who dashed up to Cospatric, until the man threw himself to his knees. All movement in the room ceased.

"The fields are on fire," he gasped, "all around the city."

In reality, no one had understood what they were up against. Blinded by their stubbornness, the Saxons still did not understand the iron determination of their Norman King. Unbeknownst to them, the garrison commander had long before succeeded in sending a messenger to William, begging for help. One appeal was enough; taking nearly all the troops at his disposal, the King had set forth, determined to teach his rebellious subjects a lesson.

While the anxious citizens milled around in confusion, William burst like magic through the billowing smoke. His sudden appearance threw the offenders into an immediate panic. Discipline vanished as every man put his own survival before their common cause. Many Yorkists took refuge in St. Peter's Minster, trusting to holy sanctuary. William put the building to the torch. Hundreds were cut down where they stood, vainly defending their families.

Many others fled the city. Declaring the day lost, Eadgar Aetheling and his companions disappeared with the rest.

Not satisfied with subduing York, William sent a strong force to Durham, intending to make a further example of them. But along the way, the army was overtaken by a fog denser than any had ever seen. Totally lost, not able to guess what direction they were to head in, they were met by a man who told them that Durham was protected by St. Cuthbert, who allowed no harm to come to his city. Abashed, the Normans turned back.

26

Margaret Aetheling

No one wanted to venture out into the storm that battered Malcolm's tower. The King was settled comfortably before a large fire, playing chess with Walter. A handful of courtiers were engaged in betting over their dice.

"You know, you are right," Malcolm said, knocking over a piece with his queen. "We should have heard from our friends by now. God's blood, I wish we weren't so isolated."

As if in answer, the door blew open, admitting a guard who pushed it shut with difficulty.

"Sire," the man said, "we have spotted a ship that seems to be in trouble, judging by the way it lists to one side."

"Yes?" Malcolm said, not paying full attention. "What of it?"

"Well, Sire, from what we can tell it carries a noble passenger. It has taken shelter in our port; Thomas said I should bring you the news."

The King sighed. "Alas, Walter, I do not doubt your friend's judgment. Will you do me this favor, and make a visit to the ship? Perhaps it belongs to someone we need to impress."

Smiling, Walter got his cloak. "You need not ask me for favors."

Taking the guard with him, Walter bowed his head to the wind, pulling the hood tightly under his chin. It was indeed a cruel night, bringing a last remnant of winter with it. The rain stung his eyes so that he could barely see; more than once he nearly slipped. He mounted a horse, unwilling as he was to leave the dry barn. Following the dim silhouette of his companion, Walter felt a rare pang of longing for sunny Brittany.

They were guided by the beacon flickering wildly at the dock, set to guide the ships safely to the port at Dunfermline. The watchman had spoken truly; before them rocked a tall ship, dangerously leaning to one side. Atop its mast flew a ragged standard. As Walter neared the flames, a recognizable face broke away from a huddled group of people trying to stay warm.

"Eadgar," Walter exclaimed, expecting the man's return by horse, not boat. The Aetheling seemed embarrassed.

"Walter, I believe," he said, then motioned with his head toward the others. "I have come with my family. We were headed back to Hungary, but were blown off course by the storm. The pilot knew of this port, so we changed direction...just in time, I think."

"Hungary," Walter muttered, "then the expedition—"

"I shall tell you of it later," said Eadgar hurriedly. "Cospatric, Waltheof are both here, along with the others. Please," he took Walter's arm, "meet my mother, my sisters..."

They walked toward the others, who were staring at them. An older woman stepped forward; her lofty bearing, even in this reduced state, gave the impression she was granting an audience. The two daughters, though less arrogant, tried to follow her lead.

Walter glanced past the mother. His eyes were drawn, unbidden, to the face of the older daughter. She was tall; her long blonde braids reached nearly to her thighs. With flushed cheeks, her soft blue eyes rested on his own, and it seemed that a rush of warm air flowed through her into him. Walter felt that he was lost in a beauty that made everything else seem dull and insignificant. She exuded peace and serenity, even making the storm seem less violent. The girl certainly bore little resemblance to her brother.

Eadgar was speaking to him. Walter had to force himself to listen.

"...and so perhaps we should wait here, until Malcolm himself chooses to take responsibility for harboring us."

"What? Oh, yes. I shall go to him now, and return shortly with an answer."

Walter stumbled off, recovering from the girl's influence. He shook his head. Malcolm will most surely scold him, for forgetting to ask her name.

Snugly inside the tower, Walter shook off his wet cloak as he told Malcolm about their visitors. The King stroked his chin.

"So the Aetheling brought his family," he said thoughtfully. "Oh, I remember his mother Agatha, the proud fool. She could never accept her dependence on the King's charity. But the girls... I don't remember much about them. Christina is the younger daughter. Full of fire she is, like her mother. But the other one...Oh yes. Margaret."

He looked strangely at Walter. "Is she really that intriguing? Perhaps the storm was getting to you."

"You must see for yourself. I think if her brother had possessed some of her refinements, he would have easily gained the throne of England."

"That's a strong statement, coming from you. However, I suppose I must greet them as becomes their station, no matter what the weather.

"Wallace," he called to his manservant, "bring my cloak, and a dry one for Walter. You other gentlemen, please break up your game and accompany us. We must impress our guests with my immense retinue."

Remembering Eadgar's warning, Walter grabbed the cloak from the servant. He placed it on Malcolm's shoulders, leaning close to the King's ear. "One other thing," he said softly, "Eadgar seemed worried about King William's reaction when he hears that you have sheltered them. Perhaps they will cause you trouble."

"Too late to worry about William now, my friend. I've already committed myself."

Gesturing for the rest to follow, Malcolm led his unwilling companions into the storm.

If anything, the winds had risen in intensity. The beacon fire was reduced to a pitiful flicker. No longer able to find comfort from its feeble flames, the party had retired back onto the ship, seeking shelter from the tent on its deck.

And yet, attempting to recover as much dignity as possible from their vulnerable position, the newcomers chose to remain on board as the Scots approached. Malcolm didn't seem to mind, and leaped aboard the boat with exceptional agility. He bowed to Agatha.

"Welcome, my lady, to Scotland. Though the heavens are less gracious than I would wish, I hope your reception in my humble tower will make up for this lack."

Somewhat mollified, the older woman allowed herself to be handed to a young man, ready to help her to shore.

Pleased with himself, Malcolm extended the same welcome to Eadgar and his younger sister. But the words died on his lips as he touched the hand of Margaret. Surprised by her unruffled manner, the King silently watched her pass from one hand to the next, ignoring each man in turn as she carefully picked her steps.

The girl seemed to have the same effect on the others.

"Well, Walter, you are right again," said Malcolm. "That woman is a marvel of her sex. See how she carries herself, as if she doesn't notice the worship of those she blesses with her touch.

"Oh, to touch that hand again," he continued as they moved on, leaving his retainers behind to unload the many trunks brought by the Aetheling's family, and of course pay the shipman.

Walter stared at him, amazed. "Why Sire, you are smitten," he exclaimed.

Malcolm turned to him, a peculiar gleam in his eyes.

"Aye, Walter, I think I am. I think I am."

The exiles gratefully allowed themselves to be given rooms and a change of clothing. One by one they came down to the great hall to share their adventure. Eadgar elected to be the spokesman.

"The movement was a success," he assured Malcolm, as a servant handed him a cup of mulled wine. "We had them trapped in their fortress, waiting for our decision. Where we failed was in not making sure the garrison was truly sealed in. Some messengers slipped through."

Eadgar took a long draught, his hand shaking.

"I tell you, Sire...William appeared as if out of nowhere. He brought all his Normans, thundering out of the smoke with enough noise to wake the dead.

"He had set fire to the crops, you see, screening his movements. Many of us were lost in the flames, or died inhaling the smoke in their flight. I took my mother and sisters, and with the others boarded the ship. My family," he added, "had been all the while at York, even when we came to you the first time."

The Aetheling dropped his voice. "William had sworn to revenge himself on me, so we thought it would be best to take refuge in Hungary."

"I hope you expected nothing else," Malcolm growled, but his voice was cut short by the entrance of Margaret who had stood, unnoticed, at the door for many minutes.

Even wrapped in a voluminous borrowed garment, she was beautiful. The King moved aside, indicating a place beside him. The room had become silent, but she affected not to notice.

Looking at Malcolm she spoke the first words he ever heard from her lips: "Your Grace, we thank you for your pleasant hospitality." The fine French words glided from her tongue as if they were native to her, and Malcolm blushed with pleasure. "I feel a great relief to stand once again on land that is ruled with humanity. For this I thank our good Lord, Whose will be done." She crossed herself; after a moment, everyone else did the same.

"We have spent many years on English soil," Margaret went on again, switching with difficulty to the Saxon tongue. "Although born in Hungary, my lineage is Saxon, and I feel most painfully the anguish of my people. My brother's cause, whether successful or not, is absolutely necessary, if England is to be saved from destruction by the tyrant. Don't you agree?" She bent such a demanding look on Malcolm that he squirmed.

Forgotten in her little corner, Isabel watched the scene a little jealously. Suddenly another woman was the focal point of Malcolm's court; her appeal was undeniable. Even Walter, usually so unemotional, appeared to be hanging onto her every word. Just what was this religious affectation?

As this was going on, Myrna entered the room, seating herself near Isabel. She immediately noticed the impression this strange new woman made on Walter, and more surprisingly on Malcolm. Suddenly Isabel didn't seem like much of a threat to her anymore.

The Breton smiled wryly at her new accomplice. She was still struggling with Gaelic—not to mention Anglo-Saxon—and could not follow the conversation. Myrna bent toward her. "Who is she?"

"The Aetheling's sister, Margaret. She is truly beautiful, is she not?"

Myrna nodded. But that wasn't enough to explain the almost mystical effect she had on all the men in the room. "What is she talking about?"

"As best as I can tell, she is convincing the King about the moral value of Eadgar's invasion," the other whispered scornfully, "whether he likes it or not."

Indeed, Malcolm didn't seem to like it, for reasons he wouldn't communicate to the righteous woman. He would have been happier to keep William far from his borders. Never expecting Eadgar's rebellion to draw the King in person to deal with it, he was already regretting giving him aid.

But on the other hand, without Eadgar there would be no Margaret. He looked admiringly at the tall woman, who had turned to speak with her brother. She had a strong will, this one, and wasn't afraid to speak out. And her lineage was truly noble; on her father's side, her ancestry extended all the way back to Woden; her mother shared a lineage with those who still commanded the Holy Roman Empire. Of more recent importance, she, too, was an Aetheling, grand-daughter of Edmund Ironside... quite a worthy woman to consider for one's queen. Shaking his head, Malcolm drew his attention back to the conversation.

Cospatric was speaking: "Given added support from the Danes," he was saying to Eadgar, "we could reinvade Northumbria before the summer is over. I say that all is not lost!" He thumped a fist on his knee, in a gesture not unlike William's.

"Would you give us your countenance, Sire?" asked Waltheof, who had been silent until this moment.

Malcolm looked uncomfortably from one person to the other, until his eyes rested on Margaret. She drew herself up proudly, turning to face the King squarely. She looked at Eadgar then back again.

Seeing the faith his sister placed in the Aetheling, Malcolm relented. Perhaps he was judging the boy too harshly.

"Only if you agree to stay with me, as my guests... and give up your plan to return to Hungary. At least for now," he added hurriedly.

The men burst into a spontaneous cheer. Margaret smiled at Malcolm, who beamed back at her. Isabel and Myrna frowned at one another.

It seemed that Walter alone refused to betray his feelings.

Walter's feelings were too private and confused to share even with his wife. Later, as she lay comfortably in his arms, he stroked her hair absently, resigned to a sleepless night. It was difficult enough to sort out his emotions under any circumstances, but especially so, tonight.

What a captivating woman the Saxon was. She had dominated

the conversation without trying; all eyes were drawn to her, so astonishing was her beauty... and something more. Her manner was forceful without being demanding, her charisma was unconscious yet manipulative, as if sharpened by long practice. When she spoke, it was as if she was giving a speech.

It was odd that her brother Eadgar seemed unaware of her influence, as if all the attention was meant for him.

Malcolm was clearly taken with her, in that unsubtle way an older man could be. He was twice Margaret's age, though still in his physical prime; her very youth was, in a way, a trap. How much younger a young woman can make a man feel. He knew; it was so with him and Isabel.

The King was impulsive; there was a kingly attribute. He always seemed to know what he wanted, and when he decided on something, Malcolm stuck to his choice. And Walter could tell: he had undoubtedly chosen Margaret. An involuntary shudder came over him, disturbing Isabel. Her eyes fluttered open.

"Mmm, you're thinking about that woman, aren't you?" she murmured.

Pulling the cover over her shoulders, he assented. "You know, Isabel, I think I'm jealous."

She laughed at that notion, waking up all the way. "Let me tell you a story, my husband. When I got to know you, especially before our wedding, all you would talk about was Malcolm, Malcolm. I was so jealous of this Malcolm I thought I would despise this person when I met him. And do you know what? I found him perfectly wonderful. It was impossible to hate him."

She sat up, tucking the cover under her chin. "And yet, Walter, I still had to adapt to a secondary role, in relation to him. It took some doing, you know. But I succeeded. Honestly, if you were put into a position where you had to choose between him and me, I don't know how you would choose."

Surprised, Walter didn't know what to say. He opened his

mouth, but she silenced him with a shake of her head. "I'm not looking for an answer. So now, you find yourself in the same position. Maybe, in thinking of me, you'll understand your own feelings better."

He curled around her. "You never cease to amaze me. I'm so happy you love me."

Easing herself beside him, she continued: "There's more. Tonight, when I saw the effect this woman had on everyone, especially you, I too was jealous. Oh, don't deny it." She kissed him. "I was envious of her. But, seeing your own feelings, I think I can be more understanding. She can't help being the way she is. Perhaps she will be good for this court. Even good for Malcolm. He needs someone like her.

"I'm afraid there are some things even you can't do for him."

Pulling her close, Walter covered her mouth with his. "You are so right," he managed to say, as they began to make love.

Margaret and her family made themselves right at home in Malcolm's court. They were kept company by the many Saxons who were still coming north, unable to tolerate the stern Normans who made England their home.

Malcolm fell daily more and more under the Princess's influence.

The Saxons watched Walter's cavalry training with interest, having experienced firsthand the strength of the mounted enemy. Not a few volunteered to learn this different method of fighting, though Thomas stubbornly clung to his old training. He incorporated many of the others into his new guard.

Walter's students graduated to a new type of quintain. This one was in the shape of a wooden Saracen, an infidel whom the enthusiastic youths took pleasure in striking. The Saracen held a long wooden scimitar in his right hand. It was so designed that when struck on the shield, the form would twirl around, smiting the rider with the sword if he was not quick enough to ride or duck.

His little band had grown by twenty more, though the newcomers had to bring their own mounts. These, unfortunately, were mainly Scottish ponies; they were more suited to the rocky and mired geography of the country, but smaller, less able to support an armored knight. They were welcomed, nonetheless, and the riders adapted their leather armor to the combat.

Training was stepped up; the new cavalry was to prove its worth in the upcoming campaign of Eadgar's in August.

Meanwhile, Malcolm lost no time directing his own campaign against Margaret. The Princess was friendly—even encouraging—but he seemed unable to make any progress in his suit. There was something about this girl, so distant, so untouchable, that continued to baffle him. It was as though she kept a part of herself firmly away from the rest of the world... and of course, it was this private place in her heart that he coveted for himself. Gifts brought a smile to her face, but nothing else. He imported the best jongleurs, the most exciting storytellers, but her reactions were never more than casual.

Finally, one day late in July, he offered to take her on a tour of the surrounding countryside, unaccompanied except for one servant. Much to his surprise and pleasure, she gave her consent.

The brisk air did marvels for the girl's countenance. Her face flushed, she laughed gaily at the new sights Malcolm pointed out to her. On a little cliff overlooking the firth, he laid out a lunch, carefully packed that morning. She accepted a mug of wine with a smile that made his heart leap.

At first, the King kept the conversation general, telling Margaret of the local history, and of the Celtic influence still strong among the people. He told of the old gods, and how badly his people needed guidance. This last theme was introduced for her benefit; Malcolm knew that any topic touching religion interested Margaret. But he didn't yet realize how much.

"The Scots are in need of a bishopric nearer our capitol," he was saying. "Durham, powerful though it is, lies too far to the south. St. Andrews, of course, is nearby. I must take you there some time soon." He looked sideways at her. "But it is small yet, and our people need to be encouraged to visit its shrine..."

Margaret nodded her agreement, smiling in what he already recognized as her religious enthusiasm. Seizing the moment, Malcolm took her hand.

"Margaret, my dear, I cannot do it all alone. I need someone strong to rule beside me... someone dear to me who will ease the trouble of my people. And the trouble in my soul. Margaret, I cannot keep it to myself any longer. I am in love with you, and I wish you to be my queen."

Slowly, she turned to him, the smile fading from her face. For the first time, the woman's assurance turned to confusion. Years of carefully cultivated poise fell away, revealing an uncertain little girl, who clung to her faith as an answer to all her ills. Malcolm was astounded by the girl's naked insecurity; and he found himself all the more taken with her. For once, he could relate to the woman he loved.

"But Malcolm," she started hesitantly, "I am destined for the church."

"The church," he repeated dully, not quite understanding.

"Yes, Sire. I am to become a nun, as befits my upbringing and my inclination. By devoting myself to God, I hope to aid my oppressed countrymen in the best way I know how. My heart belongs to God... I know not how to give it to a man." She paused, uncertain.

"The best way you know how," he answered miserably. "What makes you so sure a nunnery is the right way?"

She pulled her hand from his. Unwilling to commit herself she said nothing, looking away.

Later, Malcolm visited her mother. Questioned on Margaret's decision, the woman shook her head sadly. "Yes, both Margaret and Christina have set their hearts on the church." Agatha bent over her sewing to hide her face. "They were most inspired by King Stephen, and King Edward of blessed memory."

"But isn't one daughter enough for such a good cause?" Malcolm pleaded. Agatha sighed, aware of the unexpected privilege offered to her favorite daughter. She couldn't have planned this good fortune any better.

"Sire, the choice has always been hers. She is a very headstrong girl."

The King paced the floor. "Agatha," he said, stopping short. "I'm sure you have some influence over your daughter. Why not persuade her to accept my suit? Surely she cannot defy her mother."

Drawing herself up, the woman looked scornfully at Malcolm. "Are you suggesting I force my daughter to give up the most important thing in her life? That I force her to do my will? Never would I consent to such a thing."

Seeing the panic on Malcolm's face, she relented a bit. It was obvious that he was very much taken with Margaret. And after all, his request did not differ from her own desire. Putting aside her sewing, she stood up, as if dismissing her visitor. "But I will try," she added, allowing him to hug her in response.

And try she did, until she was red in the face and puffing from Margaret's refusal. But Agatha reassured the King that the girl's obstinacy was only temporary. Given time, her daughter would come to see reason.

By mid-August, Eadgar's party was prepared to move south again. They had been in contact with the Danish King, who agreed to send three of his sons in charge of an expedition. They would join the Aetheling in Northumbria, and move toward York together.

As it turned out, Malcolm was unable to join the venture. Learning of a minor insurrection in Galloway, the King determined to put it down before it gained momentum.

"Go with the Aetheling," he said to Walter. "His life has become dear to me, and I want you to protect him from himself."

Walter paced the floor. "I don't mind telling you, Sire, I don't like this campaign at all. One doesn't willingly invite Norse to come raiding. They are hard to get rid of."

"As long as they stay out of Scotland, I don't care what they do."

Walter stared at Malcolm. But the King wasn't in an arguing mood.

"See here, Walter. As long as Eadgar keeps William busy, the Bastard will leave me alone. Having Northmen for neighbors is no worse than Normans. They are all of the same stock, after all.

"Just keep Eadgar under control. Try to lend him some backbone, eh?"

And so it was settled. Fifteen hundred men were sent with the Aetheling; they were all that Malcolm could spare. Eadgar had expected more, but no one listened to his grumbling.

As it proved, he hardly needed more men; all Northumbria was prepared to follow him. Eadgar's force met the Danes on the Humber, as agreed, then made a leisurely march toward York, stopping at friendly villages along the way. Everywhere they went, they were joined by more enthusiastic Saxons and Danes. For as they knew, Northumbria was still inhabited by a considerable Danish population, who had given up their roaming ways decades ago.

Walter was impatient. He tried to urge the Aetheling to a faster pace, before William discovered their movements. "Don't you understand?" he rasped, exasperated. "William is no sluggard. You are giving him time to gather his army."

He knew he was wasting his breath. Eadgar was already annoyed at his constant presence; he thought Walter a spy, and did his best to ignore him. But this last criticism was too much for his delicate ego.

"This is my expedition, not yours! I beg you to remember

that."

Walter took a deep breath, controlling his anger. "And it would be best you remember just whose countenance you act under. King Malcolm will not continue to give support to a losing cause."

That just made things worse. Shooting Walter a look full of daggers, his jaw stiffened. "All right then. What is wrong with our show of strength?"

"Nothing. Except that by now, you have lost the element of surprise. Messengers are undoubtedly on their way to King William at this very moment. He won't be long in responding."

"Ah, but that's where you are wrong. I happen to know that the commanders at York recently assured William that they could defend themselves for a year. He has turned his attentions elsewhere."

Despite himself, Walter was impressed that Eadgar was so well informed. But he wasn't entirely convinced.

"Don't you think your invasion could change all that?"

"Perhaps," said Eadgar with a sniff. "But he might have trouble disentangling himself from the west. It is a chance I am willing to take."

However, Eadgar's show of strength brought on a totally different response than he expected. Cheerfully advancing on York, no one seemed to worry too much about the dark smoke in the sky. But they discovered quickly enough that the fire was coming from York itself. Eadgar sat astride his horse, mouth open, oblivious to the curses of astonishment. His eyes nearly bulged from his head. People were grabbing at him, pulling his arm, but he just sat there, unable to move.

Walter watched him for a while, wondering if Eadgar was losing his mind. Then he decided that the Aetheling was merely bewildered. What else could one expect from such an inexperienced boy? Shaking his head, Walter rode closer, and put his mouth to the Aetheling's ear.

"Send some scouts ahead," he said urgently. "See what has happened. Perhaps William has preceded us, after all."

Somewhat abashed, the Aetheling looked slowly at him. The words seemed to have sunk into his brain. "Yes," he answered, unsteadily.

"And get those Danes under control," Walter urged.

Trying to look stern, Eadgar persuaded the others with some difficulty to halt. Although lusting after plunder, the Danes were reminded why they were there. All dismounted, deciding to leave their horses behind.

Six scouts dashed away. They weren't long in coming back. The first threw himself to one knee before the Aetheling.

"The Norman garrison has set the city on fire," he gasped.

The commanders swore their surprise.

A second scout followed, his information a bit more complete. He had talked with some of the citizens who had been scrambling about, and who had babbled that they didn't know who presented more danger: the Normans or the invading Danes.

It developed that the garrison had been afraid of another siege. They had feared that the Saxons would tear down the houses near the castles and use the wood to fill the ditches, making it easy to storm the fortress. To hinder that, they set fire to the buildings. The blaze quickly got out of hand and spread over more than half the town.

That was all the Danes had to hear. "Let's go!" shouted their chief, Thorkell, who led them down the hill, delighted that their work was half done.

Cursing bitterly, Walter dashed in pursuit. Their allies were already out of control. Not forgetting Eadgar, he turned his head, spotting the youth in Waltheof's company, scowling.

The flames rose way beyond the stone walls of York. Even from a distance Walter could hear the crackling of burning timber, and his skin tingled from the intense heat.

The army was jammed together at the few Roman gates, with

the Danes trying to force their way through first. This was no orderly entry; if the enemy had been thinking clearly, the Danes would have been easy prey.

Eadgar caught up with Thorkell, shouting over the din. "What are you doing?" his voice cracked in panic.

Walter shoved his way to the Aetheling's side. He grabbed Thorkell by the arm. "These people aren't our enemy," he growled, bringing his face close to the Dane's. "We are here to fight the Normans."

Daunted by Walter's ferocity, the Jarl pulled back. He sneered, but couldn't wrench from the other's grasp. "We'll fight your Normans for you. But do not expect my men to leave without their reward."

Walter's grip tightened, making the Dane flinch involuntarily. "You do not plunder the people you defend."

Thorkell brought his axe around with his free hand, laying it threateningly against Walter's chest. He wanted no trouble with King Malcolm, but Walter was pushing him too far. "We plunder whom we please."

Walter was about to respond with his own weapon, when a hand clamped around his wrist; then Waltheof stepped between them. His commanding presence cooled their anger somewhat, and Walter reluctantly loosened his grip.

Glaring for a moment at his antagonist, Thorkell swung on Eadgar, who stepped back. "Keep him away from me," he snarled, then disappeared among his men.

The Aetheling turned on Walter in his humiliation. "That's not how to handle them!" he snapped.

"You are wrong, Eadgar," interrupted Waltheof. "They only respect a stronger man than themselves. Listen to me. The Danes will fight like they promised. Our only recourse is to get them away from here as soon as the battle is over."

Frustrated, Eadgar plunged after Thorkell.

"Thank you, Waltheof," Walter said, liking this man more and more. "I was about to lose control."

The other smiled. "That was a brave but foolish gesture. Come, let us stay together."

Taking a halfhearted look after Eadgar, Walter gladly joined him. The throng was beginning to thin, and Waltheof summoned a large following of his own men. They began to push through the gates, past the frightened residents, who strove unsuccessfully to force their own way out of the city, before it was too late.

So far, the Normans had stayed safely inside their fortresses. Waltheof headed directly for the older castle, planting himself beside the gate. He shouted out a challenge to the fortress walls, as though ready to take the whole garrison by himself. The Danes were already gravitating toward the same spot, looking for a fight. In their wake, unhappily shouting orders that no one heard, followed Eadgar.

The Normans seemed anxious to join with them. Very soon, the gates flew open, disgorging the desperate garrison.

Waltheof was ready. He grasped his great Danish battle axe, feet spread wide, muscles bulging. Walter took his place at the Earl's back, almost in awe of the man's raw power. Waltheof was truly his father's son. Every Norman who approached him fell dead to the ground, missing a head, or with a chest opened wide, or a limb hacked off. The Dane was emboldened by his success and strengthened by every foe who bloodied his slashing axe. Never did an enemy's blade touch his flesh. Invincible as the old Norse Gods, Waltheof fought on, tirelessly.

Walter had little time to appreciate the great might of his companion-in-arms. He strove to protect Waltheof's back, while at the same time he kept his eye on Eadgar, whose skill was less than marvelous. The Aetheling moved closer to the invincible pair, acknowledging their ability to protect him.

Finally, the Norman ranks thinned; there were no reinforcements. The aspect of the fighting began to change. Where once the thick crush of Danes supported the deadly thrust of the

Northumbrians, now they began to melt away. They knew that the spirit of the garrison had been broken; the Normans were nearly extinguished. They had more interesting pursuits to follow.

Walter shouted at Eadgar to control the mob, but it was too late. The Aetheling and a tight guard moved through the city, attempting to restore order. But the Prince lacked authority, and his closest supporters were stamping out the last of the Norman resistance. For the rest, discipline was gone. The Danes plundered the town at will. As far as they were concerned, the alliance was over.

The rest of the Northumbrians set about destroying the fortresses, the symbols of Norman oppression. Walter was concerned with putting a stop to this counterproductive measure; he located Eadgar, but to no avail.

"Let them do it. That is why they came."

Exasperated, Walter shook his head. "Don't you see? We can hold York against William if we man these castles ourselves."

But Eadgar wasn't listening. "It's over. Our task is done. We have destroyed the Norman garrison."

Leaving the Aetheling and his misplaced glory, Walter searched for Waltheof. He found him at the cathedral, trying to organize a crew to fight the fire before the church was totally destroyed.

"It's hopeless, Walter," the other said, wiping the soot from his eyes. "We are too far from the river."

"Waltheof," Walter said, grabbing his arm, "You must help Eadgar impose some discipline. He can do nothing with these people."

Shouting a direction to one of the workers, the Dane gave Walter an angry look. "Can't you see? It is too late. The Northumbrians will soon be returning home."

"We can't let them go," cried Walter. "There is too much to be done yet."

"Walter... forget it. It is finished."

"It is finished because you let it be!" Walter found that he was shouting. "Your rebellions have no substance. You must give these people direction. They were better off staying home, rather than risk the trouble this war will bring to them."

Cospatric came upon them, heard the last remark. "Mind you, Walter. This is our war, not yours. We shall do as we see fit."

Walter had had enough. He searched out Eadgar and confronted him with this maddening lack of action. The Aetheling shrugged blandly. "What did Waltheof say?"

"I want to hear what you have to say!"

"All right. I have had enough of your meddling in my affairs. Leave me be! Bear my message to King Malcolm that I will continue my alliance with the Danes... and I will defy William in my own way."

"Is that the best you can do?"

"That is my decision. I don't have to answer to you for it. Now leave me. I am sick of the sight of you."

Walter didn't need to be told again. Finding his horse, he took one last look at the burning city and rode away.

Malcolm had already returned to Dunfermline, having quickly broken up the local rebellion. He was not happy to see Walter return, alone.

"It was disastrous, Sire."

Malcolm crossed his arms. "Well? Doesn't that give you more reason to stay with him?"

"I couldn't communicate with the boy. Eadgar has no sense that I can see, any more than do his friends. He absolutely refused to see reason."

"What is this about seeing reason? I sent you to watch his back."

Walter gaped at the King in amazement. Surely this wasn't the rational man he had come to know and love. Always before, they had understood one another.

"Sire," he went on more slowly. "The alliance with the Danes got out of control almost immediately. The Norman castles were destroyed, and the Norsemen plundered the city then returned to their ships. Then the Northumbrians went home."

"That doesn't sound like a disaster."

"It doesn't?" A momentary note of anger slipped out. "They could have made use of those fortresses. Instead, they destroyed their only hope of resistance and destroyed the city as well. It didn't have to happen like that."

"Come, Walter. That is the way of things."

Walter turned away. "William will take his revenge on Northumbria...the land you coveted." Angrily he strode to the door.

"Did I give you permission to leave?" Malcolm's voice was icy. "You still haven't explained why you deserted him."

Him. As if this selfish lad meant anything to Malcolm.

Turning, Walter felt a sadness wash over his heart.

"I tried to reason with Eadgar. I lost my temper at the needless waste of effort and lives. They were throwing away their advantage! He told me to leave him...to tell you that he would go on fighting King William in his own way."

A scornful snort from the Scot betrayed his true feelings. But he wasn't about to stray from his position.

"You should have stayed with him, Walter. On my command, not his. I am very displeased."

All Walter's anger had gone, leaving a heavy despair. Malcolm had never spoken to him like that. He looked at his friend, silently begging for mercy. None was forthcoming.

"You may go," the King said shortly.

Sighing, Walter closed the door softly behind him. Was he losing his mind? Was he the one that was wrong? Surely his years of experience taught him something.

He stumbled out of the tower, down the hill. His feet took him away from Dunfermline, tripping him, slipping in the grass. Walter leaned panting against a tree, staring up at the tower, now small and insignificant against the horizon.

What had happened to their friendship? Is this where it was all to end, with a scornful woman taking his place in Malcolm's heart—and she incapable of loving the man the way he did...

He felt betrayed, abandoned. It was true, what they said about the ingratitude of kings.

Messages soon came pouring north, confirming Walter's predictions, although this didn't serve to soften Malcolm's attitude toward his disgraced friend.

The Danes, taking Eadgar along with them, proceeded to plunder south along the coast of England.

As soon as William gathered his forces, they were his first target.

The Norman King posted watches on the Danes, following their movements until he deemed it right to descend on them. During a particularly lively raid, out came hundreds of Normans from the hills, swooping down on the unsuspecting Northmen. Many of the invaders were killed immediately, but the others banded together, forming a strong defense as they backed up slowly to their ships. They were amazed that the Normans allowed them to board, but did not let their surprise stop them from leaving as quickly as possible.

Since he knew how difficult it would be to drive the Danes from his shores, William decided to negotiate with them instead. He offered them a handsome sum of money, if they would consent to refrain from any further contact with the Aetheling and his following. They were given permission to plunder the coast for the rest of the winter, just so long as they would go back to where they came from in the spring. It didn't matter to the Danes where their money came from. They consented and sent Eadgar on his way.

Once William had dealt with the Danish threat, he was ready to do his own plundering—in the name of discipline.

Waltheof and many of the leaders deemed it prudent to move on to Durham, having lost most of their forces. They hoped that William would be more lenient with York if they weren't present. Cospatric had disappeared.

How little the Saxons understood their new king.

William proceeded to lay waste to all the land between York and Durham. No town, no farmstead was spared. All went up in flames before the vengeful force of the Norman. Any unwary villagers were murdered, all the livestock was taken for the hungry army. Thousands of emigrants crossed the borders into Scotland, even selling themselves into slavery to avoid starvation.

The once hardy country was destined to become a desert for a generation to come.

Eadgar soon reappeared at Malcolm's court. He was alone, and none the wiser for his experience. He didn't seem particularly disturbed by the consequences of his thwarted ambitions. He pointedly avoided Walter, concentrating instead on pleasing the King.

But Malcolm was surprisingly unresponsive to his advances. If anything, Walter noticed that the King had to struggle to contain his scorn regarding the campaign.

Finally, reverting to his usual self-centered attitude, the Aetheling complained that he was tired of being criticized.

"Sire, excuse my presumption in asking, but are you sure you could have done better, given the resources I had to work with?" He glared at Malcolm, a born follower trying to assert himself.

The King paused for thought. "Perhaps. Perhaps not. I suppose there is no choice but to try and see." He leaned toward Walter. "We must move quickly," he emphasized in a low voice, as though continuing some open-ended discussion, "when we are least expected. My army will be easy to reassemble."

Unbidden, tears jumped into Walter's eyes. It was the King's first amiable move since Walter's return. It was as if all tension between them had dissipated, once Malcolm had the opportunity to slide back into his accustomed role.

With a quick wave of his arm, Malcolm sent his servants running.

"Come, Walter," he said, putting an arm around the other's shoulders and drawing him off. They went walking down the hill below the tower, where Malcolm was building a new church.

"Walter," he said, his eyes softening, "I cannot say I am sorry for what happened between us. For I am your King and you disobeyed my orders. But I would not have us be like this, especially over that worthless man."

Relieved, Walter let out his breath.

"Remember," Malcolm went on, "he is Margaret's brother, and it is for her sake that I concern myself about him."

"Of course," Walter said. He reminded himself that this woman was a reality he would have to deal with. If only Malcolm would not withdraw his affection, perhaps he could learn to accept her.

They walked in thought.

"But no more of that. It is my plan to invade England, and at the first opportunity. It is obvious that such a campaign needs a strong hand if it's to go anywhere at all."

Walter ventured a question. "Why do you feel the need to start hostilities against William?"

"In some respects, William has started them. He is already demanding the surrender of Eadgar into his hands; though I don't think I want to tell the boy. He's already too impressed with his own importance.

"But more than that, it is a matter of borders. Northumbria is so situated that its borders are always changing. It is time Northumbria came back to Scotland. Why not turn Eadgar's cause to my own profit? We can arrange it so that when William is done plundering, I can move in and take over."

He handed his cloak to Walter. "I'm sorry this is so close to Isabel's confinement. I need you with me, Walter. She'll be well taken care of." Smiling wryly, Walter agreed. She had already told him she accepted her secondary role after the King. How right she had been!

When Eadgar found out about Malcolm's decision, he forgot his resentment in the dread of yet another dreary march. He had had his fill of luckless enterprises; the Aetheling had no stomach for more fighting. He was happy to turn over the responsibility to someone more adept at taking it. Malcolm's motives were of no concern to him.

Eadgar chose to move in another direction. He decided to cross over to Flanders, in an attempt to gain foreign support. Life on the same island with the Conqueror had proven too uncomfortable for the luckless exile.

27

Campaign into Northumbria

Thus began Malcolm's infamous campaign into England. Initially, he chose a route avoiding the lands of his allies. Plunder was a major factor in this foray, and parties were often sent back home, laden with treasures and slaves. Taking the conquered people for slaves was not uncommon to residents of either country; there were as many Scots made prisoner in England as the other way around.

Even more to Malcolm's taste was the pleasure of raiding the land under the Norman's sovereignty. There was no longer any doubt that the two kings were irreparably at odds; the opportunity for friendship had passed. Since Malcolm had taken the Aetheling and his family under his protection, William had flooded him with demands for their return. What was more, Malcolm's policy of political sanctuary was enough to infuriate the Norman. Malcolm took delight in goading William; it was only a matter of time before the issue would reach a climax.

It was the poor Northumbrians who suffered the wrath of first one king, then the other.

Walter didn't appreciate the campaign as it was going; this was unlike anything Malcolm had done before. But he didn't want to jeopardize his new-found favor with the King, so he rode well back in the ranks, keeping to himself. Malcolm was too busy to notice his reticence.

As the weeks drew on, the men took plundering to heart, becoming more difficult to control. And still Malcolm didn't seem to mind.

It was on the day they reached Wearmouth that news started pouring in. Malcolm sat astride his horse, grimly watching the burning of a cathedral, when a scout rode up to him, covered with dust. Walter moved closer, filled with foreboding.

"Sire," the mán gasped, "it has come to my notice that Cospatric has made his peace with King William, and has been created Earl of Northumbria." He paused as the King turned away in disgust.

Malcolm looked at Walter, who stared back, not changing expression. Then he returned to the scout. "Go on," he growled.

"It seems, Sire, that since then Cospatric has been raiding in Cumberland."

"My own lands!" Malcolm shouted, pacing back and forth. "That arrogant bastard, who turned traitor as soon as he saw a benefit to himself. May he rot in hell!" His face red, he turned back to the trembling man, who was bracing himself against the King's wrath.

"Sire, he has returned with great booty to his castle Bamburgh."

"Why didn't you tell me that in the first place, boy?" Malcolm exclaimed, pacing again. His report concluded, the scout took to his heels.

Clenching his fists, Malcolm stared at the burning buildings. Walter was the only one within hearing.

"I should have known," the King grumbled, "By God he will regret it." He mounted his horse mechanically, hands working the reins.

Suddenly, with a burst of anger, Malcolm viciously spurred his mount downhill, shouting for men to gather with him and move on to Bamburgh.

Cospatric's castle was far to the north, along the coast. It was in the heart of the land Malcolm had carefully avoided. But no longer. As the Scots gained momentum, Malcolm shouted his orders to spare no man, woman, or child, to burn every farmstead, kill every animal in all of Northumbria.

Spurring to Malcolm's side, Walter put a hand on the King's arm. "Malcolm, are you mad?" he cried. "This isn't your way. Control your anger. Put it to better use."

The Scot shook off his restraining hand. The look of fire he shot at Walter indeed showed madness.

"Look back on what your mother told you!" He spoke curtly, cutting short the words. "This is no concern of yours. Remember your place, Walter!"

Shocked, Walter backed off. He wanted to be nowhere near this feverish stranger.

Lacking the will to be part of this calamity, he pulled away from the army. But something kept him from leaving altogether. The sting of Malcolm's reprimand was giving way to a dull ache, but he tried to fight his feelings. The King was his friend. Was it possible that Malcolm was right and he was wrong?

"Look back on what your mother told you," he thought. "What did he mean?" Walter slowed his horse to a walk, searching his memory. Then he came across a discussion he had with Malcolm... how many years ago?

Not so many, though it seemed like a lifetime. He nodded to himself. His mother had told him that one could never judge a king, even though his actions seemed wrong. It was because of this that he saved Gruffydd's life and brought such shame on himself.

When he told Malcolm of her words, the King had said he was beginning to find out what she meant. And now, so did Walter. Had Malcolm sensed this anger in himself, even then? He sighed, wishing he had Isabel to talk to. She always knew the right thing to say.

Passing burning farmsteads, he needed only to follow the billowing smoke to track the marauding force. Whole fields were aflame, huge tongues of fire cutting through the black clouds.

Walter caught up with the rest of the army by nightfall, as they were setting up an uneasy camp. Leading his horse, he learned that Malcolm's orders had been eased. They were commanded to take prisoners rather than kill the locals, but the plunder was to go on as before.

Malcolm had summoned Walter, and Walter's manservant had been looking everywhere for him.

Taking time to cool off his mount and set up camp, Walter finally made his way to the King's tent. He found Malcolm seated before his pavilion, staring morosely at the camp fire. Two haunches of mutton sizzled on a spit.

The Scot looked at Walter as the latter bowed, then gestured for him to sit.

"You must have thought I was hard on you today."

Walter shook his head, saying nothing.

The King reached for a cup of ale.

"There you were behind me, lecturing me, scolding me... ME, your King. Walter, you must take a care. You are my loyal subject, and I love you as a brother. But like a vassal, you are subject to my orders. I shouldn't have to tell you this."

He wiped his mouth with a sleeve.

"Don't you think that I would have come to the same conclusion as you did, just as soon as the anger passed?"

Letting out a sigh, Walter had to admit that he was right. "But at the cost of how many lives?" he asked.

Malcolm frowned. "Your preaching saved no lives. It is possible that you made the matter worse."

Troubled, Walter basted the meat. "That, Sire, is a heavy charge."

"Then mayhap you will better understand the weight on my shoulders. It never lessens, Walter. It only gets heavier. The privilege of sovereignty is also its bane. Think of the power of life and death over all others. Is it not wonderful that I use it so seldom?"

He finished his ale, holding out his mug for more. A page scurried forth to fill it.

"I intend to get drunk tonight, Walter. Will you join me?"

Relieved, Walter assented; he already felt such a need himself. But he wondered if things between them would ever be the same again.

The next morning the Scots were on the move again. For a week they plundered steadily forward; Malcolm wanted to make sure that word of his revenge preceded him to his traitorous cousin. By the end of that time, Walter was glad to see they had reached their destination.

Overlooking the ocean, surrounded by sand dunes, Bamburgh was a picturesque fortress perched on a long ridge. Cospatric had stocked his castle for a siege, stripping the surrounding land so the Scots would have nothing to forage.

Malcolm camped below the ridge.

He paced back and forth. "Walter, send my trumpeter forward. Go yourself with him. The coward will listen to my terms: tell him to surrender his castle, and present himself before me. If he does this without delay, I shall spare his miserable life."

Restraining his objections, Walter left to do the King's bidding. The outcome was what he expected.

Making a grand flourish, a pair of trumpeters announced the royal messenger. Walter stood forward, his voice ringing against the castle walls, communicating word for word the King's command.

He was answered by silence.

After waiting several minutes, Walter returned to Malcolm.

"Sire," Walter began, clearing his throat. "Perhaps you didn't offer him enough."

"More than he deserved. And more than he shall get, henceforth!"

Walter looked at the castle. It seemed that, for once, Malcolm did not have the advantage. Was the King thinking clearly?

"I shall waste no more time in talk," Malcolm said finally, making one of his abrupt decisions. "On the morrow, we shall attack."

But the morning came and went, without any command from the King. Indeed, no one saw him leave the pavilion.

The day dragged on, while Malcolm's army fidgeted before the stern walls of Bamburgh. The inhabitants of the castle, no doubt as anxious as the Scots, still refused to parley with them. One day stretched into two, then three, while Malcolm kept his own council. Their scant rations had already been used up, and the army, so close to home, began to desert by the hundreds.

Some of Malcolm's most trusted chiefs searched out Walter.

"You must talk to him," they said, "He will see none of us."

Walter shrugged. "We are not as close as we were."

"Nonsense," interrupted a border lord, "he will see you. We all know how much influence you have with him."

Walter sighed. Some sort of new confrontation was inevitable. The army was shrinking daily.

None of the guards challenged Walter as he slipped into the pavilion. He was prepared to duck; he was braced against the shouting, the spiteful abuse the King was so ready to hurl at anyone since the campaign began. Walter thought he was ready for anything. Except, that is, for what he saw.

Malcolm was lying prone on a thin blanket, his fists gathering and loosening the frayed edges. Food lay untouched by his side; dark circles under his eyes bespoke a lack of sleep. His hair hadn't been combed, nor had he bothered to change clothes.

Before Walter could speak, Malcolm waved him off.

"I know. I know. You don't have to tell me what is happening."

Any words of criticism were already forgotten.

"I've never felt so betrayed before," Malcolm said, his voice a caricature of its usual tone.

Walter's accumulated resentments vanished in a surge of empathy. He knelt by his friend.

"But Sire. You have always known what kind of man Cospatric was."

Malcolm shook his head, cutting him off.

Not knowing what else to say, Walter stood up, looking for a pitcher of water, wine; he would have grabbed anything to make the King feel better.

Malcolm turned his head, following Walter with his eyes.

"Yes," he sighed, forcing himself to sit. "Over there, next to the oak chest. Perhaps a sip of wine would help."

He stared dully at Walter, watching him pour with an unsteady hand.

"I didn't mean Cospatric," he said thickly, taking a deep draught. "I meant myself. Betrayed by my own feelings. Indecision. Abandonment. Depression. Walter, all I can think of is what Margaret will say when she hears about all this. How will I ever get her to accept me?"

Walter gaped, astonished.

"What? Don't you think I have feelings, Walter? Don't you think I have a heart that can break?" His thoughts became more lucid as he found expression in words.

"Can't you see that woman is driving me mad? Preferring the church to myself...to my crown! How can she do this to me? Her thoughts are so pure, so virtuous. And I must be ruthless, or lose a kingdom..." Malcolm's voice broke, and he buried his face in his hands.

"It will never work. Walter, we must leave this place now. It will avail me nothing to stay here. Go, give my command to break camp."

Appalled to witness this side of his master, his hero who could do no wrong, Walter nearly leaped to his feet. But he was brought down hard, pulled by a strong fist.

"Tell me, Walter. Am I doing the wrong thing?"

His bloodshot eyes were pleading. Walter swallowed hard. "Sire, it is your command."

"To hell with that! I'm asking you to help me...I cannot think straight."

Walter's natural self-possession ebbed back, in the face of his friend's extremity. This was no time for disillusionment.

"Malcolm. Sire. You have little choice. Our army is deserting. We have no supplies, no siege equipment. We did not provide for such a strategy. Are you prepared to face King William should he decide to raise the siege?"

"Aye. No. You are right, Walter. It is good. Go to; I am all right." He loosened his grip.

Hesitating a moment, Walter obeyed. At the door to the pavilion, he heard the King say "Thanks, friend."

When Malcolm next appeared, washed and dressed in his traveling clothes, he seemed to have regained composure, to everyone's relief. Beckoning for Walter to ride beside him, he supervised the troops, then gave the order to go home.

They were to move within two hours. No one seemed reluctant to leave Northumbria. They had plundered enough.

As the tired army spilled into Dunfermline, Myrna ran up to Walter, cheeks flushed. He leaped from his horse, taking a hold of her shoulders.

"Walter... it's a boy!"

Stunned, he stared at her as the simple statement made its way down the ranks of his companions. Malcolm soon came riding up.

"When, girl?"

"Three days ago." Myrna took Walter's arm, drawing him to the palace. "A healthy boy. She named him after her father, knowing you would understand."

Walter grinned; a sudden lack for words had come over him.

Isabel was supported in bed by two feather pillows. Her face was pale, but the smile was genuine as Walter knelt beside her bed. In her arms nestled a chubby baby, with a full head of black hair and the blackest eyes Walter had ever seen. The infant smiled at him.

Relieved, Walter threw his arms around his wife.

"I was so worried about you," he said.

"It was not an easy birth. It took much too long... almost a whole day. If it weren't for Margaret..."

He raised his head inquiringly.

"Oh yes. I was wrong about her. She was absolutely wonderful, holding my hand and wiping my brow. She sat by my side the whole time, even after poor Myrna fell asleep from exhaustion."

Isabel looked up, seeing Malcolm at the door. "I don't know what I would have done without her," she told the King.

For a week Walter slept away from his wife, though he might not have, had he remembered his own infancy. For it was on one of these nights that little Alane was visited by those beings his father would have recognized with a shudder. Or, since their message was not for his ears, perhaps he might have slept through it anyway, like Isabel did.

The room filled with a deep haze, swirling into a mist that encompassed three bent forms, as though created from the very air. Intent on the fitfully stirring child, they intoned their fateful will, bestowing on him a grand purpose, of which he was a minute part:

Our eyes will be on you, our tempest-tost child,
We've fashioned the fortune to which you're entitled.
Your father will start a remarkable role
That you must endeavor to greatly ennoble.
We give you a role that thou mayest not shun;
Thou shalt 'get kings, though thou be none.
You'll follow our rule 'till thou givest a son
Who bears the same burden when your life is done.
It'll take many more until finally we'll see
The king who'll 'get kings that has long been decreed.

As the last words were spoken the mist quickened, until it

became like a whirlwind that grew smaller and smaller, finding its way outside through a chink in the stone.

Margaret was feeling more comfortable in the palace, finding her little niche in King Malcolm's court. She spent much time with Isabel and the baby, unaware that Malcolm watched her every move. Little Duncan came often and again to see her, finding comfort in her caresses; he was usually followed by Myrna, searching for her young charge.

One day, Malcolm offered to take her across to Edinburgh, and she assented, happy for a change. She wrapped a cloak around her shoulders, for even in summer the air was chill for this slender woman.

Crossing the firth, she faced directly into the brisk wind, though it made her eyes squint and her cheeks redden. Malcolm enjoyed her pleasure, feeling so much more alive in her company. She didn't seem to notice his hungry gaze, though he suspected that she was, quite the contrary, very aware of him.

"I must have her for my own, no matter how long it takes," he thought, admiring her profile. Remembering Margaret's first refusal, the King trod carefully with the girl, trying to note all her changes of mood, so he could pick her most receptive one.

Pretending to act aloof, Malcolm took her through the great hall at Edinburgh castle. She seemed charmed by the buildings, but was most drawn by the view. They looked across the firth toward Dunfermline.

"Oh, it is so beautiful here, Sire," she sighed. "It seems so serene to me, even though right here, in this very spot, decisions affecting your whole kingdom take place every day."

Biting his lip, Malcolm felt like he was going to say something foolish. Sure enough, he did.

"Margaret, my dear, I so want to share all this with you. Can you not find it in your heart to accept my suit?"

She looked troubled and turned her head, hoping he wouldn't

notice the conflict on her face. He took her silence as encouragement.

"Oh, I know Scotland is cold and rustic, not comfortable or refined like you're used to on the continent. But with your help, we can improve the standard of living in this poor country. It only takes a guiding hand like your own..."

She put a finger on his lip to stop him; the touch thrilled through his body. But then he noticed how wet Margaret's eyes were.

"Stop, please. You are torturing me, and yourself. I have told you my vocation. My decision. All this talk is to no purpose." Her voice was pleading.

Sighing, the King gazed at the Forth. The country looked ugly to him, the sun seemed cruelly dull, giving no warmth. Only her words were sweet, and they, too, were like little knives thrust into his heart.

"Come. Let us leave this place." His voice sounded harsher than he meant.

Taking one last reluctant look over her shoulder, Margaret followed meekly after him.

Arriving home, the Saxon took refuge in her room. She passed by her mother without a word. Observant as always, Agatha followed and sat quietly by her daughter's side, waiting for Margaret to pour out her troubles. After a long wait, the words came tumbling out.

But Agatha proved less encouraging than Margaret had hoped.

"My dear," she said when her daughter had finished, "perhaps it is time you reconsidered your...our position."

Stopping in the middle of a sob, Margaret turned an incredulous look on her mother.

"Well, think about it," Agatha went on. "At least consider the rest of your family for a change." She looked at her nails. "There's your poor brother, wasting away in Flanders. He dare not venture to England for fear of the Conqueror's wrath. Even in Scotland he doesn't feel safe.

"And here we sit, healthy and secure, because of that man's charity. Nay, under that man's power. Let us speak the truth. One cross word and he could turn us out. And there you go, stubborn as you please, refusing the best offer you are ever likely to hear for your hand in marriage."

"I'm not looking for marriage," Margaret reminded her patiently, as she had done many times before.

"Oh, all right. Say it how you will. That doesn't change the basic problem. King Malcolm wants you as his wife; everyone knows it. Many a girl would give everything they had for such an opportunity; he's certainly not an undesirable man. And yet, you persist in your selfish refusal.

"Let me tell you, daughter: think it over well. You do us all a disservice by your obstinacy. It may happen that his patience will run out someday, and we will find ourselves beggars once again. I, for one, do not cherish the thought."

She gathered up her skirt to go but paused, waiting for an answer.

Margaret wiped her eyes. "I refuse to believe such a thing about that kind man. I'm sorry we have to differ, mother."

Exasperated, Agatha left in a huff.

Christina seemed to agree with her mother. Never before had Margaret felt so totally alone.

The bewildered girl went to bed soon afterward, but tossed and turned for hours, unable to sleep. Finally, she put on a cloak and wandered about the tower, hoping to find comfort in the chapel. To her surprise, passing through the main hall, she found Walter sitting near the hearth, staring into the embers.

Seeing that he was deep in thought, Margaret sat quietly next to him, waiting until he noticed her presence. After a few minutes he stirred, sighing, and jumped when he found her at his side. Indeed, he had just been brooding about her.

"I'm sorry, Walter. I didn't mean to startle you."

Smiling sheepishly, he said, "It is for me to apologize for my rudeness in ignoring you."

She leaned forward, stoking the fire. "No. I am bothering you. But I can't help myself tonight. I feel so troubled...actually, I'm glad to have somebody to talk to."

Walter was not sure how he felt about that. He always found this woman so disturbing, his feelings about her jumbled. He resented her, yet was drawn to her at the same time.

"Is there a way that I can help?" he said finally.

"I'm so glad you asked. Yes, you can help me in a way that no one else can. For I see that you know the King better than anyone."

He sighed again. "That was the very thing I was thinking about as you came up. Sometimes I wonder if I know him at all."

Margaret wasn't really listening. "Walter, I just don't know what to do. The King has asked for my hand in marriage, as you must know." She stopped abruptly, but he said nothing.

"It is true that I feel kindly for him," she went on. "Perhaps I even love him, but I do not know. I have been so intent on the church that love has never been a concern of mine. Not love between people, anyway." Her smile was lit by an otherworldly source. "But I don't know what I'm supposed to feel for a husband."

Walter looked at her with a mixture of sorrow and wonder.

"Oh, don't feel sad for me. I have been justly recompensed." Margaret crossed herself. "But my mother warns me that I am putting my family into jeopardy by refusing him. I don't want to marry for that reason."

Her eye flashed in anger. "Never will I do that."

"Wait," he interrupted, holding up a hand. "You never have to worry about that. I would wager my life on it."

"All right," she hurried, not wanting to offend, "I believe you. But the doubt has crossed my mind as to whether I am taking the right course. Perhaps I can, after all, serve my people better as queen."

Walter studied her, a steady long look that ruffled even her composure. "If serving is the only question you have, it seems to me that the quiet of a nunnery only serves the individual. How can such seclusion help a whole country's misery?"

"By... prayer, as I see it."

"Well, that is not for me to say..."

Margaret interrupted him. "Do you mean to tell me you are not Christian?"

"I am not, nor do I wish to be."

She moved imperceptibly away from him on the bench.

"But that is not really the point," Walter went on. "Let me tell you a story. About King Malcolm. I must tell someone, if you can bear to hear it."

Shivering, she nodded.

"Perhaps it's not all that bad. I don't know. When I first met Malcolm, he was still a Prince without a country. I came with him to Scotland to help win back his father's throne.

"Oh, what glorious days those were, and I in the midst of my youth."

Moved by the thought, his face took on a glow in the ruddy light. "He was so pure...so perfect. I worshipped him...not that I don't now." His voice didn't sound so convinced. "But of course, I was less bitter then, less disillusioned.

"I wasn't with him all those years in between, for many reasons." Walter paused, remembering. "Never mind what they were. But I wasn't always near in his most difficult times. It is something I will ever regret.

"Perhaps something happened to destroy his faith in himself. Perhaps kingship just has a way of ruining a man's temper. I don't know. But what I saw this last campaign..."

He frowned. Anxious to hear more, Margaret said, "Go on."

"Things did not go well. First it was Cospatric, shamefully

raiding King Malcolm's lands, just to please William, his new master. It was a terrible thing for him to do. My King had never been betrayed like that before. Something in him just snapped."

He looked at Margaret, pain in his eyes.

"I have never seen him like that. He raved like a madman, swearing to destroy every inch of land in Northumbria. He was like a man possessed."

Walter put his hand in his chin. "He didn't, of course. Wreak the bloody revenge, I mean. He couldn't," he said, more to himself. "But Margaret, that day will haunt me until I die. I hope I never see him like that again."

"I heard something of all that," she said, her voice taking on a note of disdain.

"But my lady...what you didn't hear was why he stopped his campaign. It was because of you."

Not thinking, Walter took Margaret's hand; she had sense enough not to pull away. "If you ask me what you should do, I can only speak from my own heart. Your influence on the King is strong; you are the best thing that ever happened to Scotland...to him. It is your sweet will, your gentleness he needs...to keep that from ever happening again."

Troubled, she slipped her hand free and stood up; Walter turned back to the fire.

She would never know what it cost him to say those things, to encourage the woman who was the cause of all his troubles. And yet, he felt a strange comfort, doing what he could to make Malcolm happy.

At that moment, if Walter had taken thought to look at her, he would have seen the glimmerings of new decision in Margaret's eyes.

28

The King's Oath

Walter was discussing the purchase of new saddles when he paused, hearing a familiar voice in the courtyard.

"Alain," he cried, bursting into a run. The Count was handing over his horse to a groom when he heard his name called. Turning, his eyes brightened at the sight of his good-son.

"Walter, my lad. It is good to see you."

Alain looked like life in England was agreeing with him. Increased activity in William's service had converted some of his excess weight into muscle, making him seem younger than before.

Malcolm came up behind them. Walter introduced them, grinning.

"So William finally sent an envoy more agreeable to me," Malcolm laughed. "Though I'm sure his messages are the same."

"Why no, Sire. I've come to pay a visit to my grandson. The King doesn't even know I'm here."

"Then the more welcome you are, Alain. Come in. We'll find Isabel for you."

Putting an arm around Walter's shoulders, the Count followed Malcolm into the tower, chattering happily.

"Thomas," he said, seeing the Saxon just inside the door. "You seem to have recovered your strength." He shook the man's hand, though Thomas looked less than happy to see him. Alain's face brought back to mind the painful memory of Hastings.

The Count saw Thomas's expression, and for a moment his eyes became hard. His new role, requiring a constant assertion of superiority, came easier to him as time went on. But his automatic reaction faded when he recalled that he was a guest in a different country.

This new facet of Alain's personality was not lost on Walter.

He stepped back, allowing Malcolm to draw his visitor away; the King lost no time questioning him on the state of the government in England.

"He seems like a good man," Thomas said uncomfortably. "I suppose I'm not fully recovered, am I? I can't help holding a grudge against Harold's enemies." Realizing what he said, he looked anxiously at Walter. "Most of his enemies, anyway."

"I understand, Thomas. I don't fully forgive myself for the part I played." Walter looked sadly at his friend. "If the same thing happened to King Malcolm, I can't imagine what I would do… No, that's not good enough. This is a cruel world, Thomas. It is we who make it that way." He shook his head. "I understand your feelings toward Alain. You don't have to explain yourself to me."

He started off, but Thomas stopped him. "Walter, you have always been my friend. Let's talk no more of this. What is done, is done. There's no changing it."

By the time Walter found Alain again, the Count was happily holding his grandson, while Isabel sat next to him, leaning over the baby.

"A fine boy, my namesake. Looks a lot like me, don't you think?"

Isabel giggled. "I was thinking he looked like his father."

"Well, maybe a bit. Anyway, since we are all together, I have an announcement to make. Sire, Walter, we are almost neighbors. I have been made the Earl of Richmond, and I intend to take up residence at once."

"Let me see," said the King, "if I'm not mistaken, that puts you in North Yorkshire. A fine country... or was, before William passed through."

"And two hundred manors as well," Alain added, ignoring the comment. "Not a bad spread, wouldn't you say?"

The others were speechless, even Malcolm.

"Your King certainly is generous to his supporters," the Scot finally murmured. "Two hundred manors. Nearly a kingdom by itself."

"They are not all in the same place, of course. But a hundred and sixty-six of them are in Yorkshire. I plan to build a castle at Richmond town. There is a fine hill overlooking the river Swale."

At that moment, Margaret appeared in the doorway. Everyone stood up. "Margaret, sister of Eadgar Aetheling," said Malcolm.

The Count bowed. "Very happy to meet you. It was said that you are a beautiful woman. I can see that the reports are understated."

The Princess nodded, accepting the compliment.

"This is Alain, Count of Brittany, Earl of Richmond. He is Isabel's father."

She extended her hand for him to kiss.

"Earl of Richmond," Margaret said, sitting down. "The title is not familiar to me."

"It is because I am the first. Under King William's rule, Earls no longer act as under-kings, like they did to the Danes. There are no more under-kings; we just have governors of a sort. Since the title of Earl is comparable to Count in Europe, William can create more of them."

Malcolm turned to Walter. "I am glad my uncle Seward did not live to this day. He would never have stomached the loss of prestige."

No one spoke what was in the back of their minds; it was unlikely that Seward would have retained his title anyway.

Alain stayed a fortnight. After the first couple of days, the uneasiness that came with his new status faded, and he was soon back to his old self. Malcolm took an even greater liking to the Earl, keeping him mostly by his side, which gave him less time to spend with Margaret.

All too soon, Alain went back to England with a gift of two beautiful white horses. The tears of his daughter were soon swept away by the demands of her own child.

On the days following Alain's departure, Malcolm found Margaret to be in an exceptionally charming mood; he told himself she seemed almost anxious to please him. Never one to allow an opportunity to pass, he determined once again to ask her hand in marriage.

Gathering his courage, after dinner a few evenings later, the King went in search of his beloved. He found her, as usual, kneeling in the chapel he had constructed for her personal use. Determining to wait, Malcolm knelt behind her, listening to the softly whispered prayers.

He never realized just how long it took her to pray every night. He knelt as motionless as he could, until his muscles, unaccustomed to such stringent restraint, quivered in annoyance. And yet Margaret didn't look up from her devotions.

His legs stiff, Malcolm stumbled to his feet and found a bench next to the wall. He wasn't ready to give up yet.

The next thing Malcolm knew, he was being gently shaken awake. His eyes flew open, rested upon the worried face of the Saxon.

"Sire," she spoke softly, "I knew not that you were here."

He shook his head to clear it. "How long..."

Margaret sat next to him. "I do not know. A few hours, I think."

Recalling his purpose, Malcolm gently took her hands. Surprisingly, she responded with a slight pressure of her fingers.

"I know of no better place to ask you this... one more time," he began, bracing himself for a refusal. "Margaret, would it hurt to ask you once more to be my wife? I need you so badly."

Malcolm saw a quick succession of emotions cross her face: first relief, then a last residue of denial, then finally a softening, as a quick smile brought an answer to her lips. A thrill of hope warmed his body.

"My King... Malcolm. I think I have found the answer to my

prayers. Yes, I will be yours, and work the will of God as Queen of the Scots."

Unable to contain his joy, Malcolm whisked her up in his arms, carrying her from the chapel. As he set Margaret down at the door to her chamber, the King satisfied himself with a quick kiss on her upturned lips, then disappeared.

He might have lingered had he seen the look of longing on the beautiful girl's face.

As Margaret put an unsteady hand on the doorknob, the first rays of dawn were breaking over the hills of Fife.

The wedding was set for the day after Easter, April the fifth, 1070. When the King of England heard of Malcolm's nuptials, his face went red with anger. But he restrained the outburst of rage everyone expected to see. This was a bad sign; there were times when a healthy temper tantrum was preferable.

Malcolm didn't care about William's reactions. He was too far north, and William had too many troubles to launch a major campaign against him.

Or so he thought.

But King William was used to fighting wars on more than one front. With this marriage, Malcolm had made a definitive stand on the issue of Eadgar Aetheling. There was no way the Scottish King would ever surrender his own good-brother now; Eadgar had firm ground from which to launch another campaign, if he so wished. The only way to make him ineffectual was to put Scotland under England's power. Somehow.

It was only a few months later that the dreaded news came that William was on the move. It was much worse than Malcolm expected; William had launched an extensive campaign specifically against the Scots.

Malcolm summoned his chiefs and thanes to Edinburgh, sending messengers to the far ends of the kingdom. Puffed up with their own importance, Thanes and Earls obeyed the summons, heading little companies that flew their own banners, eyeing distant neighbors whose numbers may have exceeded their own. Negotiations became complicated; Malcolm had to muster his most convincing arguments to persuade the others to forget their differences. Often and again, shouted arguments broke out among the attendees, and blades were drawn in anger. Usually there were enough level heads to break up the disputes. Only occasionally did blood get drawn.

The debates went on for a week. Finally, one of the Thanes took his men and left the castle. As the mid-summer setting sun turned brilliantly pink, the King bid Walter to join him atop the battlements and they watched the little band ride away. In the privacy of the moment, Malcolm allowed his face to relax, though in doing so he looked haggard, exhausted.

"To think that all this comes back to Eadgar," he groaned. "William fears repeated insurrections in his name, and to tell you, Walter, so do I. I have no faith in his ability to see a campaign through to the end.

"Though I would have no peace with my dear wife if I were to turn him over to the Bastard, surely we can work out some sort of compromise. I can no longer involve Scotland in his hapless cause."

Surprised, Walter glanced warily at Malcolm; he was surprised at the King's willingness to antagonize the Queen, though he hardly disagreed with him.

"I don't think William wants to fight any more than I do," Malcolm went on. "He has so many more... crucial enemies to destroy. I think he wants to impress me with his power; or maybe he wants to scare me into submission.

"Well, maybe I'll let him scare me, for now."

Walter was nervous. "Remember... this William is tricky. You may find yourself caught in one of his tangles."

Malcolm nodded. "What you say is true. But we are not strong enough... united enough to fight. I need more time to bind my chieftains to myself.

"That's what I intend to do, Walter. Buy time. Oaths have been broken before, not necessarily with the dire consequences Harold had to face."

He looked at Walter. "Yes, I know that's what you were referring to. Don't think I haven't given it much thought. I hope to God I am right in my thinking.

"But we must bring a full army to meet him, anyway. Just in case. Come, Walter, I can't leave my troublesome nobles alone too long."

Negotiations lasted for another week, but Malcolm finally got what he wanted. The chieftains parted for their own lands, to raise a hasty army in defense of Scotland.

William was already on the march. Word reached Malcolm that he had launched a combined sea and land invasion. The King laughed bitterly.

"Just like old Seward's campaign. Do you remember, Walter? It seems that the Fates are laughing at me."

Sitting with them in Malcolm's private chamber, Margaret shook her head. "There are no such things as Fates, dear. You are speaking nonsense."

The King looked at Walter, shrugging. "Old habits, like old religions, are hard to shake."

"I noticed," she said, getting up to rub her husband's shoulders. "But what are your subjects going to do, when they see the example you set? You must be more careful."

Knowing where this conversation was headed, Walter left the room. The Queen watched him go.

"And there's another example of what I'm talking about. You are the King. Your subjects should not just leave, without asking permission first. I see it at dinner all the time. When they are through eating, they dash away from the table without a by-your-leave."

The King sighed, pulling Margaret onto his lap. "I understand what you are saying, love. But I just can't suddenly ask my friends, like Walter, to treat me like a stranger. He observes certain conventions in public, but I myself told him to forget them when we are alone. It would hurt his feelings if I were to ask him to change now."

It was her turn to sigh. "Very well, my husband. The harm is already done. I must find a way to alter this thing, without creating stress. But you must take on a more regal stance."

He kissed her as she said the last words. "As you wish," he murmured trying to distract her. But she wasn't finished.

"But about that other issue," she said smiling, pushing him back. "Your abbots, your bishops. They conduct themselves as if they belong to a different hierarchy than Christian. Not even deigning to take communion. They even observe the wrong date to celebrate the holy Easter. Malcolm, they are more pagan than Christian. We must work to bring them to the true path."

The King sat back, resigning himself to his wife's insistent policies. "Very well, my Queen. We will summon your bishops, and host a debate on these very issues. I will translate for you, if you wish. But not now. We have more important matters before us." He played with a wisp of her hair, escaping from her veil.

Satisfied, Margaret leaned into his arms. When he wanted to, Malcolm could easily distract her from the issues closest to her heart. His lips were so soft, his eyes so inviting.

She ran a hand along his powerful arm, tracing the lines of his muscles with curious fingertips. She hadn't been prepared for the allures of the flesh. Forgetting the mental objections, which continually chafed to intrude on her pleasures, Margaret kissed her husband hungrily. He picked her up and carried her to their marriage bed.

What Malcolm did not know was that afterwards, when she spent so many hours in prayer with her precious black rood, she was desperately praying for forgiveness. She was enjoying—to excess—that act of love designated by the church as a necessary function of procreation.

By the time the Scottish army had assembled, William had passed through Lothian and was nearing Stirling. It was too late to try and stop him there, so Malcolm determined to make a stand at his old capital of Abernethy, under the ancient stone tower.

They waited for William, who arrived during the night. In the morning, the Scots were amazed to see an endless line of soldiers, rank after rank of spears sparkling in the sun.

A small group broke away from the main force, carrying William's flag. They stopped halfway, letting a brightly dressed herald come the rest of the way alone. He drew himself up before the Scots and filled his lungs with air, giving his voice power to carry through the last row of the waiting troops.

"Hear me, O King of the Scots. My master, the powerful King of England and Duke of Normandy comes here to negotiate a treaty between yourself and him. Your recent ventures into Northumbria have caused him great bitterness and pain. He extends his hand to bring peace between our two countries."

As he paused, Malcolm gave Walter a wry smile. "The only thing that pains him is a loss of plunder for himself." A runner was sent with a small purse of gold coins for the herald, and a message that Malcolm would send his response presently. They watched the herald bow and return to his master.

The King gathered a few men around him, then turned to Walter. "Go tell him I will meet with him, in full view of both our armies. Here, on the field. That is all; do not let him force any concessions from you. I will await you here."

His request was soon done; a hasty pavilion was erected between the armies.

Malcolm put on his robes of state and rode the short distance to the meeting place with five of his men. William was already seated and waiting when they arrived; he was facing the door so it would seem as if he was conducting an audience. And so it was in truth; William's host was more than triple the hastily assembled Scots. Malcolm sat across from him in the only other chair provided.

For a moment the two kings studied each other: William, brittle and harsh, eyes glinting like steel, against the calm, speculative Scot. Then the Conqueror spoke, and his words were biting.

"Malcolm, who calls himself King of the Scots. By what right do you invade my Northumbria?"

Already on the defensive, Malcolm knew what tone to take with his wily enemy.

"It is only yours if you can hold it." He spoke low, menacing. "Besides, after you were finished with them, there was nothing left for me to invade."

William sat back, surprised by such confidence. He was used to intimidating his victims.

"I imagine this is what you have come all the way here to discuss with me," Malcolm continued, "or haven't you finished conquering yet?"

William set his jaw, secretly enjoying the challenge. But he was careful not to push his opponent too far. He had already seen the result of Malcolm's rage.

"If I am not mistaken," the Norman said finally, "your Scots are even more difficult to rule than the English." His eyes carelessly rested for a moment on Thomas. "That is a chore I gladly leave to you, King Malcolm. If you leave Northumbria to me."

Malcolm nodded thoughtfully. "I leave it to you, then," he said, as if it meant little to him. "But you should take one word of advice: it would be better if you let Northumbria be ruled by one of their own. You will find them more amenable if you do. Take young Waltheof, for example. He has already shown considerable promise."

Suppressing a sneer, Malcolm was sure William knew about the hundred men Waltheof killed at York. But to his surprise, William looked thoughtful in turn.

"You are right in what you say. I just may consider this move." William's face suddenly became hard again. "But that is not all we must agree on, of course. There is the question of the Aetheling."

Everyone knew that the subject would come up, but still the others held their breath. Malcolm looked at his hands. "Question," he said, rolling the word around. "There is no question. He is not here; he resides in Flanders, I think."

"Where all my enemies reside!" William's voice rose threateningly. "Listen to me, King of the Scots. He will come back. That type of man always does. Never again will you aid him in his campaigns for the crown of England. Or I will return to your country, and I will spare no man, woman, or child in my wrath."

Malcolm stood up, desiring to end the negotiations at this point. "That much I will certainly promise," he said decisively.

"There is more I would discuss with you." William's tone was uncompromising, demanding. Malcolm faced the Norman without sitting.

"I would have you swear to be my man."

Walter shivered; this scene was too reminiscent. "With this promise," William continued, "I will feel confident enough to return to England...without the fear of retaliation."

Malcolm seemed uncomfortable for the first time. The implications were dangerous, and he did not move.

William decided to help him. "Do not force me to fight," he said.

The Norman never bluffed. Malcolm put his hand out. "Done."

One of William's companions pulled out a Bible, kissed it and presented it to Malcolm.

"From this point on," William said, "I claim Lothian to be annexed into England, for you, King Malcolm, to hold in fief to myself. And after me, to my heir. Swear to me in front of our witnesses that henceforth you will be my man, King Malcolm of Scotland, and will uphold my interests there."

So this was to be Malcolm's concession; and he did not have the resources to refuse. The Scot turned his head aside, deep in thought. Lothian, ever contested, ever the battlefield for invading armies, was to be reintegrated into England. Well, so be it; originally it was a gift from King Edward, anyway. Besides, borders are easily changed. Malcolm straightened up. "To this I do swear," he said, solemnly and clearly.

"Swear that you will not give aid to Eadgar, called the Aetheling, in his attempt to claim my crown."

To this also Malcolm swore.

With the King's hand on the Bible, William made one more demand: "To confirm this oath, and to see that it is well carried out, I demand your oldest son, Duncan, as my hostage."

Malcolm's hand shook slightly, but with a great effort he stilled it. "It is done."

Later that night, Malcolm summoned Walter to his tent, not realizing that he was already standing ready outside the flap.

"Tell me," the King said, pointing wearily for Walter to sit. "What the men are saying about me?"

Walter sat among piled boxes. "They grumble, of course. Many of them wanted to fight, and think the Normans are cowards for going away."

"The fools," said Malcolm unemotionally. "And my oath?"

"Word of that has not yet leaked out. Your people are confused, and await a word from you."

The other sighed heavily. "Walter, do you think I did the right thing?"

Walter was worried. Fearing a repetition of the scene at

Bamburgh, he considered the question carefully.

"He couched his words in the vaguest terms..." His voice faltered, then he took strength from Malcolm's hesitation. "I think you were right. He was as intent as you on not fighting. Both of you can save face, now."

Shaking himself out of his stupor, Malcolm smiled weakly. "Thank you, my friend. Yes, it could have been much worse...but oh, my son." His voice cracked.

Of course, Walter thought. Here is the crux of the problem. "It is a regular custom on the continent," he started bravely. "No harm will come to him."

Malcolm waved him silent impatiently. "I know all that. But Walter, he will take on Norman characteristics, Norman values..." He frowned in thought. "He will cease to know me."

Walter couldn't think of an answer.

A small contingent of Normans accompanied the Scots back to Dunfermline, to bring the boy back to William. Myrna burst into tears as Malcolm gently disengaged Duncan from her arms. She threw herself at the King's feet.

"Oh, don't let them take him away from me! I'll never see him again...my Duncan. Please, don't."

Watching her weep so piteously, Duncan began to cry, squirming from his father's grasp. He put chubby arms around her neck.

Somewhat at a loss, Malcolm sat on the floor next to them. He put out a hesitant hand to his son.

"Duncan, you are ten years old now...almost a man. And you are heir to the throne. You must act like one, especially in front of your new companions."

Sniffing, the boy looked at Malcolm with wide eyes.

"Am I really going that far away, father?"

"Yes, very far. You are going to see many new and wonderful things."

At those words, Myrna moaned aloud. But Duncan, remembering his new-found status, stood up straight, putting a hand on her shoulder in a gesture reminiscent of his father's.

"It's all right, Myrna. I'm old enough to take care of myself, now."

"That's a good boy," Malcolm said, relieved. "You will be my man in England, and show the King what a real Scot is made of."

Smiling through her tears, Myrna looked up to see Margaret standing unnoticed at the door. The Queen came closer, leaning toward her ear.

"We will soon have a need for you again, my dear. I am with child."

Myrna's gasp was drowned by a shout of pleasure from the King. "My Queen...my love. Why didn't you tell me?" Malcolm was on his feet, swinging Duncan around by the arms. "Did you hear, Duncan? You are going to have a brother."

"I didn't tell you because you weren't here, of course. And how do you know it will be a boy?"

Carrying Duncan over to Margaret, Malcolm gathered his wife into his other arm. "If not this time, then the next."

Momentarily forgotten, Myrna began to pack Duncan's things. But she had to keep stopping to wipe her eyes.

29

A Place of Honor

It was said by later chroniclers that William's Scottish campaign did him no good. But perhaps this wasn't quite true; Malcolm honored the treaty for nine years.

What astonished everyone was that the King of England stopped at Bamburgh on his way back to London. Accusing Cospatric of taking part in the earlier revolts of Northumbria, he deprived him of the earldom and gave it to Waltheof, notwithstanding the Saxon's participation in the same revolts. Cospatric fled to Flanders, to join the others who took refuge from William's wrath.

Some time later, Cospatric appeared once again in Scotland. No one knew why, but Malcolm treated him as if there had never been trouble between them. Cospatric's eternal luck was still with him; Malcolm created him the first Earl of Dunbar.

Waltheof was a good choice and reigned well; he soon married a niece of William's named Judith. But his fortune was short-lived. Three years later, a trumped-up charge of supporting a plot against William's life was brought against him. Judith was one of his most vehement antagonists.

Regardless of the cries from his people, Waltheof was brought to Winchester and beheaded as a traitor. The last of the Saxon earls was greatly mourned, and miracles were soon reported at his grave site.

Two years after the Abernethy treaty, William chose to go back to Normandy and settle some affairs there. No sooner did he set foot on the continent, than Eadgar and all his friends set sail for Scotland.

He was received with less enthusiasm than he expected.

Agatha was the first to rush out the door, covering him with kisses, admiring his Flemish clothing. She turned with a glowing face as Malcolm and Margaret came regally forth.

"He is back among us, at last," she exclaimed happily. "My Eadgar has gained enough strength to defy that usurper."

Irritated despite his mother's best efforts, the Aetheling hastened to declare that his intents were otherwise. On this assurance, Malcolm's face softened.

"Then you are welcome, my brother, to court. For I can ill afford the resources for another war."

Thinking that her husband lied, Margaret shot him a look of contempt. "Come, Eadgar," she said, loosening herself from the King's grasp. "Let us welcome you in a manner more becoming your status."

As the feast was being prepared, Margaret took her husband aside.

"I do not like your attitude toward my brother," she said, preparing for an argument. "It does not suit your reputation. Nor mine. And what of the falsehood you spoke, about not affording a war? There was been peace in our land, and prosperity."

"Wait a moment, wife." He pulled her onto a seat beside him. "Think about what you say. Was it not Eadgar who finally brought William north, when I was forced to swear that shameful oath? If I break it by sheltering and aiding him, I will have committed a sin against God. William will bring his full army upon us; and this time he will not hesitate to fight. And what of poor Duncan, left all alone as his hostage? I cannot bear that aught evil would come to him, and all for the sake of your troublesome brother."

Margaret bowed her head, reluctantly accepting Malcolm's argument. When she raised it again, her eyes glittered with tears. "The poor boy. Of course you are right. What is it we should do?"

Malcolm rose. "We shall see what he wants. I suppose he wants something, after all. He usually does."

Eadgar did want something. He was all too eager to tell Malcolm the cause of his visit.

"I received a letter from Philip, King of France," he said the next day. "He is a good man. He offers me the castle of Montreuil."

The King was amazed. "From which to harry his neighbors, I suppose. His Norman neighbors."

The Aetheling smiled smugly. "Well, yes. I could be of service to him in this regard."

"With your background of fighting, I suppose," Malcolm added, ignoring the red color seeping in to the man's face. "Let us get to the point. You need my aid in setting you up in this castle."

Defensive, Eadgar stiffened. "I have had no money for these three years. If it weren't for the Duke of Flanders..."

"I know," interrupted Malcolm. "I am perfectly willing to help you, provided you make it soon."

After a moment's thought, Eadgar decided to hold his temper. "It shall be as you say, Sire."

A week later, Malcolm gave Eadgar and his retainers a worthy farewell. They were presented with rich furs, mantles, and treasures, so fine that Eadgar forgot his resentment. With a showy retinue, the King and Queen bid him farewell, and sighed with relief to see the ship recede on the horizon.

But they didn't relax for long. That very night, a terrible storm came from the sea, battering Eadgar's ship against the rocks. Many lives were lost, but enough gold plate was saved to buy the survivors some miserable old horses on which to limp back to Dunfermline.

Malcolm and Walter watched from a window as the ragged troop straggled up the hill. A surly frown curled the edges of the King's lips.

"Shall I never be rid of this accursed man?" he said softly. Below them, Agatha ran to her son, scolding and encouraging him at the same time.

"He alone has caused dispute between my wife and myself. I

would sooner bid him be gone, but her charity stalls me. Oh, for the quiet of my earlier years."

Walter smiled. "Did it seem so quiet at the time?" They both laughed. "But I do have a suggestion," he went on. "Why not propose a reconciliation between him and William. I half believe he might be comfortable, keeping Duncan company as hostage."

Malcolm made disagreeable noises, shaking his head. But he began to look thoughtful. "You might have the right idea, Walter. No one but him would consider such a thing. However...yes, he might, at that. It would certainly solve my problem."

Later that night, Malcolm told his wife about the idea. Her first reaction was the same as his, yet on reflection she agreed. "My poor brother has been a refugee long enough. I really don't think it agrees with him."

"Then it is settled," Malcolm said happily. "We have only to convince him."

For six hours the next day, the King and Queen kept Eadgar locked up alone with them. Even Agatha was forbidden entrance, though she paced before the door in a righteous heat. Finally, it was opened a crack, and Eadgar's haggard face appeared, even more pale than usual. The last person he wanted to see was his mother, but he couldn't close the door against her foot.

"What is the meaning of all this? Why lock me out of hearing, away from my son?" She pushed her way into the room.

Malcolm and Margaret sat opposite her, tired but triumphant. Eadgar disappeared as soon as his mother looked away from him.

Sighing, the Queen got up, taking Agatha's hands in her own. "Eadgar had decided to make his peace with King William."

"He has not," the older woman cried, snatching her hands away. "He would never do such a thing."

"Mother, would you have him forever running away from that man? And finding himself responsible for all those deaths in his lost cause?"

Agatha threw herself in a chair, refusing to let her daughter touch her. "His cause is lost because you let it be! How could you?" She burst into tears, the first time in Margaret's remembrance. The Queen threw herself at her mother's feet.

"Oh, stop, please. I can't bear it."

Agatha covered her face with her hands. "I will not accept this thing," she sobbed.

Exasperated, Malcolm got up to shut the door.

"Good-mother. You have no choice; nor did Eadgar, nor did we. We cannot expose Scotland to William's wrath again. You do not know how lucky we were the last time."

He shifted his weight from one foot to the other. "If I had any faith in his cause, I would not abandon it. But he has failed too many times."

Agatha's sobbing subsided. But when she looked up, her eyes were unforgiving. "Failure is one thing I understand," she said, leaving the room and the two people to stare at one another.

However, the reconciliation proved agreeable to both Eadgar and William. The Aetheling formally rescinded any claim to the throne, and William granted him lands and a title in England and Normandy, preferring to keep him within reach.

Malcolm was surprised one day when a ship docked at Dunfermline, bearing passengers of noble bearing, but dressed as Normans, all the way to the shaved back of their heads. A closer look revealed one of them as Duncan.

Malcolm, of course, remembered his son as the ten year-old boy; but that was five years ago. Even so, he was not prepared for the transformation into a nearly full-grown man, who had adapted the garb and mannerisms of his unfriendly neighbors; here was his greatest fear in the flesh.

The King's welcome, though genuine, was awkward at first, as he fought with conflicting emotions.

He was relieved at the arrival of Thomas, whose insistence on accompanying the King wherever he went proved sometimes annoying but often useful.

"My son, Thomas, though greatly grown up. Do you recognize him?"

The Saxon responded with a bow.

Pretending not to notice his father's reticence, Duncan turned to his companion. "Father, this is Robert, the eldest son of King William, and my good friend. We have come to pay you a visit, and so I can meet my step-brothers."

For a moment Malcolm studied the man critically, but found little of his father's arrogant attitude. He affably invited them back to his tower.

Robert proved to be an amiable person, and showed a great liking for Duncan, who was four years younger than himself. Malcolm was delighted to learn that the visit was undertaken without the knowledge of William.

"I must admit," Robert said, enjoying himself, "it grates against my father that he cannot control his sons any better than his conquered people. But I thought it was high time I saw what the country is like to the north of England; so here we are."

Malcolm grimaced at this easy disobedience. He saw the change in Duncan, and noticed that the boy seemed to like his new life; he, too, had lost control of his son.

"And what of you, Duncan. Do you obey the King of England like a respectable noble should?"

Duncan grinned. "Of course, father. I am not likely to get away with aught else. Robert cannot protect anyone but himself from his father's anger."

"It is true," the other laughed. "Whenever Duncan acts like he may follow my lead, he is taken out of my influence. Then it is I who behaves better."

The two young men looked at each other, smiling. Malcolm watched them for a moment, then turned at a sound from the door. "Ah, Eadward," he said, beckoning the boy forward.

"This is your brother Duncan, who has been living at the court of King William."

The child looked at his brother with wide eyes.

"He is the eldest of three," Malcolm said, "and there is another on the way. Eadward, go get your brothers."

The boy ran from the room. Duncan laughed. "How old is he?"

"Five. Eadmund is three, and Aethelred is two. The next is due in another month."

The children were back, crowding around their new-found brother. "But there are four of them," Duncan laughed.

"Yes. This is little Alane," Malcolm put a hand on a black-haired boy. "Walter's lad."

The children talked all at once, and Duncan began to seem a little more like Malcolm's son again.

They spent only two days in Scotland, fearing to raise suspicion as to their absence. Although Duncan was as friendly as ever, it was obvious that his ideas were becoming radically different. He was much more warlike than Malcolm would have preferred, and seemed to pay little attention to learning. Robert said that these traits were necessary to survive William's harsh discipline.

They left on a friendly note, and Malcolm sent many gifts, encouraging them to come back often. They visited again on occasion, though not often. However, Malcolm took a liking to the strong-willed Robert, and felt much better about Duncan's stay with the Normans.

The summer of 1078 was terribly dry; fires broke out all over the country, burning down whole towns. Malcolm had his hands full trying to dispatch aid to the areas most in need of help.

In the midst of one of his meetings, a messenger was allowed to enter. His clothes were dirty and sweaty; he had insisted on reporting directly to the King, without even taking a moment to rest. On his appearance, all the voices in the room stopped.

"Sire," the man said, bowing low. "The Maormor of Moray has got together an army and invaded south of the Dee. It is said that his force numbers five thousand."

Malcolm looked disturbed, and dismissed the scout to get sleep. His counselors were silent.

The Maormor's name was Maelsnectan, son to Lulach and grandson of Macbeth. Years after Lulach's death, he had seized the Maormorate and ruled there quietly, as if a prince in his own right. Many of Malcolm's advisors had urged that he move north and deal with this lurking threat, but Moray was far from his capital, and of little importance. As long as Maelsnectan remained quiet, he was content to ignore him.

He should have known that it wouldn't be enough. Wearily, he ordered Walter to gather an army, and meet the new threat. Everyone was surprised to hear that the King wasn't going this time.

"I have too much to do here. I am very confident in Walter's abilities."

Walter was thrilled; it was his first real command in Malcolm's service.

Later, Malcolm told his wife that he had a design in mind for Walter. This was a splendid opportunity for the man to excel before the others.

"I know what value he is to me. It is time they knew as well."

Walter calmly assessed the army that spread across the field, waiting for his own. His experienced soldier's eye told him that whatever else he was, Maelsnectan was not a great tactician. His men were too far apart, the lines were straggling. The geography of the field presented the worst threat; directly in front of the army was a bog of unknown quality.

It was a grim enemy that faced Malcolm's army. Born in the fierce highlands, the men resembled savages to their southern brethren. But their hardihood made up for any lack of training; a life of fighting among themselves had already weeded out the weakest.

It was time; Walter ordered the trumpeters to sound the attack.

His force split in two, flanking the bog. They attacked the Highlanders simultaneously from both sides, squeezing them together. The defenders found themselves slipping into the very mire they thought would help protect them.

From the beginning, the result was obvious. Maelsnectan's men were outnumbered, and unused to fighting together. After only an hour, a chaotic movement in their center betrayed Maelsnectan's intent to escape.

"To the center," Walter shouted, leading the chase. But they were too far away from their goal. The army seemed to part before the anxious movement of their leader, and he broke away, surrounded by his bodyguard.

The Highlanders were not far behind their chief. For these mountaineers, retreat merely meant that they would fight another day. As one, the northerners fled the field, lashing out at those who followed too closely. More than once, a number of them would suddenly turn and face their antagonists, teaching them not to be overconfident.

Walter recalled his fighters with a trumpet blast. The day's work was at an end.

For a week they pursued the Highlanders through the mountains, breaking them up, accepting the surrender of lesser chiefs, until Walter was convinced the rebellion was at an end.

The plunder was respectable. Maelsnectan's stronghold at Inverness was filled with treasure, and a large herd of fat oxen was brought back to Malcolm, along with an even greater prize, Maelsnectan's mother. Her confinement was enough to keep her wayward son from rising up again. With his spirit broken, the Maormor lived out the rest of his life in obscurity.

The army's homecoming was all Walter could have wanted. People lined the road to Dunfermline, cheering them on. There was a welcoming banquet at Edinburgh.

Before the feast was a short court, and Walter was surprised to hear his name called. He turned and looked at Isabel, who nudged him, motioning him forward with her head.

It seemed like the longest minute in Walter's life, approaching the King. Never before had he been celebrated like this. His ears pounded with the oppressive silence as he knew that all eyes were upon him.

"Walter," Malcolm announced, standing before his throne, "in gratitude for your victory over my enemy, and in honor of your years of faithful service, I am pleased to call you Knight, Walter son of Fleance, grandson of Banquo." He tapped the astonished man on his shoulders with his sword. "Stand, Sir Walter, and strive to be a good knight this day forward."

The room burst into a spontaneous cheer. Walter was dazed, and could not for a moment find the strength to stand. Then he got unsteadily to his feet; yet Malcolm stopped him from retiring.

"Wait, Sir Knight. Long have I considered the need for a Steward in this realm, to collect my royal revenues, to see that my court is properly directed, to aid myself in the trials of ruling this country. I hereby appoint you, Sir Walter Steward, first high Steward of Scotland, and give you this hereditary post to pass to your children into perpetuity.

"I also give you a grant of land in Fife, so that you may reside always near my person."

For a moment the court was silent, as the attendants considered the import of what had just occurred. Then a great cheer, more deafening than the first, expanded within the walls. It filled Walter's ears with a din that matched the whirling inside his head.

He, a bastard, had risen to knighthood and a place of honor next to a king. His wet eyes rose to Malcolm's, and he saw a smug, happy smile spread over the King's face as he leaned gracefully back in his throne.

Walter went about his new duties with astonishing energy. Aware of the great honor in making the post hereditary, he began to take Alane with him on minor excursions. The boy was mature for his age, his attention span long, and he was a fast learner.

It was while King William was off in Normandy, dealing with his son Robert's new insurrection, that Malcolm thought it time to expand his border again.

"Do you know what you are doing?" asked Walter, who had become more bold in his new position. "You will be the first to break the treaty."

Malcolm looked around, making sure his wife wasn't near. "One of us was bound to do it, sooner or later. Why not take advantage of his absence?" He leaned forward conspiratorially. "Besides, I have heard that there is much unrest in Northumbria, since he brought in his new earl, Robert de Moubray."

Walter sighed. When the King was like this, there was no stopping him.

A large expedition set out after the feast of the Assumption of St. Mary in 1079. It was the middle of August, and the King assured his wife he would be back well before winter set in.

With her usual resignation, Margaret went off to pray for the victims of her husband's policies. Her face was gaunt and strained these days, and she was large with her fifth child. Each birthing had taken its toll, yet she saw it as her duty to give Malcolm as many children as she could. The last was a daughter Editha; her husband hoped for another son.

Malcolm was home before winter. William made a half-hearted attempt at reprisal, but was soon back on the continent.

There, the Norman met his death, wounded by the pommel of his own saddle while burning the city of Mantes.

William Rufus, called by some The Red, was crowned King of England. He was the second son; Robert Curthose, the first, would have to be content with his inheritance as Duke of Normandy. Luckily, for the most part he considered England secondary to his native home. Rufus sent Eadgar Aetheling packing as soon as he was crowned. Once again, the exile made his way north to the Scottish court. Impoverished, homeless, Eadgar had nowhere else to go. This just gave Malcolm another excuse to invade England.

Alas, he didn't realize how quick Rufus would be in bringing retribution. The Norman King was set on teaching Malcolm a lesson, from the very beginning.

The two armies met face to face at an estuary called Scot's Water, in Lothian. Malcolm studied the enemy carefully, noting the distribution of cavalry, infantry, and archers. He saw Rufus's banner, and Eadgar pointed out the one belonging to Duke Robert.

The very same banner broke loose from the army and advanced to a parleying point. Eadgar volunteered to meet him.

Malcolm agreed. "Listen to me closely," he said. "We must find the strength of this army. I cannot tell from this distance. Tell Robert that he is invited to come speak to me personally. I guarantee his safety. I'll send hostages if it is necessary."

Eadgar nodded hurriedly, anxious to move off. Malcolm pulled him up short. "And Eadgar, see if Duncan is among them."

The Aetheling went forward with six men. Malcolm watched him greet Robert, who paced his horse back and forth as they spoke. Eadgar sat still and quiet on his own mount. Then Robert sent someone off to Rufus to gain approval.

"William Rufus will want hostages, if his reputation is true," Malcolm said.

Events proved him right. After much hesitation and bickering, Robert came to meet Malcolm alone; Eadgar and the rest stayed behind.

Robert hadn't changed much, except to thicken around the middle. His eyes brightened as he dismounted before Malcolm.

"Welcome, my old friend," said the King. "How goes it with my son... is he with you?" He tried to keep the anxiousness from his voice.

"Duncan is well," said Robert, grasping Malcolm's extended hand. "He deemed it unworthy to accompany me, and I agreed. I left him in Normandy, happily training in the art of the joust."

Malcolm sighed with relief. "That is well. He is a good boy."

Robert set his mouth. "He prefers Normandy to England. I am the Duke there, now."

"Congratulations. But I would have preferred you as King of England."

"My father wished otherwise. Besides, my brother wears the crown well."

"Still… is it not time for Duncan to be released as hostage?"

Robert busily adjusted his saddle. "King Malcolm..." He turned back. "William had him knighted before his death. And gave him his freedom."

Malcolm stared for a minute, uncomprehending. "Then why hasn't he come back?"

"Sire, he isn't coming back. He prefers to stay where he is."

Malcolm turned away.

"Sire... he didn't know how to tell you."

"If he doesn't come back," Malcolm's voice cracked, "tell him he is disinherited."

There was an uncomfortable silence. Malcolm stared at Walter for a moment, then turned to face the Norman army.

"Listen," he said, his voice a growl. "This is how I see it. When I swore fealty to your father for Lothian, I swore also to his eldest son... to you. Not your brother. I owe him nothing. Lothian was a gift from Edward. It is mine."

Robert cleared his throat. "Times have changed, Sire. The laws of Edward exist no longer. What he did is nil. You know that." He waited, but Malcolm stubbornly refused to answer.

"The power," continued Robert, "is with my brother William. His army is well trained, and mounted."

The power of the Normans was of a kind Malcolm didn't really want to test. He knew the weight behind Robert's reasoning.

"I shall think on what you have said. Come. Let me serve you some dinner."

"No. Thank you Sire. I must return directly. The King awaits your answer. Sleep on it, King Malcolm. I will return in the morning for your answer. Meanwhile, we will entertain our... guests."

Robert stiffly remounted his horse, bowing slightly to the King. As he rode off, Malcolm leaned his head toward Walter. "I don't have much choice, do I?"

Walter shook his head. "I hate the thought. Perhaps you should at least get his measure." The answer sounded as lame as he felt. The Scots were in no condition for a full-scale war.

The next morning, Robert returned with an escort. Malcolm was ready for him. The Duke nodded, wordlessly, and led the others back to a pavilion which had been erected, reminiscent of the last such event.

William Rufus received Malcolm in state. The English King was seated on a portable throne atop a raised platform, surrounded by his great officers.

Despite himself, Malcolm's eyes were drawn to William's; never had he seen such an emerald green color, nor eyes that shone with such malevolence. The right side of the King's face was covered with a red splotch, which gave him the nickname Rufus.

William carelessly put out a hand for him to kiss. Malcolm barely brushed the proffered hand with his lips, thinking he would rather be dealing with this man's father.

In a hurried ceremony, Malcolm renewed the terms of the

treaty of Abernethy, swearing to be William's man for the earldom of Lothian. In return, Rufus promised to return twelve vills, or hundreds, to Malcolm that were in the English possession during the Conqueror's lifetime.

Eadgar Aetheling was reconciled with King William, and returned to England with him.

The next day, the armies were gone.

30

William Rufus

By Christmas, Duke Robert and Eadgar Aetheling left King William's court, disgusted that he had neglected to fulfill any of the promises he had made to both his own brother and Malcolm. They went to Scotland, to spend the winter there until fair weather made it possible to return to Normandy.

Malcolm entertained his guests graciously, not surprised by the turn of events.

But even he was astonished when, the following year, King Rufus invaded Strathclyde, intent on gaining the city of Carlisle. This was clearly a violation of the treaty, and Malcolm was incensed. But he had problems at home that hindered yet another extensive campaign.

For one thing, Margaret was sick again. She had given birth to their sixth child, Alexander, only a year after Edgar's birth, and had not recovered from the exertion.

To make matters worse, word had reached Dunfermline of Nell's death at Forteviot. The palace he built there had been finished for some years now, and his mother had continued to reside in peace at the quiet little mill on the Earn. Walter read the dispatch to Malcolm, who received the news with an unsteady countenance.

"We must go to her funeral, wouldn't you say, Walter?"

The other nodded. He sent ahead the necessary funds to inter the woman properly.

The next day, King Malcolm and Walter rode hard for Forteviot. They took two days to cross the thirty miles, but the local priest waited for them before conducting the quiet service. The townspeople stood a respectful distance away from Malcolm, commenting to each other about his unusual sentimentality; Nell had been long ago accepted as his old wet-nurse. Malcolm showed his grief by staring, tight-lipped, at the priest.

Suddenly, Walter felt the King stiffen beside him. Looking up, he followed Malcolm's eyes to a small group of horsemen, standing in a tight clump the other side of the fence. He could tell that they were Highlanders by their wild appearance; the leader, standing a bit before the others, was studying Malcolm with an unfriendly expression.

Walter's hand strayed to his sword, but Malcolm grasped his wrist. As the two of them watched, the leader gave them a curt salutation and turned, leading the rest away quickly and quietly. They melted into the forest.

No one else seemed to see the disturbance; the service ended shortly and the villagers filed out of the graveyard, leaving the King alone. None but Walter noticed that his mind was already on other thoughts.

"Who was it?" he whispered.

For a time he received no response. Finally, Malcolm whispered in a hoarse voice, "My half-brother, Donald Bain."

Walter shuddered. The last time he had heard that name was in this same village, and he still remembered the venom with which it was spoken. He looked about, half-expecting them to reappear.

"I don't think we have to worry about them coming back," said Malcolm. "He just wanted to make sure I know what he knows..." His voice trailed off. "He must have very good spies."

He would say nothing more. But on his return to Dunfermline, Malcolm sent out his own spies, to discover Donald's strength. They returned with no answers.

It was as if Malcolm had seen an apparition.

"My dear brother is biding his time," the King said. "He has lived in the Highlands all this while, gathering support from those savages. Perhaps he was in league with Maelsnectan..."

It was one of those beautiful May days that made one feel glad to be alive. It was Malcolm's turn to visit the Earl of Richmond in his new Yorkshire castle. For many months they had sent letters back and forth between Edinburgh, Alain and the nunnery at Wilton, where Malcolm's eldest daughter Edith was receiving a distinguished education. Malcolm had conceived the idea that Alain would make a splendid husband for his daughter, especially considering his wealthy status. Margaret gave her blessing to the espousal, and all parties were content. There only remained one task; receiving permission from the English King, since Alain was his Noble subject.

Malcolm mounted his steed, turning around to face into the breeze. "Ah, I do love the spring flowers," he smiled, turning to Alain. "Our season is too short, but glorious."

The rest of the party was ready to start. The English King resided in Gloucester, which was over two hundred miles away, but no one seemed to mind the trip. For once, their journey was peaceful rather than military, and a festive mood captured all the men. Walter couldn't be happier, riding between his two favorite people—aside from his wife and son, who he was missing already.

Rolling hills never seemed greener and they were blessed with a fair number of days without too much rain. Townspeople opened up to them, for the populace sensed that this informal party would be lavish with their funds. And so they were; Malcolm was enjoying himself. For a while.

As they got closer to Gloucester, his mood darkened. There was no disguising his distaste for the task ahead of them. "I am so happy that you are on good terms with King William," he said to Alain. "For otherwise I would not venture near his court."

Alain shrugged unconcernedly. "I trust that he has no problems with me. We have ever been cordial; his father may he rest in peace has given him a good example."

"Alain, you are a powerful noble and a good friend," Malcolm nodded. "I hope to see you carry the day."

Walter listened to this exchange with a frown. He feared for Malcolm and somehow felt responsible, for without Isabel, Alain and Malcolm may never have met. If all went well, then he could congratulate himself. If not...

Malcolm looked at Walter, almost reading his thoughts. "What could go wrong?" he murmured.

They were soon to find out. Although they were received without delay, William Rufus was evidently not having a good day. He scowled when Alain knelt before his throne, and he barely looked at Malcolm at all.

"To what do I owe the honor of your visit?" he asked Alain, pointedly. The Earl glanced at Malcolm and rose.

"Sire, King Malcolm has agreed to wed me to his daughter Edith." He bowed graciously, and Malcolm did the same.

William looked down his nose at the pair. "He what?"

Alain cleared his throat. "He has offered his daughter to me in marriage."

There was silence in the room except for the drumming of William's fingers on the arm of his throne. "You would marry the daughter of King Malcolm."

Malcolm spoke up. "Yes, Sire. It is both our wishes."

"But it is not my wish." William stood up slowly, raising his voice. "I refuse my permission."

Alain stepped back, stunned. Malcolm clenched his teeth, not trusting himself to speak.

Alain tried again. "Sire, I do not understand."

"You don't understand," the King said mockingly. "Of course you don't understand. Why in heaven would I want the King of the Scots extending his influence into my kingdom? Why don't you stay on your own side of the border?"

The last sentence was directed at Malcolm, and the King of the Scots was not loath to respond.

"Sire," he spat, taking three steps backwards. "I will do so gladly. For now." He turned on his heel and stomped out of the room, followed by his retinue.

Alain stared at King William until the other sat down in his throne, motioning for someone to bring him a goblet of wine. He did not offer anything to the Earl.

Speechless, Alain bowed then followed Malcolm. The Scottish party was waiting for him and they rode to the east, glad to put the King's court behind them.

They rode at a gallop until the city was far in the distance. Slowing their horses to a walk, Malcolm paused until Alain caught up with him. Walter rode in the next rank, still within hearing.

"Well, Alain. I suppose we should have expected this. Perhaps we should have approached the King differently."

The Breton sighed. "I do not know if it would have made any difference. His behavior is most unkingly."

They rode in silence for a moment. Malcolm turned in his saddle. "Alain, I don't dare leave my daughter in this kingdom. I have drawn William's attention to her, and she may not be safe. Will you come to Wilton with me? Then we shall decide what to do." He smiled grimly when the other nodded his head; they both had a lot to think about.

Wilton nunnery stood to the west of Winchester so the party turned south. The convent had a long and distinguished history, and most recently had been rebuilt into stone by Edith of Wessex, Queen of Edward the Confessor. Malcolm's party was expected, but the happy reception soon turned into a hushed conference. Luckily, the nuns knew how to deal with their unhappy guests. Their house was known for providing refuge.

The princess welcomed her father solemnly, but inadvertently broke into a quick smile, quickly squelched when told about their reception with King William. Walter suspected he knew why; she was only a teenager, and Alain must have seemed like a grandfather to her. She was an obedient daughter and would have married whoever her parents demanded. But she didn't have to be happy about it.

Alain didn't seem to notice. Edith was accompanied by another woman, well into her thirties, who looked curiously at the newcomers. Malcolm's daughter turned to her companion.

"Father, Earl Alain, I would introduce you to Gunhild, daughter of King Harold of recent memory." Alain's face opened up into a large smile. It seemed that he had already forgotten about Edith, in consideration of this new opportunity. Walter looked at his good-father, amazed. He had just barely gotten used to thinking of Alain's upcoming wedding, and now Alain seemed to be looking for an alternative wife. What would he tell Isabel?

The nuns were ushering the company into the great hall, which they had laid out for a meal. Malcolm took his daughter by the arm, and Alain offered his own to Gunhild. Graciously nodding, she accepted.

As they took their places at the trestle table, Alain leaned toward his new acquaintance. "Gunhild," he said, savoring the name. "Your mother was Eadgifu the Fair, I understand." He knew very well who Eadgifu was; as William the Conqueror's champion, Alain was the lucky recipient of many estates after the Battle of Hastings; a large portion of his new lands had once belonged to this same Eadgifu, who came from a very wealthy family. Unfortunately, his tenants were more loyal to their fallen lord than their new master. Could an association with Gunhild help turn this around?

It was entirely possible that Gunhild knew all this as well, but adversity had taught her caution. She had retreated to Wilton for safety's sake, but any high office within this aristocratic cloister was unobtainable because of her post-conquest status. She was a virtual prisoner and didn't particularly relish spending the rest of her life here.

She looked appraisingly at Alain. "Yes. That is true. I haven't seen her for many years."

A little embarrassed, he coughed. Walter, sitting on his other side, patted him on the back.

Across the table, Malcolm and Edith were studying this little exchange. "Father," she started, taking his hand. "Mayhap you needn't fight with King William over me."

He smiled back at her a little crookedly. "I am loath to give up a fight," he admitted, "but perhaps this time I can force myself to see reason."

"I am not harmed in the least," she quickly assured him. "But I would return home with you."

They both looked again at Alain and Gunhild who were silently breaking their bread together. Malcolm put an arm around his daughter's shoulder. "You are dearer to me than I can ever tell you," he said. "And we will surely find you a royal husband."

The King winked at Walter, who was watching them, a little bemused. It looked like the immediate crisis had passed.

Anxious to be on their way, King Malcolm led his party north the following day. Not only did Edith accompany them, but Gunhild came away as well. She and Edith were riding inside a small wagon, fitted with extra pelts and blankets to make their ride more comfortable.

Alain seemed particularly jolly as Walter rode by his side. "I suppose this is a surprising turn of events," he volunteered to his good-son. "But we did not have much time to make a decision."

"Well, that much is certain," Walter agreed, looking forward to Malcolm. "King William will almost certainly be angry when he finds that his birds have flown. But what has happened between you and Gunhild?"

The Breton looked thoughtful. "Aside from the fact that I would have a companion," he said, glancing quickly at the wagon, "there are other factors. Gunhild is happy to go back home. Her presence will make my life much easier with her people. We both have much to gain."

Passing through Richmond on their way to Scotland, Malcolm and his retinue bade farewell to Alain and Gunhild who seemed quite satisfied with each other. Edith was happy to be returning to her mother, and even Malcolm was content to let things be. For now.

There was no word from the south for the next couple of years. Yet, in due time, Eadgar Aetheling came to visit Malcolm in an official capacity rather than exile; he had finally carved out a position for himself as ambassador. His task was to work out an agreement between the two kings.

But Malcolm did not want to discuss matters through an intermediary. For nearly ten years he had struggled with Rufus, accepting promises that were never kept, or exchanging minor incursions into each other's dominions. He sent Eadgar back to William requiring another personal meeting.

Riding hard, Eadgar found William Rufus in Gloucester, taken with a fever so dangerous that rumors of the King's death already met him on the way. But William wasn't finished yet; terrified of death, the Norman was bargaining with God. He promised to mend his ways, to quit selling churches for money, to show more mercy to his enemies and his people. In a repentant state, William graciously commanded Malcolm to come to him in Gloucester. He even sent hostages to insure his good faith.

Encouraged, the Aetheling returned to Scotland.

Margaret was desperately ill. After nine children, the Queen was spent; through perpetual fasting, she was emaciated. Her stomach ailment was critical, depleting her strength until she had to be carried to her bed, bent over double. Finally, she couldn't rise at all. Margaret had been transferred to Edinburgh, where Malcolm had built a chapel especially for her. She was safer there, and more comfortable now that she had little need for freedom. The King spent as much time as possible with her.

A gentle tap on Margaret's door sent her maids hurrying to answer it. Malcolm stood before them, finger on his lips in sign of silence. Used to his unannounced visits, the girls left the room.

Margaret sat up in her bed, propped up with pillows. Her long hair, still as golden as the day he met her, lay spread out over the pillow, and a brush lay absently in her hand as she gazed out the window. She didn't seem to notice the entrance of her husband.

Sitting beside her, Malcolm took the brush and gently ran it through her hair. Sighing, the Queen turned to him and laid her head against his shoulder.

"You're leaving again, aren't you?"

Surprised, he shifted to look at her.

"Oh, I can tell by the way you walked into the room."

Malcolm took her frail hands, stroking them. They seemed so thin, almost transparent, so that he could see the veins under the skin. One by one he kissed the fingers.

"You will be proud of me this time, my love. For once, I will cross the borders in peace. I am going to ask the King nicely to fulfill his end of the treaty."

"I thank God I am here to listen to those words."

"Hush, speak not so." Malcolm brushed his eyes with his sleeve. "We have many things left to do for our Scotland."

Margaret thought otherwise. "Kiss me, my king. I will wait for your return."

Consoled by her promise, Malcolm complied, kissing her forehead softly. He left hurriedly, unable to tolerate her pain. It was like this more and more often. Whenever he went away, he felt as if it were the last time he would see her alive.

Malcolm's escort was waiting for him, including Eadgar, Walter, and Thomas. The King mounted and sat astride his horse for a moment, looking at his closest friends. There was Walter, who turned his head and looked back, with eyes less sad now, but older and more understanding. Malcolm idly wondered just when his friend had lost his hurt look. Walter's hair was graying at the temples and throughout his beard. And no wonder; he was well into his fifties.

Malcolm rubbed his arthritic knee. Who was he kidding? He was nearly seventy himself, as far as he could figure. He hadn't much time left either. His once black hair was nearly all white now, though it hadn't thinned even a little.

At Walter's shoulder was his only son Alane, a fine young man of twenty-five who had a pretty little wife and a son of his own named Alexander. Alane took after his father in both practical and military skills; he would be a good servant to Malcolm's son, Eadward, who was the declared heir.

Malcolm looked proudly at Eadward, who sat straight in the saddle, looking neither to the right nor the left. He was a good son, and had all the right qualities for a king. But Malcolm was worried about him; unused to the cruelties of war, would Eadward be able to withstand the rigorous opposition of Donald Bain?

But at least he still had Thomas to help, faithful Thomas, whose marriage had been childless but happy.

Sighing, the King gave the command to move; they had a five hundred mile ride to Gloucester, where King William Rufus waited for them.

William Rufus had an enormous army camped around the town of Gloucester. Settling his own force well away from them, Malcolm sent Walter and Eadgar with a salutation to Rufus.

Eadgar knew his way about, and had no trouble getting introduced. But even he was surprised at their cool reception.

Far from being on his death-bed, Rufus was up and about, in good health. With his recovery came his usual arrogance; he conveniently forgot every promise he had made while in fear for his life.

As Eadgar and Walter were ushered in, the King sat with his back to them, engaged in a game of chess. He let them stand for some time. Finally, he turned in mock surprise.

"Oh, you are back," he said to Eadgar. "And who is this other person?"

The Aetheling bowed. "This is Sir Walter Steward, come to greet you in King Malcolm's behalf."

Walter bowed in turn. "I send his Grace's regards," he began, but paused when Rufus turned back to his game. He looked at Eadgar in confusion.

"Sire," Eadgar took up for Walter, "King Malcolm has arrived this very hour, and awaits your Highness's pleasure."

King William moved a piece, disdaining to answer.

Eadgar cleared his throat. "Is there a message you would send to the King?"

Rufus shook his head. "No."

"Your Grace," Walter said after a moment. "Perhaps you have misunderstood. King Malcolm has come in person, and desires to meet you to discuss the terms of your treaty."

Detecting a note of annoyance in Walter's voice, the Norman turned impatiently. "Did I address you?"

Walter's face turned red in anger. The Aetheling took a step forward.

"Sire," he said soothingly. "The Scots are allowed more freedom in their King's presence. He meant no disrespect."

Looking Walter over in obvious distaste, Rufus dismissed him with a lowering glance. He turned to Eadgar.

"Tell this King of his that I require one thing of him: to swear fealty to me as a vassal of England. Here. In front of my nobles. If he refuses this demand, I have nothing to say to him."

Although Eadgar had gained respectable skill as a negotiator over the years, he couldn't contain his surprise. He summoned his courage for a last response. "Sire, I don't think I understand you..."

"You understood what I said well enough." He turned back to his game.

Walter couldn't restrain his anger any longer, but rather than provoke a dangerous argument that could only end in his own arrest, he turned and left the room. The Aetheling stayed behind.

Malcolm was waiting in his pavilion, his expression grim. He noted the absence of Eadgar.

Walter went down on one knee.

"He barely acknowledged me. The man refused to discuss terms... or anything for that matter."

The King's eyes narrowed. "What did he want?"

"He wants you to swear fealty—"

"I did that already."

"—for Scotland as a vassal to England."

Malcolm released his breath in an explosion. "What!"

"Here, in Gloucester. Before his nobles. Or he refuses to meet with you."

The King paced his tent. "And Eadgar?"

"He stayed behind to reason with the King."

"Will it do any good?"

"No."

"Then order the men to start repacking. I should have known better."

The sun was setting as Eadgar dismounted before the King's pavilion. Malcolm came out to meet him. They both turned to look over the camp.

"Did you reason with him?"

Eadgar scratched his neck. "The man is a beast. He has already forgotten his change of heart. There is no talking to him."

Malcolm sighed. "Then he refuses to see me?"

"Unless you swear fealty to him."

"Must you stay here with him?"

"He has commanded me to."

Hearing the sympathy in Eadgar's voice, Malcolm felt a

sudden surge of tenderness for his good-brother. This poor, unfortunate man who was never able to grasp his destiny, always a pawn in someone else's game, felt sorrow for another who was infinitely more fortunate than he. Malcolm embraced the Saxon.

"I'm sorry we were never able to put you on the throne."

"We would both be happier if you had," Eadgar said sadly, mounting his horse. He turned a last look to the King, with a shadow of a smile. "But I would never have been able to hold it."

Early the next morning, the Scots were on the march again. They went without complaint; everyone knew the insult offered to their King. Proud, considering the slight as a personal affront, the Scots were ready to follow Malcolm to the grave, if necessary.

Malcolm had not been prepared to fight at Gloucester; his had been a peaceful mission. But William Rufus was going to know what it meant to anger the King of Scotland.

Malcolm meant to invade Northumbria with a vengeance.

Walter went home to put his affairs in order. Although on the surface this looked like just another campaign, there was something different about it. Malcolm's honor was at stake; he hoped to meet King William in full battle array. He even sent the Norman a challenge.

But there was a certain fatalism in Malcolm's attitude. He felt Scotland's innate weakness; more isolated than England, Scotland had developed more slowly, both culturally and militarily. A direct confrontation did not bode well.

As Walter turned his horse's head onto the homebound road, the animal picked up its pace, anticipating a warm stable and dinner. Walter wished he could share his mount's enthusiasm. But he knew that he faced a bitter argument with his wife, as he ever did when he went to war.

Worse than that was the order he had to pass on to Alane. Always before, his son followed him on campaign; he meant to earn the high position he stood to inherit. But Malcolm had chosen Alane to captain the guard he meant to leave behind, just in case there was trouble at home. And Walter knew how his son was going to take the news.

He found Alane busy cleaning his sword when Walter entered the house. His son looked up with a smile; but the grin faded at his expression.

"What is it, father? Not bad news, I hope?"

Walter picked up the sheath from the floor. He busied himself with wiping it.

"Come on. I know when you are disturbed. It has something to do with this campaign, doesn't it?"

Walter nodded. "Yes, Alane. There are times when one has to follow orders that seem to make no sense. Like the one I must give to you."

Alain sat straight up. "Orders?"

"You must know how defenseless the King's children are when he leaves the country. Especially now, since King Malcolm's half-brother has been seen near the city."

Alane shrugged, going back to his cleaning. "I heard something of the sort."

"Well, let me tell you everything. Malcolm thinks that Donald intends to usurp the throne. He has spread a rumor about the King's...birth that makes his claim to the throne...somewhat less sure."

"That's ridiculous," Alane interrupted, "After thirty years, he is more sure of his position than ever."

"But how much longer will he live? And what of his heir? Eadward is going with him this time, but who knows what may happen. Those children left behind are almost defenseless against an unscrupulous enemy."

Alane put down his sword. "I am expected to guard them. Is that what you are trying to say?"

"Yes. It is an honorable task."

"Honorable," Alane said bitterly. "To sit behind while all the glory is taken by someone else."

"Yes, glory." Walter got up, shaking his head. "You will come to find that this glory is an empty word. And what is the trust of your sovereign worth to you?"

He went to the wall, hanging up his cloak. After a moment, Alane came to him.

"You are right, father. It is an honorable task."

Walter caught Alane's hand in both his own. "It is good to have a son I can be so proud of."

They looked at each other a long minute. Then Alane pulled away, giving his father a quick hug. "You better tell mother," he said, "I don't have the heart."

Walter looked toward the garden; he knew he would find Isabel there. Giving Alane a look between anger and desperation, he went to find her.

Isabel was cutting some flowers when she heard her husband's footsteps. Jumping up, she started to run toward him, but slowed to a stop when she interpreted his expression; it was one she had seen too many times before.

He had to go to her then, knowing she would allow him to embrace her stiff, tense body. She looked up at him, eyes pleading.

"There's another campaign, isn't there? Can't you stay behind this time? Must you always go, as if Malcolm would get lost without your presence?"

The argument was always the same.

"Isabel," he faltered, brushing a strand of hair from her eyes. "This is no ordinary campaign. Malcolm faces the King of England himself...he needs all the support we can give."

"Oh, why do I bother?" she cried, breaking away. "Go. Do what you have to do. If you don't come back, you don't come back."

She ran into the house.

Walter stared after her. She had never said that before; the pain sunk deep into his breast.

Later that night, Isabel lay quietly in his arms. The tears had finally run their course.

"My love," he whispered. She gave no answer, but he knew she was listening. "There is something I should have said to you long before. I have seen much in my life: misery, hate, war, death. I have seen my King, who I idolized, reduced to a shambles of his former self. I have been disillusioned, betrayed. I have seen everything I believed in turn to dust. But always, Isabel, there has been you. You have ever restored my hope. In you, I have found truth. I still have something to live for."

Though she did not answer, her limbs relaxed, nestling against his own. And in moments, her lips found a place against his throat. Here, indeed, was a reason to live.

Margaret hadn't left her bed since spring; her wasted frame lay flat, her head sunk into the pillow. No longer could she even support a sitting position, to look from the window. Her confessor Turgot was constantly at her side now, ever ready to administer the last rites if she needed them.

But she was able to summon a weak smile when her husband came to tell her farewell.

"It was not so long ago when we last said good-bye," she said, putting her hand around his neck. "Must you leave me so soon? I feel that I may not be here to greet your return."

"Shhh. Speak not so."

"That is also what you last said. My husband, think on what you are doing. Dare you give up everything we have worked for, to satisfy your overweening pride?"

"Margaret. If I were to hide my head now, the next time my enemies will push me even farther. I must never show weakness, or I will truly be done for. They will fall on me like a pack of wolves."

She closed her eyes. "As you say. Now kiss me, for I would not have us part in disagreement."

With tears falling unashamedly from his eyes, Malcolm gathered his wife carefully into his arms, kissing her softly. She seemed exhausted by even this little show of affection, so he laid her back on the pillow. Margaret smiled slowly at him.

"Pray for me, my love," he said, as he backed from the room. Her answer was so soft that he didn't hear the fervored assent. Turgot bent over his charge as Malcolm shut the door.

31

Death of King Malcolm

In late September, 1093, the army that set out from Edinburgh was large and well organized. At its front rode the King and his closest advisors; behind them paced his son Eadward and the fourth son, Eadgar. It was Eadgar's first military encounter, and the seventeen year-old looked around with wide eyes.

MacDuff's son was in attendance, as well as Cospatric, who had been summoned with his vassals from Dunbar.

The King's second son, Eadmund, was left at home, for it had been noticed that he was associating with poor company. The boy was not altogether trusted. His next brother, Aethelred, stayed behind because of a troublesome illness of the lungs, which often left him weak and breathless.

Alane was glad of his company, and told him so as they watched the army march away from Dun Edin. Aethelred put an arm around Alane's shoulders.

"I am glad, too, my friend. I shall ill bear this solitude while such an important event takes place without us."

Little did the two of them realize that they, too, would be in the midst of an event as momentous as that waiting for Malcolm.

For just below, in the forest surrounding Edinburgh castle, the fierce Highlanders of Donald Bain were gathering. Within a week, the gates of the castle would be closed and barred against a besieging force of grim intent. And Malcolm knew nothing about them.

Approaching Alnwick castle, the new home of the Earl of Northumbria, the Scots ran across their first serious opposition. The castle was heavily defended; they could not leave it at their backs. Robert de Moubray's banner floated atop the highest tower.

Siege warfare was a tedious, uncomfortable chore. If the walls could not be breached, the defenders had to be starved into submission; that is, if the offensive army did not starve first. But there really wasn't any choice. Malcolm deployed his force on both sides of the river that ran before the fortress.

During the course of the two week siege, many attacks were repulsed. In return, there were two night sallies from the castle. Both of them inflicted little damage.

On the morning of the fifteenth day, a white flag was raised over the castle walls. Malcolm called a meeting in his pavilion, attended by all his chiefs and earls.

He sat informally on a pile of blankets, his crown laid beside him. Eadward stood to one side. When they had all gathered, Malcolm cleared his throat.

"Thomas," he called to the Saxon, standing guard outside the flap. "Please come in. I would ask you first what your opinion is."

Thomas, ever faithful, had always spoken his mind. Because he had never shown disobedience to Malcolm's orders, the King never reprimanded him, much though they disagreed at times. The Saxon shook his head worriedly.

"It is too soon. They have not starved in so short a time. Perhaps this surrender is a trick of some kind. We all know how treacherous the Normans can be." He did not hide his bitterness.

Malcolm dismissed him to his post. He often doubted Thomas's objectivity when it came to Normans.

He turned to young MacDuff. "I advise accepting their surrender," the man said. "We have eaten all we can from this area, and our scouts must go farther away to gather food. Very soon, we too will be feeling pangs of hunger.

"Already the chill November wind takes the fire from a man. Before long, we may begin to lose fingers and toes in our idleness."

Many in the tent seemed to agree with the young Earl; a rumbling assent rose at his words. Malcolm asked Walter.

"I agree with Thomas," he said simply.

The King turned to his son. "You must surely have an opinion, Eadward. What do you say?"

The Prince blushed at the attention. "I say that this may well be a trick. But we are many in number, and can stop any sally they might make in the guise of surrender."

Malcolm nodded. "Very well. Our troops are unused to a long siege. Let us put on our grandest cloaks, and accept de Moubray's surrender."

The men filed out, satisfied with the turn of events. Walter lingered, until he was alone with Malcolm.

"Sire, I feel a great uneasiness. I caution you to proceed with great care."

Malcolm turned his eyes on Walter. Those eyes were bloodshot with restlessness, tired with worry.

"Is it really such a terrible thing to die, Walter? Life has been a burden to me these ten years; my shoulders are no longer strong. I yearn to lie down beside my dear Queen and pass with her into eternity...as long as God accepts my soul, so filled with the sins a king must commit, in order to rule from strength."

Walter was alarmed. "Your Grace, I have never heard you speak so."

With a great effort, Malcolm pulled himself together. "And you never shall again. Come, embrace me, my brother...for you have always been like a brother to me."

Overcome, Walter embraced his friend. For a moment they stood thus; then, with a tired gesture, Malcolm assured Walter he was all right.

"Let us get this task over with," he said wearily.

The King's best men took their places around him, horses prancing, opening a path in the cheering army. Edward rode to Malcolm's right, Eadgar to his left.

The white flag still showed above the wall of the fortress. The little cavalcade moved slowly to the pipers and drummers, playing in their wake. It was if though they were in the midst of a festival, rather than at war.

Stopping to within fifty feet of the castle gate, a local priest stepped forward, alone. He raised a hand to the forbidding wooden doors, conscious of his mission.

"I bring you greetings from his Grace, Malcolm Canmore to Earl Robert de Moubray. The terms of his surrender are this: if you agree to throw down your arms and accept his suzerainty, if you agree to come forth from your castle and allow him to take possession, the King of the Scots will permit you to leave in peace. He promises not to take a single life, nor will he do damage to this, your fortress. In due time, when all is as it should be, King Malcolm will return to Scotland and leave you in possession of this castle, as his vassal."

The man stood aside, waiting for a response. Walter marveled at the priest's bravery; many a herald had been sent back from such a task, filled with arrows.

After the lapse of a few minutes, the great doors creaked open several inches, and a lance was thrust through the gap. Hanging from the tip was a ring with the key to the fortress.

A great cheer rose from the Scots. Malcolm, conscious of his dignity, moved his mount forward at a walk.

Alone, resplendent in his victory, Malcolm rode toward the doors. Walter watched with uneasiness, then suddenly a stab of pain shot through his chest as a similar spectacle poured into his memory: Alain's reach for the key at Dinan, and his own faintness when the Count grasped it. How clear it was now!

Malcolm reached for the ring slowly... oh, so slowly, as Walter stood in his stirrups. "Malcolm, NO!" he shouted, but thought the words drowned in the cheering.

Though somehow, momentarily, Malcolm caught the thread of Walter's panic and twisted his head toward him, before turning back and extending his arm.

But he never grasped the key. Pushed with a deliberate motion, the lance changed its angle, plunging forward with deadly accuracy straight into Malcolm's eye.

The cheering of the army changed into yowls of horror, then anger as with one accord, the Scots surged forward.

They were not expecting the ferocity of the Northumbrian attack.

The doors crashed open with exceptional force. Scores of mounted armored knights thundered forth, lances lowered. They trampled the poor King underfoot before anyone had a chance to reach his inert body.

Eadward reacted immediately. Screaming his father's name, he spurred his horse forward; the Prince moved so quickly he was among the knights before they knew it, fighting desperately against their forward momentum. He hacked wildly at the nearest targets he could reach.

But the youth was no match for these hardened warriors; as he was wrenching his sword from a shield, another man came from his blind side and drove an axe between his shoulder blades.

Walter, following to extricate the boy, watched with horror as Eadward's horse reared up, dumping the rider from its back. Walter leaped from his mount, shouting Eadward's name, then Malcolm's, bringing his sword around his head in a wide circle. In a moment, he cleared a way to the Prince. Finding Eadward's body, Walter straddled him.

One Norman tried to ride him down with raised sword; Walter was ready, and stepped aside, driving his blade into the knight's leg. He twisted around, catching another in the back. But no help was forthcoming; disheartened by the loss of their King, the Scots were already breaking and running before the onslaught of the Normans.

Still swinging his sword around his head, Walter never saw the lance coming directly for him. An unknown knight, shouting with glee, pierced his throat then moved on, pulling the shaft cleanly from its mark. Walter fell, instantly dead, across the boy he sought to protect.

Cospatric, seeing the danger to the Princes, managed to grab the reins of Eadgar's horse. Savagely plunging his spurs into his mount, he burst to the side, pulling the startled boy away from the danger.

For a moment it seemed that they wouldn't make their way out; but Cospatric, clear-headed as ever, had already drawn his sword with his other hand, using it to sweep his enemies away. Intent on pushing the Scots before them, few Normans sought to slow their progress.

In a few moments, Cospatric broke through, pulling the unwilling boy after him. Even then he didn't stop, but continued until they reached the shelter of a nearby woods.

Shocked by the murder of his father, the Prince had burst into tears. "Why did you pull me away from there? Why didn't you let me die with my father?" He buried his face in his hands.

Dismounting and transferring provisions from his own horse to Eadgar's, Cospatric let him cry for a few minutes. Finally, he took hold of the boy's knee.

"Listen to me, Eadgar. Stop for a minute and listen."

Taking a breath, the Prince looked down at him, tears still flowing.

"You must go and tell the others. Go to Edinburgh. Your mother may be in danger. Word of this tragedy is already on its way to her enemies. You must go to her."

Little by little the import of these words sunk in. Eadgar looked at Cospatric, confused.

"Aren't you coming, too?"

The Earl hesitated. "I will come part of the way. But hurry, we must go before we are found."

The Scots were in a panic; they had no real leader; there was nothing to fight for. The Normans kept coming and coming, determined to teach them a lesson.

Many of the fleeing Scots tried to cross the river, but the current was too swift and deep. The weight of their armor pulled them under the surface; many simply could not swim. Others ran downstream, but were overtaken by swift destriers. The Normans cut them down without mercy.

Only the sheer numbers of the Scots saved the rest of them; the Normans couldn't kill every one. After a time, the victors returned to the castle, satiated with killing.

But the Scottish army was diminished by half. They straggled home as individuals; as an army they were no more.

32

The Siege of Dun Edin

Edinburgh Castle was a fine example of modern construction. Perched atop a steep, craggy rock some hundreds of feet above the Forth, the castle was surrounded by a cliff on three sides. Even along the cliff's edge, a thick stone wall encircled the fortress; only the gates pointing south-east were accessible.

Donald Bain was satisfied with his position. He had kept informed of Malcolm's movements. Spies followed the army's destructive progress all the way through Northumbria, reporting faithfully back to their chief.

While the Scots paced restlessly in front of Alnwick, Donald considered attacking Edinburgh. But he waited; Malcolm was a popular King, and he wasn't sure how much support he could muster. The King could still return like an avenging angel; but perhaps when the Scots moved further south...

So when the news came of Malcolm's disaster, Donald refused to believe it. Surely his brother couldn't have been so foolish. He questioned his informers again and again, until he pieced the story together. Yes, the old King had finally gotten careless. Donald rubbed his hands together.

He was an odd sort of fellow; most people didn't like him. Perhaps it was the way he went about complaining all the time, using his misfortune to get favors. Or maybe it was the way he threatened people, reminding them that he would be king some day. And the fervor with which he called Malcolm a bastard was quite unnerving, especially when the King's men were about.

Whichever it was, everyone agreed that it was really his eyes that couldn't be trusted. He never ceased to look about, as if expecting an assassin to appear at his side. Apart from that, his countenance was almost agreeable; he bore a strong resemblance to his father Duncan.

Donald was still waiting for one more clan of reinforcements. Then he would attack.

The residents of the castle were protected by a very small garrison; of that he had made sure. The Princes—and the crown of Scotland—would very soon be in his hands.

Cospatric had parted from Eadgar on the borders of Lothian, leaving him with a retinue of six men. The boy was nervous; he knew none of these men, and was completely dependent on them even to find the way home.

But he swallowed his fear and took nominal command, as was his right. They didn't seem to mind; Eadgar forgot that these men were as afraid as he was. After thirty-seven years, they were left without a king. None of them remembered any other but Malcolm.

Eadgar bitterly cursed Cospatric. The Earl was more concerned with securing his own lands than protecting the younger son of his late King. Always an opportunist, that one.

But the boy had more bothersome issues to think about. How was his mother going to take the bad news? Or was she even alive?

It took Eadgar three days to reach Edinburgh. At twilight on the third, he stood at the edge of the forest, biting his lip in agitation. To go so far, and find the worst danger before him.

He dismissed his companions, who were none too willing to risk their skins further. They melted into the woods, leaving the Prince alone.

It was Eadgar's duty to get into the castle, much as he would have rather disappeared with the others. He knew of a secret door on the cliff-side, with a ledge leading up to it. But how was he to get through the rebel army?

Dismayed, he sat thinking until it was completely dark. Then he felt safe enough to move.

Fortunately for Eadgar, the Highlanders felt so confident that they were careless of posting guards. Huge bonfires crackled at intervals, and the men sat rowdily around them, roasting game on spits, passing around the wineskins.

Eadgar thought it best to walk boldly through this rabble. So he left behind all his traveling gear, sent his horse away, and stepped from the safety of the trees.

No one seemed to notice a lonely, shivering boy in the dark, so he took a deep breath, pulled his cloak closer, and strode forward.

The Highlanders were speaking to each other in a dialect Eadgar barely understood. Their voices were guttural, harsh from the cold. He passed them without attracting attention.

After a time, as his presence was ignored, the Prince took heart. Nearing the castle, he listened perhaps a little less carefully than he should have. Looking to the right and left, Eadgar nearly directed his steps toward the ledge when a heavy hand fell on his shoulder.

"Eh lad. Where d'e think 'eer goin'?"

Eadgar took a breath, too scared to speak.

"What say ye? I doan think ye belong here."

Without waiting for an answer, the large man pushed Eadgar around, steering him toward his leader's tent. As they passed the fires, the men stopped talking, then got up to follow. They had been lacking excitement for a while.

A large group had accumulated by the time they reached Donald's tent. The chief came out to see what the noise was about. Eadgar was pushed to the ground before him.

"Found 'im in front of the castle."

Donald looked at him, annoyed. "And how did he get so close?" he asked icily.

Expecting praise, the man shrugged angrily. "Doan know. I canna be everywhere at onct."

Donald wasn't listening to his answer. He pulled the boy's chin up, studying him.

"One of my brother's bastards, by the look of him."

The others grumbled interestedly.

"So who are you?" he asked the boy, a little less gruffly.

Eadgar looked at the men around him. "I am Eadgar. And who are you, to surround my father's stronghold like a pack of thieves?"

The Highlanders laughed. "A brave one," someone said.

Donald frowned, then laughed as well. "He won't have need of his castle any more, will he?"

Eadgar tried to get up, but his capturer pushed him down.

The boy's uncle paced back and forth, and then pointed a finger at him.

"You're here to tell your mother, aren't you? You were slow in coming, but that's all right. We haven't told any of them yet."

He turned to his men. "Take him to the gates. Announce his coming; they'll let him in. The bad news will destroy their morale. Go. We'll have him back soon enough."

They were disappointed, expecting to have had some fun with the boy. But, accustomed to obeying Donald, the Highlanders picked Eadgar up and prodded him forward. He tried to take a last look at Donald, but tripped and fell to his knees.

The sentinels at the gate announced to those inside that there was a great massing of the enemy. It was feared that the attack had finally come; Alane was summoned to give instructions.

What Alane saw instead, as he looked over the wall, was more unsettling than the prospect of fighting at night. Standing before the gate, arms outspread in his captor's hands, with bloody face, torn clothes, disheveled hair, was Aethelred's little brother, sixty miles from where he should have been.

Aethelred was standing behind Alane; his hands tightened on his friend's arms. The steward could be depended on to recover quickly, though; guessing at the meaning of their enemies' gesture, he dared to thrust his head over the wall.

"Is this young man a hostage?" he called out, looking for a leader.

There was shouting for him to open the gate.

"Tell me your intentions first," he demanded.

Realizing that Alane feared they would rush the gate, one of Eadgar's guards shouted for the others to back up. They obliged. Before the man let go, however, he jeered, "He has a message for you."

Laughing, he threw Eadgar forward and walked away.

As soon as the Highlanders were a safe distance away, Alane ordered the gate opened. The bar was quickly lifted and four men dashed out, carrying the boy to safety; he was so relieved he could hardly walk. Once they were inside, the gates crashed shut.

The men lowered Eadgar slowly to the ground. Alane had gone for water; Aethelred cradled his brother's head in his arms. He bent over the boy, bringing his lips to Eadgar's ear.

"Tell me," he whispered.

Still frightened, Eadgar began sobbing. "It's worse than you can imagine. They are all dead." He choked, trying to sit up.

Alane came up behind them while Eadgar was coughing. He knelt, offering a dipper. The boy drank eagerly.

Aethelred turned his head away, his chest heaving; but Alane bent nearer.

"Who are they?" His clear eyes gave strength to Eadgar.

"My father, your father, my b,b,brother...Oh God, why did this have to happen?"

Standing, his eyes wet, Alane told someone to prepare the Queen. He looked down at Eadgar, his lip quivering. "Come. We must tell her now. She asks about him hourly."

For a minute, Eadgar stared at the ground. Then he reached for Aethelred's hand. "He is right. But I am so afraid to face her."

The two brothers stood in a huddle, seeking comfort. Alane put his arms around them.

"What an evil day this is," he whispered.

Running footsteps interrupted them. Eadmund led a group of servants through a doorway. At the sight of Eadgar they stopped.

"Come," Alane said, pulling Eadgar gently with him. "Let us go."

They had taken only a few steps before Eadmund ran up to them. "What are you doing here?"

Aethelred took him aside, motioning for Eadgar to keep moving. The servants stood by while they talked, watching his face express anger, then despair. The two brothers disappeared quickly into the tower.

They entered their mother's sick room behind the other two.

Margaret was lying just as Eadgar left her weeks ago, clutching her black rood. She was awake, her eyes glistening in the candlelight. Showing no surprise as Eadgar entered, the Queen lifted her hand for him to kiss. The boy threw himself on his knees at her bedside.

"How goes it with your father and your brother?"

Eadgar kissed her hand carefully, hesitating before raising his eyes. "All is well with them," he said finally.

"I know that. Eadgar, I beg you, on your love for your father and me...Tell me the truth in this matter."

He looked at his mother, so frail yet full of strength for him.

"They are dead, mother. Killed by the cruelest treachery while laying siege to Castle Alnwick." He told her the story in simple words.

When he had finished, Margaret laid her hand on Eadgar's head.

"Dear God," she said, looking upwards, "I thank You for giving me this anguish to suffer at my last hour, that I may be purged my sins. By Your grace, Whose death has given life unto the world, deliver me."

Closing her eyes, Margaret's spirit passed out of the world.

Overcome, Eadgar laid his head on her shoulder and cried.

The few members of the household passed quietly through

Margaret's room, paying their last respects. Eadgar was put to bed, almost insensible. He no longer cared about the waiting army outside.

Alane took Aethelred and Eadmund from her room, bidding them to put aside their grief for the moment. They could see from his face that his own sadness was a burden he was suppressing with great effort.

"We must think of the mob out there," he said to them in a low voice. "It is your family, now, who are in danger. I thank God at least your two sisters are at their Aunt Christina's abbey. Your uncle will destroy every one of you, if he can get his hands on you."

Aethelred shook his head. "I don't care anymore."

But his brother was thinking ahead. "No. Alane is right. We must get ourselves, and our mother out of here. You don't want the man to desecrate her body, do you?"

Aethelred crossed himself. "But how?"

Alane rubbed his forehead. "I do not know. Is there any secret way from the castle?"

Eadmund was deep in thought. "No. Well, yes. But I don't see how we can use it."

"Show me."

Somewhat reluctantly, Eadmund led the way with a torch. Alane and Aethelred followed. They went through many dark passages that Alane didn't know existed, until Eadmund reached a trap-door in the floor. He seemed familiar with this route. Even Aethelred was surprised.

Throwing open the door, Eadmund gave the others a sheepish look. Then he went down a ladder. His companions followed.

They found themselves in a narrow passage that terminated in a stone door. With a tug, the Prince pulled it open.

A gust of cold wind blew into the tunnel. Alane found himself looking over a cliff. Below them, a quarter of a mile out from the granite base, flowed the Firth of Forth.

"We are on the opposite side of the castle," said Eadmund softly. "This is the outer wall. There is a ledge here, which I have used on occasion. It's the only other way out; the shelf runs along the castle wall, all the way to the gate. But once there, we still cannot avoid Donald Bain."

Taking a step onto the ledge, Alane kept hold of the friendly wall. He leaned over the summit, looking down; there was no sign of an army below.

Sucking in his breath, Alane pulled inside quickly. He was afraid of heights.

The precipice was steep, but rocks jutted out along the drop. For an army it was impassable, but for a handful of determined refugees...

"We shall climb down the mount," he said.

The other two looked at him like he had lost his mind.

"There is no alternative."

"We shall fall," said Eadmund.

"They will see us," cried Aethelred.

"Not at all. Can't you see? They would never expect such a move. Come, let us get some rest. We will start at dawn."

Aethelred blocked his way. "What about our mother?"

"We will lower her on a litter."

Astonished, the Prince let him pass.

The next morning, a heavy mist shrouded Dun Edin. Bishop Turgot, hearing the plan, crossed himself. "The Lord has sent us a cloak of fog, to hide our escape."

He and his servants carefully wrapped Margaret in a blanket, tying her securely to a litter. They carried the body through the secret tunnel, passing her from one to the other down the hole of the trap door.

The children, David and Alexander, were awakened from a sound sleep. Aethelred came to dress them, and to tell them of their mother's death. The children burst into tears, throwing themselves into their brother's arms.

"Shhh," the Prince comforted them. "We still have a difficult task ahead of us today. You will need to be brave, so that we can save mother from our enemy."

The boys trusted Aethelred implicitly, and dried their tears, trying to be strong. They knew the danger threatening them all; it took only a moment for them to be ready.

The handful of servants and two-score soldiers were gathering in the passageway. Alane followed, bringing many lengths of rope.

The litter was lowered by two ropes, held by the strongest soldiers. Two others began the long descent, finding the most secure footholds in the treacherous rock, while trying to steady the burden as it was lowered. They were soon lost in the mist.

No one dared follow just yet; if someone were to fall, they might dislodge the Queen on the way down. The watchers held their breath for long minutes. The wait seemed to take forever.

But finally, the men holding the ropes felt a vibration, as if their burden had touched the ground. Seconds later, the men at the bottom tugged the line, signaling their safe descent. Alane sighed with relief.

Turgot was next; he was too old to attempt the climb, so the rope was pulled up again and tied about his waist. The boys were lowered with him, though they were so terrified they couldn't help themselves much. Little David was crying, so Aethelred gave him his mother's prayer book to hang onto. The child was so impressed by the honor that he settled down, giving them no more problems.

The women went next, and after they were down the rest were deemed capable of descending by themselves. Groups of climbers prayed as they went down; this was an exercise no one had ever attempted before. Alane insisted that only six go at a time, so no one would knock anyone else off. Only once did a man slip; his cries echoed all the way down, cut off sharply at the end.

Alane could feel his heart pounding, waiting for shouts from rebel guards. But as the minutes passed, it became evident that no one heard.

Finally, all were down except Alane and the three Princes. They clasped hands before climbing over the edge.

Alane was never more terrified in his life; he was grateful that he couldn't see through the fog. Pretending that he was only feet above the ground, he concentrated on the position of his feet. The rocks were slippery, cold against his cheek. Beads of sweat covered his forehead, dripping into his eyes. Alane shook his head, his teeth chattering.

He stared at his fingernails, digging into the stone. Stretching, he reached with his toes for a foothold. At times he couldn't find any without twisting his body to the side.

To his left came scraping noises and a thump. Breathing heavily, Alain gasped, "Aethelred... Eadmund... Eadgar."

Nothing. He began to panic. "Are you all right?"

First a groan, then he heard Eadmund answer, "I'm all right. Took a little slide."

Alane paused, his head against a rock. "Are you sure?"

"Yes," he heard. He continued moving.

After a long time, he heard voices from below. "Turgot, are you there?"

"Careful, my son. You have not far to go."

Relieved, Alane almost slipped. But he gritted his teeth, and made the last dozen feet with relative confidence.

Setting foot on the ground, Alane fell to his knees. "I thank God for delivering me from this terror."

He looked up. "Did the others make it?"

A scrambling sound was his answer, and soon the Princes were standing at his side. Blood flowed from Eadmund's knee, but otherwise he was all right.

They were looking for their mother's litter. Turgot brought

them over to it. The blanket was torn, but the ropes binding the body were intact.

"The Lord saw her to safety," the Bishop said.

The little group carried the litter to Queen's Ferry. Expecting an attack, the ferrymen stood shoulder to shoulder, axes in hand, ready to defend their post to their last breath.

But they recognized the faces appearing from the fog. Exclaiming at the sight of the litter, they ran forward.

"Yes, it is the Queen, my children," the Bishop said. "We are trying to bring her safely to Dunfermline."

Not wasting time with questions, the ferrymen boarded the passengers. When all were across, they left the boats on the north side, refusing to cross again.

It was a sad funeral procession that conveyed its burden to the church at Dunfermline. The Queen's long-expected death was received with mourning. Never again would Margaret grace the church with her soft prayers and beautiful face. But her legacy of enlightenment would never lose its brilliance.

Alane was at the tower, gathering the regalia that had been introduced by Scotland's innovative monarchs. They needed to be safeguarded against the onslaught of anarchy.

Tying the valuables to a cart, Alane was astonished by the appearance of Thomas, who was trudging up the hill with a handful of Walter's men. The sight of the old veteran was too much for the youth; sitting on the ground, Alane gave vent to the misery bottled in his heart.

The men went inside the tower. Thomas dropped to the ground beside his friend's son.

Alane looked at Thomas. "I thought you were dead."

The old warrior hung his head. "I wish I were, Alane. I am too old to serve a new master. And I have lost my best friend."

Alane could not speak.

"I was knocked unconscious in the battle," Thomas continued.

"When I awoke, not long after, the whole army had fled. I had seen Walter fall, though, and crawled over to him. He lay where he fell, atop young Eadward. The Prince was not yet dead."

Alane looked dumbly at Thomas. "Not dead?"

"There were a few peasants searching the field. I called them over and offered a few coins if they would help. So they wrapped the Prince in his cloak and made a litter for him. We did the same for your father, though he was dead."

Alane sighed. "He wouldn't let me come."

"But look what you accomplished here. If it weren't for you, the Princes would be in grave danger. I have seen the Queen's body. We took Eadward there to join her."

"What happened after you found Eadward?"

"We carried him back to Scotland. I found those other men along the way, so we sent the peasants back to search for King Malcolm's body. I don't know if they found him." Thomas frowned.

"I would have searched for him myself, but my concern was with Eadward. For two days we tended him, though he never regained consciousness. He died in Jedburgh Forest, on Scottish soil.

"We buried your father there, for we could no longer carry the burden. I said the last words myself."

Alane could not stop the tears. "My father is buried in Scotland, at least. For that I am indebted to you."

"No. I did my duty as his friend."

Thomas rested his head against the cart. "It was terrible. I have seen so many friends die..."

After a moment, he reached for his pack and pulled out Walter's—Fleance's—sword. Handing it to the boy, he said, "He was holding it, still. Use it well, Alane. Walter once said it carries a legacy with it, but what that legacy is, you would best know."

Epilogue

Malcolm Canmore's body was found by some peasants and brought in a cart to Tynemouth, where the corpse was interred in an obscure grave. Later, it was transferred to Tynemouth Priory; twenty years afterwards, it was removed by Malcolm's son, Alexander I, and brought to Dunfermline, where he was interred alongside Margaret.

It was said that Malcolm's children were rescued by their uncle, Eadgar Aetheling. And so the exile became the protector. The daughters, and David, at least, were probably raised at Romsey Abbey by their aunt Christina.

Donald Bain easily usurped the throne of Scotland. For a time he had an influence over Eadmund, who was flattered by his uncle's smooth manners. But the Prince soon repented of his decision and, renouncing all earthly ambition, retired to a Cluniac monastery. There he lived out his life and requested, on his death, to be buried wrapped in chains.

Donald Bain was so hated by his subjects that they invited Duncan, Malcolm's first-born, to take the crown. As Duncan came to Scotland, supporters flocked to his banner; Donald Bain took fright and fled the country six months after usurping the throne.

But Duncan proved a poor choice; studying only the military arts in his youth, he was ill equipped to handle the rigors of civil government. Seeing the country's growing discontent, Donald Bain hired a murderer to dispose of Duncan, and remounted the throne after an exile of a year and a half.

Aethelred, Margaret's third son, became Earl of Fife and Abbot of Dunkeld, but died before the year 1098.

Donald Bain's reign lasted only three years; he was despised as much as ever. The Scots invited Eadgar to claim the throne. Borrowing a small army from William Rufus, with whom he had made peace, he invaded Scotland (possibly under the leadership of Eadgar Aetheling). Once again, the people flocked to his standard, and this time Donald was captured and imprisoned; it was said that he was blinded. The usurper died soon thereafter.

Eadgar reigned nine and a half years. On William Rufus's death, Eadgar confirmed his treaty with England and gave his sister, Edith, to the new King, Henry I.

Edith, who changed her name to Matilda, or Maud, became Queen of England. It was from her marriage with Henry I that the royal blood of Saxons and Normans was finally merged. From the loins of Edith came the future Plantagenets, who reigned for hundreds of years.

Eadgar died without issue, and was succeeded by his brother, Alexander I, surnamed The Brave. He reigned for fourteen years, and was succeeded by his brother David I in 1124. David married his distant cousin Matilda, daughter of Waltheof.

Queen Margaret, so instrumental in establishing the Christian religion firmly in Celtic Scotland, was canonized as St. Margaret in 1250.

Alain le Roux, Earl of Richmond, died the same year as King Malcolm. All of his lands were willed to his brother, Alain le Noir. Gunhild, who lived with Alain until his death, also went to Alain le Noir, and stayed with him until his death in 1098. After that, her fate is unknown.

Alane Steward, son of Walter, went on the first Crusade with Duke Robert Curt Hose, in 1099, also accompanied by Eadgar Aetheling. But it is said that he returned to Scotland, to continue in his hereditary post.

As for Isabel, she was blessed with obscurity.

Following is a genealogy, in which Walter takes his part, from Percy Enderbie's *Cambria Triumphans* written in 1661: *Genealogy of Charles II from the Welsh Blood*

Cadelh, King of South Wales
Howell Dha, Prince of South Wales

Owen, King of Wales

Meredith, King of Wales

Llewelyn ap Seisylt, descended from Anarawd, King of North Wales

Gruffydd ap Llewelyn, King of Wales

Nesta, the daughter of Gruffydd ap Llewelyn, was married (sic) to Fleance son of Banquo whose issue was

Walter Stuart

Alan Lord Stuart

Alexander Lord Stuart

John Lord Stuart

Walter Lord Stuart, married Margey, daughter and heir of Robert (Bruce), the first King of the Scots,and had issue

Robert the Second, King of the Scots

Robert the Third, King of the Scots

James the First, King of the Scots

James the Second, King of the Scots

James the Third, King of the Scots

James the Fourth, King of Scots, who married Margaret, eldest daughter to King Henry the Seventh, King of England

James the Fifth, King of the Scots

Henry in right of his wife Queen Mary, sole daughter and heir to James the Fifth

James, Monarch of Great Britain

Charles, Monarch of Great Britain

Charles the Second, Monarch of Great Britain whom God of his infinite goodness protect from his enemies.

It was James, Monarch of Great Britain for whom Shakespeare wrote "Macbeth", intending to honor his sovereign with an account of his ancestral roots. Unfortunately for the great bard, the play was considered cursed, and it is believed by some that even James I was highly displeased with the witches' incantations and banned its performance for five years.

Bibliography

Barlow, Frank, *Edward the Confessor*, Univ. of California Press, Berkeley, 1984

Barnett, T. Ratcliffe, *Margaret of Scotland, Queen and Saint*, Oliver and Boyd, Edinburgh, 1926

Buchanan, George, *The History of Scotland*, Blackie, Fullerton, & Co., 1827

Cambrensis, Giraldus, *The Itinerary Through Wales*, H.G. Bohn, London, 1863

Connon, F.Wallace, *The Stone of Destiny*, Covenant Publishing Co., London, 1951

Enderbie, Percy, *Cambria Triumphans, or Britain in its Perfect Lustre*, Printed for Andrew Crooke, London, 1661

Freeman, Edward A., *The History of the Norman Conquest of England*, Oxford at the Clarendon Press, 1870

Henderson, Ebenezer, *Annals of Dunfermline*, John Tweed, Glasgow

Holinshed, Raphael, *Chronicles of England, Scotland, and Ireland*, AMS Press Edition, London

Howarth, David, *1066, The Year of the Conquest*, Viking Press, New York, 1977

Keith, Duncan, *A History of Scotland*, William Paterson, Edinburgh, 1886

Lloyd, Alan, *The Making of the King, 1066*, Holt, Rinehart and Winston, New York, 1966

Mason, Emm, *The House of Godwine: The History of a Dynasty*, Hambledon and London, 2004

Roberts, Peter, *The Popular Antiquities of Wales*, E. Williams, Bookseller, London, 1815

Robertson, E.William, *Scotland Under her Early Kings*, Edmonston & Douglas, Edinburgh, 1862